AS CROOKED AS THEY COME

MBTA Green Line train, Boston, 1971. Philip R. Jordan photo.

As Crooked As They Come

*Chicanery, comedy
and disorganized
crime in yesterday's
Boston underworld*

PHILIP R. JORDAN

Onion River Press

This novel's story and characters are fictitious. However, certain buildings, neighborhoods, long-standing institutions and public offices are mentioned, but the characters involved are, quite thankfully, wholly imaginary and do not roam at will beyond the covers of this book in an effort to visit them.

Onion River Press
191 Bank Street
Burlington, VT 05401

ISBN: 978-1-949066- 84-5
Library of Congress Control Number: 2021915186

For old times' sake

Contents

Foreword

They don't make crooks like they used to. Gone are the days of the old dons, and the 'traditional' sort of shylocks, bookmakers and street soldiers who 'kicked the money up' to the top. Judges and policemen are no longer 'in the pockets' of men who wear fine designer suits but cannot pronounce the French names on the makers' labels, yet get a shoeshine daily, a barbershop trim every other week, and pay cash for their gambling and girlfriends despite having no bank accounts or credit cards.

When I first hit the streets of Boston, it was in 1971 (before I knew we had a crook of another kind in the White House). I got an eyeful of Boston's gritty, morally-depraved Combat Zone and some of the traditional crooks. The ticket for admission to this show of Boston's sordid, churning underbelly was 50 cents. Deposited in a Metropolitan Boston Transit Authority turnstile, that was the fare per person whenever my college roommate and I set out to explore the city. Anticipating careers in broadcast journalism once we graduated, we were young enough (and dumb enough) to think ourselves fearless, and went boldly everywhere we could (and probably should not have).

My roommate, a budding news hound had a press pass, earned at home at his dad's radio station. Whenever we heard of a big bust, a riot or a fire in Boston, off we went; he with a notepad and I.D., I with a camera. At the police line, he would flash his station I.D. and announce his name, the station's call letters and the word "radio" at the end, asking for admittance. "So, who is this guy?" the cop would ask, pointing at me. "Oh, he's the station photographer." "Okay," the cop would say, lifting the yellow line and grunting at performing actual work. "You can both go in."

The cops never figured out, quite thankfully, that a radio station would have no need for a photographer.

The idea for this book came to me one winter night in 2017 when visiting Boston, walking along a street in Dorchester. The area had been the epicenter of gang wars during Prohibition when Steve and Frank Wallace's Gustin Gang held sway against the Italians (until it didn't). In Boston's North End, drive-by shootings had resulted in Hanover Street being called "The Shooting Gallery" in the newspapers, but reporters were cautious in their criticism of gangsters, lest they be awarded a bullet surprise for their writing talents. Much later, as evidence was unearthed, the grisly deeds of Whitey Bulger came to light and horrified the public anew. As I walked by dark triple-decker houses from which a drawn window shade occasionally blinked in curiosity to reveal a slit of yellow light, I felt as if I were stealing past sentries guarding secrets of the violent past.

I was ignoring a car that had been slowly following me. It finally pulled up and the passenger put his window down. Relieved at not seeing a gun displayed, I ignored the offer of drugs. I pulled up the hood on my jacket and trudged on; the car left. I then thought of those innocent, long-ago college days and how crooks no longer resembled the ones of old Boston. One by one, the ghosts of the past in that neighborhood revealed themselves to me and spoke, and the characters you will soon be acquainted with came to mind and began to take shape. Some of them are humorous; others, not so much. I knew I would have to write about them before they escaped. It would be a crime for me not to tell you about what they've been up to.

Boston, just a few hundred yesterdays ago.

"If you think your boss is stupid, remember: you wouldn't have a job if he was any smarter."
—John Gotti

"If you want a story on a gangster, go to a cop. If you want a story on a cop, go to a gangster."
—Jack Kelly, WNAC TV investigative reporter

"If a man is dumb, someone is going to get the best of him, so why not you? If you don't, you're as dumb as he is."
—Arnold Rothstein

Cast of Characters

JIMMY "THE MERCHANT" CALLAHAN, a Dorchester businessman in his late 60s who owns a retail business but also an illicit underground supply house for Boston's less-than scrupulous types, whose occupations involve relieving other businesses and financial institutions of their money as efficiently and discretely as possible.

PATTY CALLAHAN, Jimmy's street-smart daughter, who has a respectable job, is too inquisitive about her father's business dealings for her own good, and is one of the few honest people you will find in this book.

ELLEN CALLAHAN, Jimmy's ex-wife. She becomes an unwitting accomplice to one of Jimmy's capers and also Patty's accomplice in unearthing an old family secret.

MARVIN "THE MAGICIAN" MAHONEY, Jimmy's store manager, forger extraordinaire and right-hand man, who quite often dips his own right hand into the till.

VINCENT "THE SANDMAN" SALUZZO, Jimmy Callahan's nemesis and don of the Saluzzo crime family. Although elderly and semi-retired, he is wise enough not to turn his semi-legitimate business over to his three not-so-wiseguy sons.

MARIA SALUZZO, Vincent's charming wife and head of a charitable, nonprofit type of business that is neither. She does Vincent's books and employs the three sons, simply because Vincent refuses to.

CHARLIE "CHA CHA" SALUZZO, Vincent's son, who has brilliant ideas that come rushing to him like runaway freight trains. Unfortunately, these trains enter one of his ears and then exit this tunnel of brilliance as quickly as they come.

BOBBY "TWO SHOTS" SALUZZO, another of Vincent's three sons. He is Charlie and Franky's half-brother and is approximately half as bright as Charlie. He likes to brag about his exploits, and believes *omerta* to be some kind of Italian sausage he's never had.

FRANK "FAT FRANKY" SALUZZO, Vincent's third son and the self-professed 'brains' of the Saluzzo brothers who keeps them in line. He is dishonest enough for all three of them.

DOMINIC "DOM" SALUZZO, Frank's teenage son, an up-and-coming con artist in his own right who is smarter than his father, his two uncles and *their* father, all put together.

JERRY "THE GIANT" GARRANTINO, A.K.A. "GELATO", king of the cons at the penitentiary and an enforcer who once worked for Vincent. He is renowned on the street (whenever he is on it) as an ape and a leg-breaker, despite his otherwise stellar reputation as an ugly piece of work. He gets along fine with Jimmy until he doesn't.

JOHN FISHER, A.K.A. HERMAN HOFFMAN SCHMIDT, unemployed musician, carny trick-shot artist and substitute hit man who has fallen off both the wagon and the radar of law enforcement.

BILLY "THE BUDDHA" JONES, a rather large man with an enormous appetite for food and cash. Billy runs an illicit rental agency of sorts, and can therefore swear before a jury without crossing his fingers behind his back and perspiring that he no longer steals to make a living.

MURRAY MALONEY, Chief Detective, Cold Case Squad, Boston Police Department. An honest Irish cop who occasionally cracks open a cold one to have with his corned beef and cabbage, but never while on duty. Well, maybe once or twice, now and then.

JACOB THAYER, retired Boston Police Detective, best-selling crime novelist and Murray Maloney's mentor. Prepared for anything, he holsters a loaded flask as well as a .38 revolver.

SAMMY NACOSTO, owner of Nacosto's Italian Ristorante, a respectable family-oriented dining spot with a well-respected gun shop of sorts operating out of the kitchen's back door. His family 'made the peace' with Jimmy's grandfather's gang in the early1930s.

SERGENTE LORENZO TOSCANINI, is a sergeant in Rome, Italy's Police Department and a member of its Visitors' Assistant Unit. He is the tall, whacky OCD guy in the P.D. who goes AWOL and comes to the U.S.A.

MIKHAIL ZUCKOFF, Ukrainian émigré and owner of several resorts, one of which houses an illegal, high-stakes gambling casino. Ever the wizard of odds, he makes sure the house always wins and that only one confidante there knows his true identity.

KATRINA VALENCHNIKOFF, the Natasha to Mikhail's Boris at the resort, so to speak. Katrina is a stone-cold beauty (and killer) who served in the Russian military in Chechnya and knows her way around a trigger, as well as Mikhail, her boss's, purview.

THE DEPARTED

ROSE CALLAHAN, Jimmy's sister and exotic dancer at a Combat Zone nightclub. She was killed in the late 1970s by an unknown shooter before she could testify in an extortion case. She haunts Patty's memories of the past.

MICKEY "MICK" CALLAHAN, Prohibition-era rumrunner and gangster who made a fortune. He was Jimmy's grandfather and intercedes, at times, as Patty's spirit guide. Jimmy hears him sometimes, too and wonders what happened to the fortune, without asking.

AND, there are several other characters in this book who are not worthy of mention here, simply because they are all innocent of any wrongdoing whatsoever.

Chapter 1

Two Crooks and a Cause

He knew he wasn't going to be caught this time. And that he wasn't going to be questioned as to what he knew about his mentor, who'd been found dead in an alleyway in a pool of blood with five bullets in his back, after he tried to break into a building late at night. That was long years ago. But memories linger.

Jimmy Callahan knelt softly, as quietly as a choirboy during Mass, before the big steel-case safe down in the dark basement. He blew softly on his fingertips just for luck. *Old habits die hard*, he thought to himself. Gently, eyes closed in concentration now, one ear pressed against the safe, the other listening for any strange noises or footsteps behind him, he began to twirl the dial, sensing the tumblers progressively falling into place deep within the four-inch-thick door that he soon opened with a practiced twist of the chrome handle, thinking, *Yep, nice to know you've still got the touch!*

Jimmy's hands moved swiftly and surely to a small drawer, from which he removed a bundle of crisp, new 100-dollar bills with the tender touch of a father cradling a tiny brand-new baby. His hands were steady, probably because in this case, Jimmy was handling his own money. He stuffed the bundle into the pocket of his shirt, gently closed the door, gave the dial a good spin, and pulled on his jacket.

He turned to face his cluttered old desk and equally-ancient computer. It was still on, and the monitor displayed the post he'd just seen on a message board of the Classic Crimebuster's site after searching, as he had been almost every day, ever since the dawn of the digital age, for clues that might lead him to his sister's killer.

The news Jimmy had just received was a long time coming and it was bad—bad in this case for his adversary. It never occurred to Jimmy that bad news—as it's so often said—usually travels fast...or never comes so easily when it is so important to resolve a feud. It was an anonymous crime reporter's post about a con's deathbed confession, in which he stated he'd helped shield a certain contract killer and create a cover story for him. The killer who'd slipped past the U.S. Marshals and offed Jimmy's sister in her hotel room in Boston, as she waited to be called as a federal witness in a sensational court case that had captured the public's attention back in '78. A case in which her testimony would likely have put an end to a certain gang boss's freedom...and also, most likely, his life.

Moreover, the reporter, gamely shielding his identity, cited other sources who stated that the dying man was likely correct in stating who he had been working for in his supposedly charitable act, one that was not without monetary return.

"I should have known," Jimmy said to himself, as he jigged the computer's mouse around to shut the machine down. "I should have known he was behind that scheme all along." When the monitor's screen went dark, Jimmy doused the lights and headed upstairs to the main floor of his store. After 40-odd years in business, the daily grind of working retail (and maintaining certain after-hours business pursuits) was starting to take its toll, but suddenly, Jimmy felt energized. He felt a change coming on, coming on fast.

The store, JC's Police and Fire Security Mart—also known as Jimmy C's—catered to a specialized crowd, the hardworking cops, detectives, firemen, and security guards who protected and served the good citizens of greater Boston. Jimmy C's was where you went if you needed a departmental ID badge, a trustworthy set of handcuffs, a blackjack, brass knuckles, listening devices, fluorescent safety vests, hard hats, extra-long crowbars or Detroit door openers, lock picks, uniforms, hats, or holsters for weapons. In fact, you could buy just about anything you needed except for firearms. "Catering to the workingman since 1977" read the sign above the barred windows of the scruffy storefront.

Jimmy huffed up the last few stairs and stepped onto the main floor. The excitement of his discovery had overcome the needling pain of arthritis that had plagued him the last few years as he had aged gracefully into his late 60s. The gaggle of keys on the holder on his belt jangled as he strode past rows of padlocks and hand tools, the key-duplicating machine, and finally, several male and female mannequins dressed in police and fireman's uniforms. The store was his special world—and for its customers, Jimmy C's was their special store. Jimmy was well known within the realm of Boston's shady underworld...and on the streets as Jimmy "The Merchant."

As a young man, Jimmy had aspired to become a professional boxer; he soon learned the ropes and that there was more money to be made in fixing matches and bouts than in sparring (or starring) in them. Indeed, Jimmy became well known and regarded as a fixer, a talented man who could determine the outcome of a fight; even an auto race, without so much as touching a wrench...he could deftly change the outcome of a horse race without visiting the track. Unlike the more prominent men who have figured in Boston's underworld history in past years, Jimmy soon shied away from the gangs who at first wished to recruit him, and soon found himself in a convenient spot, one in which he, the fixer, could get the materials anyone needed to do "a job." Jimmy "The Merchant's" number-one man among his crew was Marvin Mahoney, widely known as Marvin "The Magician" Mahoney. Marvin's specialty was in creating on short order and for reasonable fees the certain kinds of documents, passes, identity cards, and other things that were the keys to the success of any operation that was going to fly beneath the radar of the law and not get shot down in flames.

"I'm on a roll, Marv. A lucky one," Jimmy said to the rotund cashier at the counter, who appeared to be absorbed in trying to move a heavy file cabinet around, in order to do some cleaning.

"Whaddya mean?" replied Marv, spinning around to face his boss.

"I've made up my mind. Got more information than I've ever hoped for. And I need to settle the business—the old business."

Marv studied Jimmy carefully. One *had* to study this man of many talents but also many expressions, in order to get a read on him, especially when he made decisions in the moment. Jimmy was sometimes irascible and had a violent temper when provoked. And now Marv could sense the emotions of this moment surfacing. He had to advise Jimmy carefully in making any major moves; business, not rash decisions and their consequences were what mattered. Marv and his crew liked to keep things simple and on good terms with their neighbors, and liked to keep their names out of the headlines.

"I have the goods on him," said Jimmy.

"Who?" asked Marv, licking his lips in anticipation of a good story. He hoped it wasn't an old one—one that he was all too familiar with. But it was.

"Vince Saluzzo," answered Jimmy, staring at Marv, deadpan. Marv observed that Jimmy's fists clenched briefly...and guessed that, somewhere within Jimmy's brain, a forest fire might be starting to slowly take hold, right underneath his hair roots.

"Rose?" asked Marv, taking an odd chance. "Again? Is it about your sister?"

"Yeah," answered Jimmy, sighing and turning away from Marv and the cash register. Marv sensed that Jimmy was gone now—staring into a tunnel that had been bored into a mountain of his darkest memories. Those memories were now at work, drawing him into them inexorably, like a dark star pulling matter from the brightness of the universe and drawing it into Stygian depths from which no escape is possible.

"I found out he did it, Marv," said Jimmy. "I know he pushed the button. And...I will make him, and his family, pay."

"How?" asked Marv. Marv could sense trouble when it walked through the front door.

He could also sense it when something walked into Jimmy's action zone and pushed his big, not-so-easy button.

"I'm going to take him out, Marv," answered Jimmy. Marv looked back at him incredulously, as though he'd been stunned, and drew a breath. In older times, with Jimmy as wound up and bloodthirsty as he was today, it would have been a shame not to let him loose and put his opponent's family in the awkward position of having to buy a headstone without shopping around for a deal. Or at least putting him in the hospital by performing some minor blunt force brain surgery. But things were different now. This would bring more than just bad juju. This dandy little piece of work would have the feds on the boys like white on rice.

"You're gonna whack the guy? Here? In Boston? In this day and age? You can't be serious," stated Marv, obviously astounded. "Nothing's been settled like this in years. Do you know what will happen? Boss...you'll bring the heat like no one's had it. Think again. It'll be a meltdown. No one will want to make the peace if you do this."

"I know what I'm doing Marv," snapped Jimmy. "And I have two perfect guys for the job. One's a foreigner. Contract guy. Nobody knows him. Nobody in town's ever heard of the guy. He'll disappear like a spook when the deed's done, and we have a cover to make it look good. Really good. 'Cause the other guy has a score to settle and best yet...it's with the mark...he used to work for him. But he's not a shooter; that guy's an ape, a real leg-breaker. And the blame—it will all fall on the other side if I play my cards right." Marv looked at Jimmy with soulful eyes. The many years of building up JC's business...the customers...the faith...the loyalty mattered to him.

Yes, loyalty mattered. And to betray Jimmy was to take one's life and limbs in one's hands and roll the two like dice. Retribution could be swift——perhaps even lethal. One case of Jimmy extracting vengeance was that of the O'Harrigan brothers, two kids who were stars of the local high school's basketball team. They started out their careers in crime innocently enough, shaving points on state championship games that Jimmy bet odds on in exchange for bribes, then joined Jimmy's crew upon graduating. The bromance between Jimmy and the O'Harrigans was over when he discovered they were stealing from him, and that they'd been sinking the money into a Corvette they'd acquired from a local chop shop. Jimmy planned his vengeance carefully.

He put in a call to a truck driver who owed him a favor; the driver obligingly followed directions to the street where the Corvette was parked, found it, and broke the driver's side window. He then lowered the discharge chute on his cement mixer, filled the car with quick-setting concrete and drove away, a happy man who was free of his obligation.

The O'Harrigan boys, upon discovering the evil deed late that day armed themselves with lug wrenches, gathered up two friends and headed for Jimmy's store. Arriving at closing time, full of beer and testosterone, they met Jimmy at the back door just as he was locking up. Jimmy knocked them down one by one as they came up the stairs. While Jimmy stood there rubbing his sore knuckles, the O'Harrigans regained some semblance of composure and staggered to their feet, stanching the flow of blood from their broken noses with their shirtsleeves. "You bastard!" one of them muttered.

"Look on the bright side," Jimmy said. "Be glad you're not eating concrete in your Heavy Chevy ghetto sled. If you ever come back here again, you'll get a free ride to the ocean––and I guarantee you travelers won't have Saint Christopher medals chained around your necks; you'll have a boat anchor." The boys never did. Marv remembered that episode (and many others like it) well. But that was 30 years ago; things were different then. He had grave concerns about staging a sensational hit that could leave his fingerprints, and possibly those of Jimmy's five-man crew on it, as well; tough muscle they were, but they were getting on in years also. They were known in local circles mostly as "the Gray Team".

"Are you gonna tell our boys? Bring them in on it?" he asked.

"No," answered Jimmy. This is my deal. But I want your help. And that of one other person."

"One thing," Marv intervened, "really matters. Make a call. Call the bastard. Put him on the spot. Shake him down, Jimmy, for God's sake, if you've got his number. There's a way to do it. Make him pay. Before you pull the trouble down on us, on everyone; give the bastard a chance to save his ass and his family. And then, if it's war, then, okay, it's war. But—it will be war like we've never seen it—since the bad old days. There'll be fallout. And you'd better make sure your button man's taken care of. And I mean like the days of the shooting gallery,

Hanover Street...the days of your grandfather Mick, and Steve and Frankie Wallace, God rest their souls...if you know what I mean." Jimmy stood, straight as a ramrod, looking at Marv for a full minute.

"Okay," he said. "One last try." An ironic smile wrinkled the corners of his mouth. "I'll let you know how it turns out." Jimmy stalked down the stairs and into his office, dropped into his chair and with one finger, stabbed in several numbers on his telephone with the intensity of a man who is attacking an adversary with an ice pick. Upstairs, Marv shouldered the file cabinet back into position, knocking askew an old, faded photograph thumbtacked to the wall, a photo of a little girl. She was dressed in a pink bathing suit, sitting in a tiny folding chair on the sand of a beach; a gray, shingled bungalow was in the background. The little girl was Jimmy's daughter, smiling up at the camera and holding up a coloring book before the camera. Below the illustration—a stick figure—were the words: "When I grow up, I want to be just like you!" He paused to straighten it, gazed at the photograph and sighed, shaking his head.

"No you don't, baby," he said. "No, you don't! And not like your daddy, either."

Jimmy had built a nice little business with JC's, but he'd also built *yet another* nice little business on the side—strictly on the q.t., catering to a few certain individuals, hardworking private citizens who wished to remain anonymous and who had a temporary need, from time to time, for police or armored car service uniforms, construction barricades, police scanners, and duplicate security-clearance badges to suit their purposes. Or a need to temporarily store a few things that needed to disappear from public view, without anyone being seen entering, or leaving the store with the goods.

This business supplied them all—it was JC's underground store, literally...connected to the Dorchester store's basement by a hidden doorway. It could otherwise only be accessed by an abandoned subway tunnel that had a secret entrance, a maintenance hatch with a stairway beneath it, located a block or so away. It had once served a subway station, long since demolished. His men, plus one woman, were all sworn to secrecy. Only these few who knew of the tunnel and had keys to the hatch went there. All of them knew that to talk about the underground store and the connection (what was called, tongue-in-cheek, "The Callahan Tunnel") outside of anything other than jovial shop talk after hours at JC's was a certifiable death wish––like the one Jimmy had just silently pronounced on Vincent "The Sandman" Saluzzo.

Vince had a nice business going too; quiet and for all appearances perfectly legitimate, much like Jimmy's, only quite a bit larger. But years ago, it had been mostly in small-time rackets and shakedowns—his specialties when he was a younger man. Even in the earliest days when he had no street soldiers working for him, the sheer sight of his bald pate and hulking physique that appeared at the front door once a week were enough to strike fear into anyone who didn't pay up "on time," as he would say.

"Don't you know history? In the old country, Mussolini made the trains run on time," he'd bark at a quivering bookmaker or arcade owner who hadn't come across with the money for protection "and *you know* what happened to those guys who were *late*, don't you? Gonzo!" he would exclaim, pointing a fingertip at his own head to indicate where the forthcoming bullet would be lodged. Bookies who wanted to do business but complained about the percentage Vince took had little choice. "You want to operate here on my turf, you pay the rent," he'd tell them. "It's simple: no rent, you won't be operating. Period. Odds are some doctor will be operating, though—on you."

In his time, Vince had earned the nickname "The Sandman" not because of involvement in construction business, but because of what supposedly happened to those involved in it who did not pay Vince on time, or who crossed him: "The Sandman" would visit them late at night——and put them to sleep. Permanently. Legend (mostly promoted verbally by his three sons while visiting dive bars) had it that a few of Boston's departed elite, Vince's detractors and leaders in their field were still so-called pillars of society today, since many of them were parts of concrete columns that held up various highways and parking garages. Thus, when it came to construction, it could be humbly said that Vince had *some* connections. Or so the boys said.

In later years, as Vince's business interests grew, expanding into new professions such as broader-based rackets and illegal poker machines, he brought in more muscle, initially adding his three sons, Franky, Bobby, and Charlie to the business...discretely, as subcontractors. But mistakes were made, territorial lines were crossed, and many times, the sons failed to deliver. "What's wrong with those boys of yours, Vince?" his elderly father once asked him during a nursing home visit. "When I was their age, I brought something to the table when there was a family business meeting. Cash. New numbers runners. Politicians. What do they bring to the table?"

Vince looked at him wearily, sighed, and shook his head in disgust. "Mostly, Pop" he said, "they just bring their elbows."

When some profitable rackets were finally taken over by the three boys, it turned out they didn't quite know how to run them. Shots were fired in anger (sometimes in the wrong direction). Arrests were made. And when the pinches came down and the boys sang, they sang a song about working not for their father, but for a certain Garrantino capo, whereupon their father conveniently threw his aging chief enforcer, Jerry Garrantino, to the wolves to take the rap. The *Baystate Police and Detective Gazette*'s editor, who frequently advocated for capital punishment, probably saw through this scheme. He invoked humor while sarcastically referring to their actions as "an experiment in disorganized crime, pulled off by juveniles destined for the chair...who should be fried as adults." The boys got off easy and went to work for their mother's nonprofit. "Geriatric Jerry" as the boys had taunted him with their catcalls, went to prison (or, "went to school" as some people in the know like to say).

These days, Vince no longer wielded such things as weapons; Vince wielded influence. And he could be a charitable man when the occasion called for it. Vince's wife, Maria, was by all accounts a law-abiding, church-going citizen. Active in the neighborhood church (which, incidentally, she lived next door to), she also helped her husband with the books of his business. Maria was also quite active in the nonprofit organization she was the executive director of; and when it came to contributions to this nonprofit whose mission was to help the poor in the parish, Vince could be very, very charitable. Quite naturally, his sons would have become poor had they not been elected to the company's board of directors, and some of the people Vince did business with would have become quite wealthy had they not been influenced by some strange coincidence to become almost as charitable as Vince was. Controlling the finances of this nonprofit—the comings and goings—was both challenging and rewarding for Maria, who often referred to it as a cleansing process, one quite similar to that used by Vince once every day as he drove his Audi through the local car wash.

Maria, with her doe-like eyes, arched eyebrows, garrulous demeanor, and raven-black hair, was a poster child of sorts. When it came to alms for the poor during times of floods, blizzards, or hurricanes, Maria was there before the paparazzi with furrowed brow, gesticulating hands, the provocatively-high hemline on her skirt wafting tantalizingly upward in the gathering breeze, and her urgently-spoken words borne of great agitation, begging for contributions to the worthy cause, whatever it might be, on television. If a storm swept in and froze the greater Boston area in a clutch of ice, Maria was there before the cameras, clamoring for intervention and pledges of dollars to help the cold, the homeless, and the needy. It was said that one need not worry about the weather, unless he looked out his window in the morning and saw Maria Saluzzo sharing a microphone with Jim Cantore of the Weather Channel.

Despite his total disregard for the outward appearance of the building Vince "Sandman" Saluzzo based his busy import-export operations in, he took great pride in the appearance of what was within it—that is to say, for one thing, the room that was his second-floor office inside the cavernous building. This fortress-like, brick structure was one that had been used to make munitions for the military in World War II. It currently appeared to passersby on the gritty street outside as though it had been abandoned since the Japanese surrendered, and the United States gave up any idea of supporting a small family business—one operating in a crumbling factory building in urban Massachusetts.

As if sunken in a sea of old brick buildings with weathered facades, sooty windows, and sagging roofs—barnacled with patches of years' worth of repairs—the former factory's scabrous, hulking shape was much like that of a gnarled, dark oyster lying on the bottom of that sea. But although that building was an old oyster of sorts, closed in so many ways to the outside world's scrutiny, Vince's prosperous, seemingly-innocuous little business housed within it was to him that very oyster's pearl.

Vince seldom showed himself in public in anything less prestigious than one of his finest designer suits, the same attire worn when in his box seat at the Suffolk Downs track on weekends. Gold-framed eight-by-ten photographs of his dozen coveted racehorses blanketed the wall beside his massive desk. Aside from all of his various activities, including placing large bets at the window with richly-rewarding results, it could be said that whenever he had the time, he was a devoted family man––one who thought highly of his wife. In an unabashed show of this affection, a small, gold-framed 5-by-7 photograph of Maria stood on the far edge of the enormity of glass-topped mahogany that was Vince's world. Her exploits were hers; Vince's were his own, as closely kept as an oyster holds a pearl on the dark ocean floor. All things considered, when Vince thought of them in idle moments, it would be a shame if Maria were to fall off the edge of that enormous flat world some day and shatter this picture of marital bliss.

Maria was away today, traveling in the company of another man. This, Vince knew for certain, and he was very happy with this arrangement; it was for business reasons––his. Maria was headed to Italy together with a priest of the local diocese, on a mission of mercy. That mission of mercy was to pray the indulgence of the pope in a fundraising effort. An effort that Vince's company was involved in and from which it could reap many merciful benefits. It would be merciful, too, for Maria would be gone for a week, thought Vince. Vince regarded himself not only as a good provider, but above all as a highly influential and accomplished leader of men; after all, although he had had some minor scrapes with the law years ago, he had never been indicted for participating in a scheme or a racket, had never been called as a witness in any trial, and had never been convicted of a crime. Those, indeed, were significant accomplishments for a man of his background and abilities. Vince steadfastly maintained to the general public that his business, with its many overseas connections, was "strictly legitimate." Rather than stars, had this business and its owner been listed on a legitimate Internet business rating site, they would have earned a rating of four Pinocchios.

It was sad when the Saluzzo family members, like slandered royals, had to suffer the occasional rumor that Vince was a crook. It was known to have been expressed by a few people who found themselves riding in speeding ambulances afterward, looking forward to a contrite and sober recovery. To make matters even sadder, these rumors were true. Through the grapevine, Jimmy would sometimes learn of another of Vince's big wins at the track, or about one of Maria's charitable donations or acts of public service being spotlighted by the press at a gala black tie and evening gown event. And at those times he'd share the news with Marv and his crew.

"There you go, boys," he'd say. "Living proof that scum always rises to the top."

Now, as he neared the age in which most men think about what few years they have left on this planet and what to do with them to benefit mankind, Vince redoubled his efforts to benefit his own coffers. He honored his father's credo, usually a retort when the man was confronted about his ethics——or perhaps better said, the lack of them: "Nothing personal, ever. Business comes first." Vince, at this point in life, reflected fondly upon earlier times, those of the '60s and '70s. Those days referred to by his senior associates as "the bad old days." To Vince, those had been the best of times, the golden era of underworld crime; the era of the last of the dons. Vince held them in high regard, almost as much as he revered other certain powerful figures in history such as Mussolini, who had figured largely in bending Italy to his absolute rule while conning the public into granting him the status of a folk hero——until war intervened. War was about to intervene in Vince's life.

Fresh from his brisk morning commute, Vince composed himself, then focused on what was on his desk. A scant 20 feet outside his open office door, Tina and Michelle, the office workers, began their day at the office.

"And what was he saying to you, my dear?" Tina asked Michelle cheerfully. Her pleasant-sounding voice lulled first-time callers into the erroneous belief that they were dealing with a good company and an intelligent, attractive young woman, which was the only reason Vince could possibly think of as to why he had hired her.

"He said, that S.O.B. *said*," Michelle declared, pouting like a schoolgirl in detention, "that he don't wanna go out with me no more." Tina rolled her eyes the way a horse does when fed a sugar cube; this was good, juicy gossip, worthy of a Facebook post.

"Oh, damn. What a moron he is, right?" Tina asked, well-knowing the answer.

"Yeah, really," groused Michelle, crossing her arms and frowning.

The intercom line on the phone rang. Tina answered.

"Hey Tina," said Gigi, the gatekeeper downstairs, "I got somebody here, says they're with the tax assessor's office. Wants to see the boss about something important."

"Hang on," Tina blurted into the phone, then dropped it temporarily into a deep pile of papers on her desk. "Vince!" she yelled into the next room. "Tax assessor's here, waiting to see you." In the next room, Vince's neck stiffened suddenly within the crisp collar of his Pierre Cardin shirt.

"Waiting?" he said, coolly. "Okay, good; let him wait." Unruf-fled, he turned to the paperwork scattered across his desk, a small world awaiting his attention as he rose to the occasion like its morning sun. Tina picked up the phone and informed Gigi of Vince's command, which would most likely result in the assessor falling asleep in the lounge and ultimately going back to city hall empty-handed.

"Dumb bunny," said Michelle to Tina, snickering. "Third time that person's been here." The phone rang. Tina picked up; the call was for Vince. Michelle looked pensively at Tina, wondering who it could be. Tina's face was turning a ghostly shade of white.

"Oh my God; it's him, Callahan," said Tina, hushing everything, her hand over the phone. Michelle crossed her eyes, then crossed herself. Tina, not wanting to be the bearer of bad news, simply put the call on hold and buzzed Vince's line. Beneath her desk, her sleeping Shih Tzu was awakened and was treated to a tasty shower of crumbs as Tina knocked aside and overturned a box of donuts as she opened up her newspaper.

"Dear Abby time!" she announced.

It was several minutes before Vince's thunderous exclamation, "Damn!" could be heard clearly down at the end of the hallway, where Michelle was now cloistered in the bathroom, texting her friends about her latest, fast-developing melodrama. And then: "Now...you are *really* pissing me off!" Tina tried to concentrate on the invoices she was working on, hoping that Michelle would come back soon. It sounded as though her boss, like the long-dormant volcano of legend, Stromboli, was going to blow his stack, as it often did in the days of old. "You know what you are?" Vince bellowed. "You...are a cheap, rotten little worm. I should take you out, right now. But I won't. You know what? I'll start with the bottom...that's right, the bottom...where you came from, you and yours, and I'll work my way up...to finish you. For good."

Michelle rushed into the office and dumped herself hurriedly into her vacant office chair, spinning around so quickly she knocked papers off her desk onto the floor, upsetting Tina's panting, overfed Shih Tzu, who then looked up at her with troubled, goggling eyes.

"Omigod Tina; what did I miss?" she exclaimed.

"Some, but not much," answered Tina, scooting her chair closer to the doorway. "Stick around; I think the best is yet to come."

"You may think I'm done...*but I'm not!*" came Vince's voice, booming out loudly from the office down the hallway. Then, softly: "Oh, wait a minute...did I make a mistake?"

"Here we go, here we go, here we go," muttered Tina, peering around the corner, trying to see what Vince was up to.

"Omigod," said Michelle. "I think I hear the faint whistle of the bipolar express." Then the apparent verbal jousting match raged anew and both Tina and Michelle cupped their ears; hardly necessary, since Vince held forth in rare form and in verbal prowess he had not been known to engage in for years; a lengthy stream of profanity followed.

In the depths of JC's in Dorchester, Jimmy Callahan, sitting in his small basement office, got tired of waiting and slammed the receiver of his phone down. "Sonofabitch!" he exclaimed, putting his feet up on his desk. "I should have known he'd never even pick up." Jimmy reached for a cigarette—lit it, blew a lungful of smoke, and spewed a plume of it up toward the ceiling. Hiring a button man wasn't a direct process; that, he knew. You went through somebody who went to somebody else who went to the guy––you'd never know who really did the deed––but it got done. But Jimmy was going to do things his way, not that way. This was personal. And anyone who knew Jimmy could tell you that there was either Jimmy's way or the highway, and if it was the highway, you'd better be on the next bus out of town. He stared at a framed photo of his sister that was on the wall over his cluttered desk. "I'm gonna do it," he declared. He stubbed out his cigarette in an ashtray, got to his feet and headed for the stairway.

Over at Vince's office, Tina and Michelle were now checking packing lists. Chit-chat time was over and the conversation outside their door had gotten too boring for them to follow. The red blinking light on Vince's telephone had gone out...without ever being seen; Vince had not noticed it. Had not answered the call, had not talked with Jimmy. Not at all.

Vince, pen in hand, was intent on the one thing that most attracted his rapt attention every day (other than the racing form): his daily Sudoku puzzle...with the newspaper spread out across his fancy desk...and its bothersome, constantly-ringing telephone. And—damn—it was puzzling, this particular one, that little patch of black-and-white squares in the newspaper. It was annoying him greatly, although he was a numbers person. Annoying him to no end. It annoyed him...almost as much as Jimmy Callahan did.

In Dorchester, several minutes later, Jimmy emerged once more from his basement lair. "Sweep up the joint before you leave," he ordered Marv, who now stood with his arms extended, palms turned up, as if in expectation of being told what Jimmy had learned.

"So?" he asked. There was no reply from Jimmy as he stalked by the counter. "Will do, boss," grunted Marv as Jimmy let himself out the front door. Marv, keeping one eye fixed on its wire-reinforced window, bent over and finally succeeding in grasping and pocketing the stray five-dollar bill he'd spotted earlier lying on the floor, down between the cabinet and the wall.

Halfway down the block, Jimmy hailed a cab, heaved himself into the backseat, and barked orders to the driver. Like most businessmen who engaged passionately in petty crime but held their heads high above the dirty waters to preserve their images, Jimmy resented nothing more than another successful businessman who was also for all practical purposes a petty criminal, particularly one who now and then encroached on his territory and affairs. Like the horse race fixing Jimmy enjoyed some supplemental income from.

"It's seasonal business," he once remarked to Marv in an upbeat moment. "It's good for you—gets you out of the office and into circulation." The playing field for this type of business was both secretive and competitive, and it had its rules;

if you broke them enough times, you might come down with a bad case of rigor mortis.

Jimmy Callahan was formulating a plan. He pondered...it was going to take a while but it would work, this little scheme. But first, he'd have to reach out to his ex-wife, Ellen, for two simple reasons. First, he needed a runner no one would know to make a pick-up and delivery; Jimmy didn't like to leave trails of breadcrumbs behind when he made a move. And for another, his sister Rose and Ellen had been very close. The shock of Rose's death had as made as much of an impact on Ellen as it had on him. He and Ellen had been divorced for more than seven years now, and it had been almost as many since he had even had a conversation with their daughter, Patty...and there it was...his mind wandered off again, back to thinking of his sister Rose, gone all these years. And now, he knew the story, knew who'd pulled the trigger on her, and who had paid for the job. And now, who his runner was going to be. Jimmy had placed the call.

The cab slowed to a stop outside the post office at 25 Dorchester Street in Boston. Jimmy scanned the people standing on the sidewalks, people scurrying in the crosswalks to scoot across the street before the lights changed, people trudging along, shoulders hunched, head down, oblivious to the lights. Busy people. He scanned the faces of the idlers, the loiterers, too. He recognized no one. It was safe. The steady buzz and hum of traffic crossing the Summer Street bridge nearby, the rhythmic thumping sounds of hundreds of car tires hitting multiple joints in its pavement each minute throbbed irregularly, like the erratic heartbeats of patients being monitored in a clinic. He paid the fare, hopped out of the cab, and strode quickly into the massive building, keeping his head low, and stopped before a row of silver mailboxes, looking for a tag that indicated one was available. He wrote down the number of one, a large mailbox, on two scraps of paper; he took them to the window and rented the mailbox, paying by cash.

Jimmy left the counter, separating his two, newly-acquired post office box keys from their ring as he walked. One, he returned to his jacket pocket. The other, together with one of the scraps of paper he stuffed into a small, padded envelope bearing postage stamps and a Waltham address. He sealed it, stopped at a mail slot just long enough to drop the envelope into it, and resumed his walk toward Boston's downtown. *It's all going to work out*, he thought. This act of revenge would be done the way his grandfather would have done it, the way it was done in the old days, the days when there was honor. After all, he, Jimmy...was an honorable man. And, best of all, Jimmy thought—unlike the way it was sometimes done in the old days—he wouldn't have to sit down and negotiate with a council of equally-dangerous, like-minded peers or buy someone a Cadillac to make it happen.

Chapter 2

Patty Callahan

Patty Callahan settled into her seat, leaned back, and waited for the show to begin. Drama club plays she'd had parts in in high school and later on, during seasonal stints as an actress in summer stock theatre in Ogunquit, Maine (or, straw hat theatre, as the New Yorkers who flocked to the coastal town each June, July, and August called it) provided an outlet for Patty's budding creativity. In fact, she'd often been referred to as the only actress in the troupe who'd ever pulled off the feat of playing two sharply different roles in the same production. That time spent on the stage as the consummate chameleon in the '80s had sharpened her appreciation for theatrical performances. She was rarely disappointed these days in her job with the airline; each flight (during which she catered to the needs and, sometimes, undue demands of passengers) was like a theatrical production, replete with its cast of quirky characters who had to be interacted with: the elderly man who refused to wear a seatbelt and insisted that in the event of a crash, he'd rather be thrown clear; the woman swearing at the boy sitting behind her who kept kicking her seat; the baby from hell who kept bawling while its mother sat placidly through the whole ordeal, earbuds on, gazing at the

31

glowing screen of the phone she was cradling, and the unfortunate man seated next to her who had acquired the look of quiet desperation, much like that of a bruised and beaten prisoner of war constrained in a cage, shackled to an unruly cellmate.

Today, the production began, not with the drawing of a curtain, but with the closing of a door...and not on an airplane. The sound of a booming, disembodied announcement sounded ominously throughout the shiny rapid transit commuter train Patty was seated in: "The doors...*are closing!*" The two teenage girls with shouldered backpacks who had been chatting on the platform outside heard the announcement and bounded through the doorway next to Patty's seat, just as the door began to close...the train then hummed and seemed to come alive with a surge of electric power. The door rolled shut with a soft *thunk* and the train quickly began to move forward. Still standing and suddenly thrown off balance, the two girls heaved themselves into seats, giggling, and congratulated themselves at their successful effort to board at the last possible second, as the train then gained further momentum, and the platforms of Denver International Airport began to slide out of view of Patty's window.

Across the aisle, a boy wearing a Denver Broncos jacket briefly fiddled with his phone, then tucked it away and concentrated on the two girls until one of them turned around to look at him briefly, then whispered something in her friend's ear that made her laugh. He then craned his neck to look out his window and feign interest in the massive blue-green gridwork of the airport station's overhanging canopy from which the train was emerging. The train rolled along up a steep grade, climbing steadily out of the man-made ravine that held the station platforms, and out into the open where the sun burned fiercely, hot and bright. It was almost unbearable to look at, high aloft in an impossibly clear blue sky that seemed like something straight out of a spaghetti Western movie, the kind Patty used to watch on television as a young girl. This—so much of Patty's life—was a view from a window, and a seat at a theater, keeping an eye on an audience that was itself the show. Her job—no, she called it her career—had been the key to her departure from dual roles: acting in the summer, then leaving after Labor Day to work at a gourmet restaurant where she waitressed until May, back in the days of splitting costs of a third-story walk-up apartment with her friend Theresa, scraping to pay her share of the rent and to keep a battered Toyota Celica on the road. All the while, she worked six days a week on staffing schedules that turned erratically like a quirky rotisserie in the hands of the mildly demented chef/owner; he often cooked with top-shelf liquors and fine wine, and sometimes, as Patty wryly observed to Theresa one evening, even used it in the food.

And now, life for the most part consisted of a series of departures and arrivals. Each departure preceded by the ritual of boarding a plane—first, the waiting while any last-minute cleaning and catering was done. Then, the waiting while the conga lines, each 45 passengers long, formed at the gate inside the terminal...and the waiting for the first footsteps of what invariably became a thundering herd of early boarders to come thumping down the gangplank, the unruly among them acting like cowboys on a cattle drive, prodding the behinds of the unhurried waddling before them with corners of carry-on luggage.

Then came the waiting——to finish smiling and welcoming them all aboard, standing at the forward hatch aft of the cabin like Noah might have done on the ark, watching the animals come aboard; the most impatient airline passengers sometimes actually tried to squeeze through the doorway two-by-two like rival beasts. And waiting while the blockers, the sturdy souls who stood in the middle of the aisle, held up the boarding while they fiddled with their luggage, placing it this way and that in the overhead rack as if their suitcases were the perfect solution to a Rubik's Cube puzzle. There was also the occasional person who arbitrarily picked a spot between two pieces of luggage and frantically rammed his suitcase in between them, as if he were a truck driver in urgent need to park and find a restroom, jamming his rig into a parking space barely large enough for a Volkswagen.

Then would come the preflight safety briefing, an opportunity for some standup comedy. But Patty always kept to the script while the push-back took place, a small tractor rolling the plane out onto a clear runway. She held aloft the instruction pamphlet passengers would find in the seatbacks before them and announced: "Please take a moment to read through these instructions to learn about the safety features of the Boeing 727." *Read 'em before you need 'em*, she thought to herself. "Each seat is provided with a seatbelt." She held aloft the sample belts and clasp, snapping the two parts together. "Please fasten your belts now and leave them fastened until the red fasten seatbelts light is off." Patty set the sample down and continued: "There are six exits provided for your use in an emergency. Two in the forward area that have evacuation slides..." *In case of evacuation, points will be awarded for best style and most impressive landing*, Patty thought, suppressing the urge to smile. The attendant behind her, standing near the exits, pointed toward them "and four in this rear area over the wings." She pointed two fingers on each of her hands toward the exit doors, smugly thinking *Please do not use these exits during flight*. Next came the drop-down oxygen mask demonstration, and the caution to cover both one's nose and mouth with the mask. And Patty's own, silent admonition: *If you are seated next to a dwarf, you may be called upon to help him reach his mask.*

As the train picked up speed, Patty found herself chuckling about the one time she'd actually blown her lines while giving the life vest warning and verbally cautioned: "Do not attempt to use this as a toilet seat cover." The boy in the Denver Broncos jacket glanced at her briefly, probably wondering what in the world Patty was thinking, then tugged out his phone and checked his email. The man seated next to him, propped up against the window, had fallen asleep, his arms crossed across his chest and eyes closed, his face wrinkled and shriveled. Turned bone-dry with age like the desert, he could have passed for an ancient mummy—one somehow smuggled from a museum and tossed aboard the train to be hurtled into public life and downtown Denver.

The two teenage girls were now engrossed in pawing over a copy of *People* magazine; other passengers were quietly staring out the windows. This was a quiet little theater, indeed, Patty thought. Hitting its stride, now on a section of track as straight as an arrow, the train zipped along through a flat, arid landscape that roasted under the sun like a vast baking sheet stretching clear to the eastern horizon, devoid of anything green, save for scattered patches of brush. The airport terminal was receding in the distance, now looking like a far-off cluster of tall, white circus tents. Scattered near it like huge dice that had been rolled into the desert and abandoned by gamblers who walked away stood the monolithic chain hotels. In the foreground beside the train tracks there were only small rocks, scrub, the poles flitting by that held the train's overhead wire, and now and again a spot where someone had tethered a small horse or minute donkey, fenced in a tiny enclosure together with a watering trough. There were no other signs of human life. And this was the dichotomy of the desert; there was what was close, and there was what was far away—there was nothing in between.

The train lurched slightly going over a dusty highway crossing, then canted to a sweeping curve that carried the train across an embankment, revealing the view to the west and the mile-high city of Denver. From this perspective, 20 miles away, the city appeared as a collection of stone obelisks raised heavenward by the hand of some pagan giant who once lived in this remote, arid land and worshipped the blazing sun that seemed so close overhead. It appeared as if it were a mirage, or perhaps some fantasy land depicted in a travel brochure; far beyond it, the jagged saw-toothed profile of the distant snowcapped Rockies rose like a painted theatrical backdrop in a stage show set, arranged to enthrall dawdling tourists and vacationers.

Patty had decided to forsake the hub of the airport and its mammoth hotel and to seek a needed day of rest—perhaps even visiting a museum—downtown. Her thoughts turned toward her daughter, Chloe, just now finishing up her sophomore year at the University of Vermont. There were mountains there, too; the Adirondacks, visible across Lake Champlain, and another, Mt. Mansfield, that loomed in the east. The university's hometown, Burlington, seemed to be a friendly little city, the kind of place where oncoming traffic stopped to let you make a left-hand turn, where some good-hearted passerby had put money in the parking meter where Patty had left her rental car, in order to spare her a ticket, the last time she visited Chloe. Soon, it would be time for another visit...time for her father, Brad's, birthday, too. But there would be no celebration—other than a celebration of Brad's life. Brad, called up from reserves to serve in Iraq, had died in combat, a victim of an IED, a roadside bomb. There were risks with everything in life. As a soldier, you have to accept those risks; you have to do your job and do your best, sometimes to simply just stay alive. It's what you do. And Patty had had to accept his loss, as hard as it had shaken her and Chloe. That was what she'd done.

Patty had to accept certain risks, also. There was little if any thought, day-to-day, to what would happen if her plane went down. If, God forbid, it suddenly exploded in mid-air, scattering passengers, crew, luggage, and debris into the sky, seven and a half miles above the earth. True, if this did happen at 40,000 feet, once ejected from the plane if you survived the blast, you would lose consciousness from the subzero temperature and lack of oxygen. Falling quickly, you would reach terminal velocity, about 122 miles per hour after the first 1,500 or so feet, dropping rapidly like a skydiver bereft of a parachute. But you would no doubt awake with a start and open your eyes sometime during the roughly three and three-quarter minutes it would take for you to finally make your impact on the world. It would give you time—but not much—to think. But you don't think about those things day-to-day if you are a flight attendant. You simply do your job as a professional and inspire confidence in your passengers; it's what you do. You seldom think about death and mayhem...unless, of course, your family has some connections to organized crime.

There were subtle clues in the past that Patty's father might be involved in activities that were questionable. Patty thought of the first one: the time her father disappeared when she was very young, before she'd first gone to school. Gone for a month, her father returned one day to Patty's relief and her mother's welcoming arms. "Thank God you're out," was all she said. And nothing further of the 30-day absence was ever mentioned again. Then, there was the second time, when she was 10 years old. During the summer, the Buchanan family next door went on vacation and their son David, a high school student and drummer in a rock band, insisted on staying home so he could do a gig while his parents and younger sister went on to Disney World. Their son, she learned afterward, was no slouch when it came to his social life; he had entrusted the care of the house to a pal that Friday night while he went out with the band. All told, about seven or eight of *his* friends showed up to help him pass away the evening with his housesitting duties and brought an ample supply of beer to keep them in good humor. They proceeded to spend the entire evening at the house, partying and drinking 'til well after midnight out on the deck; bawdy stories of sexual encounters, dirty jokes, and the sounds of hard rock music and foul language wafted unabated through the clear night air.

The next morning, Patty, having left her window open slightly despite the noise, heard the sounds of someone vomiting next door. She arose and looked out the window. The boys had apparently drunk until they passed out and slept—either on the deck or in their chairs; one of the teens had arisen and was leaning over the deck railing, retching and moaning. Another boy stirred in his chair and groaned, "Oh, dude...I'm so wasted!" It was then that the homeowners' son David arrived, looking somewhat disheveled, and stood on the deck with a look of amazement on his face. It was also the moment Patty's father emerged from the Callahan household, strode across the porch, and stood staring at the boys. He placed both hands on the porch railing and leaned toward them like a college professor who is eager to give a dissertation on a serious and very important subject.

"Fellas," Jimmy began, "I just have to tell you, now that you're coming around...and I knew you would...how much I enjoyed listening to you all last night." The rest of the boys were now coming shakily to their feet, rubbing their eyes, and staring back at Jimmy. Another of them staggered over to the side of the deck and retched briefly. "Yes, I really, really enjoyed hearing all about your drinking and your puking, your dope smoking, your screwing, and who you were screwing, plus every detail of your little lives. Who you are, who your parents are...your brothers and sisters, too. Yes, believe you me...I did enjoy it...and I will not ever, ever forget it. It was a very memorable evening. Thank you...and I will not hesitate to recommend you to my friends and associates."

Jimmy turned on his heel and strode back into the house, softly closing the door behind him. The boys stared at the door in disbelief. David was the first to speak.

"Oh my God," he said, looking around at his uninvited guests with a crazed, fearful look on his face. "Do you idiots know who that is? Do you have *any* idea who you've pissed off, you morons?" None answered; one boy belched loudly. "That was Jimmy C, Jimmy Callahan," said David, answering his own question. He ran his fingers through his hair as if trying to rip it out by the roots. "That's his house." He looked toward the Callahan home as if he'd seen a ghost.

"Oh, crap! Jimmy "The Merchant" Callahan?" said one of boys, looking as though he'd just seen a ghost. "That's *his* house? Now I am gonna hurl." He staggered about briefly, found his sneakers after a comically frantic search for them, and then fumbled clumsily in the course of putting them on, at first attempting to put his right sneaker on his left foot.

"Oh, crap, this is a bad, really bad scene," exclaimed the kid who'd been retching over the railing. "Oh, my God," he said, as he spun around, took a step, and tripped over his shoelaces, promptly falling flat on the deck. "Shit...we're screwed."

"Dave...dude...we didn't know...swear to God," said another, pulling on his jacket and staggering toward the steps. The rest of the boys, although groggy and ashen-faced, were now showing some definite signs of animation. Within five minutes flat, all the boys were gone except David, who scurried about with a trash bag, busily picking up discarded beer cans, pizza boxes, and fast food wrappers. No teenagers ever came to visit David after that day, nor did David ever again play his drums in his room or the garage, or even hold his graduation party on the deck or in the house. A time of peace and great tranquility existed ever afterward between the two families, the Buchanans and the Callahans.

That evening, at dinner, Patty had looked over at her dad and innocently asked him: "Why do they call you Jimmy "The Merchant", Dad? Is that some kind of nickname?" Jimmy dropped his fork as though he'd been stunned.

"Where did you hear that?" he demanded, retrieving his fork and pointing it at her.

"I heard one of those kids next door say it," she replied.

"That, young lady, is something I never want to hear in this household again," he cautioned her.

"Just eat your supper, Patty," advised Ellen, blushing and reaching over to touch Patty's hand. Jimmy's face had meanwhile affected the appearance of a thundercloud. "It's just one of those silly things. You know how silly some of those kids can be. They don't have to work, and they're probably jealous, because your father owns a store and their fathers don't." Ellen looked at Jimmy and gave him one of her bright-as-daytime Doris Day smiles; Jimmy stayed silent, focusing on his dinner, and briefly sawed savagely at his pork chop with his knife. Patty looked at her mom, then down at her own pork chop, potato, and green beans, studying them as if she expected the pork chop to somehow run away and escape its fate.

"Okay, Mom," she said, looking over at Ellen and managing a wan smile. Ellen beamed at her, looking relieved. It was another one of those things, Patty guessed, that you just couldn't ask about. Like what had happened to Aunt Rose. Or why Uncle John from Florida didn't visit any more.

"We don't talk about him," Ellen had said quietly, the last time Patty asked. "Let's talk about what went on in school today. You looked so happy when you came home! What did you learn? And remember, you have your ballet rehearsal tomorrow after school." And that was the dichotomy of the Callahan household when Patty was growing up. The enigmas of the family history that loomed so large in her mind as it raised question after question about them were forever on the horizon—dark, obscure, and distant. But close by, always at hand were the small things—the trivial, the menial: school lunch menus, ballet, *Jeopardy* on daytime TV, *Happy Days* on evenings. Shopping expeditions at Kmart or Filene's Basement every other Saturday. It was what you did.

And in between the two, the distant and the close at hand...that was the nowhere land, the place that was neither here nor there, where things—and people—disappeared over the years and simply went away. These disappearances haunted Patty...but in a strange turnabout, it was the memories of Patty, ever blonde and blue, hiking off to the bus stop almost every day, a smile on her face, turned up nose, books in hand, that had haunted Ellen when Patty herself had disappeared soon after finishing her senior year at high school. She returned home that fall, tanned, world-wise, and confident, unannounced and in her own car—a real beater—after a summer spent in Maine working with a theatrical company. She also had a fiancé, Brad.

"You never told me you were leaving. You have no idea how I worried," Ellen said to Patty when her wayward daughter arrived at the Dorchester home's doorstep one drab October afternoon when the sky was filmy with overcast, the neighborhood strewn with windblown litter, downed tree limbs, and puddles of gray storm water left behind from a late-season hurricane that had swept through. There was wind in Ellen's hair, strain in her voice, and pain in her eyes. The family television, heard faintly from within the house, rumbled with news of boats tossed up on beaches along the coastline, flooding inland, and National Guard callouts to rescue stranded homeowners. The script rattled on as Patty stared at her mother for a moment, and then the two of them embraced in forgiveness. And then, Ellen let go of what she could not forgive.

"He's left me," was all Ellen said, starting to cry. "He's gone...disappeared into that basement of his business...that hell-hole of his...it's where he lives now. It's his whole life."

This was the beginning of the process in which Patty, albeit slowly over the past many years, had begun to peel back the onion of the Callahan family history, once her mother relented: the stories, sometimes pried out of the past, came forth about Great-Grandfather Mickey, the rum-runner and about Uncle John, the bookmaker and his floozy girlfriend who'd displaced Uncle John's wife. And her dad, Jimmy Callahan, petty thief and up-and-coming safecracker who wised-up after a brush with the law, and took to running a legitimate (or, so it would appear) business, issuing great promises of family fortune and stability.

The train's air horns hooted to warn motorists to stop at a grade crossing with a Denver highway, and the sound of the signal's clamoring warning bells rose and fell as the train passed by them. Gates held back traffic on a street where a line of customers stood at a mini-mart-turned-marijuana dispensary, and a small boy and his father standing close by the tracks both waved to the train's engineer. The train slowed, coasted past freight yards teeming with grimy boxcars speckled with graffiti, and presently pulled into Union Station, gently coming to a stop before a bumping post at the platform. The window into Patty's past closed as the doors on her car rolled open and the disembodied voice sounded once more, advising that the train had reached the end of the line. She stood up, pulled down her carry-on luggage from its spot on the overhead rack and headed for the station entrance and her hotel beyond. The next day would bring another window...another departure, in itself a disappearing act, the kind that began with leaving her parents' home long ago. The act in which a person vanishes after appearing on stage, getting sawn in half in a magician's show, and goes wandering off in two different directions only to strangely reappear—whole, the halves recon-nected, years later. Back to tell, should someone ask, of how she had defied the odds to survive and return...all the while in-explicably clinging to memories of the past as if no harm had ever been done to her. And to ask, mind wide open, what had happened while she'd been gone...and why.

Chapter 3

Brothers in Crime

Friday night was the Saluzzo brothers' meeting night. The three not-so-wiseguys liked to get together after hours to discuss a little business at the end of each week. Much like the way a floating crap game moves around to various locales until it is either unwelcome or else plays out its course, the Saluzzo brothers' weekly meeting was held at a different watering hole each Friday. Variety was one consideration; another was that the vociferous trio frequently wore out their welcome at establishments.

Frank "Fat Franky" and Bobby "Two Shots" Saluzzo were enjoying the pleasures of the Knothole Lounge at Driftwood by the Sea on Boston's south shore, draining multiple glasses of booze while they awaited the arrival of Charlie, "Cha Cha". Tonight, he was late, and the duo anticipating his arrival had thus become loud and rather pleasantly (or so they thought) intoxicated. Frank, once a chubby youngster, had simply become an obese, middle-aged man in order to acquire his hoodlum nickname. His brother Bobby, on the other hand, had earned his nickname, "Two Shots", from his innate inability to fire a handgun and hit a target of any kind with either the first or the second bullet, only the third...and whatever followed.

Usually, a quick succession of bullets would follow until Bobby had emptied his clip; counting shots was not his forte.

"Hit the side of a barn? He should be so lucky," said Irv "The Nerve" Bernstein, the wily, dour-faced old fence in Medford who occasionally 'did some work' (which meant murder for hire) and otherwise procured untraceable firearms for Vince's men when necessary so they could do some 'jobs' (which were far less complicated). "Guns, I like," grumbled Irv. "Him, not so much."

The two brothers eyed the television set hanging over the bar. The news was on and it was bad: Freddy "The Fish" Funarlo, an underworld figure who had been recently caught up in a sting operation and turned state's evidence against his employer, had mysteriously disappeared. He'd been missing for several days; the worst was feared, and now the district attorney was in a jam and reaching for the aspirin bottle.

"Damn!" said Bobby in a loud voice, draining the last of his whiskey, but keeping his eyes level with the TV screen. "From what I hear, ol' Freddy isn't lyin' low and slow somewhere; he's been shot fulla holes, for sure. Maybe gettin' ripe in the trunk of his old Continental, for all I know. He sure could drink. Drank like a fish, right? Know what? Bet he can't keep his alcohol down now, can he? It'd be pourin' all outa him...just like rainwater!"

Franky tried but could not suppress a giggle that made him quiver all over, like a mass of Jell-O whose otherwise massive and glacially-calm appearance is suddenly rumpled by an earthquake.

"Yeah! Freddie the Sieve!" he chortled, coughing and spitting out a few cocktail peanuts. "And they say nobody dies of lead poisoning anymore!" Betty the waitress, at all times all ears, slipped by silently, cat-like, her eyes glancing over those of the brothers slowly, warily. She scooped up Franky's and Bobby's empty glasses, placing them deftly onto her tray. She knew the two men could be total jackasses, but were stellar tippers.

"How 'bout another one, guys?" she asked, taking a calculated risk.

"Ya, sure," said Franky. "And," he added, patting his lap, "how about touching down here for a little break, Betty? On my landing strip?"

"In your dreams," Betty retorted. She then faced him and smiled a broad, defiant smile. "You don't have room for me down there; there's too much of you spreading out all over your knees." She stalked off to the bar, and both Franky and Bobby's eyes unerringly followed the fast, determined undulations of her derriere, until they lost sight of it, jiggling rhythmically as she stalked off into the kitchen. Now Bobby giggled, and Franky took offense.

"Screw you." he said to his brother.

"What?" asked Bobby. "*You* pissed her off. Now, me, the big tipper; I'm gonna have to make it right. I always have to pick up after you."

"I still say screw you," Franky said. "You ain't pickin' up my toys; I try to pick up one, you bust my chops. Shame on you." A middle-age man entered the restaurant, whale-watching brochures in hand—obviously a tourist, with his wife and two kids in tow. All wore matching, bright orange windbreakers. "Nice jackets, folks!" remarked Franky, leering at them as they passed by, loud enough to be overheard at the bar. "Halloween early this year?"

A few minutes later, Betty returned with fresh drinks and set them down, together with new napkins.

"Betty," Franky crooned after her, "Betty...Boop-boop, be-doop!" His gaze was focused just a short distance away from and at a spot located several inches below her neckline. Betty rolled her eyes and brandished her empty tray like a centurion holding off a rain of poison arrows with a shield. Franky reached for his drink; Bobby slapped his hand.

"Apologize now, you dipshit," Bobby growled to his brother.

"You know what?" asked Betty. "I don't care. I really don't." She walked off in a huff. The brothers stared down at their drinks.

A few tables away from the brothers was John Mulligan, a recently retired corrections officer. John had, up until this point, been enjoying a quiet dinner with his wife. The spot John had chosen was perfect for him, because it indulged his need for a seat with its back to a wall, for security, and afforded a clear view of both the lounge's entranceway and that of the restaurant, from which the enticing aromas of juicy steaks, succulent seafood, and top-shelf liquor wafted.

"I have to," he'd explained to his wife as he requested that spot in the lounge. "I just have to see who's coming and who's going...it's habit. I spent too many years doing it inside." And now, as was his habit, John kept one eye on the brothers, who he pegged as potential troublemakers, while he worked away at his medium-rare sirloin with a large, serrated knife. Meanwhile he discussed vacation plans for the coming summer season with his wife.

The Knothole, and the Driftwood itself, enjoyed a stellar reputation, and its owner liked to keep it that way; bad news makes people vote with their feet and leave. In fact, the Internet was fairly alive with postings of rave reviews of the fine food, the friendly staff, and the great ambience of the impressive-looking lodging and its lounge, but not so in recent years of the many other grand old resorts and restaurants in the surrounding area. One by one, they had succumbed to the public's reaction to the withering digital diatribes of disgruntled diners and guests, and closed their doors—only to be bought at auction, in many cases––and re-opened by the secretive owner of Driftwood by the Sea.

The Knothole took its name from a peep-hole in the door of a popular speakeasy that had flourished in this spot during the Prohibition days, days when fast, mahogany-hulled power-boats brought in the beer and the booze from ships that plied the waters between the deep-water ports of Canada and the parched-dry Massachusetts coastal towns. And when men of great influence and wealth controlled the flow of alcohol and money that defied the grasp of the law and the G-men who tried to enforce it. On the weekends, the parking lot over-flowed with the Packards, Lincolns, Pierce-Arrows, and Cadillacs of well-to-do patrons who'd come from miles around to drink, gamble, play, and dance away the night hours. In its latest iteration, this stylish hideaway and its ever-watchful owner looked carefully after the interests of the guests...very carefully. And so it was that this owner, watching the events of the evening taking place in the lounge, decided to dispatch the manager to the table of the two inebriated Saluzzo brothers.

"Is everything alright with you gentlemen?" Rick, the manager inquired politely, tapping Franky ever so gently on his right shoulder to gain his attention.

"Yeah, okay, but not so right," he replied.

The manager's eyebrows shot up; then he composed himself and inquired further: "What seems to be amiss?"

"A miss? You see...there's the problem," Franky declared, draining the contents of his glass and then plunging its swizzle stick briefly into the top of the manager's hand, to make sure he had his attention. "Your *Miss* Betty here, she ain't too friendly. And you know what? We here think you guys need some protection."

"Protection? From what?" asked Rick gamely, his brow beginning to wrinkle.

"The wrong kind...the criminal element," Franky said, matter-of-factly." He turned, spotted Betty, then picked up and waved his empty glass at her to regain her attention.

"What my brother means is...what he means," explained Bobby, "we know there are some people, bad people coming into this territory, who would like to take over this place. People from out of state, even...now, Franky here and me, we know you have those poker machines downstairs that nobody's supposed to know about; they'll be after you to control the action. We can help you—believe me."

"Are you cops?" asked Rick.

"No," replied Bobby, grinning like a monkey who's spotted a ripe banana that has fallen from a tree in the jungle, as soon as he spotted what he believed to be signs of relief written all over Rick's face. "You can trust us with your troubles; we're pros."

"This sounds interesting," said Rick, regaining his composure, rubbing the back of his sore hand. "Let's go see Mr. Z."

"Mr. Z, huh?" asked Franky, looking expectantly at Bobby. "Hey, does this guy have some horsepower here?"

"Absolutely," replied Rick.

"Look, guy," said Bobby. "We're waiting on our other brother, Charlie. He's way late. Have Betty here fix him up with some drinks and eats...here." Bobby plucked a roll of big bills from his pocket and stuffed two twenties into Rick's hand.

"Come with me," he told the brothers, and he led them away from the table and into the restaurant, in the process, stopping to hand Betty one of the twenties and telling her to expect Charlie.

"Where are we goin'?" asked Franky, waddling along; he bumped into a table, spilling peoples' drinks as he passed by the bar.

"Downstairs to the big guy's office. Mr. Z's," Rick answered, looking over his shoulder at the two men as they walked along, swaying slightly as they came, then at the security camera positioned over the bar.

Mr. Z's basement office was sparsely furnished. A battered desk stacked with papers and ledgers stood in one corner, near

a pile of crates of lettuce, potatoes, and onions. A motley as-
semblage of plain, wooden chairs stood before the desk. Beside
the desk stood a large trash can with a Boston Red Sox emblem
on it. Several bare overhead light bulbs provided a dim sort of
illumination, somewhat on the order of the light that reaches
Saturn from the far-distant sun. And like a far-off planet, this
room was cold and dank. Mr. Z, a tall, thin man, dressed im-
peccably (and quite improbably, for this atmosphere) in a black
suit, vanilla-white dress shirt, and a gold, silk necktie, sat impassively behind the desk. Mr. Z did not look at the two brothers.

"Sit down," was all he said, softly. Then, "So?"

The brothers resisted the urge to exchange nervous glances;
this was not exactly what they had expected.

"We," Bobby said, "are offering you some protection."

"Really?" asked Mr. Z, looking up at them, a look of mock
surprise on his face. "And why would I need that?"

"Because," Bobby said, "we were tellin' this guy here, what's
his name?"

"Rick," answered Mr. Z, nodding, and then folding his hands
together on his desk, as though he were a teacher indulging a
schoolboy who is struggling mightily to come up with a correct
answer to a tough question.

"Well, we thought that Rick, and you...you could use our
help...against the wrong kind guys, you know..."

"Tell me now, boys; are you insurance agents?" asked Mr. Z,
a thin smile spreading across his narrow face.

"Well, in a way we are," said Franky, shifting his ponderous
weight in the uncomfortable, creaking chair and struggling to
look self-assured.

"Funny," commented the thin man behind the desk. "I've
seen insurance ads. Neither one of you resembles that little
green lizard that talks with an accent. Or Flo."

"Hey!" Bobby blurted out, "do you know who we are?"

"Yes, I do," countered Mr. Z, the thin man with the wicked smile. "You're BS artists, both of you. And I know who you are...the Sleazzo brothers, we call you, the lesser guys from greater Boston. The boys their own father fired. The Larry, Moe, and Curly team who can do the work of one man. I think Boston would be much greater...without you. I have a lot of people, just like you, who try to shake me down. And I'm always ready for them. I *do* have insurance; just take a look behind you." A door behind the two brothers opened and then swiftly closed.

Both brothers turned; behind Bobby stood a huge man in a black Driftwood by the Sea polo shirt and jeans, a man who was roughly, Bobby figured, the size of a Brahman bull. Behind Franky was a punk, super-size, about six feet tall. He wore a black T-shirt, with a greasy, dirt-stained apron wrapped around his waist and his black leather pants. He had a stud in his nose and skull rings on his fingers; the narrow strip of purple hair on his otherwise shaved head stood up like the bristles on the back of a wild boar.

"Hey, hey, hey, now wait a minute here!" exclaimed Bobby, starting to rise from his chair. "This ain't right! You got us all wrong!"

"Sit down, banty rooster," said Mr. Z. A heavy hoof from the Brahman bull man shoved Bobby firmly back down into his chair.

"I think *you've* got it wrong," said the thin man, pulling a pack of cigarettes from the breast pocket of his black suit. He selected one, lit it, and inhaled the smoke deeply. He tipped back in his chair and then blew the smoke toward the ceiling, gazing at it as if he were a churchgoer studying frescoes. He then lowered his gaze to look at the brothers.

"I think it's *you two* who need some insurance. Do you know where your brother, Cha Cha is?"

"Yeah, he's headed here now," Franky said.

"Wrong," said the thin man. "He's already here. Take a look." Mr. Z pointed at one of the three security monitors next to his desk.

"He ain't here," declared Franky, looking at one of the split screens. "Our table's empty."

"Of course it is," the thin man replied, kicking back his chair and putting his feet up on the desk. "He's in another room. Your brother got here early...and we found a table for him. We're like that; we're good people...see?"

He pointed to one screen in particular, showing the indistinct figure of a man, alone in a large room who was bound to a chair and seated before a small table, upon which sat a baseball bat. The room was otherwise empty.

"Oh, shit," said Franky; Bobby was silent.

"This," said Mr. Z, rising from his chair, stepping over to the trash can, and pulling out an aluminum baseball bat, "is why insurance is important." He swiftly raised the bat and then brought it down with brute force on the empty chair next to Bobby, destroying its back and showering Bobby with splinters of wood. "I think you need to pay for a policy—right now."

"Hey, if you think we're gonna sit here and watch—" started Bobby.

"Too late," said Mr. Z. Bobby and Franky felt their shoulders being grabbed from behind, forcing them to stay, squirming, in their chairs. Mr. Z stepped to the wall behind them, tapped on it three times, and suddenly another murky figure appeared on the video monitor, picked up the bat, swung it, and hit the man bound to the chair. He paused, turned, walked over to the camera, and covered the lens with his hand—the screen went dark. Two or three muffled thumps were then heard from the room behind the brothers—there was a groan of agony—then silence. "Round one," said Mr. Z, smiling at the brothers, and dropping the bat back into the trash can. "As you can see, my doctor next door likes to have fun with his patients. After all...he is...a bone specialist. Gonna pay your premiums, boys? You do care about Cha Cha, don't you? Five hundred bucks apiece—now. Or it'll be just the two of you trying to do one man's work."

Five minutes later, after the pastry chef had stopped pounding the dummy duct-taped into the chair in the room adjacent to Mr. Z's office, and the Saluzzo brothers were, between the two of them, $1,000 to the bad—after Mr. Z told the brothers they would see Charles in the parking lot—John Mulligan and his wife, enjoying dessert, watched, enthralled, as the Brahman bull and the super punk, otherwise recognizable to regular customers as the bar back and the dishwasher, frog-marched Bobby and Franky up to the front door. They then tossed the brothers out into the parking lot, where Charlie was just emerging from his car, its radiator steaming.

"Hey guys?" he asked with a look of concern. "I just got here, sorry I'm late; car trouble. What's goin' on?"

"Where the hell have you been?" roared Bobby at him. Before Charlie could answer, Bobby threw a punch at him and missed; Franky pummeled him and kicked his shins, and then Bobby tried anew and connected with Charlie's jaw.

"You sonofabitch!" Franky cursed at Charlie, who stared up at them from where he'd landed after bouncing off the fender of a car, putting a small dent in it, and fell to the pavement.

"They're criminals, aren't they?" asked John Mulligan's wife, as she poked the last of her cheesecake with a fork and eyed the goings on in the parking lot outside the lounge through a large, plate-glass window that was framed like a ship's porthole.

"Yes, dear," answered John, taking the last sip of his coffee and reaching for the check. "And you know what? Most criminals have one thing in common."

"Really?" asked his wife, her eyes wide open in wonderment.

"Yes," answered John. "They're stupid."

Chapter 4

Woes in Waltham

In a sedate, leafy part of the suburb of Waltham, where things were relatively quiet and calm, and while the birds sang in the trees and people in the neighborhood on this beautiful Saturday morning mowed their lawns, or drove to the supermarket or walked out to the mailbox to get their mail, Patty Callahan sat with her mother, Ellen, at the kitchen table in Ellen's tidy little home. Sunlight streamed through the two windows of the compact room in Ellen's comfortable bungalow and was reflected onto the bright yellow walls by the surface of the Formica table, where two plates of steaming hot scrambled eggs, toast, and bacon sat while Patty caught up on one thing after another relating to Callahan family history with her mother. Outside the small house, Ellen's little old maroon Toyota sat on its somewhat underinflated, economy-grade tires in front of Ellen's garage, the aged car's sides bearing small white streaks from where it had gently kissed both sides of the doorway during the past seven or so years. Ellen's eyesight was not exactly what it used to be.

"Want coffee, Patty?" asked Ellen, walking over to the table with a percolator of ancient origin.

"Sure, Mom," replied Patty. "And may I say, Mom...it's sure nice to be waited on; you're the best!" Patty's job as a flight attendant, flying out of Logan frequently, had made her the almost-consummate and almost constant hostess. It felt nice to kick back for a few days after the return from Denver and relax without wearing a uniform, engaging passengers in small talk about their in-flight movies, and attending to their many personal problems. Most of them involved their small lives and increasingly large demands, all the time while the airplane moved rapidly over the land thousands of feet below, itself a work in miniature glimpsed through pressurized windows. It was one seen as a crazy-quilt patchwork of landscape, like the ones bomber pilots of World War II had seen when they looked down at their targets and most likely determined, since they were being shot at from below and were targets themselves, that everyone living in that patchwork beneath them was as crazy as they were.

And, speaking of targets, security concerns posed a night-mare in regulations and protocol; as her favorite pilot often ruefully said: "Before 9/11, flying was fun." The dark-brown coffee plunged, steaming and gurgling into Patty's cup in a steady stream, almost overflowing the rim.

"Whoa, Mom! Enough already!" Patty shouted, beaming up at her mom and looking into her blue eyes. Mom had had a tough time of it after Jimmy had left her, filed the divorce, and moved on, leaving with a then-new car, enough money to buy a house (a small one, built in 1947, thank you, Jimmy), and some other means of support while she finagled a job at the lo-cal grade school, working in the lunch room. There were crows' feet around Ellen's eyes now that evidenced the stress of a working person, a person who was at the age in which golden parachutes open for many, but not for people like her. A rising tide lifts all boats, but not the ones chained tightly to the bot-tom.

"So what's this deal with Dad, Mom, and why did you call me?" Patty asked. Ellen poured a cup of coffee for herself and sat down heavily. She stared into her cup, Patty thought, as if she were a clairvoyant reading tea leaves. But Ellen was not looking solely into the future—she was looking into the past. Recalling the golden days of old long before Jimmy had gotten mixed up with the the Monument Hill boys, before he'd gotten into a close relationship with the beer and the booze, before the late night business meetings that kept him away from home that were followed by the cops knocking on the front door the next morning, asking him if he knew someone who was on the run. And finally, before that epic night when Jimmy came home late, liquor on his breath and lipstick on his collar. And, perhaps, now she had indeed glimpsed a bit, just a bit, of what the future might hold and what it meant for her and her daughter...if a certain family issue that had long lain buried could be resolved.

"Your father," Ellen said, "is up to something again. He's asked me to help him with a problem."

"Oh my God, Mom; you're not going to do it, are you?" Patty inquired, leaning across the table and staring at Ellen, who now sat with her arms crossed defensively, a sure, sign that she had obviously already made up her mind. Outside the small white house and its garage, with the lawn that did credit to the appearance of the manicured greens of a miniature golf course, a mail truck puttered by. It stopped and then started, and then there was the sound of the lid of the mailbox at the end of Ellen's short driveway slamming shut, signaling that the mail, with its customary allotment of bills, magazine subscription renewal notices, and solicitations for various nonprofits had been delivered.

"I think I am, Patty," said Ellen, who'd lowered her head and was now studying the ashtray on the table, rather than her coffee grounds. "He's said it's something for old time's sake...and it's something about your Aunt Rose."

"My Aunt Rose?" queried Patty, eyebrows arched to the max.

"Yes," continued Ellen.

"*My aunt*, the ballerina goddess?" asked Patty.

"This may come as a shock to you, but she was...she was not a ballerina, Patty," said Ellen, reaching for her cigarettes.

"*You* have never told me this!" said Patty. "You've never told me about her, about what really happened to her," Patty said strongly, folding her arms, forming a blockade of sorts across her end of the table.

"And there's good reason for that," said Ellen, seeking to reopen the conversation in earnest. "But, well...now...I think you're old enough to know. I think I need to tell you."

"Old enough to *know*? Ma...what are you saying?" Patty shrieked.

"Don't call me Ma, Patty. And please, please, eat something," said Ellen, who calmly lit up a cigarette, her lighter flaring briefly, the cigarette glowing and its smoke spiraling upward toward the ceiling of the kitchen after her lighter clicked, like an automatic pistol being cocked and then snapped shut. Ellen tapped the butt on her ashtray, sculpting it carefully, regarding it the way a master craftsman regards a piece of marble while slowly crafting it into a work of art. She briefly studied it, then returned her eyes to the level of those of her daughter.

"Your dad's older sister, Rose, she was in some trouble, back before she was almost your age. Your dad helped her. She studied ballet, acting...all of that stuff. Like you did. High school days. But a job? There were no jobs. Yes, your dad did some awful things, as you know...but so did your Aunt Rose. We've all done things we had to, hon, when we had to get by."

Patty sat, stunned, in her chair, her arms dropping down and dangling at her sides, her mind attuned to her mother's story.

"Your aunt, she worked at a club," said Ellen, swigging her coffee, dragging on her cigarette and then taking a stab at her breakfast.

"Omigod, Mom; a club? What *kind* of club?" Patty asked, elbows scooting in on the table, both eyes focused keenly on Ellen.

"Well," came Ellen's reply, "nothing bad; she was a dancer."

"Oh God, Mom, you mean, like, an *exotic* dancer?"

"Yes, dear." Ellen puffed on her cigarette, looked out the window in embarrassment, then snuffed her smoke out. "And she got mixed up with the wrong kind, you might say. She made money—good money. Had plans to get out of performing at all those places...you know, the old Combat Zone, we called it, down on Washington Street in town. And then it happened."

"All you've ever told me—all anyone ever has—is that she died. That she was murdered."

"Well, sure enough," said Ellen, lighting up another smoke. "That was in '78. Shot dead late one night at the club where she worked. That's how the story went."

"Mom...*the story*; what do you mean? What story?" asked Patty.

"She got shot. But she didn't die there in '78." At this, Patty jumped to her feet, knocking her chair back against the wall, and then paced the room like a caged animal, pulling her fingers through her hair. "Stop it, Patty, and sit down. You'll yank your hair out," said Ellen, authoritatively.

"I just might, Mom, before I get all the answers I need from you," said Patty, reclaiming her chair and sitting down heavily, then staring, wide-eyed, at her mother. "So, now I find out...my aunt wasn't a dancer; she was a stripper, right? And she was a murder victim. Okay, so what's the story? I want to hear it...from A to Z."

Ellen took a deep breath, stared out the window, and then continued. "Your aunt witnessed a murder, a murder in cold blood. A gangster shot the manager of the old Mayflower, the club where your aunt worked. It was late at night after a show...everyone but your aunt and the manager had gone home; Rose had misplaced her car keys and had been looking for them all over the place...and finally walked backstage, over toward the manager's office, trying to find them. She stopped and looked around the corner down a hallway into the room, just in time to see a man...oh, God; it was awful...strangling her boss, shoving him up against the wall. 'Where is the money?' he kept yelling. Another man, his accomplice, said the job wasn't going fast enough...he looked wild, crazy. 'Let him go—he's useless—I'm out of patience,' he yelled. He pointed a gun at her boss's chest and shot him—two or three times. And just then...he turned around, saw that she'd come in, and obviously seen and heard everything...and then he shot her."

"Now," said Patty, throwing her hands up, "I am totally confused. Aunt Rose and the manager are the only people, other than this gunman, in the whole place; the manager's dead, and since Aunt Rose is dead...I need to know...*who* told you this story?"

"Simple," said Ellen, draining her coffee cup. "Your aunt...and the FBI." The television set in the living room Ellen had left on when Patty arrived blared loud music suddenly, announcing a rerun of an ancient episode of *Jeopardy* that had somehow triumphantly survived the passage of time.

"Your aunt," stated Ellen, "did not die that night. That gunman shot her because she'd witnessed a murder, after all, so he took no chances...or so he thought. Rose was just an innocent person who was in the wrong place at the wrong time. But he didn't do his job. His small-caliber bullet took out her left eye; but she lived. He and his partner must have left her for dead. The building super found her lying unconscious on the stage when he came in to check the boiler and wondered why the lights were still on. He found Bernie Finnegan, the manager, too, stone-cold dead...with a letter opener in one hand and a playing card, the ace of spades, lying on his chest. Was it a clue? If it was, no one ever found out anything about it."

Patty sipped coffee and listened to her mother.

"And when she recuperated," Ellen continued, "weeks afterward, she talked to the police, once she was able to. Then the FBI came in—because of who this manager was mixed up with—and they put her in the witness protection program. They moved her away. Away from everything and everyone...all of us."

"There was a funeral...I know, Mom; I was there...I was a little kid, but I saw it," stated Patty emphatically, the words falling out of her mouth slowly. Tears formed in her eyes, a gathering rainstorm. "I know what I saw."

"Yes," said Ellen reflectively. "I remember, too; it was closed-casket, Patty. It had to be that way; they buried an empty coffin. Your father...he and I knew the whole truth of the matter, but nobody else. I was sworn to secrecy. I agreed to things because I had to. But...Patty...the truth never did seem to matter much to your father. I made my choices. For me—and for your sake. I didn't want them finding out about his business...and all those friends he had in that crew of his. I had my own life to look after. I kept them away from him, from finding out about him."

"So...Aunt Rose...she's...alive?" queried Patty, looking askew at her mother.

"No," said Ellen, staring down into her now-empty coffee cup. "She was shot dead that winter in the lobby of some cheap hotel on the south side the FBI had put her up in. They'd called her back from out West to testify before a grand jury. Someone knew...someone had to know she was there...someone set her up." Ellen looked up at her daughter; tears were in her eyes now. "Patty, her face was disfigured...she said she could never work again, never see people again...never go out in public."

"So, what, Mom; you're on board with what, Dad's revenge?" fired back Patty.

"Patty...your aunt and I were...we were so close. There has been so much of this that I want to end...all of the old business. The business from your father's days. Those bad old days. Can you...will you help me, please? It's for old times' sake. And then, I hope...it will be over."

"Dad! Dad! Go Dad, go!" whistled Ellen's pet cockatiel Skylar from his cage in the corner. Skylar, wings aflutter, paced back and forth excitedly on his perch, and Ellen turned to offer him a piece of crust from her toast, which Skylar proceeded to nibble on.

"Besides, Mom, why wait to tell me this, all this, now?" Patty entreated, digging into her breakfast, now gone stone cold, with sudden, renewed interest.

"Because!" Ellen replied hotly. "And because I knew your aunt. She was a good person."

"But she died, Mom. How?" Patty wailed, tugging at a strand of her hair again.

"Murder. Plain and simple. And your father says he knows who did it now," Ellen answered.

It was 9:00 a.m. and on that mark, Ellen's television blared forth the latest news from its spot in the living room amid a collection of tattered magazines and crossword puzzle books; the TV was usually left on 24/7 regardless of when (or if) Ellen went to bed. Skylar nibbled on the last of his toast, scattering crumbs into the bottom of his cage. Save for the latest on disasters, storms, killings and political mayhem from that televised source, all was silent in Ellen Callahan's bungalow...until Patty spoke.

"You know, Mom? I'm a lot like Skylar. Yeah, I fly, but I'm in a cage. A cage with a couple of hundred people who aren't like me. People who have to be cocktailed at 35,000 feet to keep them happy and quiet. People who like to fight with each other. People who treat luggage like religious objects. And now I'm thinking, really, really thinking about all this...because I am who I am, not somebody else. Remember what Dad said? When I still liked him?" Ellen was silent, but attuned to what her daughter was saying: "Honey, if you're going to be just like me...who's going to be just like you?"

Patty paused, reflected, and circled back, saying "But, because I love you, Mom, whatever you need my help for, I'll do it...just this time...for old time's sake."

Chapter 5

The Silver Bullet, 1978

Patty left her mother's Waltham home early—shortly before lunchtime—because she knew that she had to clean her apartment, pay bills, do laundry during the afternoon, and pack for her morning departure from Logan the next day. Storm clouds that had been gathering in the west soon overtook her car, and heavy rain began to drum on its roof and windshield. The traffic leaving Waltham moved slowly, the local weekend drivers dawdling, going from mall to mall, being cautious in the gloom and downpour and it was just as well, due to the poor visibility. Patty daydreamed and poked along, and the windshield wipers on her car brushed away the raindrops, which fell aside and trickled down the side windows like long, drawn-out tears on this dreary, gray day. The repetitive sound lulled her into letting her mind wander and engage in a certain feeling of sadness and a longing for the past, the sense of the present seemingly flowing away in the slipstream left behind her little car as it churned its way along through the storm, splashing gray, foaming rainwater to the sides of the road. She soon thought back to her favorite childhood visit with Aunt Rose, on a sunny day long ago when Rose took her to the beach on the south shore for a weekend in hot, sunny August.

"She's here!" Ellen had announced, pulling aside curtains and looking out the bay window of the living room in the Callahans' Dorchester duplex. "The Silver Bullet has arrived!" Ellen then turned around quickly, padded in her slippers to the television, and turned it off; the Looney Tunes image of Bugs Bunny running across a field of carrots instantly narrowed, turned into a tiny white dot on the screen, and then vanished into a black morass. Patty, all of 5 years old, jumped off the couch from where she'd been watching cartoons and ran to the window, chock-full of curiosity to see just what the Silver Bullet (which she'd heard so often about) really was. She then stood on tiptoe, grabbed her mom's waist, and looked out at the street, where a shiny, silver-gray Pontiac Firebird Trans Am had pulled up to the curb.

"That's her," said Ellen.

"Aunt Rosie!" exclaimed Patty, a smile bright as sunshine beaming on her face; she waved her little left hand at the figure behind the wheel of the car; the figure waved back.

"Do you have all of your things? Your bathing suit and towel?" asked Ellen, looking down at her little daughter.

"Yes Mommy," replied Patty, turning and looking up at her mother. "We're gonna go to sit...sit...skit..."

"Scituate, Patty," said her mom, smiling at her. "It's a funny name. But there's a big beach, and a lighthouse, and Aunt Rose's little old beach shack. You'll have so much fun! Now don't forget to have Aunt Rose help you put on suntan lotion. You don't want to get sunburned, Honey. And remember, don't go into the water unless Aunt Rose is with you."

Then there was the *thunk* of a car door being slammed, and suddenly the thudding of Jimmy Callahan's stockinged feet pounding down the front hall stairway from the bedroom, quick time, sounding like a buffalo stampede in a corny, old-time Western movie, the kind that Patty loved to watch on television. Just having finished getting dressed and fastening the last button on his shirt, he opened the front door just as Rose, forever flamboyant, this time in short, rhinestone-studded denim cutoffs and a tight black T-shirt, swung open the aluminum screen door.

"Hey Sis!" Jimmy said, giving her a hug and almost pulling her off her feet. "You're looking good. Been working out or something?"

"Yeah," answered Rose, giving him a saucy-looking smile. "Been working out a way to convince everyone you're really not my brother!"

"I see you're still drivin' that old hot rod, huh?" asked Jimmy, peering out at the Pontiac. "Don't you know gas is gonna be up to 65 cents a gallon by Labor Day? You must be making the Arabs a fortune!" They both laughed and turned to watch Patty come running toward them with open arms.

"Aunt Rose!" she exclaimed. Rose scooped her up, and gave her a hug and a kiss.

"I think Patty's adopted you!" observed Ellen, joining the welcoming reception, still dressed in her bathrobe, coffee cup in hand. "Good grief, Rose!" she exclaimed, looking askance at her in mock disapproval. "You're showing off a lot of your famous fast figure today. I hope you don't go walking around the Combat Zone like that!"

"Yeah," commented Jimmy, nudging her with an elbow, "you've gotta be like a banker; keep your assets under cover!"

"What time do you think you'll be back on Sunday, Rose?" Ellen asked.

"I'll shoot for 4:00, before dinnertime," answered Rose, adding with a sly, eye-shadowed wink "unless she's a bad girl. Then, it'll be early."

"Oh, I won't be!" promised Patty breathlessly, clasping her hands together.

"Okay, Patty; you're on," said her aunt. "And it will be 4:00, because I have two shows to do Sunday night in town. Now, we should go, before we hit traffic. Do you have your things, Hon?"

"They're right here," Ellen answered for her daughter, presenting Rose with a small pink duffle bag with Patty's change of clothes, bathing suit, toothbrush, comb, and towel.

"Take it easy, now, Sis," Jimmy cautioned. "Remember," he said to Rose, with a grin, "Jesus jumps out after 70!"

"Better kiss your mom and dad goodbye now," said Rose to Patty. "We have to get going."

This time it was Jimmy who scooped up the little girl, brought her up to the height of his head and shoulders, and Patty gave him a kiss. Her dad's cheek was rough; he hadn't shaved yet. It felt like sandpaper to her, the sandpaper her dad used when he made Patty her dollhouse out of wood, cardboard, and wallpaper; she had watched him in awe, working down in the basement. Patty gave her mom a kiss and then Patty was out the door, holding her aunt's hand tightly and walking with her toward the car, a car that stood long, low, and sleek. Its grille, divided by a slim chrome bar, yawned wide open, dark as a chasm inside like the maw of a hungry, great gray shark that would eat up the miles between Dorchester and the seacoast.

Rose opened the door for Patty, gathered several eight-track tapes from the front seat, and tossed them onto the backseat. She reached around behind her seat, grabbed an old boat throw cushion life preserver that was lying on the floor, and placed it on the front passenger seat for Patty to sit on, so she could see over the dashboard. Painted on the cushion was a name: *Bad Penny*. Patty hopped onto it, and Rose helped her with the seatbelt.

"Buckle your butt in, Honey-bunny," she said. She walked around to her side of the car, got in, buckled up, and started the car; its mammoth V-8 rumbled into life, its exhaust burbling from two chrome-tipped tailpipes. Rose dropped the gearshift into drive and let off the brakes; the Pontiac glided away from the curb. "Wave goodbye to your mom and dad!" said Rose. And Patty did, realizing she had never been away from home without her parents, and that she had never seen the ocean.

The car threaded its way, stopping and going, turning this way and that, through streets and intersections that Patty did not recognize at all. Here, there was a block of three-story buildings, all the same size, shape, and color; there, a brick fire station with firemen in blue uniforms, washing a long red hook-and-ladder truck out front. And there were churches and malls, schools with empty playgrounds with swing sets hanging idle like the pendulums of silent clocks and even an armory with olive-green Army trucks lined up in its parking lot, and men raising an American flag that fluttered in the morning breeze on a tall flagpole in the front yard, while they saluted and stood around it like toy soldiers in a storybook picture.

And then Rose steered the car onto a ramp to enter I-95 and put her foot down; the big V-8 engine responded with a surge of brute power, and the Silver Bullet rocketed forward like a hungry lion lunging for swift-footed prey. The small, jeweled crucifix hanging by a silver chain on the rearview mirror swayed wildly.

"That," Rose said to Patty, turning briefly to look at her, suppressing a giggle of satisfaction and then eyeing traffic both ahead and behind on the highway, "is what the old Silver Bullet does best!" Rose deftly merged with the southbound traffic heading out of Boston and her car became part of a procession of multicolored autos speeding along together, like mismatched components of a mile-long, runaway train. It was a fast-moving one, of people—working people, tired people, frantic people running away from their homes, their jobs, and their concerns to spend the weekend slowing down, in the more quiet places that appealed to them.

"We're almost there, Patty," said Rose some 40 minutes later, glancing over at her niece, whose head was swiveling back and forth, taking in the sights. "Want to see a lighthouse?"

"Oh, yes, I would!" Patty exclaimed, smiling at her aunt. Rose turned onto Jericho Road and followed it, driving slowly, and stubbed out the last of three lipstick-smeared cigarettes that had sustained her during the drive. The first of many houses to be built on this stretch of ocean front were going up, and carpenters were at work framing them, roofing them, and putting up walls—pounding busily at nails as if they were woodpeckers jackhammering away on trees—even on a Saturday.

"Those places are a lot bigger than my little old shack—you'll see," commented Rose. "I've got the last one of the old places on the beach."

She soon veered off onto Lighthouse Road, following it until the road ended in a small circle with a parking lot near it. The tall, white tower of the old lighthouse stood stoically there like a spindly-looking sailor assigned to some lonely seaside sentry duty, drawn to attention in his dress whites. At its feet were the keeper's rustic little house and shed that seemed like the sailor's well-worn shoes. Beyond them and a jumble of large rocks, the ocean appeared, the far-off horizon seemingly drawn across its farthest visible extent like a thin blue pencil line. The white sails of the small pleasure craft of weekend skippers appeared as tiny foolscaps scudding across the distant waves. Rose parked the car and turned off the ignition; the hungry lion rumbling under the hood went silent.

"Come on, Patty," she said excitedly. "Let's go see the ocean!"

Patty grabbed her aunt's hand as they walked toward the lighthouse. It was low tide, but they could hear the *whoosh* of waves surging and rippling around great stone breakwater that stood far out toward the open sea. A strong breeze blew up from the east, buffeting Patty and her aunt, whose long hair blew out in a horizontal stream, which she struggled to regain control of with both hands; Patty's hair blew into her face. She and her aunt exchanged glances and laughed; they looked far out to sea and held hands. Except for the noisy jangling of the snap hooks on the nearby flagpole from which the stars and stripes flapped and fluttered at its uppermost reach, and the rumble of the surf that came like distant thunder, all was silent at this hour, except for the little girl and her aunt.

"Aunt Rose," asked Patty, looking up at her, breaking the bond of their hands, and their silence, and pointing out to sea and the horizon line, "is that the end of the world?"

Her aunt laughed and retook her hand.

"No, Patty dear; that's just one of its beginnings," she answered. "Let's go to the beach shack." After a short jaunt north along the coastline in the Silver Bullet, Patty and her aunt pulled into the driveway belonging to Rose's small gray cottage that fronted the beach; beside the cottage was a little tool shed with a cupola, from which a weathervane surmounted by a green shamrock wiggled and waggled in the strong sea breeze.

"This is it, Patty," announced Rose. "My humble little beach shack. My home away from home...my bachelorette apartment home in Boston."

Rose stepped from the car, bringing along a beach bag, and produced a rusty key from her pocket, with which she unlocked the front door to the little house and stepped inside, beckoning her niece to follow.

"Wow!" said Patty. "It's so neat." The cottage was indeed neat, and compact. It smelled a trifle musty and redolent of salt air, seasoned pine and cedar wood, and faintly of alcohol and tobacco smoke...aromas Patty did not recognize. On one wall hung a brass ship's bell and beside it, a framed black-and-white photograph of a long, low, wood-hulled powerboat. Patty stood on tiptoe, craning her neck to see it better. There were men wearing funny-looking suits and hats standing on the deck of the boat among several wooden crates and rows upon rows of big bottles. Five of the men held guns; two of them were pointing their guns at each other and looked like they were laughing.

"What's that, Aunt Rosie?" asked Patty, pointing at the sleek-looking boat.

"That's *Bad Penny*," answered her aunt, walking over and reaching down to take Patty's hand. That's your Great-Grand-dad Mickey's boat. "And that," she said, using her free hand to point out a jaunty-looking young man in a fedora, who had one leg propped up on a wooden crate and was looking straight into the camera, "is your great-granddad."

"What's a bad penny?" Patty asked Rose, looking up at her quizzically.

"Well," said Rose, gazing at Mickey's smiling face in the faded old picture, "it's a lucky name...they say a bad penny always returns. His boat always came back from the sea."

The beach shack's main room contained a dining table, covered with a red-and-white-checked tablecloth with three mismatched chairs to keep it company, two easy chairs that had tattered cushions, and a small bar with tall glasses and shiny bottles of various libations set up in one corner with a stereo system nearby. Two small bedrooms stood off to one side, and a screened-in porch faced the ocean and a stretch of beach, where sandpipers skittered about and a flight of black cormorants flapped in silhouette across the view to the east, flying low like dark, demented beings on the run, close across the rippling surface of the water.

It didn't take long for Patty and her aunt to change their clothes and then to dabble and wade in the water, explore the tidal pools, build a sandcastle, and then set up chairs on the beach outside and retire to them. Except for a couple catching the sun on loungers much farther down the beach to the south, she and her aunt had the ocean, or so it seemed, to themselves. Rose had brought out a small transistor radio, turned it on, and tuned in a Boston station. Suddenly, music from *The Nutcracker* ballet came forth from the radio, a public service announcement on WBZ about a performance to take place in town in the late fall season. Aunt Rose took to her feet and looked at her niece.

"Have you ever been to the ballet?" she asked.

"No, Aunt Rose," said Patty. Without hesitation, her aunt stood, slowly untied her terrycloth beach robe, and then tossed it with a flourish onto her chair, revealing her purple, two-piece bathing suit. A small one. To Patty, it looked small enough to be her own...and very much like her mother's underwear.

"It's a bikini," said Rose, grinning and sensing her niece's apparent wonderment at the appearance of this unfamiliar garment. Then, "I've studied dancing" smiling and hoping to get Patty to understand the ballet. "And...I dance. See?" She then pirouetted and performed a series of plies, waggling briefly in the sand in her flip-flops. Patty noticed that the man in the lounger farther down the beach who had been looking at ships with his binoculars was now training them on her aunt. The lady sitting next to him seemed to notice this new attention, rolled up her magazine, hit him on the backside of his head, and then said something to him. The pair then collapsed their loungers and left the beach.

Patty doodled in the coloring book she had brought along, scrawling with her crayons that were getting close to melting temperature, now that the sun was rising high overhead.

"When I grow up, I want to be just like you!" Patty scrawled in purple on a page that showed her rendering of Rose as a stick figure sitting on the beach, with a tiny red boat floating beyond on blue water, and proudly showed it to her aunt; Aunt Rose rummaged inside her beach bag to get her Instamatic camera.

"Hold it up, Patty! Let me take a picture of you!" said Rose as she held compact camera in her hands. Patty did, and her aunt snapped the shutter. "Now, I'm going down to the beach store to get some things," said Rose to her little niece, as she and Patty arose and walked the short distance back to the beach shack, Patty carrying her coloring book, crayons and towel. "I'll get some Moxie, some hot dogs and chips, and some other stuff for lunch. I'll be gone a few minutes—so *don't* go into the water. Stay on the porch or inside...okay?"

Rose looked at her closely to make sure her niece was paying attention and Patty nodded gravely...and then her Aunt Rose was gone, the front screen door banging and rebounding on its creaking hinges as she left, leaving a whiff of perfume and a faint scent of cigarette smoke behind her.

Patty looked out at the ocean and the distant horizon. There was a big ship on it now, miles away. Gulls wheeled and soared over the rocks, where the waves broke and crashed like rolling thunder; closer to her was the sand and the two chairs, but nothing more. No one else had emerged from the other houses far down the beach. There were no cars, no trolleys, no televisions; no cars, no airplanes, and no interstates. There were no dark, forbidding buildings like the ones she'd seen in Boston when her parents had driven downtown at night to have dinner, buildings standing like rows upon rows of tall, black dominos with white dots of light in them in the darkening hours after twilight.

This was the sort of barren seascape Patty sometimes thought of later on as the background she'd seen in a Popeye cartoon. But it was also the kind of seascape so often captured in an Edward Hopper painting, the kind she would see in later years, ones in which the focus invariably entreats the adult viewers to envision themselves, each one of them, alone on a shoreline that they and they alone inhabit...not as castaways but as characters, and in which they must find their true selves. This empty-looking world began to resonate with little Patty, standing silently, looking out to sea. And Patty felt a new sense of comfort falling over her, like some warm blanket that protected her from something—from what she did not know—and a sense that she was, even though very, very young, well on her way to becoming someone like her aunt, who would never be afraid to be...alone.

Hung on the wall over the kitchen counter in Aunt Rose's beach shack was a plastic clock, a likeness of a black-and-white cat with eyes that turned back and forth with the passage of each second. And its tail twitched back and forth as each second passed slowly by...*tick tock, tick tock*, while Patty stood, then sat, in the kitchen and waited for her aunt to return. Suddenly, car horns blared like trumpets.

The windshield wipers on Patty's Honda Civic called out to her: *tick tock, tick tock, tick tock.* And Patty jolted—blinked—as she listened to their sound...and she suddenly found herself staring through the windshield at an unfamiliar intersection somewhere east of Waltham, where the wipers on her car still slapped, *tick tocking* in slow time, and her foot was planted firmly on the brake pedal. It had stopped raining. Her car was standing still; traffic had piled up behind her. She was not in the Silver Bullet. Aunt Rose was gone, long dead. The traffic lights overhead showed green—as green as

shamrocks on St. Patrick's Day. Patty flushed in embarrassment, tromped on the accelerator, and sped off. She concentrated now on the traffic...and returning to work tomorrow
and to other business at hand—and left whatever was in her
rearview mirror, and in her childhood memories, behind. She
would also find out what her father was up to.

Chapter 6

Recruiting the Muscle

Jerry Garrantino, known in most circles for his tall stature and exceptional strength (and no hesitation to use it when a situation called for it) as Jerry "The Giant," awoke with the sure sense it would be the last time he would ever hear the morning alarm sound. But it was not, for example, heard with the sense one has upon awakening when the alarm clock clatters noisily on the long-dreaded day when the IRS auditor is due to call, papers in hand. Or the day a bail hearing is set and the bondsman has told you to pack a change of clothes or two—just in case. This alarm buzzer was heard clearly and its sound was welcomed as warmly as the sound of a dinner bell by a hungry man...and it was received with a sense of relief. The noise was loud—loud enough to be heard throughout the entire cold, castle-like prison.

In fact, the sound was as loud as the period buzzer at a hockey arena when the Boston Bruins do their best to keep the speeding pucks within the clutches of their out-of-town as-sailants out of the hometown net, and the fans who are safely ensconced at home and too impaired to drive are sensibly placated by what they've been consuming...and thereby refrain from throwing their empty beer cans at their televisions. The old guy down at the end of Jerry's cell block had had the worst of it; the alarm was mounted on the wall right next to his cell, and the old bird claimed to have lost a lot of his hearing in the last five years he'd been in residence. But Jerry was not tone deaf, nor being fatalistic in his thinking: he had served his time and he was getting out today.

Jerry rolled over and looked at the floor on his side of the bars; sure enough, it was there...a pack of Marlboros that had been dropped "by mistake" (most likely after bed check at 5:00 a.m. by some janitor who wasn't above making a little money on the side). He eased his six-foot, two-inch frame out of the rumpled bedding in his cot and stooped to pick up the pack. Taking care to make sure no one on the opposite side of the hall was looking, he turned around and carefully peeled back the tax stamp. Yes, there it was: the telephone number he'd been waiting for, one beginning with a 617 area code. It would be his springboard to "the job." The job he'd been enticed to take, even at his advanced age, because it was "for old time's sake." An old score to settle is still a score, no matter whether it's with a hockey stick, or some other means at hand.

Jerry read it over several times, trying his best to commit it to memory, but finally gave up and rolled it up into a tiny ball, stuck it between two of the smallest toes on his right foot in order to conceal it, and put his socks on. By the time he was dressed, the motorized gates on the entire cell block unlocked and rolled back, making a sound not unlike that of a speeding rollercoaster derailing. It made Jerry think back briefly to the days when he was a kid, when he'd ride the old, thundering rollercoaster at Revere Beach, play pinball, and ogle the girls hanging out along the beach. Those days...those bad old days. But it was time to move on now. Jerry was soon dressed and ready for breakfast. And the job. For old time's sake. Hell;

mostly, it was for the money. And hell, it was for something else, too...to send someone straight *to* hell.

Jerry had the odd nickname "Gelato", one he did not care for. It had come about as those of some criminals do in a bizarre and freakishly humorous way: as a 13-year-old kid growing up in the Boston suburbs, pilfering merchandise from various stores (he also beat up small kids and stole their pocket change to stay busy and augment his income) he had come up with a plan to make more money—real money. This rare and elusive stroke of genius that did not involve stealing bicycles from kids, or snatching purses from comely women on the subway came to him after he watched a late-night TV movie. The film about the Great Brinks Robbery that had taken place in 1950 in Boston. A light, albeit one of low wattage and brief duration, glowed in Jerry's brain. Like the Brinks bandits, he planned his scheme methodically, rehearsing it in his mind, over and over. For a kid who was the quintessential straight D student, this took most of one of his summer vacations to plan. He decided, after carefully noting its route and schedule, to steal the Good Humor ice cream truck that made its weekly rounds through his neighborhood. The hapless driver proved to be quite literally a pushover and sustained a concussion when Jerry committed his crime...and threw the poor fellow from the open cab.

The joyride was short-lived. True, Jerry was a big, strong kid, but not a skilled driver. In fact, he had no driving experience whatsoever. Furthermore, he was color blind. Not realizing the traffic light at the intersection with the turnpike was red, he drove straight through it, striking a bus in the process. The Good Humor truck careened off the road into a shopping mall's parking lot and crashed through the front window of a women's lingerie specialty store. This did not escape the notice of the two beat cops, brothers Tom and Duke O'Hara, who had been parked on stools in a nearby diner enjoying coffee and donuts, as well as the sight of the various customers coming and going.

"This kid," said Duke to an alert *Boston Globe* reporter who had sped to the scene upon hearing of the crash on his car's police radio, "is dumber than a box of rocks." The reporter then snapped a photo of the handcuffed kid. He was being taken into custody and holding a novelty Italian ice cream treat he'd pilfered from the truck and been eating while he drove. Jerry was thereafter known to his teenage peers as "Gelato" (although there were also those of lesser means and accomplishments in his neighborhood who derisively referred to him as "the ice cream bandit").

Frequent brushes with the law invariably led to terms of suspension from school for Jerry (much to the dismay of the coach of the football team Jerry played on). Because of his hulking physique and formidable appearance, the pep squad voted him "player most likely to come out of a bottle if you rubbed it." Once Jerry left high school, he grew into a young man of boastful (but little monetary) means and strove to make a name for himself. Jerry "The Giant" earned his moniker by going to work on the streets as an enforcer for a small-time gambler dabbling in rackets and doing some freelance petty larceny work on the side. This eventually led to Jerry's first conviction and prison term. Once "outside" and asked by fellow felons what his line of work was, once he had returned to it, Jerry would boast that he was in the numbers racket.

"Father, I like to play with numbers," he said when asked the same question by the local priest, Father O'Brien, who naively assumed that this meant the young man would someday become a mathematician and tried in vain to encourage him. What Jerry meant was that for the most part, he more or less figured he had a future in making money as an enforcer...and when he was not doing that, that he would be making license plates for the Commonwealth of Massachusetts, as long as there was sufficient help available to assist him in reading the work orders. By the time his former high school classmates were working on their senior-year term papers, Jerry was serving his second prison term; by the time some of those classmates were seniors making the dean's list at BU, he was on the parole board's list for early release from his second grand larceny conviction. A job, after all, wasn't a nine-to-five thing; to be respectable with the bounds of the criminal element, a "job" was usually a robbery, a burglary, a shakedown, or a collection call. And Jerry, upon going to work for Vince Saluzzo, who had bigger and better things to do in those days, became a very effective enforcer in making those collection calls.

But now, like many of the great sluggers who have gone to bat for Boston during the years, aged gracefully and hung up their jerseys, Jerry's golden era had come and gone. The kicker had come when Saluzzo's three sons botched a job they'd been entrusted with that required Jerry's follow-up. The boys lied to their father about what had gone down and rolled the blame on old Jerry. Vince, who promptly flew into a rage when he heard their story, refused protection to Jerry when the heat came down. It was tantamount to being let go. Well, hell, it *was* being let go. It was probably not too smart, Jerry thought afterward, that in defense of his actions he told the boss that the problem was not with what he was in charge of, but what Vince had entrusted to the brains of the operation: "Your three sons: Larry, Moe, and Curly." And now, being close, so close, to getting out of the big house and with a new opportunity awaiting him outside, Jerry knew what he was going to do with this caper: he was going to get revenge. *An eye for an eye—that's how it works*, thought Jerry as he donned his flash orange prisoner's jumpsuit.

"Gettin' out today?" yelled one inmate to Jerry as he descended the staircase from his block. "When's your retirement party?"

"Hi five, tutti-frutti! Where's yo *ice cream?*" yelled another. But most of them, the younger men, ignored the passage of the old man they termed a "silverback con." Jerry grinned and waved to them, put his head down and headed for the prison library, where he then sat down, furtively removed a shoe and sock, unrolled the tax stamp, and tried to concentrate on the numbers, trying unsuccessfully once more to memorize them. He soon hit upon an elegant solution; borrowing a green pen from the librarian, he wrote down each digit of the 10 telephone numbers on the tax stamp, in turn...on each of his fingers. *Perfect*, he thought, *like Jake and Elwood, right?* No one would be the wiser. Gelato tossed the tax stamp into the trash and signed out of the library. It was time to eat.

There was a lot of revenge...thoughts of all kinds of it...all manner of hideous, brutal, depraved acts of violence, stewing in many of the minds of the thousand or so men penned up in the prison that morning; it brewed in their heads, percolating like particularly strong morning coffee that spiked their energy and quickened their steps as they marched along toward breakfast. Old though he was, Jerry was one of them. The longing to inflict pain and suffering on those who had put them away simmered—it bubbled and boiled in them.

Any seasoned prison guard can tell you he can almost smell that bitter, toxic brew when the heat of anger is turned on under it. Unlike a real percolator, a criminal's mind—much less his head—has no glass top so that you can see what's going on inside. It's not until that mind boils over and you "wake up and smell the coffee" that you realize there's trouble. And then, you are frequently too late to prevent mayhem, or a murder...perhaps even your own. White, black, yellow, and red, the thousand-odd men, all clad in flash orange jumpsuits, tramped along the hallways of the prison with a quickening pace, all the while under the sullen but watchful eyes of the armed prison guards, guards who were ready to act at a moment's notice. No matter whether the mind of 1, or of 20 or 50 or more of the men in orange moving en masse toward the mess hall suddenly boiled over, went into high gear, and made trouble.

Jerry had taken good care to make sure no one had seen what he'd done underneath the table in the library...after all, nobody "in the system" hated anyone more than a snitch, a rat. And Weasel, good boy for what he would soon do in his role in Jerry's "export," wasn't one, nor would he be one...of that, Jerry was certain. Jerry was cool with that—as cool as iced coffee, brewed the day before.

Chapter 7

A Plant in the Office

Vince Saluzzo arrived at his company's tumbledown building at 9:00 a.m. sharp as he usually did, strutting into its entranceway like the highly-decorated commander of a mighty fortress. And Vince looked sharp in his freshly pressed suit, fitted dress shirt, and silk tie, just as he usually did, although his men—his soldiers—were already hard at work inside. The foyer of the building was—in contrast to Vince's crisp attire—drab, dimly lit, and dusty. It contained (perhaps as a measure designed to dampen the desires of visitors who wished to interrupt Vince's valuable office time with their pleadings for money, deals, or favors) two uncomfortable chairs, a selection of tattered, dog-eared magazines, and a coffeemaker whose contents resembled used crankcase motor oil—its usual appearance. He rapped on the office window in the foyer to get Gigi the gatekeeper's attention. Gigi, who looked up from her tasks and then waved hello to him, obligingly pressed a button on her desk to briefly unlock, with a loud buzzing sound and a *click*, the steel-case door that opened on the stairway leading to the upstairs offices and storage rooms. He ascended the stairs, and after reaching the second floor mumbled a good morning to Tina and Michelle as he passed by their desks, his head bent over, his eyes intent this morning on scanning the headlines of *The Boston Globe.*

Vince entered his office, where the morning sunlight was now filtering through the blinds hung on the east-facing window. He closed the door behind him, heaved the newspaper onto his desk, and then sat down heavily in his high-back, leather-upholstered chair. It would be good, he thought, to run a quick check on the financials this morning, if for nothing else, just to see who might be trying to steal from him this week. Maria would look after the books otherwise as soon as she returned from Italy. He switched on his computer and its large screen sitting on the credenza beside his desk flickered into life.

While he waited for the computer to boot up, he rifled through the pages of his paper to find the sports news; racing season was on, and Vince had a considerable chunk of change riding on certain horses in certain places. He briefly toyed with the idea of taking a side trip to Saratoga; it would be a pleasant diversion, with Maria away on extended travel. The computer's screen blinked and came alive with informational options. It occurred to Vince that with the world figuratively at his fingertips, now poised over his mouse and keyboard, that he had the opportunity to explore other closer, more interesting and lively diversions for the next few evenings. The financials and whatever disloyal thieves might be among his crew, and their comeuppances, could wait a bit. Vince opened an email whose subject matter seemed very compelling. A message appearing to be from a discreet service he subscribed to, one that could engage the computer in a search that, 35 or 40 years ago, would likely have been made in the old red-light district of the Combat Zone. Vince's heart began to pound softly, like that of an old racehorse approaching the starting gate at post time, one who suddenly spots an attractive young filly frolicking about near the stables. He opened the message.

Suddenly, through the thick door that barred the way to Vinnie's office, both Tina and Michelle could clearly hear Vince's first, thunderous oath as it erupted, followed by a string of mighty curses. Across the screen of Vince's computer, an endless procession of cherubs now pranced, holding harps and bright red Valentine's Day hearts. The words "Looking for love in all the wrong places?" in pink letters flashed on and off on the screen like a neon sign advertising a Vegas night-club show. Below that, a bright green shamrock appeared, and in tiny letters, the words: "Your network has been locked. If you want to play now, you must play my game. To recover files and get decryptor, click here. Pay in two days, or fees double. Payable in bitcoin only. Sorry."

There was no doubt about it in Vince's mind; this was the handiwork of Callahan and his Monument Hill Gang pals of years gone by, come back to pay him their disrespects. The gang that had now come back to taunt him in the digital age. Vince gave the computer the command to quit; nothing happened. Then to restart; nothing. Gave it the command to go to his internal server; no change. He counted to 10, as his doctor had told him to do in stressful situations. He took a deep breath, then slowly exhaled. He briefly imagined pulling out the loaded Glock he once kept in his desk only for emergencies and special occasions, and discharging all of its bullets into his PC. Next time, Vince swore, he would get a Mac. *Callahan and his crew can pull his crap, but Freddy will know how to fix this*, thought Vince. *God knows, the kid spends half his life in front of a screen and a keyboard. Small wonder he's the size he is—it should say Goodyear on his shirts.*

Vince leaned toward the telephone, but before he could touch it, it beeped; the light for Gigi the gatekeeper's extension was on. Vince took another deep breath, exhaled, and picked up the receiver.

"That tax assessor's here again," said Gigi.

"Tell him I'm busy," retorted Vince. "Tell him to make an appointment. For next month, next year. I don't care."

"It's not a he," informed Gigi. "It's a she." There was a long pause while Vince stared at the light on his phone, his brows furrowing and his mind wandering. Gigi stared at her phone, waiting for instructions. *Perhaps this was not going to be a bad day after all*, thought Gigi's bald-headed, fuming boss upstairs.

"Boss?" asked Gigi.

"Okay, send her up," replied Vince, before hanging up the phone. *Perhaps this was going to be a pleasant interaction after all*, he thought. He could and would, ultimately, be charming and diplomatic; it would be an excellent diversion from his Callahan problem...but he would be on his guard. If this was going to be a scam, a shakedown, or something that was going to cost money, this woman was going to go straight to hell without passing go or collecting so much as a single dollar.

Vince stood, straightened his necktie, and stared into the mirror strategically placed near his desk. He stuck out his jaw, folded his arms, and assumed the posture that had placed fear into the hearts of so many adversaries so long ago. There; that was the power stance. And now, there was the consummate man of power and authority in the Saluzzo territory...the only one. It was the pose he knew his sons would never be able to assume in order to further the family business. Vince allowed himself a small smile and shook his head slightly. He heard footsteps. Those of high heels. His visitor was climbing the stairs to the office.

The visitor, Marina Valoccik, as she identified herself, paused briefly at Tina and Michelle's desks, briefcase in hand, her ID card encased in plastic on a cord dangling around her neck. A tax assessor's job, she knew, is simple and straightforward, but the life of a tax assessor is complicated. Sometimes dangerous. It involves such things as measuring buildings to determine whether or not any unauthorized additions have been made since the last visit, determining whether or not the building's current uses match those that are permitted, and if any uses other than those permitted have been taking place, and, accordingly, what fines or remedies may be involved. It sometimes, understandably, involves threats to the assessor's well-being...and sometimes, even his or her own life.

"Should I go in?" she asked Tina cautiously.

"Yes, but just give a little knock first," Tina answered while eyeing the tax assessor's formidable-looking black leather briefcase, "just to be sure."

"Come in; close it behind you," Vince said softly, when he heard the knock. His visitor twisted the doorknob and slowly, tentatively pushed the door open, inquisitively pushing just the tip of her dainty-looking nose inside. "C'mon in if you're coming in," Vince muttered, his attention focused purpose-fully on the sports news.

"Mister Saluzzo?" she inquired. "I am Marina Valoccik from the tax assessor's office. I am so very pleased to meet you to-day." She smiled a pearly-white smile and thrust out her hand in his direction; Vince ignored it. He was going to toy with her a bit, after all.

"Have a seat," he said, staying behind his paper. She folded her tall, shapely frame, sensibly dressed in a gray jacket and skirt, into a side chair and sat there, regarding him warily. Vince turned to face her and suppressed the urge to react. Her skin was angelically fair; her hair was blonde wisps wrapped like folds of sunlit honey around a spoon, and her eyes were a piercing, clear, cold blue. Like a radar station opening up to scan the skies for any foreign attention or visitations, the tax assessor then stretched out her long legs and her spike-heeled shoes and displayed them where she knew Vince could not help but see them.

"So," Vince began icily, keeping his emotions well in check, "tell me what this is all about." The woman laughed heartily.

"Oh, sir, please. You must understand; this is only routine, this visit. Not one of us from my office has been here in a dozen years. It is time to make sure we have complete information. Have there been any additions made to the building recently, for example?"

"No," said Vince, impassively.

"Constructed circa 1928, am I right, sir?" she asked, pulling a tablet from her briefcase and consulting it, regarding it almost casually, pensively tapping a pen on her right cheek and then smiling at him engagingly.

"Yes," said Vince. "At least, that's what they tell me. I wasn't around back then." Then he smiled. A warm-up smile. Just to get her started. Vince reached for a pen on his credenza and bumped aside the computer's mouse. The computer, his damned computer, started up again and the dancing cherubs pranced across the screen once more. Vince quickly turned to switch off the monitor. And a knowing smile, unseen by Vince, flickered across his visitor's face and swiftly vanished.

"Oh, you know," the woman blurted, suddenly taking an interest in the display of framed photographs on the office wall, "I do so love horses. Can you tell me about those?" And so Vince told Marina about his many racehorses. Marina, observing Vince carefully as he digressed, named the horses, and explained their exploits one by one, slowly pulled a small, cylindrical device the size of a watch battery from her pocket. She palmed it, pulled a strip of paper from it to reveal its small, self-adhesive strip...and then stuck it to the bottom of her chair, all the while watching him to make sure her movements were not observed.

And Marina then told him about the horse she rode as a little girl, growing up on a farm in the Ukraine, before she came to America.

"And," she giggled, "I would throw a blanket on that horse, and my father, he, the farmer, would say 'Now, come on, you learn to ride that horse, I tell you...or you will never go on to anything farther from this farm. You must learn not to be afraid!' And so I did; I rode horses in a circus after I lost my fear, and I did other things, and then I came to America with that circus and I left...you know, I...guess you say...I hopped off the bus. It was in those days when there was so much that was so bad going on. And so, in search of so much that is good, in America...here I am."

Vince still regarded her cautiously, but he was warming up to this very cool, tall blonde lady. One who had put on big, schoolgirlish reading glasses to read what was on her tablet. "What do you need from me?" he asked. And then, suppressing a smug smile, "What do you need to see?"

"Just a quick tour of the premises," she answered. "As soon as I confirm measurements of the building and that there are no changes, I will go. And then I will fill out my report." Vince pushed a button underneath the edge of his desk. Down in the garage and in the warehouse, buzzers sounded and workers sprang into action. In swift compliance with this well-known warning signal, cartons of illicit goods and open crates of munitions of staggering capability disappeared as quickly as an eight-grader's dirty magazine in study hall when the teacher calls his name. Vince pushed his chair back, arose and accompanied Marina down the stairway and into the warehouse.

"We're an open book," declared Vince, smiling broadly as he told the lie, swaggering along. He proceeded to show Marina every inch of the building--those inches that he was willing to reveal.

An hour later, the tall blonde woman posing as Marina said goodbye to Vince and left the premises, her high heels clacking loudly on the concrete, walking a block down the street to the place where she had left her car. She removed her ID card and its cord from around her neck, and tossed them and her briefcase containing the tablet onto the backseat. She retrieved them later on that day when she arrived back at her office and shredded the falsified City of Boston assessor's identification, as well as the false driver's license she had been carrying.

"He suspects nothing?" asked Mikhail Zuckoff, raising his eyebrows.

"No, nothing," answered Katrina Valenchnikoff, looking at him with her cold blue eyes—the ones that had served her so well in Chechnya as a Soviet sniper.

"Then good," said Zuckoff, known to his employees only as Mr. Z, a smile crossing his narrow face. "All of those men...those old men...they play checkers. All of them; Saluzzo, Callahan...and here, as you know, we play chess. Old school, old fool, I say. There is no need to kill; I let the killers destroy themselves. To come to an end that they so richly deserve, as they leave the playing field to us. And now, we can listen to Saluzzo's every move...thanks to you."

"Yes," answered Katrina, smiling. "Of course. And, I can tell you...now that he has that virus on his computer, he will of course put the blame on only Callahan. God only knows what he will do."

"Then," said her boss, Mr. Z, "you see that *we* do not clean up the mess. That is not our function. We have no need to. We are the overtakers, not the undertakers. Not like those old men who waste their time. We merely reap the benefits of our labor. We have no need for guns...or even the wire around the neck. Tell me: do you hate cats, Katrina?" he asked, reflectively, resting his head upon one hand pensively, staring at her.

"I do not...care for them," she answered.

"Then," Mr. Z responded, "here is the answer to that problem. So, you wish to get rid of cats. So, you take the two cats that are bothering you in your neighborhood, because they wish to fight, so you oblige them. You bring them together, tie their tails together and then you hang them over the clothesline. And, then they tear each other's guts out. Problem solved.

You own the playing field. But...*you* did not kill them; they killed each other. You have solved the problem. And now, the neighborhood is yours. There is no guilt upon you."

Mr. Z produced a bottle of vodka, uncorked it, and poured some of its clear contents into two glasses. "Za vstrechu! To our meeting!" he said to Katrina. The two did not clink glasses. They drained their glasses in a gulp, eyeing each other closely. Suspicion, as well as mutual trust, was part of their shared culture's somewhat curious and ambivalent nature.

"We knew each other in Chechnya, colonel," said Katrina, "and we worked together so well. So, it was a disappointment to establish this business here with you and to work so hard without results, other than the restaurants taken over...all for you. Until now, but we have hope here today, for something much, much bigger. We are on the edge, grasping on hard...and I have my hooks into it. I assure you."

"So true. Za to, chtoby sbyvalis mechty! Let our dreams come true!" said Mr. Z. He winked at Katrina and reached for the bottle again, thinking of the near and, insofar as he was concerned, irrefutable future of his Boston syndicate that was growing bigger by the day, as his hackers, young men pounding keyboards downstairs, poured disinformation and false news into the mainstream of Boston's social media and its many devoted advocates and followers. He poured himself, and Katrina, another two glasses.

Chapter 8

Delivering the Goods

It was a beautiful, sunny spring day for most people in Boston and the surrounding metropolitan area. The dark clouds that had hung low overhead at dawn as if clinging to the top of the Prudential Building, obscuring the sunrise and even the blue beacon of the Custom House tower from view, had simply blown away and vanished. And now, people were out and about, enjoying the notable sights of the capital. College students who had skipped class were rowing boats out on the Charles River; the first busload of laughing, happy schoolchildren on a field trip was marching en masse up the gangplank of the *U.S.S. Constitution* to take a tour; and tourists were strolling on Boston Commons, feeding pigeons and taking pictures of the swan boats paddling about on the pond. Old men who had nothing better to do sat on park benches under leafy green trees, peeling apples or oranges to snack on, and fending off marauding squirrels while otherwise fussing over crossword puzzles in their rumpled newspapers.

Chuck Warssel, also known as "The Weasel" was at that very moment busily engaged in peeling a few things himself—peeling cobwebs off his face while crawling on his hands and knees through the darkness of a dank, filthy ventilating shaft that led from the wall behind the kitchen to the laundry room, deep within the massive walls of one of Massachusetts's most notable prisons, just to the west of suburban Boston. He had let himself into the kitchen storage unit by prying open a vent in the wall located underneath a table after loosening its two screws with his thumbnails. He had first taken care to open a box of donuts that were on the table, helping himself to a few. Still munching on the last of a sugar-frosted jelly donut and wiping away the crumbs from his mouth, he had disappeared into the labyrinthine depths of the inner workings of the prison after pulling the vent neatly back into place behind him.

Chuck then made a sharp right, burrowing into an opening someone had cut (and later concealed) in a previous escape attempt, one that led into a large steam pipe, one he knew was safe to access because it would not be used until the laundry shop swung into production at 11:00 a.m. He continued wriggling along toward the daylight showing dimly at the far end of the pipe. "The Weasel" had earned his nickname due to his scrawny frame and his uncanny ability to crawl through small, obscure openings in the prison that would have, one amazed con thought, denied access to a Burmese python. He was therefore very much in demand when it came to deliveries of illicit goods within the prison, goods that had to defy the eyes of the guards, even the ones who were said to be on the take.

He had kept the 7-by-14-inch padded manila envelope that Jerry "The Giant", the big lug on block three, had given him inside his jumpsuit in order to keep his hands free.

"You really *do* need to do me this favor," Jerry had told him the day before, drawing himself up to his full height to loom intimidatingly large over Chuck as he handed over "the export" "both because of those cigarettes I got you...and because you never know what things could happen to you, bad things, when you get out. Now, *you* get this package out, Weasel, and trust me," Jerry said, grinning enough to bare his spectacularly jagged and discolored teeth, "you *will* have a future after you get out next month."

Chuck had looked at the envelope, concealed it, nodded, and walked away. On the envelope was scrawled the numbers 021271331. *Now, just what the hell did that mean? A secret code? That's not a con's number*, Chuck thought. He knew enough not to ask. That would have been too much like trying to take a banana from a hungry, 500-pound ape. *Be cool. Don't do anything stupid*, Chuck thought to himself, as he inched his way along. That was what he, "The Weasel" had said to the lady of the house he was burglarizing several years ago in Wellesley when she'd come home late at night, hit the light switch, and caught him red-handed, plundering her jewelry box. That—and her husband, who'd slipped silently downstairs from the bedroom and was standing right behind him unseen (no wonder his wife was smiling) and cracked a table lamp over Chuck's head—had eventually landed him where he was right now. The arresting officer's asking if he had "seen the light?" in committing this crime that carried a hefty sentence, only added insult to the injury.

"This is justice being served?" Chuck remarked in court when the judge handed down a lengthy sentence for the crime. "You know what? If this was a diner...you'd be one lousy server and I'd be one hungry man." That got him an extra six months.

Chuck reached the end of the pipe. "Thank God!" he muttered. Here, a hinged grate that looked as though it had recently been welded to its steel frame gave him a bar-striped view of the loading dock below where an idling garbage truck stood; its hopper was yawning wide-open. *Here we go; now, again, don't do anything stupid*, thought Chuck, looking momentarily at the graffiti on the wall. It said: "Eat my smoke, suckers!" It had been left there a year ago by a self-described

Houdini who had jimmied the locked grate off its hinges, opened it and wriggled out, only to find himself hanging from the grate in mid-air because the would-be escapee hadn't thought to bring along any means of descent, such as bed sheets knotted together, or to time his departure with the daily garbage pickup. The guards soon found him dangling from the grate housing with tower 13's German shepherd circling beneath him, jumping up and down, trying in vain to rend apart the seat of the hapless con's pants with its teeth. Houdini (more recently known as "Genius") got an extra three years' time for his troubles. *Yeah,* thought Weasel, *a plan; you gotta have a plan...and not do anything stupid.*

"Here goes nothin' Jerry, you big bastard," Chuck said through clenched teeth, sliding "the export" through the opening and carefully releasing it. It dropped straight down and landed with a soft *plop* amid the candy bar wrappers, soggy newspapers, empty coffee cups, *TV Guides*, and Twinkie wrappers collected from the guard tower, where it was now indistinguishable from the garbage.

"Done deal!" said Chuck, yanking the frayed electrical line on the wall and thus making the exit sign on the dock blink. This pre-arranged signal did not go unnoticed; the truck's air brakes released with a *pheew*, its gears crunched as the driver shifted out of neutral and let out the clutch, and the truck started lumbering slowly toward the south gate.

Once the guards had checked the truck inside and out and cleared it, the vehicle quickly covered the next five miles to the Miss Concord Diner; there the driver parked and nonchalantly left the truck idling again and unattended while he went inside. Presently, a bedraggled figure with the look of a homeless person—someone who'd been idly sitting on the curb nearby—waddled over to the open hopper of the truck and started sifting through the garbage. The bum took time, as bums do when they're foraging, much like bears pawing through unattended picnic baskets in a park when all the campers are off swimming. The bum showed no hurry or concern in picking up "the export," examining it, walking over to an opening in the eight-foot-tall fence behind the truck, and disappearing through it. Once on the other side, the bum quickly dumped the attire (an Army surplus rain poncho, ragged gloves, and baseball cap) into a nearby garbage can and climbed into a waiting car—a maroon Camry. Its driver quickly started it, dropped it into gear, hit the highway, and headed toward Route 2, the expressway, and downtown Boston.

Inside the Camry, Ellen took her watchful eyes off the road, shifted her glance to the rearview mirror, and then looked nervously over at her daughter, who had buckled her seatbelt and was now examining the package she'd retrieved from the garbage truck.

"Patty...what's in there, girl?"

"I don't know, Mom," Patty declared, first shaking the package, then feeling it to try to gauge its thickness. She shook her head, brushed away some dirt from the sealed, padded envelope, and bounced the package on her lap. She then brought it up to her ear and listened to see if it was ticking. It was not. It was almost featherweight, rectangular in size, and thin as a wafer. She shook it; two metallic things inside clanked together. It was as if the package was remaining silent, holding a secret; silent like her father...silent about his shady business dealings. She shook it again, and its contents rattled this time.

"Mom...what are we—no—what are *you*, supposed to do with this?" she asked, looking back at her mother. Ellen took her eyes off the road momentarily and the Camry strayed slightly toward the centerline of the highway; a big rig headed in the opposite direction sounded its air horns, and Ellen quickly swerved back into her own lane.

"Just deliver the damned thing. Take it to a mailbox at the post office on Dorchester Street in Boston...that's what the zip code on it means...and leave it there," she snapped. "And this is the end. Just so you know. This is the end of all these things, the things I've done for him and will ever do. Ever, for your father. Even if this is for his 'old times' sake'...whatever that means. What are *my* old times' sakes? For God's sake!"

She peered apprehensively into the rearview mirror again, as if part of her past life with Jimmy Callahan was motoring up behind her, roaring along on four brightly burning, hot wheels from the hell of her marriage, shooting flames as they came. Catching up with her to burn her, now that she had a quiet home, a garden, a house in Waltham, and a relationship with her daughter. Those wheels were from the hell of Jimmy's business interests, forces she feared that wanted to push her into a collision with the law. Jimmy's vehicle would be a dark, ominous-looking vehicle, too, maybe an old black hearse that was dragging along the grief of his sister's murder behind it like a partially severed tailpipe. But it would not come quietly, oh no. Its engine was roaring with fury. This death vehicle would come up behind her as quickly as a stock car racing on Saturday night, with a revenge-crazed driver at the wheel and a long-unearthed corpse in the back—the corpse it had carried along for 40 years—and a mammoth, chrome-plated bumper on its front. That bumper was set to crash into her, Ellen feared. It would send her and her sensible old Camry, like a dispossessed Egyptian queen in her sturdy chariot, hurtling into the afterlife upon the fateful collision, to be forever with the king of her hell on earth.

"What's the end of all these things, Ma?" asked Patty. The Camry, ever Ellen's faithful servant for the past many years, hummed along the highway unperturbed, its radio babbling the latest traffic report. Ellen pondered.

"The end is, Patty, your dad's done some bad things. This...is my end...my end of doing anything at all with him. Patty, open up my purse." She did so. "Now...do you see that old brass key stamped with the letters MBTA, that has a tag with some code numbers on it?"

"Yes Mom," answered Patty. "Good...take it...and when we get to the post office, leave that key in the mailbox for your father. He probably doesn't even remember he gave it to me...made me swear never to tell anyone about it."

"What is it, Ma?" inquired Patty, pulling the large, ornate key from the purse that sat between her and Ellen and studying it. "It's the key," answered Ellen, "to the secret entrance to the tunnel—and a warehouse he calls a "hide" and the basement of his store—the root of all the crooked business he started, about the time your aunt died. I'll tell you about it someday. And Patty, please. Don't call me Ma."

Inside the prison, Chuck, filthy dirty and exhausted from his ordeal, elbowed his way up the steam pipe and back along the ventilation ductwork to the kitchen area. Taking care not to make any sound, he gently grasped the vent, pushed it out and set it down silently, wriggled through the opening, and was back underneath the kitchen table. *Excellent*, he thought, *most excellent.* He then reached for the two screws, lying amidst a scattering of powdered sugar he had left behind on the floor. Weasel suddenly felt someone grab his right arm and begin to drag him forward. And he suddenly had the feeling a condemned man has when he finally spots the priest walking toward him on death row, Bible in hand, in the company of the warden.

"Be cool now, Weasel," said Ronnie, the worst of the guards one could hope to cross and to whom that heavy, grasping hand belonged. Ronnie was holding a jelly donut in his other hand as he slowly hauled wiry little Chuck out from underneath the table on which he had left the open pastry box. A triumphant smile was on Ronnie's face as he asked Chuck something, with a twinge of sarcasm in his voice: "Didn't your mommy ever tell you the story about Hansel and Gretel, and how *anyone* can follow a trail of breadcrumbs?"

Ellen pulled over to the curb and stopped at the post office entrance. She looked at Patty.

"Know what, girl?" asked Ellen. "Seems to me that you and I are kinda like Jake and Elwood." A wan smile spread across her face, and Ellen leaned over to hug her daughter. And like Jake and Elwood, they symbolically rapped knuckles together. Just for luck.

"Just go, girl and get it done," she whispered into Patty's ear, adding: "I'll be back in 15 minutes," as Patty bounded off with the package in hand. Better to circle around and come back than to wait and be a sitting target, or "get made" in a surveillance video, Ellen thought. She'd helped Jimmy with his little games before. But, Ellen pondered, why was Patty, her daughter with a bright, blossoming career with the airline, now agreeing to be part of this new, and, hopefully final (possibly crooked) little game that she, Ellen—despite her protests, her divorce, her disassociation with Jimmy—had agreed to be dragged into, just for old time's sake?

Patty probably would not have answered that question...she had too many questions of her own at the moment. She opened the mailbox and placed the envelope inside. She pulled the old brass key out of her pocket, turning it over and over. She returned it to her pocket, closed the mailbox, and headed toward the door. She was going to keep it, for now, for old time's sake—and that of her burgeoning sense of curiosity. It might—just might—be a key that would unlock the door to the secrets of the past.

Chapter 9

The Loan Officer

It was late afternoon two days later when Jimmy once again stepped from a cab outside the Dorchester Street Post Office building. After paying the driver and, upon looking about not spotting any familiar faces in the flurry of pedestrian traffic, he darted into it. Jimmy went to his mailbox, pulled a key from his pocket, inserted it into the lock cylinder, and turned it.

Jimmy slowly, gently—expectantly—opened the door, the way a baker carefully opens an oven to ensure that he doesn't fumble and make his cake fall. There it was—the object of his affection and his trip today: the "export"—a plain, padded manila envelope with a zip code and four-digit appendage for his mailbox written on it in large, crudely-formed numbers. Jimmy grabbed it, felt it, and estimated its dimensions. *Yes, this is it*, he thought. *Perfect.* He nodded in silent approval as he slammed the mailbox door shut. *But, don't open it and look at it now. Don't jinx it.* All things considered, although this was going to be an expensive game, he would knock the proverbial ball out of the park; of that he was certain. He was going to play the game old school style, he thought—because he *was* old school——and by his rules. But, in fact, there were none this time around.

Jimmy left the building and walked purposefully, head up, chest out, not trying to call any attention to himself. He headed toward a parked cab that was empty, its driver absorbed in reading a newspaper. A paper coffee cup perched on the cab's dashboard jiggled in time to the vibration of the idling engine. *Don't look back.* The thought briefly popped into his head, startling him momentarily. That was a warning Grandad Mick gave him, long years ago, but for a reason other than to remain inconspicuous. It was a day in the late '60s, the day after Jimmy left the boxing ring for good after Bernie O'Sullivan trounced him in a match, inflicting some major battle damage in the process. Jimmy's pride was also wounded, and he held forth with a litany of complaints as he sat at his grandparents' dinner table that night: Jimmy's luck had been better with his old manager, he said; his girlfriend had dumped him and her predecessor had been better; the whole world had dumped him——except for his creditors.

"Don't look back now, Jimmy," said Mickey Callahan gruffly, looking at the bandaged young man sitting across from him who was nursing a long-neck Bud, besides his grievances. The old man fixed him with a razor-sharp gaze, then looked away momentarily before turning back to impart further advice. It was March 17, St. Patrick's Day and from outside the cozy triple decker on Dorchester Avenue came the steady *thump——thump——thump* of a basketball being dribbled as kids played in the street, weaving among parked cars and clumps of dirty snow, dodging traffic in the last rays of the late afternoon sunlight. The tantalizing aroma of beef stew cooking on Grandma Laureen's little four-burner gas stove in the kitchen wafted into the dining room, and Jimmy heard the *thunk* of the door being gently closed on the old GE dome-top refrigerator once his grandmother finished adding two shots of whiskey to the simmering pot. "That's where your ghosts live, back there. If you look over your shoulder too many times, they'll follow you. They'll run your game tomorrow and forever after, wherever you go. You'll never live to be who you could be."

Jimmy need not have turned around; there was no one following him. There was no one shadowing him. Nothing was going wrong. The substance of his grandfather's warning had glimmered briefly in his mind like a check engine light and then flickered out, like the last rays of the setting sun on that day in '69 as kids played basketball and stew simmered on Laureen's stove. Stew that simmered like the vengeance in his mind did today. He smiled, hopped into the cab and told the driver to head toward Logan Airport.

Pilgrim Park 'n Fly had an expansive parking garage and a well-utilized courtesy shuttle service to the airport. It was into its dark, refreshingly cool subterranean entranceway just off Maverick Street that Jimmy soon walked after the cab deposited him outside the building. Inside the attendant's booth sat an unusually large man who was reading a magazine, holding it in one hand while his other was engaged in stuffing the last of a slice of pizza into his mouth. Jimmy stepped up to the booth's window and rapped on it.

"Jimmy! M'man!" mumbled Billy Jones, the attendant, upon looking up. He put the magazine down and unhurriedly wiped crumbs and tomato sauce off his lips using the cuff of his jacket. Judging by the color of Billy's face and his fragrant exhalations Jimmy smelled coming through the open window, he made an educated guess that Billy was on the bottle again, well before dinnertime. "Got a good'n for you this time, I do!" Billy chortled.

Billy had started out as a salesman upon graduation from high school, and soon became remarkably proficient at selling things that did not belong to him. His financial needs and stellar abilities soon won the attention of more law-abiding people, who thoughtfully chipped in and sent him on an all-expenses-paid, two-year vacation in a large gated community in Walpole. While attending this unaccredited junior college of sorts, Billy commiserated with his peers about his unfortunate career choice, and eventually learned that having a rental business made much more sense than being in direct sales.

Billy was short and fat––obscenely fat. His enormous bulk obscured from view most of the chair he sat on in the parking lot attendant's booth, much as the mass of a bullfrog conceals the rock it's squatting on. His physical immensity and calm, serene composure made him seem almost Buddha-like. In fact, "Billy the Buddha" was what certain independent contractors called him. Billy, big guy in a small but thriving cash-only business, the ultimate big frog in a little pond, was the mastermind of the illicit car-rental business that he and he alone controlled in this small part of East Boston.

"Done talkin', Buddha-boy," said Jimmy. "As you know...I've got a job tomorrow. Nice, clean, no dirty stuff. Back well within 48 hours and no mess."

"Got ya' covered," said the Buddha, stamping out his Camel that was smoldering in a cluttered, expansive ashtray, itself a miniature likeness of Hiroshima after the atomic bomb had made its impact and the plane that had dropped it had flown back to its base. Grunting and struggling to rise to his feet, Billy squeezed himself out of the narrow doorway and flop-footed down a dark passageway in his overlarge sneakers, by-passing a barricade that read "no entry," and following yellow arrows on the pavement pointing toward a lower level. "Just follow me," he said.

"This," said Billy, while huffing and puffing to catch his breath, "is *it*." He reached for another Camel and lit it with, of all things, a kitchen match, scratching it alongside the fender of a rusty Ford with Vermont plates that was parked alongside the dove-gray Lincoln in order to light his smoke. "Your Holy

Grail, m'man. A nice, super-clean, kinda late-late-model Town Car. Got a little holy-roller sticker in the back window, but that's all. Squeaky-clean. Ta-da! All the toys. Prestige ride. Not too new, not too old, not too flashy, not too shabby. Long-term parking gig; old goat who owns it is gone 'til the end of next week. It's gotta be true; I saw all kinds of luggage go into the airport shuttle van."

"Don't you bullshit me," demanded Jimmy.

"No sir," retorted Billy, his chin now jutting out like a rock outcropping along a river, as if he were telling the one true story alongside a quickly-running stream of lies.

"If this ride ain't clean," groused Jimmy, "you're gonna get me what I want, pronto. And if it's gotta be another ride, it better be American, like this, not some shitbox."

"Hey," the Buddha replied, pulling the registration from his pocket and displaying it before Jimmy's piercing gaze, "just be cool. Check it out. Here's the ticket, too. Look at the registration. Read it, for Christ's sake. Here's all the stuff from the front desk. Except," (here Billy smiled, a knowing smile) "his credit card number and the name and phone number of his lady friend."

"Mileage?" asked Jimmy.

"It'll get wiped. All spoofed as soon as you get it back to the barn," said the Buddha. "All with the miracle of modern electronics."

"As usual," said Jimmy, pulling from the inside of his jacket and then handing over to Billy a plain white envelope fat with unmarked bills. "And no questions."

Satisfied with the consummation of the deal, Billy tucked the envelope into the pocket of his elephantine gray trousers, turned away, and waddled back up the ramp toward his booth. Jimmy popped open the massive trunk of the somewhat elderly-looking Lincoln. Yes, it was clean. He stood there a moment, thinking ahead...he made himself a mental note to take along a plastic drop cloth to protect the unspoiled carpet liner the next evening...just in case. A shovel might be called for also.

Jimmy slammed the trunk shut, hopped in the car, gunned it, and quickly exited the garage...and he briefly chirped the tires upon leaving the first stoplight he encountered. He was headed to Fenway to meet the kid. And things were beginning to rush through his head. Jimmy smiled. *Well, okay, he is a triggerman*, he thought, *but the triggerman is a kid...hell, he's younger than my daughter.* Two blocks down Commonwealth Avenue he caught another red light and heavy traffic, but Jimmy grinned. He hadn't driven in quite a while, and finding himself behind the wheel of a powerful luxury car was exhilarating And, suddenly, it didn't matter to be old enough to retire. To be watching some of his hair go down the drain in the shower every morning—to put up with some aches and pains. This was better than old times. Jimmy was a heavy in this game—his game. It wasn't going to be Vince "The Sandman's" anymore. *Yeah...eat sand, Saluzzo*, he thought to himself. Curiosity overcame him as he sat at the stoplight, the Lincoln's engine idling smoothly under the long hood. He turned, picked up the padded manila envelope, and ripped it open. There they were, his custom-commissioned babies: two perfect replicas of the license plates assigned to the deputy commissioner of the Boston Police Department. Like magic charms of sorts, they would soon find a place on the Lincoln's bumpers, thereby providing special immunity from any curious cop sticking his nose or his gun barrel into the car while Jimmy and his hired men were using it to get some work done. Or so he hoped.

Chapter 10

The Hit Man Plays Ball

Jimmy, growing more impatient by the minute because of the slow-moving traffic, was forced to drive the big Lincoln in a series of fits and starts, fast and slow along Brookline Avenue, accelerating where there was room in traffic, stomping on the brakes now and then, muttering curses at the jaywalkers, dog-walkers, and out-of-state cars that impeded his progress until he finally turned onto Landowne Street. He was striving to look calm...but was as alert as any fox could be upon feeling daylight burning his back outside a barnyard chicken coop. Jimmy scanned everything from left to right, and right to left. Yes, to be sure, he was scanning for men on rooftops, men in dark-colored full-size sedans and in unmarked panel vans occupying no parking spaces. He was also looking for the kid, who was supposed to be waiting for him near Gate E, with bells on as they say, good to go. He'd told the kid to watch for a car with an upside-down Uber sticker on the windshield—a bogus sticker Marv had created for him. Marv had jokingly told Jimmy the pickup instructions constituted a death wish for the kid, the way Jimmy had laid them out.

"You told him...*what?* To be wearing a *New York Yankees jacket* and be standing on the sidewalk in front of *Fenway?* That putz—he'll be dead in half an hour for sure!" Marv proclaimed, holding onto his ample belly and chuckling like a grade-school kid who knows a good prank when he sees one in the making, and can't keep it a secret. Jimmy had just laughed. But of course, in Jimmy's mind it was the perfect setup for the kid to prove his mettle as a tough guy...and a stone-cold killer.

Besides having the reputation of an expert marksman with an impressive list of kills, the kid came with a pedigree of sorts; his great-grandfather had been a sharpshooter, one of the best (albeit, on Germany's side) in World War II. Herman Hoffman Schmidt, casually known in some underground, dark web circles as Herman "The German," a 30-something soldier of fortune, was the gung-ho, go-to guy if you were in a business that you wanted no one else to mind and wanted to send your enemies to the other side without putting a stitch in your bankroll. At least...that was what Jimmy had found out about him through several time-consuming internet searches.

While it is entirely possible in this digital age to get a good reference for, say, a reputable plumber or a reliable roofer via a home services website, getting a referral from a reputable criminal source (that in itself an oxymoron) on a good hit man may be an entirely different matter. Jimmy's searches and inquires had not gone unnoticed, nor had someone at a keyboard overseas wasted any time in providing exactly the right man for Jimmy's 'work order' and at the right price.

What Jimmy's per diem hit man had found out, not too many hours ago before getting his assignment and assuming Herman's alias, was that he'd have to play along and take Jimmy's lead...until his handlers were ready to intervene and provide further instructions on a take-down. He knew well enough not to ask more questions. "Do not call...under any circumstances" was the text message he had received upon arriving in Boston. He then deleted it, per the instructions he'd been given.

Soon enough, Jimmy spotted him. Skinny kid...Coke-bottle glasses...Yankees jacket; that was him, alright. Herman was alone (good, that was a major part of the deal) and also not carrying...at least not carrying a piece or anything that looked like it would conceal one. Jimmy pulled the Lincoln over and lowered the passenger-side window a few inches.

"Uber?" asked Jimmy, in case anyone was looking and snooping.

"Yah, I'm the Yankee nut who emailed you. Thanks for coming; glad you're here," answered the kid.

"Okay," said Jimmy, acknowledging the prearranged pickup line. "Get in the car."

The kid was tall, wiry-looking, with an unruly, rat's-nest shock of hair and a pair of wire-rimmed glasses with thick lenses. *Yes, those are Coke-bottle, John Denver–style glasses*, Jimmy thought, as the kid hauled open the door and plopped himself into the seat. It was a stretch for Jimmy to believe the kid was actually a renowned contract killer and not a geek who'd hacked the identity of someone, a guy the likes of which Arnold Schwarzenegger would need a bazooka to dispatch. Perhaps his appearance was little more than a disguise? Truth be told, he looked more like a librarian than the triggerman who'd iced more than two dozen of Europe's notorious underworld figures that certain interests—none of them legitimate—had wished to dispose of. Before the kid could buckle his seatbelt, the Lincoln took off, snapping Herman's head backward in the process, and scooted along Landowne, then took a right onto Ipswich Street.

"Where's your gear?" asked Jimmy, glancing sideways quickly at the kid. "And how does your kind get firepower into my territory without showing up on my radar?"

"Oh, well," answered the kid modestly, removing his glasses in order to clean them with a white handkerchief he plucked from a jacket pocket, "I am, as perhaps you know, a devotee of music. Classical music."

"Okay—so?" continued Jimmy, now casually eyeing the rearview mirror.

"Well, you see, I play the organ proficiently, and I am as well a repair person for pipe organs. That is my...actual profession. I am well known, and I travel to many countries. I must ship pipes in to repair damaged ones...so, why not gun barrels in small pipes? Or in pipes that carry cleaning rods, too? Not too conspicuous. Nobody sees them...nobody finds them. Metal in metal. It is easy. I have such a job now, working on an organ in Cambridge...most convenient."

"Uh-huh," affirmed Jimmy. "Good cover. Look, here's the deal," he then said, slowing and pulling over, after turning onto Boylston Street, in front of a bar where an altercation between two brawny-looking men was taking place on the sidewalk. "This guy," said Jimmy, handing Herman two photos of Vince, "is the target. The whole deal goes down tomorrow night. Logistics are all set."

"Logistics? I do my own logistics usually," said the kid calmly. "Him?" he queried quizzically, pointing at Vince's swarthy, somewhat rotund image in one of the prints. "I have seen him before...I am sure of it."

The fight outside was heating up now, and several people had emerged from the bar to watch the fisticuffs. The two pugilists, weaving left and right and unsteady on their feet from their excessive infusion of alcohol, were wearing baseball jackets of different colors, an aspect that apparently incited excitement between two factions in the gathering crowd.

After some staggering, clumsy footwork, finagling, and a few preemptory swings and insults that were exchanged, the man wearing a blue jacket and cap emblazoned with the red

B of the Bosox caught the man wearing the black jacket with a vicious left hook. It landed him with a loud *thump* on a fender of the Lincoln, against which the victim laid with the blank-eyed look of a deer that has been bagged and is about to be dragged out of the woods and lashed to a hunter's car. It took about five seconds for Jimmy, vigilant about anything that could possibly damage his borrowed chariot and thus incriminate him, to emerge from the Lincoln in fighting trim as if he were back in a boxing ring, yelling at the man to get up and get off the car.

Circling around the front of the car, Jimmy quickly grabbed an arm of the unfortunate man who was draped over the right front fender and hauled him upright. His opponent suddenly jumped forward, grabbed Jimmy's collar, and started swearing. The blank-eyed man suddenly came to, lurching forward toward Jimmy.

"This is friggin' Boston. And who," he asked, pulling a small black pistol from a concealed holster with amazing ease, "are *you* to tell me what to do?"

"And what's your game, dude?" asked the other man, hauling Jimmy backward to prepare to deliver a punch...but he never had the chance.

"I don't know where that guy came from," said the bartender to the police afterward, "but he sure as hell cleared up the mess. It was like...he was Spider-Man or something." The person who cleared up "the mess" was the kid, who'd sized up the situation, jumped from the car, and quickly grabbed the gun. He tossed it away and then grasped the jackets of the two fighters, rapidly pulled the two men toward each other and handily cracked their skulls together; both men went down on the pavement in a jumbled heap of sports apparel and alcohol fumes, leaving a befuddled and still-blustery Jimmy Callahan on the sidewalk with no one else left to quarrel with.

"There was a fight...a guy got out of his car and tried to break it up and one of them pulled a gun and then another guy just came from nowhere and did this Kung-Fu thing...and it was all over; very cool," said one man to the cops much later on, after Jimmy and Herman had quickly driven away to find another meeting place, a neighborhood bar that was several miles away. At the bar, Jimmy shoehorned the Lincoln into a too-small parking spot. He emerged from the car with a triumphant smile and new faith in his subcontracted hit man.

"Kid," he hollered, "let's go in here. Everyone can use a sharpener when they're talkin' business. And by the way," Jimmy paused, rummaged in the inside breast pocket of his leather jacket, produced an envelope, and handed it to Herman, "here's half now; the other half when the job's done." Once inside, Jimmy and Herman sidled onto barstools and began to plan the finer details of the hit.

"I don't drink," professed the kid.

"What?" retorted Jimmy, eyebrows uplifted, spinning a trifle on his barstool just in time to address the first visit of the bulldog-visaged bartender, who quickly barked a question.

"What'll it be, fellas?"

"Bourbon," answered Jimmy.

"Water," said Herman.

"*Water?*" exclaimed the beefy-looking bartender, all eyes suddenly, furrows forming on his brow, working their way slowly down to his grizzled jowls.

"Give him a Moxie," crowed an old-timer who was sitting a few stools down, and looked like he was about to fall off his perch.

"You want water in *this* place, sonny," the bartender said, with a shark-like smile that displayed a veritable sawmill of jagged teeth, "you'd better *pray* for rain!"

"No prayers said in this place, kid," said Jimmy, turning to Herman, and then back to the bartender, adding, "Pour the kid a shot of bourbon."

It was later—much later that day—well into early evening, in fact, when Jimmy returned to his store, somewhat mollified about being caught up as a lightweight nonentity in the fight, and his breath perfumed to the extreme by several liberal doses of bourbon; the borrowed Lincoln was safely ensconced in a trustworthy parking lot, whose owner owed Jimmy a favor, just two blocks away. Marv was waiting for him.

"How did the deal go down, Jim?" he asked as Jimmy let himself in, appearing to be rather unsteady on his feet. The store was darkened; Marv never liked to do the cash-out and safe deposit with all the lights on, with the place lit up "like a circus" as he once said to his boss. And since Marv had stayed late after closing to talk some business with his boss, he saw little need to turn on any lights besides the one nightlight now burning over the front counter.

"Smooth, Marv...really smooth," came the reply. "I think this whole deal...is gonna work out. The German guy seems legit––a killer. He can take care of someone, for sure. I dropped him off at St. George's Cathedral...his cover—it's perfect—is that he's an organ repairman. Working on that monster pipe organ they have...it hasn't been tweaked or tuned since '85. Sneaks his iron into the U.S. under cover of organ parts. Pipes...man, pipes. Pipes and a gun barrel. Would you believe it?"

"St. George's," said Marv almost reverently. "That's Father O'Donnell's church. A brute of a Latin teacher, that guy was, back when I was in high school, that old buzzard. He's gotta be in his late 80s now."

"I'm sure he is," replied Jimmy, adding, "So I dropped our guy off there and I looked at the piece."

"What is it?" asked Marv, obviously curious.

"An OSV-96. Russian-made, 108 mm, with the DS-6 night sight. Full boat," said Jimmy, obviously impressed enough to tell Marv how he felt about the encounter. "You know what I like about the guy?"

"No," answered Marv. "How the hell would I?"

"He doesn't sign anything," replied Jimmy, grinning ear-to-ear. "Just like me and you. You know what he does? He's like—old school; he's showing me the piece, right? And he hands me two or three bullets. Puts them in my hand. And he looks at me and says, 'Treat them carefully; those are my signatures.'"

A scant 30 feet away from where Jimmy and Marv were talking stood a display of several mannequins, each dummy wearing a different type of uniform. Normally, there were four of them: a firefighter in full gear, an EMT, a policeman, and a policewoman. Had either Jimmy or Marv been paying attention, they would have noticed that tonight there was a second policewoman, its figure standing just beside the first. They would have seen the ordinarily dull, lifeless eyes of the new policewoman blink...and blink again upon Jimmy uttering the word "killer" and then focus on Jimmy.

"You've got the line on the big guy, right?" he asked Marv.

"Yeah," answered Marv, reaching into a cooler on the counter. "Want a beer?" he asked Jimmy.

"Indeed," answered his boss. Marv produced a brown bottle and passed it to Jimmy, who grasped the cap, twisted it off, and tossed it carelessly over his shoulder. It bounced off the policeman's motorcycle helmet with a loud *plink* and clattered to the concrete floor; the policewoman blinked again. Her head shifted, ever so slightly, as if she were trying to hear every word the two men were saying. In fact...she was.

"Here's to the deal, boss," said Marv, cracking open his own bottle of brew. The two men clinked their beer bottles together and then each took a hefty pull of beer from his bottle and eyed the other.

"This is where it goes right again, Marv," said Jimmy. "This whole deal goes down right after dark tomorrow night. Do you have enough of those no parking cones to put out on the street in front of the church?"

"All set, boss," affirmed Marv.

A fly buzzed lazily down from its precarious, upside-down perch on the ceiling and landed atop Marv's beer; he quickly shooed it away. It woozily flew off into the depths of the store and buzzed about in erratic circles like an old biplane in search of a landing field. Marv wiped off the top of the bottle with his shirtsleeve.

"Goddamn flies," observed Marv dourly.

"Yeah," observed Jimmy, taking another pull from his bottle, looking about for more of them. "They're dying off, like rats. All over the place." A heavy truck rumbled by outside, its exhaust rattling the store's windowpanes, then all fell silent...until the fly resumed its antics, buzzing about in random, ever-widening circles. And then landed on the policewoman's wig...and started crawling down toward her left ear.

"It's all about rats...when you get right down to it," proffered Jimmy, swaying now and clearly feeling the effects of the beer mingling with the bourbon. "Someone finally ratted on Vince Saluzzo; it's all on the Internet. That's where I found it, after I got that tip. That Classic Crimebusters site somebody posted on. It had proof positive that one of his own boys took out the triggerman, the guy who took the job Vince sent him to do, to shut him up. The guy who killed my sis, Rose, may she rest in peace. After he went boo-hooing to the FBI looking for cover, because he's a rat.

"You're sure about this? Some of those sites are poison. Run by scumbags who take over your computer and hold it hostage; then, they've got more ways to screw you than the Kama Sutra or something. Now, that kid——which one of them——Charlie? He's a mama's boy, right?" asked Marv, taking a swig from his bottle.

"Yeah," said Jimmy, glowering. "I'm sure. Dead sure. And yeah; Mama and Daddy's boy. Daddy's gonna be home tomorrow night, and he's gonna get clipped there."

The fly, emboldened by its success in making a touchdown, suddenly decided to stretch its legs. It wandered down a strand of artificial hair and onto the top of the policewoman's left ear. Just as Jimmy turned back to face Marv, the policewoman fidgeted.

"Then Mama's gonna be solo," barked Jimmy. As if reenergized following its initial exploration, the fly walked briskly down the ear of the female figure that was inside the blue uniform, scooted across her cheek, and stopped to rest on her lips. The figure in the uniform that was now beginning to show faint perspiration stains resisted every possible urge to squirm and swat the fly...and struggled to keep on listening.

"Where's the big guy—the muscle you brought in?" Marv asked Jimmy.

"He'll be over at the old Liberty Bell," answered Jimmy, "where I put him up. No high-profile types or nosey tourists stay there; he'll blend right in. He's gonna hang close by. And why shouldn't he? We're the only game he knows now. The trigger—the guy I told you about—he's doing his own thing. He's lying low and undercover, fronting a legit job...who could blame him? He's a clever kid. Smart. I'll pick them both up tomorrow night, about eight. Then, we're going up to the North End to take care of business. Once it's all over...it'll be like nobody knows anything. Right?" Marv nodded gravely, then contemplated the remaining contents of his beer bottle.

"No second thoughts now, are you sure?" he asked.

"None," said Jimmy, draining the last of his beer. The fly took flight, buzzed about, and landed squarely on the tip of the policewoman's nose, as if relishing its victim's torment. What seemed like a stifled cough...suddenly sounded within the bounds of Jimmy C's store.

"What the hell was *that*?" Jimmy exclaimed, a perturbed expression on his face, setting down his beer bottle as he looked about the darkened store. Had Jimmy been sober, he no doubt would have looked again to discover the source of that noise, and discovered that the dummy's eyes were crossed.

"Shit, Jimmy," answered Marv, "it could in fact *really be*...rats. I've caught a few down in the basement. They come up through the tunnel, you know."

"Ya know what, Marv?" asked Jimmy, setting down his empty bottle on the sales counter. "I'm done for the night. Let's call it a day. We've got work to do tomorrow."

Both men headed for the front door. Jimmy heaved his empty beer bottle into a wastebasket and then let himself out the front door as Marv reached for the alarm keypad; Patty at long last scratched her nose. Now, catlike in the darkness, she slipped stealthily away and padded softly down the stairs to the basement before the alarm could be set. She entered Jimmy's office, opened the door concealed as a bookcase and let herself into the storage room beyond, carefully closing the door behind her. Using her pocket flashlight, she hurriedly found and donned the sneakers she had slipped off earlier. She quickly strode to the access to the tunnel, passed through it, closed the door and turned to face a rusty green metal box bolted to the concrete wall. Python-size cables with insulation flaking off them in places snaked away from it, up to the grimy, arched ceiling of the tunnel. The time-faded warning "DANGER––600 volts DC, LIVE WIRES was painted on the box. She pulled the key from her pocket and consulted the tag to find the instructions and alarm code, as she had when she had entered. With some effort, she opened the box and lifted the huge throw handle of the circuit breaker––something that looked like it was a component of Doctor Frankenstein's electrical experiments––to reveal the small keypad cleverly hidden behind it. She entered the reset and time delay code for the door alarm, then stepped back into the cavernous, musty-smelling tunnel to continue her journey home, taking care not to trip over the rusted rails and dusty ties. But there were no trains to beware of there, only shadows of the past.

This, the MBTA's long-abandoned Castle Island Branch, once ran from the busy Red Line at its bustling Broadway station to the bucolic seaside. It had led a short life, serving just East and West Broadway and Pleasure Beach, a recreational spot whose weekend popularity in season was cut short when World War II's curfews and night-time blackouts of coastal businesses and night spots took effect. The line closed in 1942––and never reopened. Bricked off from the Broadway station after the war, and with its Castle Island station later bulldozed into the pages of history, the obscure branch's subway tunnel was by now off the radar of even the canniest urban 'T' spelunkers, teenage graffiti artists and winos who frequented other such eerie, dank grottos of the system.

Soon, in a far corner of a small, quiet park about two blocks away from Jimmy's store, a trap door made of rusty, diamond-plate steel stamped with the words SUBWAY KEEP CLEAR slowly arose from its berth inside a crumbling perimeter of low, concrete curbing. Patty peered out from under it, like the commander of an army tank cautiously peeking from its hatch to see if any enemy is about; the coast was clear. She hoisted the steel access plate a bit farther, climbed up the stairway, turned and gently lowered the door until she heard the lock click into place. Besides the police uniform, she was leaving with something else she had not entered with: an entirely new perspective on her father's enterprises and devious plan––and with a plan of her own in mind. Intervention.

Chapter 11

Getting Out of School

Jerry left the prison's properties office, walked through the number two inner gateway, stepped briskly into the courtyard, and headed toward the main gate. He heard birdsong and distant traffic, also shouts of excitement and sounds of basketballs bouncing off backboards, the sounds coming from the maximum-security exercise area behind far-off loops of razor wire where prisoners were shooting hoops. The air smelled strange to him—not sanitized, like it was inside the air-conditioned cafeteria, the laundry or infirmary, but like that of a city at rush hour—an aromatic amalgamation of diesel exhaust, airborne dust, burned rubber, the faint aroma of garbage, and a hint of the sour perspiration of several hundred thousand frenzied people. People doggedly hurrying to work, lemming-like, in bumper-hugging packs of speeding vehicles scurrying over the 495 loop and Route 128 toward Beantown. The air, in fact, smelled quite like that which escapes from a punctured basketball, as it does now and then when a fight breaks out and one prisoner takes a swipe at another for good measure with an illicit weapon, but misses his mark.

Turn slowly now and give a proper salute. 'Cause they're watching, Jerry thought. He stopped walking and turned around. Sure enough, there they were, watching him leave. High up in one of the buildings behind an enormous, bullet-proof glass window, there were two figures standing side-by-side, appearing as prim and proper as the miniature bride and groom figures on the top of a wedding cake. It was the warden and his amiable consort, the prison's head nurse. Jerry gave them a one-fingered salute, laughed, turned on his heel, and then continued on, shuffling along the pavement toward the main gate in his scuffed old loafers. The pockets of his baggy-looking old suit, seriously outdated and sporting the effects of some years in storage, bulged with a slightly moldy wallet containing $493 in small bills, a motley collection of loose change that was now possibly of considerable numismatic interest to coin collectors, and an array of old, crumpled-up business cards. The properties checkout guard had produced these from the depths of a large manila envelope and tossed them at him through the cutout in a chicken-wire fence at the booth's counter.

"This is all yours and that's all you've got," he barked.

But that's the deal with prison when you've done your time, Jerry had learned. Everything is strictly by the rules, almost like a hotel that likes to keep its towels and ashtrays: You don't leave anything that you brought with you, and you don't leave with anything you didn't bring.

Once out of sight of the security cameras and the sight of the warden and nurse, Jerry caught up with another con, a short-timer who was on his way out today, Bob Smith. Quickly, Jerry swapped ID cards with him, pressing a 50-dollar bill into his hands in the process. Bob, happy at having made a few bucks, scurried off to the van that was waiting to take Jerry to a halfway-house for indoctrination back into society; Jerry walked past it, and kept on going down the street.

Have to make that phone call, Jerry thought. *Have to find a pay phone. Don't ever trust the phones inside the slammer. Too many busybodies. Have to find that old bar, too. Sergeant Sully's. A great place.* Jerry, thinking both of his need to call whoever had placed the hit to get instructions for the job and the desire to reacquaint himself with his old haunts, walked purposefully up to the first bus stop he encountered. When the bus came, its air brakes hissing, its diesel snarling and smoking, it pulled up to the curb and disgorged a dozen or so dour-faced commuters. Jerry stepped aboard, dumped a handful of quarters into the receptacle next to the driver, and heaved himself into an unyielding, slippery plastic seat that looked like it would better serve patrons of a bowling alley or a fast-food restaurant. But comfort didn't matter. He was headed for Boston, and the old neighborhood. His neighborhood, for the things he remembered.

An hour later, after changing to the MBTA green line, Jerry stepped off a streetcar at the Commonwealth Avenue subway station and walked up the stairs to the street. The buildings seemed all too familiar to him—the big building that had been the Kenmore Hotel, the brownstone farther east across the way with a verdigris-colored roof shaped like a witch's hat, the enormous Citgo sign perched atop a high building close by. But there was not a pay phone in sight. He hailed a passerby, a scruffy-looking teenager in a New England Patriots jacket who was twiddling with his iPhone as he walked.

"Hey, kid, where's there a pay phone?" Jerry asked him.

"Huh?" said the kid, turning briefly to pause, look up, and stare up at the huge man. "What's that?" So, Jerry asked several other people he encountered during the next few minutes; they shunned him as if he were a deadbeat asking for spare change. Tired from this effort, Jerry recalled there was a Baskin-Robbins store on the corner and thought of having some refreshment. The urge to savor a vanilla cone with jimmies (only in Boston are chocolate sprinkles thusly referred to, and that by the old-timers) suddenly socked Jerry in his taste buds like a baseball bat swung at him by a heavy hitter.

Jerry looked, wandering like a displaced bigfoot improbably dressed in a frumpy-looking suit, his arms swinging at his sides, in search for the store with its distinctive pink sign, right on the corner of Commonwealth Avenue and Brookline. But it was gone; instead there was a busy-looking McDonald's and also several small shops. Jerry's mouth became dry. Parched. He swore he could taste sand in his mouth now. *Okay, ixnay on the ice cream...beer, then. A cold one. Or two.* He would go to the old bar—his bar—Sergeant Sully's.

Sully's was a neighborhood bar within pub-crawling distance of both Kenmore Square and Fenway, as the area's bar-hoppers and night owls used to say. It had seen a lot of the college drinking crowd's spending money in Jerry's younger days, a crowd that spilled over from Katie's and other bars when their tables overflowed with late-night revelers and baseball fans after a big game had packed the stadium. The bar's owner, Sully, was a Vietnam vet of some repute who had a steel plate and possibly some recurring, post-traumatic fireworks—leftovers from two combat tours—implanted in his head. He celebrated a notable Red Sox victory one evening by making the rounds of several other bars in friendly fashion, then riding his Harley Chopper through the open front door of his own establishment shortly before closing time, as he couldn't focus clearly enough to find a suitable parking spot outside.

It was somewhere along Brookline Avenue, *or...had it been?* Jerry had been at Sergeant Sully's before, many times...and now it was Sully's that Jerry sought, the way a nostalgia-stricken college alum seeks the familiar frat house and cordial company he left so many years ago when he attends home-coming week. *Damn. What was the street number? Number, hell...what was the street name?* Numbers...well, Jerry was good with them when they were close at hand, but when they weren't, they quickly eluded him like partners in crime when the phone starts ringing, the money's gone, and the cops are pounding on the door.

Jerry's pace settled into a solid rhythm as he strode along the sidewalk, starting to reminisce about Sully's old joint. Presently, he could imagine himself within the bar, looking about its dark, dank interior...smelling the pleasant funk of stale beer, the aroma of bar polish and cigarette smoke being stirred by the *whoosh* of the big paddle fans wind-milling away overhead...hear the *clack* of a rack of billiard balls being broken as yet another game of 8-ball began on the pool table out back. Out back where the ancient Wurlitzer jukebox was coaxed into life with an infusion of clattering quarters and sometimes a swift kick to make it go if it hesitated, making Connie Francis's voice come alive from the neon depths of that great old-time machine like a wailing siren on an old fire engine. Those were songs the old guys played.

And they would all be there—the old guard, the boys—hunkered over their beers at the bar (even at 10:30 a.m., when someone who'd been out late and just arisen would come in for "an eye opener"). Or someone who had some 'work' like Jerry's would come in, a piece hiked up tight in his belt, an extra clip stashed away just for luck, blood money in his wallet, and a mission in his mind, and have "a sharpener" before he hit the streets to do some business.

The telephone booth was also out back, far beyond the pool table. In its beige metal wall were two large round holes, holes made by a regular patron possessing a handgun. He'd become pissed off at overhearing someone making a very unwise and decidedly untimely telephone call to someone...someone known to be undercover FBI. Someone who was apparently going to put a finger on him. The shooter, Jerry noted at the time, having had a couple of eye openers before unleashing his weapon, had hit his mark after the first two shots. No worries; as they say, the third time's always the charm.

Jerry's large, usually clumsy feet felt now like they were floating over the curbs and sidewalks. The very thought of draining an ice-cold mug of beer (or two) at his old haunt was intoxicating in itself. And for all practical purposes, now, he *was* drunk—dry drunk...skunked, falling-down, dry-drunk when at last he spotted the big, familiar gold letter "S" embedded in the foyer of a building. Jerry sagged against its door, which slowly opened as its hydraulic cylinder gave way, thereby depositing Jerry's limp body into the barroom—his body arriving somewhat like the condition an octopus is in, when dumped out of an astonished fisherman's net onto the deck of a seagoing trawler. *Clack* went the brace of billiard balls on the backroom table, as a game of 8-ball began. But then the game stopped abruptly. The two sleek-looking young men dressed in tight shirts who were playing pool both put down their cue sticks and stared at Jerry.

"Help you?" asked the bartender, dabbling daintily at a glass with a spotless white dishtowel. Jerry stared at him, then at the pool table, then the jukebox. The jukebox was silent. The big paddle fans went *whoosh-whoosh-whoosh* and stirred the air, which faintly smelled like old booze gathering in the bar's drip rail and somebody's strange-smelling perfume. Bad perfume. The place was empty. No cigarette smoke. No floozies hanging out. No 'hunkers' hunched over beer mugs, with elbows firmly planted on the bar.

"Beer," Jerry managed to whisper, looking at the bartender.

"Beer?" asked the bartender. "We don't start serving that 'til noon."

"What kinda bar is this?" demanded Jerry, regaining his composure somewhat as he pulled himself up and assumed a vertical position.

"Don't be silly, big guy; this is a sushi bar!" the bartender snickered. The two men at the pool table giggled and resumed their game, after one of them briefly used his cue stick and thumb and forefinger to stroke it in pantomime of a lewd act.

"My, he's a tall one," commented one of them. "You don't suppose..."

"Do you, like...want to go upstairs or something?" asked the other, looking quizzically at the new arrival.

"Oh!" said the bartender, brightening up visibly. "*I know.* You're one of those old-timers, aren't you? Sergeant Sully's honeys, we call 'em. Culture shock, I know." He grinned like a chimp at a zoo looking at curious visitors. "We get that here from time to time."

"Forget it," snarled Jerry. "I just gotta make a phone call." Free from his momentary lapse into the Sergeant Sully's of yesteryear, he walked—swaying unsteadily like a storm-tossed schooner as he went—toward the back of the barroom, giving the pool players an ample berth. He then went down a dark hallway where—miracle of miracles—the old Bell System pay phone booth, resplendent with its little round, blue-and-white porcelain sign, still stood in a dark corner like an ancient automobile, marooned and long forgotten, sitting in a dark corner of some abandoned garage and awaiting a call to duty.

He squeezed himself inside and—too big to sit on the tiny round stool—slammed the folding doors shut. Immediately, the booth was bathed in a pool of dim yellow light from a tiny incandescent bulb in a recessed overhead fixture. Jerry gazed reflectively at the two bullet holes in the steel-case wall for a moment, fumbled for change in his pocket, then dumped quarters into the phone, making its ancient innards jingle; he dialed the numbers he had written on his knuckles. Thank God he'd taken that paper out from between his toes. This obviously, he realized, wasn't the kind of place where you'd want to bend over to so much as tie a shoelace. Several miles away,

Jimmy Callahan's burner phone rang. Jimmy eased the Lincoln over to the curb and answered the phone.

"Facilities management," said Jimmy cautiously, always fearing an FBI set-up.

"You want that order delivered to your job out there?" asked Jerry, knowing it was best not to let on too many details, in case the conversation was being monitored.

"Yeah," said Jimmy. "The estimate looks good. Real good. You've got the job. For now, take a cab to Dorchester; you've got a room at the Liberty Bell Hotel. All paid. It's on Highland Street. I'll pick you up there tomorrow about 8:00 p.m. for the conference."

Jerry hung up the phone, a triumphant smile spreading across his grizzled face. He ripped a page out of the phone book dangling from a chain in the phone booth and wrote down the hotel's name with the stub of a pencil he found on the counter. He squeezed out of the phone booth with the aplomb of a portly woodchuck shimmying through a hole in a garden fence, let himself out the back door of the bar into an alleyway, and hailed a cab as soon as he hit the street. Twenty minutes later, the speedy little white Metro Cab deposited Jerry at the front door of the Liberty Bell, a monolithic, gloomy-looking building with the forlorn ambience of some ancient, decommissioned warship that had washed up on the littered shore of a desolate beach, awaiting the attention of the ship breakers. Two statues of rampant lions that might have been works of art in Boston's bygone days flanked its front entrance. One was missing its head; the other, however, was complete in every detail, and some wag, not missing an opportunity to put his mark on the establishment's reputation, had daubed with red paint the parts of the lion that established the beast's gender as male. The lion seemed to be glaring at the boarded-up movie theater across the street, whose tattered marquee, replete with broken light bulbs, sagged over the sidewalk as if protecting the rusty shopping cart that had been abandoned there.

Jerry, grunting at the effort, tugged at the tarnished brass door handle and the hotel's massive door reluctantly gave way by degrees, its hinges croaking in almost frog-like fashion. A strong but not totally unfamiliar smell hit him—the funk of old stale beer, the aroma of cigarette smoke, and of sensationally musty carpets. It was stirred like the leftover dregs in a foul diner's dirty dishes by a huge, old-fashioned paddle fan hanging precariously from the ceiling over the check-in desk.

In this, the hotel's state of ultimate decrepitude, the building was certainly showing its age. In fact, parts of it were so badly weathered and deteriorated that any passerby unfamiliar with the hotel's past might well have imagined that perhaps the Sons of Liberty had actually stayed there, shortly after plotting the Boston Tea Party. Any one of those passersby who stopped and stayed, possibly some out-of-town cheapskate, might also have thought the lodging had likely not seen a significant renovation since the Sons of Liberty left, no doubt to find a more congenial place to stay and take out their frustrations against the British at Bunker Hill.

"A room, one night. Jerry Garrantino's the name; I got a paid reservation," the giant grumbled to the rumpled, sleepy-looking desk clerk, a woman in a black terrycloth robe who was slouched over a magazine at the front desk, a lipstick-stained cigarette dangling from her lower lip. She looked up, smoke wafting lazily from her nostrils like that of a sleeping dragon in a child's storybook being gently awakened. She took a long drag and then removed the cigarette from her mouth with gnarled, nicotine-stained fingers.

"Honey," she rasped, looking at him and thus displaying her two, rather different-looking eyes, "you've come to the right place. Rooms are all we've got here!" Looking about the foyer, which contained two baggy-looking black sofas that were hemorrhaging stuffing through holes, an ailing potted palm plant, a stereo set perhaps fashionable when Johnson was in the White House, and an analog-era television set with a black-and-white image of a Dragnet episode flickering on its screen, he could only imagine what his room upstairs was furnished with; perhaps a cot and a bare, 40-watt light bulb. But it sure as hell beat the prison cell that he was accustomed to. Jerry signed the register.

"Now remember," said the clerk, sternly fixing her one good eye on him (the other, he was sure now, was made of glass) "don't leave anything that you brought with you, and don't leave with anything that you didn't bring."

Chapter 12

The Heist

It was indeed Rome, but, *Is this really Italy?* Maria Saluzzo thought to herself, as the Mercedes taxi she was riding in slowed to a crawl as it caught up with a flotilla of slow-moving taxicabs and buses cluttering the lanes of the Autostrada Roma, just a short distance from the airport Hilton. She had expected to encounter chaotic traffic and the lunatic drivers Italy is reputed to have, every one of them seesawing at the steering wheel of a careening automobile the size of an amusement park's bumper car, but thus far along in this overseas junket with Father DeTomasi, the pace was sedate, to say the least. Most of the lunatics had been the unruly passengers on the airplane.

But this was, of course, a business trip, a trip for the good of a nonprofit charity, the one that benefited children's playgrounds. The charity for which Maria, one of Father DeTomasi's flock, was treasurer and chief cheerleader. The contributors to this nonprofit were generous and included, besides Maria's husband, a clique of businessmen who moved quietly and surreptitiously within Vince's low-profile social circles. The benefactors of this fund included, besides the several playgrounds in Father DeTomasi's parish, the various construction companies that maintained them, using uncommonly expensive materials and supplies, while charging exorbitant labor rates. They existed mostly on paper, using undocumented subcontractors and conveniently operated at a loss, due to high and poorly documented expenditures. It was much like a laundromat in which soiled quarters dropped into the slots of washing machines soon magically emerged, walking out the doors in pockets of the clean pants of those who operated it.

Maria and Father DeTomasi's audience with the pope would cement the relationship between the Holy See and the parish in Boston and lend, like a valued testimonial, further credence to Maria's fundraising efforts. Maria carried a contribution from the fund in the form of the number of a certain Cayman Islands bank account and a password, contained in a phone in a secret compartment of her handbag. No one, except her husband, who she'd emailed the day before, knew these details. After all, the less said when it came to these things, the better.

"Look, Father," Maria said to the priest sitting beside her, nudging him gently with an elbow and pointing to a shopping center that loomed in the distance. It was a jumble of box-like structures that looked as though they had been dumped onto an open field, one perhaps wrangled for a few thousand Lire from the farming families who had worked the land for untold generations and been promised a bright, shining future if they accepted an offer little more than good enough to buy them a train ticket to another land. "There's another place named for Leonardo da Vinci," Father DeTomasi sighed and then made a whistling noise through his tea-stained dentures.

"Oh, da Vinci this, da Vinci that," he scoffed, turning to Maria to display a thin, rather sardonic, off-white smile. "Leonardo da Vinci Airport? It is, you know, after all, really *Fiumicino Aeroporto*. Check your history books, my dear; da Vinci never flew there."

"Of course not, Father," said Maria. "Father," she asked, rolling her expressive brown eyes toward him the way two fried eggs roll over almost lovingly toward bacon in a hot frying pan, "do you think the Holy See agrees that Peter the Second will return the church to Christ?"

"I don't know, Mrs. Saluzzo," replied the priest, dabbing at the perspiration on his forehead with a pocket handkerchief. "Only our Lord can tell us. But I'll be glad if we do not meet him today and can return to our hotel safely at day's end. I detest traffic...and as you may know, I prefer to have my own chauffeur, wherever I go." He glanced at the taxi driver, looking gravely concerned.

Maria peered out the tinted window to look for anything interesting that spoke of local culture—a bistro with tiny tables shaded by orange, white, and green umbrellas, perhaps, or two *nonni anzianos*, gray and distinguished looking grandfathers in rumpled suits and fedoras, facing off in a friendly game of chess in a shady park where squirrels begged and pigeons pecked for handouts, but there was none of this. There was concrete and pavement and steel girders, and there were enclaves of bunker-like buildings crowding the drab-appearing street—a flat, gray-toned landscape that looked more like that of Lowell, Massachusetts than Rome, Italy.

The driver, thought Maria, *is not so bad.* He was a powerfully built, swarthy-looking man with a wild crop of curly black hair. *Hair—a full head of hair!* thought Maria. *That's it. Ahh. That could make it Italy! Perhaps even tonight!* The taxi slowed a bit more and the object of Maria's attention grumbled, honked the horn briefly and made pretense of ramming the rear bumper of a small white Alfa Romeo convertible in front of him. The driver, a large woman with sensationally-long blonde hair flowing out from beneath a colorful and expensive-looking scarf, looked in her rearview mirror, raised her right hand, and extended a middle finger.

"Shameful!" grumbled Father DeTomasi in disapproval. "Sinful!" The taxi driver peered into his rearview mirror to look at the priest. It was the way a dog looks at his owner after being caught peeing on the living room carpet, and, fully chastened, begs to come back into the house. The driver gunned the gas and the taxi surged forward, then braked sharply as it encountered a line of stopped cars, red taillights blinking as if in alarm.

"If we're late, Father, will His Holiness still see us?" asked Maria, her forehead wrinkling in concern.

"Maria, I have every confidence that ample time has been set aside for our audience," replied the priest calmly. The taxi ground to a sudden stop at a small traffic circle as the cause of the slowdown was revealed to them: a Birra Moretti truck carrying cases of beer had run into and driven over the rear half of a tiny Fiat Topolino. The bulbous little subcompact now resembled a bug whose posterior had been stepped on.

The beer truck had in turn been hit by a tiny Vespa motor scooter; a brawny policeman was now trying to extricate its mangled remains from underneath the truck's rear axle. Beer bottles littered the roadside. The scooter's owner, still wearing his helmet, had helped himself to a beer to steady his nerves and was sitting on the island in the middle of the rotary enjoying it. Two more policemen were struggling to keep the burly truck driver from connecting his fists with the pudgy Fiat owner, who was standing his ground, expressing great distress and doing a credible imitation of a baritone opera singer who was having his fingernails pulled out.

"Impossibile!" yelled the driver, who thumped the steering wheel soundly, ran his fingers through his hair, and then laid on the horn again. The blonde lady saluted him a second time, adding a circular motion to this repertoire for added emphasis.

"Find another way, please!" ordered the priest, now becoming somewhat nervous and glancing at his Rolex. Suddenly, the traffic moved forward; spotting a break in it, the driver seized this opportunity and squeezed his Mercedes past the Alfa, coming so close that Maria could see that its driver wore earrings much like her own. There was the brief scraping sound of the two cars' outside mirrors brushing against each other, then the taxi driver put his foot down, and soon the car was hurtling along side streets, finally entering the Via Portuense, where it came to an intersection and stopped when the traffic lights turned red and pedestrians scurried across the street. A group of nuns had gathered on the corner like a gaggle of penguins huddled on an ice pack. As the light changed to green and the taxi rolled forward, one of the nuns suddenly darted across the road in front of it; another turned toward the car and casually flicked her cigarette butt into the gutter.

"Disgraceful!" rumbled Father DeTomasi, peering at the smoker.

"Gesù Cristo!" shouted the swarthy driver, swerving quickly to avoid impaling the nun's flowing habit on the hood ornament.

"Blasphemer!" barked Father DeTomasi at him, kicking the driver's seat. *Oh God*, thought Maria. She turned around to see what had become of the nun—and saw that the white Alfa convertible was following them.

The Mercedes passed a soccer field where a group of bare-chested teenage boys were doing calisthenics. Father DeTomasi craned his neck to get a good look at them.

"Oh my!" he mumbled.

"Excuse me?" asked Maria. The driver took his eyes off the road and turned slightly to peer at her, then at the priest; his eyebrows were in a V-shape expressing sincere interest in what was being said.

"It's so good to see the youth getting exercise," explained the priest, whose attention was then diverted by a group of boys on racing bicycles; crazed on hogging the road and slathered in perspiration, they briefly kept the Mercedes at bay and led the way. "Goodness, but those boys are fast!" he mumbled, squirming in his seat badly enough to garner Maria's attention as the car pulled abreast of them, then sped on.

Whatever reverie that was playing in the mind of Father DeTomasi was cut short as the white Alfa suddenly pulled swiftly alongside the Mercedes, scattering the cyclists like confetti in a windstorm. Its driver yanked off her sunglasses to reveal a large, rough-looking visage, a pair of bloodshot eyes, and an evil-looking smile.

"My God!" screeched the priest. "That's a *man!*"

"Ferma l'auto! Pull over, *now!*" roared the person in the Alfa, brandishing a rather nasty-looking weapon that resembled a machine pistol. And suddenly, the day devoted to a papal visit and the furtherance of Maria Saluzzo's business interests turned into a nightmare.

Chapter 13

Pandora's Box

Katrina Valenchnikoff thought about the events of the past several days as she left her boss's office and drove out of Boston through the heavy, late-afternoon traffic. She felt the slight tug of a smile at one corner of her mouth. Things were going well: not only had she been successful in planting the bug in Saluzzo's office, but Little Bear, Mikhail's code-named mole within the Ukrainian embassy in Rome, had succeeded on short notice in setting the main wheels of the operation into motion, carelessly, or so it would seem, leaving the keys of a staffer's car in the ignition so that it could be "stolen" by a trusted contract man he had hired. The man had carried out the robbery of Maria Saluzzo perfectly and gotten away clean. Maria's cell phone, once in the hands of Little Bear, an accomplished hacker, had proven to be a treasure trove of information, account numbers, and passwords. Even now, money was slowly being drained—starting with small amounts, in order to test the proverbial waters—from several of the Saluzzo family's accounts. Quite naturally, some was being deposited into one of Jimmy Callahan's accounts in order to lay the groundwork for Vince Saluzzo to place the blame on his old enemy—and start the war Mikhail had planned so carefully.

And, conversely, Little Bear had easily penetrated the website for Callahan's business and gotten into Jimmy's email...probably laughing all the while. The last coded dispatch from Little Bear indicated that the German contract killer was on the move in the greater Boston area and in contact with Callahan...although his exact whereabouts were still unknown.

"Excellent! Let it roll!" Mikhail had said upon hearing the news.

Executing the plan—that was the part Katrina enjoyed. And she did her job with the zeal of a seasoned executioner. Mikhail had his fingers in many pies, and none of them were the famous dessert offerings of the various restaurants he had acquired. Katrina was the expert in getting the pies of other people's businesses within Mikhail's grasp. His syndicate, which had grown silently but steadily during the past several years, was beginning to flex its muscle in the underworld and it was making money—lots of it. His commercial holdings, such as Driftwood by the Sea were much like icebergs; what little was above the surface of the water was what the public saw and expected to see. Most of the syndicate's business took place under the surface, where business that was sometimes legitimate, but largely illegitimate, went on, on a day-to-day basis.

The money, thought Katrina, was good; it had brought many things, among them the pearl-white Audi she was driving...a secure and very comfortable condo...the handy little 9 millimeter Beretta Nano handgun she always traveled with...and a membership at a rather exclusive fitness club, where she had struck up a personal relationship with one of the trainers several months ago. It had started innocently enough, with an exchange of furtive glances during an arduous, sweaty exercise session, and later, it led to drinks and dinner on two successive weekends. And finally, one early evening after a workout, led to a discreet but rather wild tryst in an otherwise unused locker room, with a shared and rather relaxing hot shower en-joyed by the pair afterward.

Katrina guarded the secrets of her job closely, and the secret of her personal relationship with the trainer even more so. On the surface, she was a professional woman in upper manage-ment of a chain of well-known resorts and restaurants, which of course had its own proprietary information to be kept from the public. Katrina's new conquest asked her a question about her work one night that seemed to strike a nerve. She remained silent, totally impassive...and then the trainer, breaking the awkward silence, chuckled and said something: "Oh, yeah, I get it...if you told me...you'd have to kill me!" And then laughed and changed the subject.

It was closer to the truth than Katrina's new friend could ever have guessed. If there was one thing Katrina admired most, it was loyalty; the other thing was discretion. This new person in her life quite thankfully possessed both of those qualities, and with a sly wink had set a date for this evening saying, "We can make it another one of our training ses-sions...no business, and nobody's business but *our* business!"

As the miles slipped by and the traffic seemed to thin out, Katrina's thoughts turned toward the Irishman, Callahan's underground operation...and the Italian businessman and his three boys who were all at odds, and would soon be at each other's throats in a bloody war. How silly. How stupid they all were. And how they all deserved to die at each other's hands. All those old men...and their old ideas, ideas that even Saluzzo's foolish boys believed in. That was the old guard for you, as outdated as Elliot Ness and his gangbusters. Katrina had booked an adventure, a date tonight to take her mind off her work—nothing to do with spilled blood, but all about someone who had new ideas...ideas about her. It was time to play.

It was almost dark when Katrina pulled into the driveway of a small but fashionable brick house on a quiet side street in Cohasset, strode down the curved walkway through a pergola and an Oriental-style garden, and arrived at the home's side entrance, the one she had come to use most frequently in her many nocturnal visits. Warm yellow light glowed from the windows and from an ornate lantern in the entranceway. The heavy, red-enameled door hung from massive iron hinges and in cast-brass, dead center on the door were three Chinese characters representing the name of the owner, sole occupant of the house.

Katrina rang the doorbell; footsteps sounded from within the house and presently a slight but athletic-appearing woman of perhaps 40 answered, clad in the workday outfit Katrina was familiar with: a white, sleeveless polo shirt, black gym shorts, and sneakers. The woman held a glass of red wine in one hand.

"Come in, Kat," she said, smiling broadly, setting her wine down on a side table and brushing back her long black hair with both hands.

"Zhang Min," said Katrina, "I am *so* glad to see you again." She paused, turned, pulled the heavy door closed, then turned around to face Zhang Min Liu.

"Are you with me tonight...all night?" she asked.

"Yes, indeed I am," replied Katrina, who surprisingly caught herself quivering slightly. The two women paused momentarily, then hugged, kissed, and held each other closely for several moments.

"Would you care for some wine?" asked Zhang, finally disengaging herself from the tall blonde woman, regarding her thoughtfully now with inquisitive, large brown eyes.

"Please," answered Katrina. "You have such a beautiful little home here," she added, looking about. "I still can't get used to it." Zhang turned, sauntered down a hallway, and returned a few moments later with a glass of wine for her guest. "It's just awesome," stated Katrina, still looking about the room.

"Thank you...and you," said Zhang "are...oh! *You* are so awesome!" She tugged Katrina over to a couch, where they sat down, drank, conversed, and cuddled. Magazines and wine glasses were pushed aside on the table by the sofa as the encounter became more and more amorous, and vigorous; an empty teacup that had been left on the tabletop overturned.

Zhang, smaller than Katrina but as lithe and limber as a panther pawing playfully over one of its cubs, eventually clambered atop Katrina. "You...do not know...my big blonde girl...how long I've waited today to get my hands on you!" she said.

"And you, girl of my dreams...my dream...you do not know how long I've wanted to get my hands all over you!" replied Katrina, now gaining the initiative, suddenly rolling Zhang over and running her hands up and down her new partner's tanned legs before she unbuttoned Zhang's polo.

"I've been thinking," said Zhang, running her fingers through Katrina's blonde hair, kissing her neck, then moving on to nibble gently on Katrina's left earlobe, "about some things I'd like to do to you."

"You know," chuckled Katrina, nuzzling Zhang's cheek with her lips, "that's a great coincidence; I've been thinking about a lot of things I'd like to do to you." The two women giggled like schoolgirls planning a prank.

"Well?" asked Zhang, looking at Katrina with her huge smile of pearly-white teeth framed by dark-red lipstick. "You know what? I think I'd better put you to bed right now without your supper. You know what my name means in English, right? It means quick!"

"Is it a Pandora's Box night tonight?" Katrina asked Zhang.

"Yes!" exclaimed Zhang with great enthusiasm. "And it's my pick."

"No," said Katrina, pouting. "It was your pick last time."

"Was not," said Zhang defiantly, pulling back from Katrina. She stretched her arms, pulled off her polo, and tossed it aside. "I'll flip you for it. C'mon...let's see how tough you are!"

"You've got it. You know how I play...it's as hard as I work, and it's rough," her partner said grumpily, kicking off her shoes and pulling off her jacket.

"Go ahead," countered Zhang, "I like it just as rough as you do." Both women stood up, walked to the center of the room, and stood opposite each other on Zhang's ornate Oriental rug; a bright gas-log fire burned cheerfully close by in a fireplace flanked by two large vases, reproductions of Ming Dynasty treasures. An ornately carved, gilded dragon in miniature sat atop the mantel, its oversize eyes appearing to gawk at the spectacle about to take place. The women suddenly grappled with each other; a brief struggle ensued, and then they both dropped to the floor, a Yin and Yang of two forces, perfectly balanced in their impromptu conflict with each other.

Katrina tried to scissor her legs around Zhang's, but her skirt interfered; the two women tumbled and rolled briefly, grunting and groaning. Then Zhang got the better of Katrina in one lightning move, wrapping her powerful legs around Katrina's waist and squeezed—hard. Katrina thrashed and twisted in a vain bid to get free; her feet tangled with an electrical cord, suddenly knocking over a lamp that crashed to the floor. Zhang then triumphantly went about the process of pinning Katrina's arms and shoulders to the rug. Savoring the moment like a small but nimble spider does when it has captured a particularly large and tasty-looking bug and has begun to wrap it up, Zhang slowly brought her left leg up, gently resting her shin over Katrina's right shoulder, tipped forward to place her weight on her left knee, then brought her right leg up and completed her victory by planting her right shin over Katrina's left shoulder. She then brought her full weight to bear. The tall, blonde woman flailed and kicked her long legs to no avail.

"Give?" asked Zhang.

"Okay, I give," wheezed Katrina, panting for breath. "It's your pick tonight. I'm yours."

"Good girl," commented Zhang, picking herself up. She extended her hands to Katrina and helped her to her feet. Katrina retrieved her jacket, and the two women joined hands, smiling at each other as if nothing odd had happened, and headed upstairs.

Pandora's Box was a large, black, lacquered jewelry box inlaid with the initials *PB* in ivory; Zhang had bought it long ago at a tag sale. The initials had inspired the nickname Pandora's Box; so too had the discovery that once the chosen woman reached into the box and produced (at random, with her eyes closed) a bedroom novelty item and made erotic use of it with her partner, more and more items eventually came out of the box and came into playful use within the same evening. It proved difficult, if not impossible, to put all of those evils back in, once the box had been opened and the night was still young.

"It's all about the three E's, Kat. This box is," Zhang once said, "all about excitement, erotica, and enjoyment."

As the women undressed and Katrina placed her jacket on the dresser, her Beretta pistol tumbled out of one of its pockets and clunked to the carpeted floor. Katrina flushed with embarrassment.

"Your gun? You brought it again? Kat, you are a bad girl!" exclaimed Zhang. "Tsk, tsk!" Zhang shook a finger at Katrina and picked up the gun, placing it on a nightstand, before she removed her sneakers, one by one, and tossed them into a corner before removing her shorts.

"It's time for me to pick!" exclaimed Zhang. She stepped over to the box, covered her eyes with one hand, and with the other reached inside. "Now, I will use the *very first* item Pandora has to offer," she said. She withdrew her hand and opened her eyes to see what it was; a short length of clothesline, tied up neatly with a festive red ribbon, speckled with silver stars. "Ooh," she cooed, looking at Katrina with a huge smile on her face, "it's *the rope*. And you know what that means; you know the rules. Come over here...turn around...and put your hands behind your back." Katrina, shaking with anticipation, did as she was told. It was doubtless going to be a very long, very kinky, and extremely enjoyable workout session with her trainer tonight, she thought, as Zhang bound her wrists together tightly.

"Now, kneel," commanded Zhang. "I have a surprise for you. Close your eyes." Katrina did.

"Oh, yes; surprise me, please!" she implored. Then she heard a small *click*, and then another, imagining Zhang had chosen another item from Pandora's Box. Why had she not announced it?

"Yes, I *do* have a surprise for you," Zhang continued, drawing close to the woman kneeling before her, still trembling all over.

"Now, open your eyes. Surprise!" said Zhang. Katrina's eyes opened and suddenly grew wide as she tried to say something. Zhang wasted no time; she swiftly forced the barrel of the small black Beretta into Katrina's open mouth—and quickly pulled the trigger.

Chapter 14

Facing the Dragon

The back of the dark-green dragon rose and fell, slowly...again and again, as the lungs below its taut, bony spine rhythmically expanded and contracted, first drawing in air as it took a breath, and then as it exhaled, making a faint whistling noise as it did so. The dragon thus slept soundly and with good reason; roaming the bounds of its territory the previous evening, it had at first rampaged at large within its lair, then romped about establishing its dominance, toying with and finally devouring the victim who had come calling and had willingly entered its deepest den. The few who had seen this formidable beast in its present vulnerable, naked state were never so unwise as to tell of the tale afterward and thus suffer the sharp claws and scorching fire of the dragon's raging fury.

The dragon, the dark-green tattoo on Zhang Min's back, rippled as she awoke and stretched. The first light of dawn was beginning to show at the bedroom window. She slowly rolled over in her bed and gazed at the pale white body lying next to her. Katrina lay motionless, her face a study in angelic beauty. *How peaceful...and how beautiful*, thought Zhang. Suddenly, Katrina opened her eyes, fixing Zhang Min with a cold, steely glare that briefly paralyzed her with its icy intensity, as if she were a corpse come to life.

"Zhang Min Liu, don't you ever, ever, *ever*..." she said crossly, "dry-fire my gun again."

Some 30 miles away, in a cathedral in Cambridge, the man calling himself Herman Hoffman Schmidt groggily awoke. Through the darkness, a scant 10 feet away, appeared a large green dragon. The dragon seemed to move...slowly...and it went in and out of focus, as if trying to change its shape. Herman rubbed his eyes in disbelief. Almost as soon as he had awakened, Herman regretted that he had; a headache of monstrous proportions throbbed with the intensity of a blast furnace's trip-hammers at the back of his skull. The early morning dawn's first light, as the sun now came over the horizon, dimly illuminated a nearby stained-glass window, which he saw completely once he raised his head from the stiff and uncomfortable place he discovered himself lying on, flat on his back, arms crossed across his chest. From his many visits to churches, he quickly recognized the figure and the beast depicted in the window: the human figure was a knight in shining armor, riding a rearing white horse. The knight brandished a spear, preparing to strike it with brute force into a hunkering, dark-green dragon displaying bloodstained teeth and sharp-looking claws that lurked dangerously near the horse's hooves. It was St. George, busily engaged in the process of slaying a dragon. The spear seemed to move; it wobbled about in St. George's gauntleted hand.

Herman laid his head back down and looked straight up; there was nothing above him to be seen. If there was a ceiling overhead, it was either blackened out...or else it was light years away. Perhaps there was no ceiling...*perhaps*, Herman thought, *I am floating in space—deep space.* Whatever Herman was lying on slowly began to rock to and fro...and then Herman felt himself being transported, upward. Yes, he was going up, up as gently as a coffin is lowered down, smoothly and silently, into a grave that is yawning wide open. Stars appeared on either side of him in the blackened atmosphere. Then the stars began to streak by, as quickly as shiny points of apartment lights seen from a speeding train in the depths of night, a train...hell bound? Or bound to heaven? It was like being on board a train leaving a station on a journey toward an unknown destination. Herman was moving. Moving as quickly, now, as the Starship *Enterprise*. Moving through space and time at warp speed. A cool, narrow beam of light soon appeared overhead, seeming to focus on his forehead...then, his eyes. It grew brighter and brighter; there was no other possible explanation for it, Herman reasoned: he had died and was going to heaven.

"Dear Lord...what have I done?" implored Herman. The source of the light came closer; it revealed itself in the black-cloaked person of Father Clancy O'Donnell, who was holding a penlight flashlight over Herman's head. He was shining it into Herman's eyes in order to ascertain whether or not his newly-hired organ repairman had expired during the evening while sleeping on the seat cushions of a back-row pew. Certainly, if he had, the lifeless body would need to be removed before the next service, and the seat cushion disinfected.

"Son," said the priest, "I hope you won't mind me so much for me tellin' ya, but I think, judging from the smell of things...you had a wee bit too much to drink last night." The priest patted him on the shoulder. "You'd best get on with it now. We have a host of folks coming for the big recital, night after tonight."

The priest scuttled off to go about his rounds, and Herman sat up...although not without great difficulty. His headache thundered now like the pounding surf of the tide rising off the Massachusetts coastline, and when he coughed to clear his throat, he sounded like a mist-enshrouded foghorn. What was he doing here? Oh, yes...repairing the organ. The pipe organ that would be used for a recital in two days. Herman rose to his feet, trying to clear away the cobwebs; he stood, took an unsteady step...and tripped over his shoes that were lying on the floor. It was the bourbon...that was what it was. The après-fight bar-hopping and the bourbon...and the beers last night that had chased down the bourbon. And tonight was the night of the hit. Callahan's.

Booze. That was the dragon in this man's life. The one he had ridden a white horse on, to spear and destroy the beast in his life. He'd been clean for six years and now, just to see this job and his cover through, he'd gotten off the wagon, left the white horse behind. Herman fished in his pockets for his glasses and came up empty-handed...searched beneath the pew. Nothing but a few cashew shells, an old hymnal, a couple of gum wrappers, and a penny. Where were they, those glasses? He ascended the stairs to the organ loft...groped along the key-board; nothing there but rows upon rows of white and black keys. He sat down heavily...and in so doing, located his lost glasses, which had been lying on the bench all the while. He stood up, swaying from side to side and retrieved the mangled spectacles, twisted them back into some modicum of shape, and put them on. The world came slowly, almost hesitantly into focus...but still writhed and spun rather like the innards of a churning washing machine.

And then, the question occurred to him: what had he done with his rifle last night? It had to be concealed. He knew that he must have hidden it—but where? Herman pawed open the canvas wraps that contained his replacement pipes and gear that had been shipped from Frankfurt in a crate. The three-section rifle and its scope were nowhere to be found. Neither were the bullets. Herman gazed up at the massive pipe organ before him. The real Herman was of necessity an expert at es-pionage, and at hiding things. He would never have written himself a note as a reminder—too risky; someone could read it and then the jig would be up. The rifle had to be hidden in one of those pipes—that's what a sober Herman would have done before last night, but Herman obviously had not been sober last night. He had no recollection of what had happened after Jimmy Callahan had picked him up, other than Callahan's admonition not to be late at the arranged meeting point.

The grand Cathedral of St. George in Cambridge boasts the second-largest pipe organ ever built, a massive thing made by the Midmer-Losh Organ Company. Its intricate, lavish woodwork rivals that of replications of the grand staircase in the *RMS Titanic*. But it plays second fiddle, so to speak, to its larger, superior brother, one constructed in the Depression years for the Hall Auditorium in Atlantic City, one that contains 7 manuals, 449 ranks, 337 registers, and 33,114 pipes. Herman looked up at the various pipes, the stops, and keyboards. He longed for coffee. And he briefly longed to return to Frankfurt. Herman looked down...and found that he had overlooked something. He had left himself a trail of breadcrumbs after all.

There was a note on a piece of paper lying beneath the bench. On it was a drawing...it was an outline of a human hand...it exactly matched the size of one of his own hands, with the number eight inscribed within the letter *V* upon it.

"Shit!" exclaimed Herman, recognizing his own work at last and drawing a significant conclusion. "Handel! Voluntary Number Eight!" He planted himself on the bench, switched on the organ's blower, and coaxed the massive instrument into life. He then played the first few notes of Handel's work, knowing it, as he did, by heart; as soon as he did, a small pipe in the front of the organ snorted and made a sound not unlike an elephant does when in extreme distress. "That's it!" Herman exclaimed, getting up from his bench and removing the pipe from its place; within it was his rifle. Suddenly all was well in the world, but the headache persisted. He spotted the small, silver liquor flask lying beside the gun. *Where*, he wondered, *had that come from?*

He replaced the hefty pipe and then sat down heavily again on the organist's bench. Perhaps, he thought, by playing some music he could begin to bring himself around enough to go out and find breakfast somewhere. A music book was open, its pages spread out on the stand above the keyboard. Herman tried to read the notes, but they swam like goldfish in a bowl before his eyes and the fogged lenses of his mangled glasses. He decided to play a few bars of Madonna's *Material Girl* from memory, just for fun. The first few notes had barely escaped the towering pipes when he noticed, in the small mirror over the organ's keyboard, furtive movements going on behind him within the murky depths of the cathedral.

Dark, spectral forms were flitting about the pews, as if they were bats sweeping through the sky at dawn. Filtering through the pews, row by row. And now...they were getting closer to him. Herman stopped playing in order to listen for footsteps, wondering if he was dreaming...but the thundering headache hammering away on the anvil of his brain interfered. The specters moved closer...and suddenly, in the mirror, he saw two small black objects hurtling toward him; he turned to inter- cept them, to fend the demoniacal beings off, but he was too late. They pounded against his chest with a one-two punch, and then fell to the floor. They were his shoes, the shoes he had left by the pew he had recently vacated and tripped over. Standing before him at the railing were four nuns.

The tallest one—her facial features somewhat resembling those of the many gargoyles that lined the church's para- pets—glared at him and shook her head in disapproval. As if on cue, the quartet of sisters turned on their heels and were gone, disappearing into the vast chamber of the cathedral. Herman breathed a sigh of relief...and looked for the organ pipe he had recently disturbed. Perhaps, in this moment of need, he reasoned...he needed a sharpener.

Chapter 15

An Eye for an Eye

Jerry was not sleeping well; the bed was soft...way too soft, especially in comparison to the cell block bunk he had grown accustomed to during the long-term sentence he had served. The previous afternoon and early evening had not gone well. His lengthy, diligent search for alcohol in this part of Dorchester had finally resulted in the discovery of a small package store in a neighborhood seven blocks away, which he cased thoroughly before entering, thinking that someday he might return to burglarize it; it was a perfect mark. He wandered the aisles and pawed through the newspaper and magazine rack, at last selecting a copy of the *Baystate Police and Detective Gazette* and then a package of pickled Polish sausages, a bag of chips, and a six-pack of beer. He returned to his gloomy-looking room and consumed the beer, the sausages, and chips in stages of gulps and belches well into the late hours as he idly turned pages of the newspaper, looking to see if he recognized anyone in the photos, and then watched television before finally retiring. He now awoke after several hours' slumber, and tossed and turned in the bed in the darkness; the mattress springs groaned their displeasure at both bearing his weight and his sudden, shark-like thrashing movements. A thumping sound, repetitious and rising in volume, had awakened him.

The window of his room, room 156, overlooked a defunct movie theater across the street and otherwise afforded a view that encompassed a neighborhood of small shops and two- and three-story homes. Because it was early May, it was still warm outside and the neighborhood had seemed quiet enough when Jerry had drained the last of the six beer cans of its contents, pointing its bottom toward the ceiling in the process. He had decided to leave the window open slightly in order to have the benefit of any breeze. The room was starkly furnished, possibly by someone in charge of the hotel who received kickbacks from a local secondhand store. The ceiling over the bed had water stains that curiously resembled Rorschach test patterns, as if left untouched as a source of entertainment for the more quizzical and intelligent guests who did not enjoy watching television. A multitude of cigarette burns covered the surface of the small writing desk like dark, ugly tattoos. The lampshades on the table lamps and floor lamps were pockmarked and knocked askew, and only two of the three light bulbs in the bathroom were working; they cast a soft, amber glow into Jerry's room like a warning light on an old, decrepit car's dashboard.

The thumping sound from outside the door now caused Jerry to stir. He stirred like a hibernating bear does when his slumber is disturbed and is aroused before spring thaw sets in. Like a muffled drumbeat, the noise continued unabated until Jerry, groggy from sleep and the impact of drinking six beers, at last rolled over and drifted off to sleep again. The thumping resumed; Jerry awoke once more, thrashed, and pulled the covers and pillows over his head. The noise immediately stopped, and Jerry once more fell asleep. The thumping began anew; this time Jerry threw back the covers and rolled out of bed, his bare feet landing on the hardwood floor, just as the noise that seemed to be teasing him...ceased again. *Who-what the hell is that?* he wondered. He padded, barefoot in his boxers and T-shirt, over to the door of his room, unlocked it, and cautiously pulled the door open as far as the security chain would allow to have a look into the hallway: there was no one there. A dim nightlight at the end of the hallway, located under its cathedral-style ceiling provided meager illumination of the spot where the stairs led down to the lobby and front desk.

"Where the hell is that sound coming from?" he muttered to himself. Jerry stepped into his pants, hauled them up, buckled his belt, and sallied forth from his room, prepared to crack a few skulls, if need be; he needed his sleep, not noise at this late hour—no matter who was causing it. Stepping softly, he crept, hunched over, swinging along, ape-like almost, down the hallway. The doors of the rooms—all of them—were open, he noticed, and all of them were dark and vacant, as silent as churches on a Tuesday night. The beds appeared in the gloom as though they were catafalques with white coverlets draped over boxy coffins, the dressers like tall, dark mahogany altars. None of this made sense; Jerry had heard snoring from the room next to his when he had turned off the lights in his room, as well as a brief but spirited domestic argument in progress across the way. But now, all of these rooms were apparently devoid of any human life. He reached the end of the hallway and paused before sneaking quietly down the flight of stairs. There was a light glowing down there in the lobby—a warm, bright light. And the noise—*ca-thunk...ca-thunk...ca-thunk*—resumed, and it was louder now. It was definitely coming from the lobby.

He set one bare foot on the first step, as cautiously as a swimmer does when he tests the cold waters of the Atlantic Ocean at Revere Beach in early June, then brought the other down, tiptoeing very slowly and gracefully—as large men find they sometimes can do as well as a dancer when they are under duress—along the stairway. The lobby was deserted, save for the two black overstuffed sofas that lurked in the shadows under the leaves of the potted plant like bulbous, recumbent hippos snoozing in a jungle. A tiny red light glimmered on the front of the stereo, inside which, Jerry observed as he stepped over to look inside the open cabinet, an LP record spun, the tone arm rhythmically hammering against the last groove of it. And the sound—*ca-thunk...ca-thunk...ca-thunk*—resumed once more, amplified by the speakers. Jerry picked up the tone arm and set it aside.

The warm, bright light he'd noticed was coming from the hotel lobby's two plate-glass windows; fogged with grime and smoke, they certainly were...but they were also—inexplicably—fogged with condensation. Jerry spun around, his well-honed prison habits working full time, to make sure no one was sneaking up on him. He turned back, stepped over to the closest window, and rubbed away a small patch of the accumulation of soggy smudge with his thumb. *There's frost on the outside of the window, too—what's up with that?* he thought. Jerry rubbed some more. What he saw confounded him, made him rub his eyes in disbelief. It was winter outside. Yes, it was definitely winter; it was snowing outside.

And snow also stood, in clumps and piles and patches on the street and sidewalks, where it was besmirched with brown mud and salt, and puddles of whatever ice and snow had melted reflected the lights blazing on the marquee of the Majestic Theater. It was apparent that the evening's shows had concluded, although the flickering chase lights on the marquee still hyped the twin features in bold letters: *Rocky* and *Freaky Friday*, as kids, boys in bell-bottom jeans and jackets (some distinguished by either their shoulder-length hair or their Afro hairstyles) and girls in maxi coats, jackets, and high boots, were streaming out of the twin doors and onto the sidewalk, laughing and shouting. Alongside the sidewalk was an

idling black-and-white Town Taxi that Jerry recognized as a
'69 or '70 Plymouth Belvedere, the kind of cabs that used to
idle awaiting fares at the taxi stand outside the Baskin-Robbins
store on Kenmore Square, and behind it, a yellow Checker cab.
A Checker? When the hell did they stop making those?

Jerry rubbed his eyes again...rubbed the window, too, as if
it were a lamp containing some sort of genie that might make
this scene disappear. A snowball fight suddenly erupted outside the theater: two boys pelted another who'd ducked behind a Gremlin and an Olds Vista Cruiser. A Domino's Pizza
delivery vehicle—a Pinto wagon with an illuminated red, white,
and blue sign atop its roof—sped by, splattering slush onto
the sidewalk. And despite his watchfulness, absorbed as he
was in looking out the window, Jerry did not detect the approach of the person sneaking up behind him. Suddenly he
heard footsteps padding softly, footsteps of someone close at
hand, someone standing now right behind him.

"Would you like to come upstairs?" the voice of that person
called out softly, in almost a purr.

All 223 pounds of Jerry spun around to face the figure
that had quietly emerged from the depths of the office. The
woman's face, pale and finely sculpted, caught the light from
the theater marquee. It glinted in the whites of her green
eyes, eyes that glowed like fireflies in a darkened field of what
could have been his wildest dreams. The woman who was
wrapped in a black velvet robe. The woman who stepped—no,
floated—slowly toward him.

"I have something for you," she said, picking up a roughly
12-square-inch packet from the registration desk. In one
smooth motion, she pulled an LP record from it, never taking
her eyes off Jerry. *They're green, yes,* thought Jerry. She placed
it on the turntable of the stereo, after moving and then setting
the tone arm down on the now-spinning record. *God,* thought
Jerry, *this could be heaven.*

After a brief hissing and crackling sound, the record began to play; it was a song Jerry remembered from years ago. Something about a hotel. In California. The woman in black stepped back, staring at him with unabashed curiosity. "Welcome," she said as she, the beautiful green-eyed woman in the black robe, began to dance. The Eagles' voices floated across the gulf of time, from 40-plus years ago on the old stereo...and then the woman, the beautiful green-eyed woman in the black robe, began a strip-tease show. It was a slow one...and it was tantalizing. As tantalizing as a cold beer and a cash bar suddenly appearing on a desert island, when you know you are shipwrecked, but have all the time and all the money in the world to spend. And, as with any dream, all things now seemed possible to Jerry—in this wretched hotel in Dorchester. Suddenly, somehow, he knew he had all the time in the world to spend there.

She moved slowly, in time to the music, and finally unwrapped her robe; untied and undone with one smooth, fluid movement, it slithered off her shoulders and down her cold-white thighs to the floor. She stepped out of it. The woman was mouthing the words to the song now. And now they were both floating, Jerry and the woman with the green eyes; they were drifting closer and closer together in a jet stream that set Jerry's heart to pounding. And he could not move, could not say a word.

The Majestic's lights blinked out. Illuminated now by only the streetlamp outside the hotel, the woman's face, her bare arms and legs, moving languidly in time to the music, all set against the darkness of the room—all of this captivated Jerry. And then, the woman let her hair down in a ribbon-like waterfall of beauty. She spun around, almost luminescent in the darkness of the room, letting the last of her garments fall; she plucked them off and tossed them to him like confetti pitched toward awestruck parade watchers.

"An eye for an eye," said the woman softly. And as Jerry watched, horrified, she plucked out her left eye. She bent down, lowered it and rolled it toward Jerry—rolled it the way a person rolls a bowling ball down an alley. And then Jerry's newfound heaven quickly turned to hell.

The eye took its time getting to him; it slowed and it stopped twice along the way to look up at him, peering at him carefully—thoughtfully almost—before proceeding farther. And, Jerry noticed, it was getting bigger; yes, surely, it was getting bigger as it came. Jerry tried to speak, tried to run. But the eye was now upon him, circling his feet the way a rancher's dog circles a runaway calf, holding him in some strange, almost magnetic way, the way that people's feet seem rooted in concrete when strange and awful things befall them in a dream. A dream of the most horrible kind. The woman, facing him now with one green eye and one empty, black eye socket, was naked—bare as a newborn child, in the bluish light cast by the streetlamp outside. And Jerry saw, saw because he could not take his eyes away from her, that she was coming closer. But something was changing. She was morphing into something...something hideously strange. And very, very old.

Jerry tried to move, tried to scream, but could do neither. The eye, now the size of a bowling ball, planted itself fully on his feet, rooting him to the spot where he stood. It then looked up at him, as if in innocence of any evil or wrongdoing that might be going on. And the pupil of this eye, the huge, green eye, suddenly pinpointed as a raptor's eyes do when the bird of prey's emotions shift. And now Jerry saw the woman, the once-beautiful woman, begin to dissolve; her flesh began to melt before his eyes. Her cheeks became hollow; her breasts sagged like empty grocery sacks, her brow wrinkled, her hair turned to gray, then to white...and began to fall out, slowly, and her ribs became distended. Hers was a body turning from living flesh into the rotted hulk of a corpse, one long since dead...but it was a walking, fully awakened corpse.

Through the peephole he'd cleared on the window, Jerry glimpsed, in a brief moment of panic, great dark clouds scudding down the street, driven by a sudden gust of wind that was scattering litter; the wind rattled the window of the hotel. The cars, the kids, the snow; all of those things swiftly vanished in the clouds. But the woman—or what was once a woman, now turning into some horrible, demented being in this room tonight, perhaps a corpse that had lain at the bottom of the Charles River the whole time Jerry had served his time—was now getting close, very, very close to Jerry. It was floating so near to him that he could now smell the decay of the hideous figure as its desiccated lips pulled back to reveal blackened stumps of teeth and a tongue writhing like a small cobra menacing its prey. Her one green eye now floated like a lonely moon in the dark sky of a hollow in her skull, and from the depths of that foul-looking mouth of hers, in time to the music, came the last words Jerry heard.

"Jerry, you can check out any time you like. But now, Jerry, you can never leave."

She—it—reached out with the long, skeletal fingers of her left hand. The last thing Jerry remembered seeing was her fingernails—long, yellowed, and gruesomely stained—as she grasped his right arm and he howled in pain. And then there was total darkness—one in which Jerry woke up suddenly. It was 1:56 a.m.

Soaked in cold sweat and badly rattled, he fumbled for the table lamp and turned it on, checking to make doubly sure he had not soiled the bed, as he had as a small child, when bad dreams occurred. Checked—more importantly—to make sure he was alone in bed, alone in his room. He looked up at the ceiling; there was the stain on the ceiling that he remembered. His door was still locked and the chain secure. Thus, somewhat assured of his safety, he arose and walked unsteadily over to the window, stumbling over an empty beer can. Yes, he ascertained; it was May in Dorchester. He, Jerry, had left that beer can on the floor. He wasn't crazy after all. The curtains ruffled slightly with a sudden warm breeze. Jerry looked out the window.

The movie theater across the street was still vacant and boarded up, and wires and broken light bulbs dangled from its long-neglected marquee, swaying gently in the breeze. The abandoned shopping cart he had seen yesterday was still sitting underneath it. Jerry watched as a burly-looking 2019 Dodge Charger police car cruised slowly down the street, its headlights probing the dark corners and alleyways for anything of a sinister nature lurking in them, as if it were an inquisitive, muscular tomcat making its evening neighborhood rounds, protecting its territory. Jerry went back to bed...where he slept in nervous fits and starts until dawn, when he decided to leave. Early.

"Surely, sir," said the swarthy young desk clerk attending to Jerry's checkout, "I do not remember you." He twirled a toothpick and poked unashamedly at the food particles lodged between two of his front teeth and regarded Jerry with a puzzled look that bordered on suspicion. The smell of exotic, overly spiced food and strong coffee wafted from the innards of the office.

"I checked in with that old lady," Jerry said, bringing his face closer to the clerk's and furrowing his brow, sensing impending conflict. The clerk, confounded and dismayed, shook his head.

"Sir, to be most certain, I can tell you: we have no woman working here. It is only me and Saleem, my brother and his young son, who are learning this trade. We are always here." Just then, Saleem emerged from the office, a steaming mug of coffee in hand, glowering at Jerry.

"Please sir, tell us, what is this all about, now? Is there a problem of some kind?" he inquired, looking warily at Jerry.

"Nothing," said Jerry, "I'm out of here. Have a nice day." Sure...he would return tonight and wait outside for Callahan, that was a given...but he would never set foot in the Liberty Bell again; that he knew. And when Jerry left the great, gray, ancient warship of the hotel, walking out the doorway in a huff, thinking now only of breakfast and the job awaiting him, he was blissfully unaware of the small—but not insignificant—purple bruise that was slowly forming on his right forearm.

Chapter 16

Cops and Robbers

Outside one of the large police stations in Rome—this one an imposing, multistoried building made of dark-gray granite—two armed policemen stood, as stiffly as if they, too, were made of stone, on guard duty on either side of the main door. The sky was as dark as a sheet of slate; driving rain and violent thunderstorms were predicted. The gaggle of bright-blue police cars, among them a hefty-looking Lamborghini with the word Polizia boldly emblazoned on its doors, lined the curb and lent some color to the otherwise somber downtown scene and to the station's towering, drab-looking edifice that loomed above the parked police cars and the busy street teeming with traffic, its vehicles scuttling about like busy beetles just beyond the bounds of the station.

Both the Italian Carabinieri, dutiful and beloved soldier-policemen that they are, as well as the regular police, are often the subject of playful jokes among the Italian population. While the police themselves at this station often joked about the restricted use of the Lamborghini high-speed pursuit car and who among them got to drive it, the public joked about the wide variety of makes and models of vehicles the Polizia used. Among them stood out the ungainly subcompact, a Fiat-made

4x4 called the Panda, whose name and tiny size no doubt inspired the joke "Why did the Polizia get rid of the Panda 4x4? Because the chief tried but couldn't get 16 policemen inside it!"

Inside the station, the walls, floors, and even the chairs in the offices and interrogation rooms were as olive green and lusterless as an army tank prepared for battle. The building usually hummed with activity, but up on the third floor it was, for the most part, relatively quiet this day. Here, in his office and with its door propped open, Capitano Alberto Pellegrini sat calmly at his desk, then leaned back in his chair, stared up at the ceiling, and thought of his upcoming vacation, set to begin the next week: an entire week on the beach in a wonderful little villa he had rented. The captain leaned back even farther, relaxed, closed his eyes, and let his mind wander; soon, he was there, he imagined—seated comfortably on the warm, sunny beach in a lounger, sipping cold beer from a green bottle of Peroni and looking out at the turquoise-colored Mediterranean Sea.

Soon, not too far off shore, a woman's head bobbed to the surface. Where had she been before now? Incredibly, she waved to him; it was as though she recognized him. He watched, entranced, as she took several steps closer into shallower water and her shoulders emerged, dripping wet from the water. She stopped, briefly shook her head back and forth to clear her eyes, as the droplets of water flung from her long, dark hair glistened like diamonds in the sunlight. She raised her right hand again, this time beckoning to him to join her. This reverie was suddenly shattered by the loud, strident ringing of the telephone in Alberto's adjoining office, that of his sergeant, and a tremendous *thud* as the two enormous feet of his second-in-command, Sergente Lorenzo Toscanini, were swiftly removed from his desktop and crashed to the floor as the sergeant jolted and reached for his telephone.

Despite the fact that Lorenzo Toscanini was not related to the famous conductor, other policemen in his barracks referred to him as "Maestro" because of his name and his obsession with detail; the voluminous, pedantic reports he composed, often late at night after hours, usually ran the length of several pages, even regarding minor incidents. Nonetheless, Pellegrini appreciated having someone who was detail-minded in his department, the Unita di Assistenza per i Visitatori (the Visitors' Assistance Unit). It was also because, like the captain, Lorenzo had spent time studying in the United States in his teenage years and was fluent in English. The two men often conversed in English, just to stay sharp because their expertise in the language was often called upon to assist foreign visitors who ran afoul of pickpockets, petty thieves, and street vendors hawking stolen merchandise. The ringing of Lorenzo's telephone, the captain surmised, presaged the beginning of another such all-too-common episode. He would soon discover just how wrong he was in that assumption.

Lorenzo was soon leaning his gangling frame against the captain's doorway, dangling the printed copy of a dispatch from one hand (in earlier days when hand-written forms were in use, such a message brought hurriedly in hand might have challenged the Dead Sea Scrolls in terms of its length, but that was thankfully not the case today).

"Espresso?" asked Alberto, pointing to his espresso machine, poised at the ready on a side table.

"No, thank you," replied the sergeant. "Not unless you're having some too," the Maestro added.

"Well," replied the captain, "I am. I was just thinking of it. Caffè Americano, if you'd like."

"Well, yes, but only if you are," Lorenzo proffered. The captain shook his head from side to side, not so much as to mimic the motions of the woman he had been envisioning, but to clear his mind, and proceeded to brew the espresso, regardless of what Lorenzo Toscanini wanted (or said he did not want).

"Report?" asked Alberto.

"An armed robbery," answered the sergeant robustly. "Two tourists from America. Traveling together. Robbed at gunpoint. Armed suspect with a machine pistol, now at large, driving a white Alfa convertible." Pellegrini's eyebrows shot up...then wrinkled close together.

"A *machine pistol*?" queried the captain incredulously. "And a white convertible? Why not a white horse?" His entire face wrinkled momentarily in great consternation.

"Indeed," replied the sergeant, nodding and studying his dispatch, adding, "And, one of the victims is a priest." Alberto, seeming to forget about his espresso, collapsed into his chair and stared at the wall; his fantasy woman in the Mediterranean Sea had vanished. The machine gurgled and glugged now as steaming hot liquid trickled into the cup, like the sounds of the captain's sea-based dream, and perhaps even that of his vacation, going down a sewer.

A priest, a man of the cloth, robbed in broad daylight on the streets of Rome...this was bad, very bad. The public would be outraged upon hearing of this crime, and any misstep on the captain's part might bring the Carabinieri into this and warrant a summary investigation by the chief. Lorenzo looked longingly at the espresso machine by Alberto's desk; he hunched over it and lurked around it expectantly, the way a Komodo dragon might look at a sumptuous pond it has discovered in a jungle after going without water for a week or two. The two men regarded each other gravely for a moment without speaking, and then began to discuss the matters of the case.

"They're downstairs," said Lorenzo, at last pouring himself a cup of dark-looking brew. "The two of them, plus their driver; he's in a separate room. "Shall we interview them?"

The captain gravely nodded his consent, and the two men left the office and headed for the elevator at the end of the hallway; his cup of espresso in one hand, the captain pushed the button and looked up to see which floor the elevator was presently on.

"Oh," exclaimed Lorenzo, regaining the captain's attention, "I'll take the stairs. I try to walk at least 10,000 steps every day, without fail. I'm working toward 15,000 by next week. I'll see you at room 27, the one we always use, in the basement." Captain Pellegrini nodded once more, and his sergeant walked down the hall toward the stairway door, carefully carrying his espresso and avoiding any cracks in the tile floors as he went. The bell on the elevator door rang as it rolled open. Pellegrini shook his head, stepped inside the car, took a swig from his cup, and pushed the button marked "Seminterrato." The sinking feeling in his stomach was only made worse by the all-too-rapid descent of the elevator. The two men soon met up outside twin, steel doors in the basement; one was marked 27. The other, 27-B, was the police officers' observation room.

"I made some notes of possible questions on the way here," said Lorenzo, ripping off a page from his notepad and handing it to his boss.

"Good," said Alberto, glancing at them and then pointing a finger toward 27-B. "Now, sit tight in there, watch closely, and keep track of things." The sergeant nodded, opened the door, stepped into the dark room, whose only illumination came faintly from a window made of one-way glass that provided a view of the interrogation room, and shut the door behind him. The captain knocked softly on the door marked 27, opened it slowly, and stepped into the room.

The priest, a man perhaps 70 years old, balding and gray about the temples, was sitting quietly, perusing a prayer book. He looked up at Alberto with watery-looking gray eyes, and gave him a wan smile. He looked as though he would happily consent to be folded up in his chair and stuffed away into a closet for a millennium without complaint. The woman? Tanned, well dressed, relaxed, in her mid-to-late 60s. But despite her confident-appearing body language, there were taut lines on her face that displayed an inner tension and a need to perhaps explain something...perhaps, the captain thought, relying on his instincts, it might be something she was concealing.

"Father...Mrs. Saluzzo," began the captain, engaging in turn each of two victims with eye-to-eye contact. "I am Capitano Alberto Pellegrini of the Unita di Assistenza per i Visitatori of the Polizia Roma. I deeply apologize for the crime that has been committed against you in this, our fair city...and I am here to learn more about what happened so that we, the Polizia of Rome, may apprehend the person, or persons, responsible, as quickly as may be possible."

"Thank you, Captain," said Maria. "Now, please tell me, when can we go?"

Somewhat taken aback, Alberto proffered that he needed information first.

"Please tell me, both of you," he asked the pair, "what did the assailant look like?"

"It was a man!" blurted out Father DeTomasi, emphatically.

"It was a *woman!*" exclaimed Maria Saluzzo. The two then looked at each other quizzically. Alberto stared down at his notepad, gave himself a moment, and then looked up at the priest. And made some notes.

"There was a weapon displayed, was there not?" asked Alberto.

"Yes!" shouted the priest. "A big gun! Ugly one! A pistol."

"No, it was a *machine pistol*––I've seen them before," declared Maria.

"Where have you seen them before?" asked Alberto quizzically, quite surprised.

"Well...you know," said Maria, looking at him coyly, "old gangster movies and things."

"Well, of course," said the captain, chuckling a bit but holding both Maria and the priest in his gaze. "We've all seen those. Now...tell me...are you two here on business or pleasure?" The answers from the pair came, and clashed, almost simultaneously.

"Business," stated the priest.

"Pleasure," stated Maria. Alberto rubbed his forehead briefly in discomfort; his eyebrows nearly collided as he mentally processed this information.

"Where were you going when this attack occurred?" he asked.

"We had an audience with the pope. We were headed to the Vatican," stated Father DeTomasi. Alberto sat still for a moment, dumbfounded.

"Yes?" he asked, turning to look at Maria.

"Yes," came the answer.

"And please tell me...what was stolen from you?" the captain asked the pair.

"Cell phone, answered the priest."

"My phone," answered Maria.

"So...was any money taken? Jewelry?" Both victims shook their heads. "But," Alberto noted, looking at Maria, "the lining of your purse was slashed. What did he—or she—take from your purse?"

"I don't know," answered Maria, looking down at her lap. This movement did not escape his attention. Maria shook her head once more. "She took the purse...it was gone for a few moments...then the woman threw it back into our car and she was gone."

"He," said the priest emphatically. "He. It was a man; I am sure of it."

A knock came at the door. The captain excused himself and rose to open it, accepting a small, cardboard box handed to him by a police officer standing in the hall. It was the flimsy sort of box cannoli comes in from a bakery. He opened it, examined the contents carefully, and then dumped all of them save for two items out onto the table.

"So, here we are," Alberto said. "We have found the Alfa convertible, stolen from a diplomatic compound. We also found in it, this...a toy gun." The captain produced a plastic toy machine pistol that doubled as a water pistol and placed it on the table. "As well as a blonde woman's wig." He tossed it on the table. "Please...do not try to cover up something," he warned. "Making a false crime report is a most serious offense," snapped Alberto. He charged toward the door for dramatic effect, opened it, entered the hallway, and slammed the door behind him. Maria leaned toward Father DeTomasi and whispered to him.

"We must leave Italy as soon as possible."

"Will you call Vince before we leave?" asked the priest in hushed tones.

"No," she replied. "You know how he can get." She rolled her eyes. "I will wait until we arrive and tell him personally. It will go better that way." Alberto entered room 27-B, where Lorenzo, and now the chief, were waiting for him.

"Agente stranieros," mumbled the chief, looking not at Pellegrini but at the two people sitting in interrogation room 27. "Foreign agents, perhaps, both of them, I suspect. Their stories are fishy...they don't add up. That car was stolen—or so I'm told—from the Ukrainian embassy. Someone had left the keys in it in their courtyard—with the gate unlocked and nobody on guard duty to boot. The guards were gone...all of them. Too convenient. Too cozy. I don't believe it for a moment—and neither should you, Pellegrini. If you don't get to work on this one and solve it soon, you won't be here...you'll be working the night desk. And you'll be driving a Panda 4x4. We still have them, you know, despite what you may have heard." The rotund chief then sauntered out of room 27-B, nose in the air, thereby leaving the captain and his sergeant to solve the crime now hanging on their hands.

"The only thing we can really do for now," said Alberto to his dutiful sergeant, who always followed orders exactly to the letter, without questioning them "is to let them go...the two of them...and to watch what they are up to. Every move. Follow them. Report back only when you have something solid." And of course, Sergeante Lorenzo Toscanini did this. Exactly and precisely as he was told.

Chapter 17

What Could Possibly Go Wrong?

A search was underway. The area being scoured was not a wooded area, but a nicely-furnished two-story home several miles near the country club in Melrose, Massachusetts. However, it was not a search for a missing golf ball—it was a search for a missing person.

"Danny...where's Poppa?" Danny Smith was daydreaming about golf, and Dianne's question figuratively smacked Danny Smith suddenly upside the head, much like the question "Can I see your license and registration, please?" does, when someone, for example, is stopped by the cops on his way home from the beach, then remembers that he has several unpaid parking tickets, that he's left his wallet at home, and that he's been driving over the speed limit. *Speed 55? Darn. Forgot all about that, Officer...sorry—I was just driving home from the beach. I don't know where my mind was. Can I go now?*

"Dinner's in half an hour, Danny," his wife, Dianne called from command central, the kitchen where the cacophonic sound of pots and pans clashing and being readied for cooking, apparently with the aplomb of a ship builder riveting a steam boiler together, were coming from.

"I'll find him, Hon!" Danny hollered as he left the bathroom and walked down the hallway toward the bedrooms. Natch; Poppa's room was empty. So was the living room, the den, and the hobby room. God only knew where the kids were. Probably outside, playing softball with the kids next door. The merry search for Poppa was on.

Poppa, Danny's father-in-law, was at the certain old age at which the mind and body sometimes both decide on rare occasion to agree to go wandering off unannounced, hand-in-hand on a lark. A dangerous little combination in the suburbs of Boston, a town in which the vast majority of licensed drivers are sometimes likened by pedestrians to the largest concentration of vehicular homicidal maniacs currently at large on the highways of Italy.

Dianne and Danny had convinced Poppa to give up driving some years ago. But Poppa still had his car, the last new one he'd bought, a dinosaur of a Cadillac that resided, immobile for the most part, downstairs in the Smiths' two-car garage. It was parked side-by-side with Dianne's sensible little Prius. Poppa's car, a black, 1976 Eldorado convertible and its protected status was the sole reason Danny's black, late-model Mercedes, as far as he figured until now, would probably never see the inside of his garage again...although there was some hope. Poppa "Coach" D'Angelo had recently agreed to donate the old car as a grand prize to a fundraiser raffle for his beloved St. George's High. Danny's own status symbol, important in his life, had seemed forever doomed to endure the onslaught of the elements: aerial bombardment in the form of not only acid rain and stray baseballs but also pigeon poop; it was the ultimate in the trickle-down effect. The guys at work had taken to ribbing him.

"When are you going to stop driving a black and white and get an unmarked car, Dan-o?" one of them had said one morning. Danny checked the downstairs bathroom; it was unoccupied (an odd occurrence, in a house shared with a woman, one old man, and three kids). He walked down a short hallway, opened the door to the garage, and was greeted by the smell of acrid cigar smoke and carnauba wax, and the sound of the afternoon traffic report playing on the Caddy's radio. An AM car radio, at that. The sound jogged Danny's memory, and he thought momentarily of the days when he listened to Joe Green broadcasting aloft from the Green Machine, the WBZ traffic copter, on his morning commute; now he got his traffic reports from an app. Poppa was sitting in his Cadillac; a captain at the helm of an immense, shiny black whale of a car berthed next to Dianne's tiny tugboat of a Prius, currently docked and drawing amps from the grid, while Poppa drew down only memories.

The old goat was in gear for sure: he had put the top up, had the ignition on, the garage door open, and both hands on the car's red steering wheel. He was puffing on another of his Cuban cigars.

"Pops!" Danny yelled, "Dinner in 10!" The effect was that of a rear-end collision; the Caddy's brake lights blushed red in embarrassment, and the old man looked up in surprise, seeing Danny in the rearview mirror.

"I'll be there in a sec, kiddo," said Poppa, gently turning off the radio and then the ignition. He stared out through the windshield into the street, pocketing the keys as he did so, then swung open the heavy door of his car with remarkable ease for a man of his age and emerged, cigar in hand, pausing for a moment after he stood up. He then shuffled toward the stairway to the upper floor of the Smiths' split-level home and slowly, almost reverently placed his cigar in an old coffee can sitting on the workbench and snapped the cover closed over it. Poppa's Cadillac was part of his heritage and this ritual was almost part of his religion; using the car's virgin ashtray would have been a sacrilege. The cigar, starving for oxygen, went out.

"Pops!" exclaimed Danny, trying to shunt the old man along toward the dining room, "You know...Dee's cooking Italian tonight. Seafood. Clams Lamborghini...or something like that. I dunno."

"We were winners, kiddo," Poppa said, turning, his eyes becoming misty, to reflect upon a series of framed photographs of him and his wresting team that were displayed on the wall. Images of the high school team that had won the state championship for St. George's High for three straight years under Poppa's tutelage as coach in the early 1970s; the press had referred to the unbeatable team as "The Italian Battalion."

"Time out," said Poppa. He turned around to face the garage doorway and the driveway beyond where Danny's kids were engaged in playing a friendly game of catch with the kids next door. Poppa stepped back to the Caddy and touched the button on the remote control affixed to the driver's side sun visor, then turned to follow Danny as he left the garage and headed toward the kitchen. The garage door gently slithered down and made a soft *thunk* when it met the concrete floor, closing the one seemingly-open eye of the Smiths' garage and its view of the suburbs—just a few seconds before a baseball lofted by a youthful player impacted the driver's side of the windshield on Danny's 4-Matic Mercedes. Several kids in the immediate vicinity suddenly realized they had a good reason why they should find something else to do elsewhere and not go home until the lights were out in their parents' bedroom windows.

As Poppa loped along the hallway behind Danny, heading for the dining room, the shrill sound of the kitchen smoke alarm sounded. Danny sprinted the remaining distance to the kitchen; gray smoke billowed from the doorway. He entered, holding his breath and found Dianne at the sink, just as she was submerging a blackened frying pan in the sink that was rapidly filling with cold water.

"What happened?" he blurted out, looking to see if Dianne had been burned.

"I took my eyes off dinner for just one minute," she ruefully explained, "to answer the phone—it was my sister calling. And look what happened...oh, this is all ruined!" Poppa leaned into the kitchen from the hallway, brought out a handkerchief from his back pocket, and made pretense of fanning the smoke to get it out of his eyes.

"Phew! Mama mia!" he exclaimed. "That's some hot red sauce you're cooking there, Dee!"

"Pops," said Danny, turning toward him and scowling, "don't start."

"Di, hon," said Danny, "look, let's regroup. This isn't the end of the world. Today's Poppa's birthday, so let's celebrate it in style and go out to Nacosto's for dinner tonight. What do you say?"

"Well...okay," she answered. Just give me about 20 minutes to clean up this mess and change...and we can go. You'd better call and make sure we can get a table." Danny and Poppa dutifully left the kitchen and headed for the study to make the phone call, where there was fresh air and only the faintest smell of blackened red sauce and hot metal.

Nacosto's Italian Ristorante, a well-trafficked family restaurant in Boston, is a large restaurant that can seat up to 150 people, but is often said by tourists to remind them of the setting for a scene in *The Godfather* in which Michael Corleone settles a little score with two enemies in short order, rearranges some of the tables in the process, and skips out without picking up the tab. The movie made its debut in Boston just a few years before Poppa's Caddy was rolling down the assembly line.

Nacosto's is quite certainly a family restaurant in one sense of the word, where enjoying a meal with your relatives is great fun. In another sense, it is also the place where you can go when fun is not the focus, when you want to have a close, meaningful conversation, *sotto voce*, about business with someone in another family. A place where the discussions about the intricacies of your dealings and the other's will be completely ignored by everyone else, simply because so many other people who aren't interested in business—happy out-of-town couples in love, tourists, foodies, college students, and weekend visitors—all come here for fine food and drink. They're cooing about tall buildings or the swan boats on the pond in the Public Gardens, or Fenway as they dine. They're chatting about the news, about college courses, or where to go next, over glasses of wine or cups of coffee. They're intensely interested in chitchat about themselves, their selfies, their phones, and what they like to do—nothing else. Indeed, nothing you say will arouse the slightest interest in them or cause anyone to drop his spoon in his *zuppa* in astonishment. Nothing will go any further, where it could possibly land you in front of a grand jury with perspiration trickling down your neck, or in the trunk of a large, black Cadillac (not a convertible) headed for a date with a shovel, wishing you'd never said you wanted friends who had your back. But, then again, times have changed since the RICO law's enactment and so have tricks of the magic disappearing act for a body; after all, most cars these days do not have trunks. Who would be so indiscrete as to use a hatchback?

Nacosto's well-kept brick façade and foyer is the pride of the neighborhood; even the backdoor entranceway is attractively decorated with several immaculate, precisely aligned, matching trash cans and signs that read "don't even think of parking here and if you are found here at night, you will be found here in the morning." It's located in a lively, friendly district, one in which even the old-fashioned mom-and-pop variety stores with grills at the front counter have thoughtful owners who ask you, "How do you want your hot dogs cooked, boys, and what would you like on them?" when you stroll in with your pal, order lunch, and wander around naively looking about, swiveling your head without benefit of a map or GPS for such icons as *Old Ironsides* and the Bunker Hill Monument, or the place where the errant vehicles towed from Nacosto's might have been deposited.

Nacosto's staff is accommodating, the prices are reasonable, the atmosphere is congenial, and nobody who comes to Nacosto's goes away hungry. And of course, while they all *do* go away, even in a movie no one has ever been shot in Nacosto's dining room (although guns scrubbed clean of fingerprints and serial numbers by the ever-efficient dishwashers may have been stashed in the restrooms temporarily, a humble and discreet service for special, repeat customers). Well-concealed, short and long-term storage of items, known as "the hide," is also available. These are important services that indemnify gun owners who are exercising their constitutional rights from undue hassle, and protect their identities while they tend to other business and get caught up on things, before they take up the tools of their trades.

Old Poppa had already told Danny he might like to go out to Nacosto's for dinner some time a while ago. The food was good. So was the atmosphere, Poppa said. Danny agreed. Quiet. In fact, the Italian word, nacosto means: hidden away. A nice family place.

"Nobody will bother you there," he said.

"Perfect," said Danny.

Before making any reservations, he had to address the fact that Poppa, like Italians do, talked with his hands when he described the waitresses at Nacosto's, which he did often whenever the restaurant was mentioned. For Poppa, this was an important consideration (although, for the record, he stated he was a gentleman of the old school). For Danny, this concept of communicating images of females other than the statue of Venus (discussed beforehand with Poppa down in the garage, with only the Cadillac and the garage door listening) was not suitable behavior in public and could give people the impression of an elderly gentleman who is gradually losing his grip on the proverbial steering wheel of life. It had the potential of being rather embarrassing to his family members.

"In other words, Poppa," warned Danny, "you gotta be civil...*and* you gotta keep your hands off the waitresses." Here, Danny was referring to an incident two years previous in which Poppa had seen fit to pinch the bottom of a waitress in another restaurant, an action that did not escape the attention of the restaurant manager or a reporter for WBZ News who happened to be having dinner at the next table instead of being aloft in the news 'copter. "The place is a family restaurant...not a frat house with a party going on, Pops," stated Danny. "Just promise me, and Dianne, that you'll behave. This is not going to be boys' night out on the Via Veneto. Or else...you're going to go solo, and you're the one who's going to be pinched. *Capiche?*"

About 20 minutes after making the dinner reservation, Danny—accompanied by Poppa, Dianne, and Danny and Dianne's three young sons—went out to the garage and checked the oil in the Caddy's monstrous engine before starting the car, hoping to God nothing mechanical would fail, then dropped the convertible top. The flick of a dashboard switch caused whirring and whining sounds, as actions of various invisible electric motors and servos made the canvas convertible top slither downward like a hypnotized cobra into a cavity behind the backseat...all to the delight of the kids who stood next to the big car, seemingly mesmerized as if a genie were at work, concealed somewhere deep within the car. Dianne clambered into the car and plopped herself on the sofa-like backseat, urging the kids to hurry up and join her.

Danny started the engine and 472 cubic inches of Cadillac power gently rumbled into life. Ahead lay several miles of crowded highways, tortuous traffic lanes to traverse, and then the issue of finding a parking spot in town on a Saturday night. Danny sat quietly, pensively, one foot on the brake pedal, one poised over the gas pedal, pondering: *Question, Danny-boy: Where does one find the room to park a car the size of the* Queen Mary *(and one that has no car alarm system) when in town?* The traffic, he knew, would be hell. Poppa eased himself into the shotgun seat and closed the door with a loud *ca-chunk.*

"Here we go, kids!" Danny announced, blissfully unaware of the damage to his Mercedes, as he put the gearshift into drive; the Caddy crept stealthily down the driveway, as quietly as a hearse leaving a graveyard after a committal service, and then motored out onto the roads to downtown Boston.

Nacosto's is on a quiet street. And it was so quiet that night anyone walking past it could hear the hum and buzz of the red-and-blue neon sign in the front window advertising *Nacosto's Italian Ristorante* over the distant rumble of Boston's early-evening hubbub. Several minutes after leaving the expressway, with Danny executing a smooth but sudden traverse of three lanes of traffic and putting on a burst of speed. Dianne's hair was blowing loose, almost carrying away her sunglasses in the slipstream of the big car; the kids jumped up and down excitedly every time they passed a slower car, yelling at its driver. Poppa's Caddy, its massive engine purring in seeming smug contentment of being turned loose on the expressway and exerting its 300-some-odd horsepower, finally turned the corner onto the street on which Nacosto's was located.

And...there it was, appearing like a welcoming dockside berth of ample proportions awaiting a transatlantic ocean liner. Danny could not believe his eyes.

"Holy...I don't believe it!" he blurted out.

"What? *What*, hon?" queried Dianne, propping her sunglasses all the way up onto a brow furrowed in concern, craning her neck to see around Poppa's head and his massive, wrestler's shoulders.

"A parking spot...right out front," said Danny, a smile working its way onto his face, as he steered the Caddy closer to the curb, then backed it into a generously proportioned space between a Prius and a tiny, ancient VW plastered with peace signs and bumper stickers, without hitting either of them or scoring digs in the Caddy's whitewalls. "I don't believe it! It's...almost too good to be true."

Danny turned off the ignition and glanced at his watch; they were right on time. He felt in his jacket pocket to make sure that he'd brought Poppa's birthday card. *Check.* House keys? *Check.* Danny went to unbuckle his seatbelt; the buckle wouldn't budge. He yarned on the belt to no avail; he wriggled and writhed as if in agony, trying to escape its clutches.

"What's going on? What's the matter? Are you okay?" asked Dianne, unaware of the nature of the problem, and suspecting Danny was suffering a heart attack.

"I...I can't unbuckle my belt," he replied, tugging away at the seatbelt in vain.

"Let me help," volunteered Poppa, leaning over Danny and grasping the buckle. Dianne stood up and leaned over the two men tugging at the seatbelt.

"No, no...pull up on the buckle, not over," she said. The three kids, Bobby, Brian, and Dale, all clambered out of the backseat, wormed their way over the tonneau cover, and jumped off onto the sidewalk one by one, then approached the driver's side door.

"Pull on it, Dad!" yelled Dale. Danny heaved on the buckle and it finally gave way.

"All right," he said with a sigh, turning to Poppa. "I thought I was done for and I'd be stuck here all night! Let's go in and eat!" Danny, Dianne, and Poppa stepped out of the Caddy, slammed its heavy doors shut, and the entire family gathered, filing one by one into the restaurant. A small crowd awaiting tables had gathered at the window to watch the spectacle outside and then dispersed, quickly feigning interest in the large goldfish tank beside the cash register, as the Smiths entered.

The Smith entourage was escorted to their table, and the two waiters who promptly appeared brought with them a wine list, a basket filled to the brim with piping-hot garlic bread, and menus, all of which were quickly and efficiently deposited on the table. Sammy Nacosto himself then stopped by to greet the Smiths, welcoming them and explaining to them that he was their humble host for the evening.

"Your place," said Poppa to the restaurant's owner, uplifting his face to meet Sammy's gaze, "is...*fantastico*! I always feel welcome here."

"*Sono onorato*; I am honored," replied Sammy, smiling and even bowing ever so slightly. He turned toward the kitchen, beckoning a waiter to come and take the order for cocktails or wine. Danny felt in his jacket pocket for the birthday card; still there...but where were the keys for the Caddy? Gone. They were, no doubt about it, still in the car. Danny suppressed a brief moment of panic; his blood pressure rose but then subsided. *Who, after all, would be dumb enough*, he thought, as he reached for the garlic bread and ordered a martini, *to steal a black Cadillac parked in front of an Italian restaurant?*

Chapter 18

A Suspicious Vehicle

It was just after 9:30 p.m. when Boston police officer Samantha Adams first heard the report of a suspicious vehicle...it was not one within her precinct, but close by its boundaries. She mentally tagged it, in case that precinct called for backup. Distance and response time, she well knew, have to be calculated differently when you are on bicycle patrol and not in a squad car. And also when, as was the case with Samantha, you had a rookie tagging along with you—a rookie like Mike Swift. And swift, he was not; the guy obviously hadn't ever spent much time on a bike before now. He occasionally wobbled as if losing his balance, looking like he was about to fall off the saddle, or careened around corners at a dangerous angle. And he needed to stop along the way at places—a lot—while out riding on patrol.

"*Again?*" she asked, turning to look at him momentarily as they rolled along, side by side along Beacon Street, the unrelenting traffic scooting by them just inches away.

"Yes, again," he replied, standing up on the pedals and coasting.

"What is it this time," she asked caustically, "a coffee or a 10-100?"

"If you must know, good ol' patriot Sam Adams, it's a coffee. Not to worry; I'll drink it while I drive," Mike countered. Samantha groaned, then swerved just in time to avoid being clipped by a door being flung open on a parked, badly dented Subaru. *He can barely ride using two hands, and he's going to ride one-handed?*

If there was one thing she hated as much as being paired with a rookie, especially on night patrol, it was being paired with someone who was dumb enough not to realize that whatever he drank on a frequent basis had to make its exit eventually—indeed, riding with Mike on patrol was like taking a small child on a long-distance trip. And she especially hated being called Sam Adams because of all the locker room beer jokes that went along with the nickname.

"Take it from me," she said, "if you don't wear out your kidneys from drinking that sludge, the food you eat in this neighborhood will kill you. And we can't waste any more time making stops after this. Where to this time?"

"Titanic Pizza!" shouted Mike, who added, turning to face her with a silly grin, "Dead ahead!" The two officers slowed their bikes and pulled over to the curb in front of a shabby-looking restaurant that might have been a fairly respectable family diner in its earlier days. Atop the roof of the restaurant stood a sign, presumably made by one of the better artists in the neighborhood when he was not otherwise occupied in spray-painting things on underpasses or boxcars. It was a fairly good rendition of the ill-fated ocean liner, with a gigantic slice of pizza tearing open a gaping hole in its hull.

Oh God, thought Samantha. *Titanic Pizza, home of the day-long heartburn hero. Their coffee is probably older than his mother.* Red-and-orange neon beer signs flashed on and off inside the restaurant's murky interior like warning signs at a dangerous intersection. The heads of several people, seen dimly through fly-specked windows as they devoured pizza that looked like cheese-infused lava, tossed and swayed like bobble heads on the dashboard of a moving car. Seeing that something of possible entertainment value was going on outside, the people turned toward Samantha and Mike to gawk at them.

"If you're not back here in one minute," barked Samantha, "I'm leaving to finish my shift, and if someone steals your bike, the sergeant will have your baby-ass badge while it's still wet, with my approval." Mike turned to grin at her like a monkey trying to face down a gorilla when he knows it's a losing proposition.

"Chill, Sam," he replied. "Just tuck your beer between your gams and keep it cold."

"Right," said Samantha, "and I'll tell anyone at headquarters who asks where you are that you stopped by your mom's to get your training wheels. Know what your problem is? An RCI." Mike, obviously clueless to cop jargon as a rookie, stared at her. "A rectal-cranial inversion," she explained.

And just then, no sooner had Mike walked inside than Samantha's radio crackled to life and a call for her did come in...a call to check out the suspicious vehicle parked in a residential district just over the line in the next precinct. Samantha hopped off her bike, ran to a window on the restaurant, and pressed her face to it, hoping to spot Mike inside. A toddler on the other side of the glass, fascinated by the sight of a strange person wearing a uniform and helmet, slipped off his father's shoulder and pressed his face and hands against the dirty window, not unlike a curious squid in an aquarium, leaving a trail of cheese and red sauce instead of a splotch of ink as he went. Mike was nowhere to be seen. In desperation, Samantha ran to the door, just in time to collide with Mike, who was on his way out. A geyser of spilled coffee erupted into the air and landed on the two cops, a performance that was duly noted by the bobble heads at the windows and especially the toddler, who excitedly started making red swirls and polka-dots on the window with his tiny hands as he waved to the two cops.

"Mike! Mike! We have to go—now!" yelled Samantha, brushing herself off and grabbing her bike. "It's a 10-37 and the next precinct can't roll on it."

"Figures," grunted Mike, disgustedly tossing his now-empty coffee cup into the open garbage can by the entrance and hopping onto his bike, all in one Mike Swift move that ended with him missing the right pedal and falling over sideways into the street, with the bike crashing down on top of him. The bobble heads now swarmed to the windows to see what would happen next, and the cook, toking on an unfiltered cigarette, had come out from the kitchen to look through the windows, too. Wiping his hands on his less-than-pristine apron, he bent over and craned his neck like an old buzzard, shoving the toddler aside to get a better look outside while the child's father munched on a calzone the size of an adult snapping turtle. The mother, seated across the table and as imperturbable as a stone god, twiddled with her iPhone amidst the entire rumpus.

"A bike cop that dumb," said the cook to no one in particular, his cigarette ashes falling softly, sight unseen on the mother's salad plate, "should have training wheels."

Chapter 19

The Hit

As darkness had set in, the gray Lincoln Town Car Jimmy procured had pulled slowly into a parking spot in the North End of Boston, one that had been wisely chosen (and just to make sure that all went well, had been marked earlier that evening along with several others with orange no parking, funeral cones by Marv, who had deftly dropped them off as he drove slowly by to case the neighborhood...as he had been doing for the past several days). In addition, Marv had brought to Jimmy's attention a news snippet he had clipped from *The Boston Globe* the previous week that explained that Maria would be traveling in Italy for several days on a church-related mission. Thus, Vince, as Marv explained to Jimmy, barely suppressing a belly laugh in the process, would be "home alone" during the time the hit was to take place.

The parking spot was situated next to a small garden belonging to the local church, and partially concealed by the overhanging branches of cherry trees, well across the street from Vince's brownstone and strategically located a good distance from any streetlight. Soft lights within glowing behind ornate stained-glass windows relieved the ominously dark appearance of the Gothic-style church across the way that towered over buildings in the neighborhood. The lower casement of one of the windows was partly open, and organ music wafted through from within the cavernous depths of the building. And now, after more than half an hour spent making absolutely certain the occupants of the Lincoln were free from observation and that their moment of opportunity had come along...so, also, did a woman come along...a woman of the evening.

A yellow taxi presently pulled up alongside the curb opposite the Lincoln. The passenger door opened, and a cotton-candy-coiffed, scantily clad woman emerged; she sauntered with the self-assured poise of a lioness perusing the perimeters of a zebra pride at a watering-hole and headed over to the door of the brownstone in her glitzy dress, her high heels clattering on the sidewalk. Extending one finger dazzled with glitter and the ruby-red of an exorbitantly painted fingernail, she pressed the doorbell. A moment later, she delved into her purse, produced a ringing cell phone, and put it to her ear.

"Ya, hon; 'course it's me, Andromeda. Who? *Andromeda Galaxy?* Got it? Haha! C'mon, come let me in and the stars'll come out for ya! Let's party up and have some fun!" The brownstone's door opened, bathing her in a pool of light; she stepped in and disappeared. The door closed with a resounding *thunk*, and Jimmy, slamming his head against the headrest in the Lincoln, emitted a foul curse closely mirroring the sound of the closing door.

For Jimmy and the other two men sitting in the darkened car, waiting for their chance to get off a shot, time was weighing heavily on their hands. "He's *gotta* show himself sometime, after she leaves," he muttered, peering up at an open bay window on the brownstone's second story, from which the muted sounds of classic Italian opera wafted and where cream-colored curtains danced softly with the evening breeze. *They say he likes his opera,* thought Jimmy. *No Pavarotti for you after tonight, you bastard.*

Jimmy, dressed in formal, black-tie attire, was seated next to one of his store's mannequins he had topped off with a blonde wig and dressed in a slinky black outfit, one that revealed an ample supply of flesh-colored plastic parts that were of staggeringly generous proportions.

"You're sure this is the right address?" queried Herman, slouched behind the wheel, swiveling his head around nervously to check for the approach of anyone who might wonder why the car had been here so long, with three men inside it keeping the company of a blonde woman who looked like a Las Vegas hooker and appeared to be paralyzed. But perhaps, to any proper Bostonian onlooker who might stroll by, they were either men of the cloth hoping to reform a poor girl, or reformed Johns who should be admired for their resistance to temptation in its oldest and evilest form.

"Hey," snapped Jimmy, "I know my job—you know yours. Do it." Herman fiddled with the keys in the ignition and the key fob, an ornate emblem with a cross and Latin words on it. He fished out a small silver flask from the pocket of his uniform—a chauffeur's outfit, furnished courtesy of Jimmy's impressive array of uniforms at the store—and took a hefty swig.

"Hey—what the hell?" Jimmy blustered, his face suddenly contorted with rage. "You told me you didn't drink! No drinking on this job, not while you work for me."

"Something to steady my nerves," replied the triggerman, wiping his lips on the back of his left sleeve.

"I want no mistakes," grumbled Jimmy, "and I don't need you to get tanked. Gimme that." He leaned forward over the seat, snatched the flask away from Herman, and promptly took a swig himself before pocketing it. Herman pouted, gently picked up his sharpshooter's rifle, twiddled with the scope, and checked to make sure the safety was on—for now—and slowly, methodically, threaded a silencer onto the end of the barrel. "Now," Jimmy said, "that your nerves are steady, all eyes on that second-floor window."

"Boss!" hissed Herman, peering into the rearview mirror, which he had earlier rearranged to suit himself, "we've got company!" Two dark forms, tiny, brilliant-white lights sparkling in front of each of them, were speeding along the street a block or so away, closing the distance between them and the Lincoln's back bumper quickly. Jimmy spun around to look.

"Shit! Bike cops!" he said. "Herman, ixnay with that rifle. Make like you're sound asleep."

"Pay close attention here, Mike," Samantha cautioned her partner, as she and Mike approached the Lincoln. "Be cautious. Watch for sudden movements inside the car."

"I know the drill here, Sam," he retorted. "First, we stop and chat; we interact with the civilians."

"No," said Samantha defiantly, "first, we see who these people are; we stop where we are right now." Inside the Lincoln, Herman slowly eased the safety off on his rifle, concealed under the blanket he had left on the front seat. Jimmy, sensing the imminent danger of discovery, decided to activate his contingency plan designed to deter anyone giving the Lincoln more than just a passing glance. He pulled the dummy close to him, flipped it over onto its belly, sprawled it across the seat, and pushed it down until its head and blonde wig were firmly in place over the fly of his pants. *Let the festivities begin*, he thought to himself, leaning far back and affecting the Jimmy Callahan smile that was often seen on his face after he'd won a high-stakes poker game.

"Okay, Sam," said Mike. The two police officers stopped their bikes and glared at each other briefly. "You have to run everything, don't you?" he fumed. "This whole shift has been ugly. That scene at the pizza joint was ugly. Hell, *you're* ugly."

"*You* want to see ugly, Mikey?" asked Samantha. "When you're old enough to shave, and it might be a while, for you...go look in the mirror." She beamed the bike's headlight at the Lincoln's rear license plate and whistled softly.

"What now? asked Mike, somewhat chastened. "We call it in, right?"

"Hey swift boy, I don't think so," Samantha replied softly, putting one hand up as a stop signal to keep her rookie partner from keying the microphone of his radio. "I know that plate...it belongs to the deputy police commissioner. So––do you want to call it in now? With him parked here for a funeral and maybe staying late to talk with a priest or family? Sure—go knock yourself out; you'll end your career before it's barely started."

"Okay, no then. But I say we still need to investigate," Mike hissed, shoving off toward the parked car on his bike.

Samantha tried to stop him, but it was too late. Mike picked up speed, pedaling briskly down the street. He then coasted over to the Lincoln, puffed up his chest, and prepared to say, "Good evening, sir, I'm officer Swift with the Boston Police Department," the line he'd been longing to deliver the last two days on patrol. But no words came out of his mouth as he peered inside the car—his gaze following the revealing beam of his flashlight—and his jaw dropped. Badly flustered (after all, he was looking, as far as he knew, at the second-in-command of the police department, a respectable man who was now en flagrante with a blonde floozy, while his chauffeur dozed, completely unaware at the wheel) Mike went for the brakes as he executed a quick U-turn. He never finished it.

Mike was halfway through his turn when Samantha, now pedaling toward the Lincoln, collided with him; both bikes and riders went down with a rousing clatter that caused the curtains in the brownstone's bay window to stir as if someone took a peek from behind them.

"Crap!" muttered Herman under his breath; the activity at the window had not escaped his attention.

"Shit," said Mike, picking himself up and pulling his now-battered bike upright.

"Yes, you are one," said Samantha. Now, get *yours* together and let's get out of here."

"Damn," grumbled Mike, pedaling off beside Samantha, "so *that's how* the number two fearless leader spends his evening hours. If I'd been that chauffeur, I'd have had one eye on that rearview mirror. I'll bet that dummy's still in driver training."

Time dragged on. Jimmy checked his watch; the minute hand seemed to be slowing down in its orbits. And just then, a pool of light emerged as the brownstone's door opened and the lady of the evening stepped out, again pawing for her cell phone. Within the space of two minutes, a cab appeared, the woman entered it, the cab's roof light blinked off, and the taxicab quickly motored off. "Now, gents," said Jimmy, "we've got some work to do."

"Amen," muttered Jerry. A mile-wide grin spread across his craggy face, as he turned around to face Jimmy. "Let's put this wiseguy out of our misery! Hey––don't you think our mark didn't last too awfully long in there? And one more thing...where's my advance?" Jimmy produced an envelope and handed it to Jerry; the big man grabbed the envelope that had a short stack of hundred-dollar bills in it and stuffed it inside his jacket. Jimmy turned his attention back to Herman, who was intent now on watching the brownstone's second story through his scope, as intent and focused as a cat watching a mouse hole in a wall.

The curtains at the bay window rippled in the evening breeze, and what appeared to be the figure of a man's head and shoulders appeared in silhouette at the window. With a sense of relief at seeing this target, and before Jimmy could re-act, Herman gently squeezed the trigger. Inside the apartment,

Vince had just moments before placed his marble bust of Mussolini on the table inside the bay window and had walked back to the bar, where he poured himself a full glass of red wine, and then, stoppered bottle in hand, turned off the lamps in the room, leaving only the chandelier in the bay window lit. Standing astride his prized polar bear rug, thinking himself the master of the universe, he stared toward the open window, savoring both his recent conquest and the night air, not to mention the concert playing softly on his sound system. So Vince did not hear the muffled, popcorn-popper *pop* of Herman's gunshot from below, did not feel the impact from the chandelier hitting his head after the bullet shattered the bust of his hero and cut the light's cord. He did not realize that men in the street below were trying to kill him. Vince fell to the floor, unconscious, his wine spilling in a great, sweeping, red arc from his right arm.

"Got him," stated the hit man coldly, as convincingly as possible, drawing back the bolt on his rifle and ejecting the spent cartridge. He was intently watching the window for any sign of life, as the spent cartridge bounced off the front seat and rolled onto the Lincoln's floor. "Get that, would you?" Herman matter-of-factly asked Jerry, who obligingly put it into the pocket of his pants.

"Go get him!" Jimmy ordered the giant, slapping the back of the man's massive head. "Go in there...break the door down if you have to. I want to make sure he's dead...bring me the damned body!" The big man bolted out the car door and sprinted into action. Breaking down the apartment door? That was a simple matter. Jerry had broken down many doors in his lifetime. Having crossed the street and forced the brownstone's door open in a matter of seconds, he quickly ascended the stairs. By the dim light coming through the window, he saw exactly what he expected to see: the body of his former boss, lying face-up, splattered with dark liquid, and sprawled awkwardly across a rug. It was the quintessential black-and-white, front-page newspaper picture, one he was all too familiar with: one of the end of a crime boss's life.

Jerry stood astride Vince for a few seconds in the darkened room and looked down at him, savoring the moment, and grinned. Yes, the man who had crossed him—thrown him under the bus—was apparently dead. But this was a mess. Realizing there was no time to waste, he quickly stooped and gathered up the limp body, wrapped it in the rug, heaved it over his shoulder, and headed down the stairway. It was just then that a taxi appeared at the brownstone's entrance and two figures emerged as the driver got out and lethargically rummaged for his passengers' suitcases in the trunk. One of the figures was Maria Saluzzo; the other was Father DeTomasi. Except for a second taxi that soon cruised by, its off-duty roof light winking on as it passed, there was no other traffic.

The good priest, despite the fact that he was shaking off the effects of jet lag, never missed a beat. Upon his arrival at the parking garage he had been irked, finding that his car was unavailable, with no explanation given other than that the garage's elevator was out of service and the car could not be retrieved until the next day. He looked at the Lincoln parked across the street, rubbing his eyes. He saw the men sitting in it, and, instantly recognizing the familiar-to-him St. Anthony of Padua decal on the rear window, summoned up the courage to emit a yell as loud as Paul Revere's warning that the British were coming to Boston. "What are you doing? *That's my car!*"

"We're screwed, we've been made!" Jimmy hissed to Herman. "Crank this heap up and get us out of here!" Herman did as he was told, and the Lincoln roared to life and laid rubber...leaving only a glimpse of its red taillights behind—and the unfortunate giant, Jerry, now clomping down the stairs with a heavy load––to fend for himself.

Patty Callahan, out of breath from running, mentally cursed her luck at being delayed by traffic as she arrived at the entrance to the small garden near the church. Dressed in the police uniform she had taken from her father's store, she crouched behind a park bench in order to conceal herself, just as Jerry made his appearance.

Jerry hot-footed it out the front door, expecting to find the Lincoln waiting for him, its engine running and its roomy trunk yawning wide open. Presumably, the German guy would drive them to some construction site, perhaps near the New Hampshire border, and the body would be neatly disposed of. Instead, he was greeted by the sight of two obviously distraught people...a priest and a woman...running down the sidewalk in pursuit of the Lincoln's red taillights that were rapidly disappearing down the street. His conclusion of what had gone wrong was immediate: he'd been had. He'd been set up to be the fall guy—again. So, Jerry ran. What else could he do? He ran until he felt that his lungs would burst, that his legs would collapse. He ran, turning left-right and right-left, for four blocks. Stopping and working heavily to catch his breath at the turn of the last corner, he realized that he needed to find himself a car, soon, in order to escape. Sirens sounded in the distance. Sure, it could be fire engines, but why take a chance and wait to find a car to escape in?

Walking slowly now, looking into each parked vehicle he encountered, one by one as he went down another street, which was, thankfully, deserted, he finally came upon an old black Cadillac convertible parked outside a restaurant. Its top was down; the keys were in the ignition. Jerry's basic instincts, those of a born thief, kicked in. "There is a God after all," the giant grumbled to himself as he heaved the limp body of his former boss onto the backseat, then threw himself into the front, started the car and drove along slowly, hoping not to attract undue attention. He was savoring the breeze blowing across his face and his freedom...however temporary it might prove to be this time.

Chapter 20

Payback Time

Father DeTomasi stood on the sidewalk, stunned, having observed the departure of his treasured car. It was bad enough that the trip to Rome had been a debacle—that the audience with the pope had been ruined—and now, this. Maria left him, ran back to the brownstone, and climbed the stairs—and soon let out a scream upon seeing the destruction that had taken place in her living room. Almost as if summoned, a uniformed policewoman appeared, sprinting forth from the darkness under the nearby trees. She immediately ran over to the priest.

"Father...is there something I can help you with?" she asked sympathetically, shining her flashlight on his worried face.

"There is...oh, yes—I dare say that there is!" he exclaimed, wringing his hands in despair. "My car has been stolen! Gray Lincoln!"

"Father!" called Maria from the open second-story window, "Vince is gone! We've been robbed! Again!"

"I'll call it in," said the cop. "Which way did the car go?" she asked. The priest pointed a finger down the street. "I'll handle this," she said and sprinted off...after a few moments, she turned around to see if the priest was still watching her. When

Father DeTomasi finally did turn away and disappear, the policewoman ran around the corner of the block, following the large man she had seen leave the building with something that looked suspiciously like a body slung over his shoulder.

Exercising discretion, Jerry slowed the car a block later, pulled to the curb, stopped, and raised the convertible top. It would be far better to be concealed...even if being conspicuous by virtue of driving a car more than 40 years old, a car that only the bosses in his old neighborhood could afford when he was a kid. Jerry drove off again, keeping a close eye on the rearview mirror. It was then that Jerry's charge arose like a horror movie mummy from his temporary tomb in the backseat...and peered into that mirror.

"Who...who the hell are you?" Vince asked, shaking his head as he fought his way toward complete consciousness. Jerry slammed on the power brakes; the Caddy came to an abrupt halt, and Vince's head slammed into the back of the front seat. Jerry turned to face Vince.

"So," said Vince haltingly, recognizing Jerry after regaining his composure somewhat, "I see you're back. When did you get out of school?"

"I've been out...out of your turf...a long time, creep," countered the giant, fixing his old boss with a steady gaze. "I did time for you; you did nothin' for me." The Caddy's massive engine rumbled as it marked time with Jerry's over-large foot on the brake pedal holding it back, as if waiting for his next command. "Seems to me some payback's in order." Jerry's clenched left fist caught Vince squarely in the forehead; he collapsed like a sofa bed being quickly laid flat for an unexpected overnight guest, instantly disappearing down behind the front seat of the Caddy. "Got any complaints, Saluzzo?" asked Jerry. There was no reply. "No? Okay; didn't think so."

Jerry drove down Boylston Street and stopped close by the Public Gardens. The source of the wailing sirens he had heard earlier was now apparent: there was a fire raging in a building nearby. A jumble of fire engines, police cars, and ambulances with lights flashing red and blue had converged at the scene, where the cops had set up a police line and were holding back a sizeable crowd. *An excellent diversion*, thought Jerry, *while I pull a few things.* He looked out into the gardens where the swan boats were. They were clean...white...pure as ever. *Thank goodness some things in Boston never change*, thought Jerry. The gates were open.

Jerry turned off the Caddy's headlights and drove cautiously into the park, where he stopped short of the pond, got out of the car, and looked around; there was no one to be seen. Jerry wiped down the steering wheel of the Caddy with a handkerchief to clean it of his fingerprints. He then dragged Vince out of the backseat and, after some finagling, placed him in the driver's seat. He ran Vince's hands all over the steering wheel, then onto the ignition keys. He took the spent cartridge ejected from Herman's rifle out of his pocket and placed it in the Caddy's virgin ashtray, leaving it wide open where it could be seen. He removed his coat after taking care to transfer the money envelope to his pants pocket, then fumbled with Vince's body as he put the coat on it. He took the small bottle of wine he had snatched from the apartment and placed it on the seat beside Vince. "Picture perfect," observed Jerry. "A real, old-time Kodak moment. See you in the morning papers. Hope you enjoy the ride." He stomped his right foot on the brake pedal temporarily, moved the gearshift lever into drive, and stepped back as he quickly slammed the door shut. He watched for a few moments as the Cadillac bumped across the lawn and slowly, like a hippo wallowing into a watering hole, eased into the pond in the Boston Public Gardens...with Vince Saluzzo passed out behind its steering wheel.

Chapter 21

Spreading the Net

"Why am I just finding this out now?" asked Bob Tranten, the FBI agent who had just learned he had been appointed by the Washington office as the SAC, Special Agent in Charge, of locating someone he had never heard of before. A someone who had been another person's responsibility...and then dumped unceremoniously like an orphan into his jurisdiction by handlers who didn't want him, and didn't want to play nice.

"The CIA knew," replied Dave Dobson, the agent sitting across the desk from his boss, Bob, "and somebody dropped the ball. Our people at the foreign desk in D.C. never found out until yesterday." Bob drummed his fingers on the top of his desk and looked out the window at traffic crawling along the highway outside the agency's high-rise building in Chelsea.

"Perfect," he opined sarcastically, suddenly throwing his arms out for dramatic effect. "So what's it now—a terrorist? An arms merchant? Defector who wants to write a novel? A soldier of fortune at large? Wait—don't tell me—I know! It's another great case of outstanding interagency cooperation." Bob took a few moments to fume, then looked down and inspected his fingernails while he calmed himself and got his mind in order before looking up at Dave and asking, "So, who is this guy, anyway?"

"His name is John Fischer," answered Dave, opening the manila file folder he had brought with him and then pawing through the many papers it contained. He knew enough of Bob's predilections to always appear with a pen and folder when summoned...even if the folder usually—today being the exception—had nothing stashed in it but a few pieces of blank white paper. For one thing, he would always look as though he'd been working on something important, perhaps second-guessing his boss and bringing forward new, relevant information. Otherwise, the sheets of paper provided a blank slate of sorts. Dave sometimes sketched cartoons while Bob gave one of his lengthy, coma-inducing presentations...quite frequently, they were cartoons of his boss. But today, it did have something noteworthy.

"Here it is," Dave said. "An American staying out a visa in Frankfurt, studying music...30 years old, unemployed; last worked repairing musical instruments for a contractor in Pennsylvania. Before that, he worked in a gun shop as a machinist and was an organist at a community church on weekends. His father ran a shooting gallery in an amusement park in Weirs Beach, New Hampshire, where Fischer was born. The boy learned his way around a gun, that's pretty obvious; he earned merit badges for rifle shooting and shotgun shooting, and a Ranger's Award in shooting sports." Dave thumbed through more pages. "Captain of his high school wrestling team. Hmmm. This guy's a funny duck."

"Wait a minute, wait a minute," said Bob. "you're not telling me anything here. I don't care whether he's a duck, a goose, or a gander. First of all, why is he here?"

"He's here," said Dave, matter-of-factly, "to take the place of somebody else. A professional, international assassin." Bob Tranten stared at him.

"Oh...I get it now, like a substitute teacher?" he asked, sarcastically.

"No, not at all," Dave said wearily, having read the entire report beforehand. "He's here to take the place of the hit man Interpol just bagged and has on ice. The whole operation was under wraps. The CIA wants to see where the chain ends...so they put in a body double and let the game roll." He paused a minute. "They let it roll our way."

"So the spooks inserted him after they worked with Interpol—who brought down Herman Schmidt—to take his place?" Bob asked.

"Right," answered Dave. "Fischer was on their watch list...due to some inquiries he made about weapons on the street and on the Internet, plus the fact that his visa was timing out. And because the guy *looks* like Schmidt and needed work, and because he had no money to get back home, it was kind of a no-brainer to contract him, short-term...a doppleganger...just to let Schmidt's game play out for a few days and see where he goes and who tries to set him up for work, because nobody outside these walls, Interpol's, and the CIA's knows that Schmidt got taken down. And because Schmidt was smart, he kept no records...at least if he did, nobody's found them yet."

"That's a no-brainer, for sure," commented Bob, swiveling back and forth in his chair thoughtfully, adding, with a wry smile afterward: "All those spooks are no-brainers." Dave stared down at the floor and Bob's wastebasket...perhaps where his recommendation from Bob for a promotion would find a home if he made one slight misstep in this matter. Bob looked up at the ceiling, failing to suppress a laugh, and said, "Great. So we get stuck with the Teutonic Plague, imported from Europe. I love it."

"There's more," added Dave, hunching over the open file folder to peer at something, and then looking up at Bob. "Ever heard of the Steel Pipeline?"

"Yeah," said Bob, "that international weapons channel...kind of like firepower on demand...all on the dark net, I gather. Anything you want, short of an army tank, provided you've got the money...or the Bitcoin...whatever. I hear even the Chinese are in on it now...they have ops all over the place; it figures they'd want some of the action."

"Well, it looks like someone started pitching Schmidt's services just a couple of weeks ago," said Dave, pawing through more pages of reports, "like he'd suddenly become Schmidt's handler, although Schmidt never had, or needed, one. The two of them never had any contact with each other. And there was nothing in it for him, which is the suspicious part. Nobody does favors in that game. You want in, you've gotta pony up."

"Who is it?" asked Bob, a bit more interested now.

"We don't know...CIA and NSA are both working on it. I told them to get their asses moving, in the spirit of cooperation for anything moving forward. The guy—or guys, we don't know; it could be a room full of trolls or just one—is Little Bear. That's his handle anyway, and Little Bear's got Steel Pipeline honey on his paws."

"Crap," said Bob, shaking his head and going back to swiveling his chair back and forth, more rapidly this time. He clasped his hands together, stared out the window, deep in thought, and then said, "I hate this alphabet soup. This is bullshit," he groused. "FBI, CIA, NSA, Interpol, the BPOL in Germany...why the hell don't we throw in the Italian Carabinieri and cops, too for good measure, and get it all over with?" Not getting a response from Dave, he got up out of his chair, stretched, suppressed a yawn, and turned to look out the window once more. The traffic was moving outside on Maple Street. That's where he wanted to be, yes; moving along in a car, headed to the beach—it was a perfect day for it.

The beach would be long...and warm, Bob imagined. In his mind, as it began to wander in his daydream, he could almost hear the surf—it would surge and crest along the rocks at the beach's far end, with aqua waves that relentlessly pounded at the shoreline. There would be dazzlingly-bright sunlight, sand hot enough to burn one's bare feet, and umbrellas along the beach to take shelter under. And surfers riding on the waves, skittering about on the sea on their boards, and well-tanned women with sly eyes and cunning thoughts of mischief would be lying under those umbrellas, waiting just for him, reposing languidly on their loungers, drinks in hand, wearing brightly colored bikinis. Each of them would coyly invite him in turn, as he sauntered down the beach, to stop off and visit, plying him all the while with cold beer, vodka, gin, and conversation...perhaps even a card game or some other game of chance—and enticing him to stay a bit longer. Yes, Bob definitely thought he wanted to stay a bit longer on his dream beach. But it didn't work. There was silence momentarily, then Bob pulled himself back to the present...and turned to face Dave.

"Is he armed? Please...tell me he isn't," he inquired.

"Yes, he is," answered the other agent. "The Germans gave him a duplicate of Schmidt's rifle, complete with Schmidt's ID, his backpack, even his shoes; they're the same size. Pretty thorough of them, if you ask me." Bob Tranten stared at him as if he had three heads...then smacked himself squarely in the forehead.

"So...he's armed...and, where is he?"

"He's somewhere in the greater Boston area."

"Where?" demanded the Special Agent in Charge, now finding it hit home that he was ultimately the one responsible for putting a tail on the man with the alias of Herman Schmidt. And, presumably, making sure the doppelganger didn't off someone before some good, hard evidence was produced that would lead to the arrests of some underworld figures. Dave fidgeted his two feet under the table, trying to pull up his socks, trying to think of another way to say it.

"At this time," he began, but stopped himself short of rambling on; there was no way to sugarcoat it. "We don't know," he admitted.

"You're not helping me out here!" thundered Bob, color working its way up his face and tainting his cheeks red as his blood pressure rose; he now paced back and forth behind his desk, as if trying to wear a pattern in the carpet. "What's the plan? Don't keep bringing me problems; bring me solutions!"

"Well," said Dave, perusing one last document, "I see a couple of things here that might help us out. The guy's a reformed alcoholic. My guess is, with money in his pocket and with falling in with the criminal element, it's just a matter of time before he falls off the wagon again.

"That's one," said Bob, pouting. He continued to pace like the worried captain of a ship in grave danger of running aground, and is waiting for a tugboat he has summoned to arrive and save his vessel. "What's the other?"

"Well," Dave went on, "it's what we don't know. We do know how dangerous Schmidt was; we don't know how dangerous Fischer could be." Bob just stared at Dave as though he'd been asked to swallow a live frog, much less a tall tale.

"And just what does that mean to me?" he barked.

"Without any proper weapons training, it's likely this fellow couldn't hit the side of a barn at 20 feet, never mind his youthful accomplishments, even if he threw his rifle at it. We should be able to put a tail on him and keep tabs on him...and I don't anticipate trouble."

"Well, then...get going, Dobson!" said Bob. "Get a BOLO out; get whoever you need to get working on this now...get people on the street and in the bars. And I want reports; be back here before the end of the day and give me an update. Or there will be trouble...and it will begin here."

Chapter 22

Dutiful but Doubtful

"Where is Toscanini?" The question, posed by Sergeant Stefano Bianci, who had just arrived at Capitano Alberto Pellegrini's doorway made the captain, absorbed in writing a report, jolt...and then sit bolt upright. This was the question—the inevitable one—he had been dreading to hear. It was posed innocently enough, as Stefano had only asked based upon his observation that the other sergeant's office had been vacant for a day now.

"Off on a case," remarked the captain matter-of-factly, not glancing up from his paperwork.

"This one?" asked Stefano, producing a copy of *la Repubblica* he had bought at a newsstand this morning, opening it up and handing it to the captain. Alberto looked; there they were, the priest and the woman from Boston, in a color photo on the front page. The headlines decried both the unfortunate robbery of the pair of visiting Americans, and the apparent inaction of the Polizia in apprehending the perpetrator, much less their failure to come up with any clues as to that person's identity. Alberto finished sending yet another text message to Sergeant Lorenzo Toscanini, imploring him to check in; Alberto was under increasing pressure to produce results of the investigation. He had updated Lorenzo with startling new information he had discovered about who had attacked and robbed the American visitors.

Alberto sighed and looked up at Stefano. "Have some espresso?" he asked, gesturing to the desktop machine and then returning to his paperwork. "Want some caffè Americano?" The sergeant nodded his assent, poured himself a shot, added water, and settled into the captain's spare chair. "There are some considerations here," said Alberto, turning to face Stefano. "At first blush, the stories those two gave me didn't add up...not at all. And the motive of this robbery? To grab two cell phones? That makes no sense at all...the woman had something of intrinsic value concealed in her purse. That much was apparent—as it was to whoever helped himself to it." Stefano sipped the hot espresso and tipped back thoughtfully in his chair.

"Go on," he implored emphatically. Stefano was, in fact, killing time before his shift began.

"This caper was planned," continued the captain, "and is not the simple matter the papers make it seem to be. The car that was stolen—or so the story goes—taken in broad daylight from an embassy, with not one single guard on duty at the time, and the gate left open, to boot. Of course, we were not allowed to interview anyone; the entire staff invoked diplomatic immunity. But, here...look at this." Alberto swung the screen of his computer around so that the sergeant could see it: a staff listing of the Ukrainian embassy, each person's headshot appearing over their name, staff position, and, if they had one, an email address. "Look at this man's face," said the captain, reaching around and tapping the eraser of a pencil on one man's photo. "Recognize him?"

"No," answered Stefano, after leaning forward and squinting at the image.

"I didn't think you would. Now, see how the magic of facial recognition works wonders," remarked the captain. He tapped a few keys and moved the computer mouse, and a new image, a grainy black-and-white mug shot of the same man looking much younger this time, appeared on the screen. Stefano let out a low whistle as the information accompanying the photograph quickly unrolled on the screen beneath it.

"Ivan Kuznetsov. A Ukrainian, born in 1971," explained Alberto. "After the Soviet Union broke up in '91, he fell in with another guy, and the two of them started stealing. Little stuff at first...later on, plundering arms caches and hijacking shipments of Russian military weapons that were going to all points of the earth, then selling them. Ivan was the muscle and the recruiter; the other was the brains. Then a Russian army officer, David Mikhailov, a man who was born in America of Russian parents on diplomatic assignment, caught onto the game, after returning from Chechnya. He wanted in on the action. He had the goods on Ivan, muscled in, and took over the operation. No one ever saw Ivan's partner alive after that. It became a huge business, known as the Steel Pipeline once the dark net came into being, operated by a gang the two formed. Mikhailov eventually got found out, was court-martialed, went to prison, and escaped after being inside for two months. He went underground and eventually made his way back to America...where he is now, living under another name, most likely a composite of his old one, I suppose. And probably engaged in criminal activity. As to Kuznetsov, he was arrested in the Ukraine but disappeared in 2013 just before President Yanukovych was ousted."

"And Mikhailov? Where is he exactly?" asked Stefano, clearly astonished. The captain paused for a moment before answering.

"Boston, we think. There's some kind of connection tying all of them together: Saluzzo, that daffy old priest, Kuznetsov, and his buddy. I'm sure of it, but I need time to work on it."

Alberto looked at his watch. He would try calling Toscanini again soon; hopefully he would eventually pick up his voice-mails and finally start answering his calls. Alberto needed to bring him up to speed—wherever he was—and find out what in the world he was doing. Alberto knew he couldn't cover up his sergeant's unexplained absence much longer.

"Well, thank you, Captain, for the espresso and the news...but, I have to begin my shift," said the sergeant, looking at his watch, arising, and heading for the door. "Oh," he exclaimed, stopping abruptly and turning around to face Alberto, a sheepish expression suddenly appearing on his face. "I almost forgot...the chief wants to see you."

"I figured as much," replied the captain gloomily, looking at the computer screen and Kuznetsov's mug shot.

"Oh, one other thing," added Stefano, now looking down at his feet. "He said to bring him the keys to your vehicle."

Chapter 23

Trust, But Verify

Several time zones away, Patty Callahan, still posing as a policewoman, raced down the dark street on foot, still intent on trying to find out what was going on, who was involved, and where the Lincoln—and the large man carrying what looked like a body wrapped in a sheet—had gone. Also, whether or not someone had actually been killed tonight. Three blocks away, after circling back as close as Jimmy dared to come within range of the Saluzzo family's brownstone, Herman pulled the Lincoln into a parking lot opposite Nacosto's Italian Ristorante, parked it in the second row of cars, and doused the headlights. Jimmy wriggled out of his formal coat, yanked off his necktie, and donned his leather jacket, his usual attire.

"Stay here," he said softly to Herman, "and keep the engine running. If you see that big lunk Jerry Garrantino, flag him down and get his ass into the car...tell him to wait for me." Jimmy headed off toward the brownstone, turning up his jacket collar and jamming his hands into its pockets.

It was a few seconds later when Jimmy saw a woman, a uniformed police officer, running toward him. He suppressed the urge to hasten his pace and instead lowered his head, hunched his shoulders, and stuffed his hands deeper inside his pockets. The cop hustled past him. That's when Jimmy noticed the sneakers the cop was wearing: clean, white sneakers. *When the hell did beat cops in Boston start wearing sneakers?* And then along came another person, a tall, thin young man, running for all he was worth down the middle of the street, wearing black trousers and a black leather jacket. *No reflective clothing, no brains...had to be one of those whacko marathon runners,* thought Jimmy; *they just can't ever use the damned sidewalk.*

Before turning the corner onto the street the Saluzzo residence was on, Jimmy slowed his pace. He pulled a discarded newspaper from a trash can, folded it, and tucked it under one arm to take on the appearance of a man casually strolling home, perhaps from a late work session at his office. He stepped around the corner; the street beyond was empty—no cops, no cars. He looked at the brownstone; the building was lit up like a carnival. He walked slowly past the front door, which apparently had been closed and secured, and just beyond the building. He then ducked into an alley, looking about for Jerry; there was no one to be seen.

"Dammit," hissed Jimmy under his breath, turning around and leaving the alley in the direction he'd come, "the big bastard's pulled an end run on me." Jimmy retraced his steps. If Vince Saluzzo had been murdered tonight, his old lady was taking it pretty well, Jimmy thought. Perhaps the priest was administering last rites while Maria prayed and awaited the arrival of the meat wagon? Something wasn't quite right. He sensed it. Jimmy headed back toward the Lincoln, walking briskly now.

Arriving at Nacosto's, he found several people standing outside the restaurant's front door; Jimmy crossed the street in order to avoid them, ducked behind a parked Volvo, and then peeked around its fender to briefly watch them and to listen to what they were saying. A cop, the lady cop he had passed on the sidewalk, was talking to a teenage kid wearing jeans, a

T-shirt, and a white apron that had dark, greasy stains on it. The kid, nervous perhaps, wiped his hands on the apron while he talked, then ran the fingers of one hand, then the other through his hair. There was something vaguely familiar about the cop's appearance.

"You wanna know what happened?" the kid asked the cop. "Okay. I came around the corner from the alley from puttin' the garbage out back, just in time to see that dude hop into that big Caddy and take off. Older guy, had a big gray jacket on...and a bottle in one pocket. Looked like a wino to me. Maybe some lot lizard who hangs out down street. Never seen him before." The cop scribbled furiously on a pad while an elderly man standing behind the kid was waving his hands and having a shouting match with a younger fellow, while a well-dressed woman and three small kids stood by like statues.

"What's your name and date of birth?" asked the cop.

"Brian Jones. April third, 1998," he answered.

"Thank you for your help. Now, I have to call this in," said the cop to the kid. "I need to use your phone; my radio's back in the car three blocks away. And I'm not walking back there. I need your help now." The kid and the cop disappeared into Nacosto's; Jimmy slinked back into the dark depths of the parking lot, found the Lincoln, and hopped in.

"Let's go," he said to Herman. "Downtown. Take it slow."

The restaurant's aproned garbage boy with the slicked-back hair let the cop—Patty Callahan, playing her quickly improvised role perfectly—through the foyer and down a short hallway that led to the manager's office. He pointed to the phone on the desk and an empty chair.

"Go ahead, you can use the phone—the boss is out back talkin' to some ladies, if you need to talk to him," said the kid. "I got stuff to do. My shift's almost over." He turned on his heel and sauntered off down the hallway. Patty looked about quickly; there were no security cameras to be seen, only monitors showing activity in the cocktail lounge and dining rooms. On one of the screens, Patty saw a tall man dressed in a suit, most likely the boss—perhaps even the owner himself—standing beside one of the tables and chatting with several seated customers. A small television on the manager's desk had been left on, and Patty noticed that an old episode of *Law and Order* was playing. In it, a holed-up gunman had taken hostages and was threatening them. Something clicked. It was what her father used to say: "A plan. You've got to have a plan." Patty formulated one—quickly. She focused immediately on the telephone on the desk. And turned up the volume on the TV.

She hit the speakerphone button and punched in three numbers: 9-1-1. She removed her hat, pulled off her badge, and stuffed them into an empty Nacosto's take-out bag while she waited and listened. Upon hearing someone on the line pick up and answer "9-1-1, what is your emergency?" Patty turned up the collar on her blue jacket, headed quickly back up the hallway, and slipped out a side door into the alley.

"If none of you can get me out of here, I'm going to start blowing heads away. Maybe yours, first," hollered the gunman in the TV show. He fired a shot into the wall, missing the hostage's head by inches. "That cop you saw outside? That's how you'll look––soon."

"Wait, wait, please!" implored the women who was the hostage. "If you want a way out, I'll find one. And there's money here, too. Look! You have to believe me!"

"Again, 9-1-1, what is your emergency?" sounded the exasperated voice on the telephone. Then, on the TV show, another shot was fired. The Boston Police Department, thereafter alerted via its frustrated 9-1-1 dispatcher, quickly took notice of a possible hostage situation (and of an officer presumably down) unfolding at Nacosto's, and fired off a volley of police officers toward it. All who were available within a two-mile radius responded—with exception of the two bike cops processing Vince Saluzzo for grand theft auto, DUI, and drunk and disorderly conduct.

Patty moved slowly, cautiously toward the back of the alley. She turned left at its end, walked around the corner, and found herself at the restaurant's back entrance, its doorway flanked by two signs reading: "don't even think of parking here and if you are found here at night, you will be found here in the morning". *I don't intend to be found here*, thought Patty, moving cautiously and trying to figure out her next move. All was still but for the humming of the big ventilator fans in the wall pumping the delicious aroma of fresh-from–the-oven lasagna and just-baked garlic bread into the night air; they overcame the strong odors wafting from the nearby open dumpster.

Indeed, all was still but for the voice behind her that suddenly called out. "Officer!" Patty spun around, almost dropping the take-out bag. A tall, gangly-looking young man with intelligent features stood before her. He'd evidently spotted her entering the building and then gone looking for her outside Nacosto's after not discovering her inside the restaurant. The man shielded his eyes to shut out the harsh glare from the floodlight beaming down from Nacosto's rooftop behind Patty; he squinted in an effort to see her better.

"Oh, I apologize," he said, almost bashfully. "I think I am mistaken."

"No problem," said Patty coolly. "Anyone can make a mistake. What's going on?"

"I think I have just witnessed a crime, but, I am not sure. In fact, I'm not sure exactly what I saw...it may have been an abduction."

"Oh," countered Patty, "you mean that little fracas a few blocks away? I saw that, too. I know the neighborhood. It's...what you might call a family problem."

"Well...it looked suspicious to me," he said. *Shit*, thought Patty, *the guy's inquisitive.*

"You mean," said the man, "something like a family feud?"

"Oh, yeah," answered Patty, turning around and stepping along toward the street. "That kind of thing goes on here all the time. Boston thing...been going on for years." She picked up the pace; the young man—Lorenzo—walked along with her.

"So, why were you here?" Lorenzo asked.

"Just passing by—curious, you know." A siren sounded in the distance, its sound rising and falling, drawing closer. "You?"

"Same as you," answered Lorenzo. And then, after a nervous pause: "Perhaps we shouldn't be here." He had seen and read the warning signs.

"Suits me," said Patty," her mind pinwheeling in an effort to find a way out of being caught on security cameras, seen by the police, or with this stranger...or having anything to do with him tonight. "I need to walk back to my car," she said, doubling back from the alleyway and heading toward the street. Regaining the sidewalk and heading briskly toward the intersection farthest away from Nacosto's and the approaching police car, with Lorenzo tagging along beside her, she popped a question, turning toward him to ask it.

"Tell me something: Do you know the Saluzzo family?" Lorenzo, absorbed in his habit of avoiding cracks in the sidewalk and trying to think about his next move, jolted. He stopped.

"Saluzzo *family?*"

"Yeah. That's what I said."

Lorenzo looked at her, astonished. "No. They are some people I have been asked to investigate. That is why I am here tonight."

"Investigate? Pal, who are you?" queried Patty, making sure to stop under a streetlight before turning to look at him. "And, more important...who do you work for?"

"Police," answered Lorenzo, fumbling for, and finally pulling forth from his black jacket, the badge of the Polizia. It dangled from the lanyard hung around his neck and glittered like gold in the streetlight's glare. Patty's heart skipped a beat.

"You're investigating...the Saluzzos, right?" she asked.

"Right," he answered.

"And you are...Boston PD? A statie?"

"Neither," replied Lorenzo. "I will admit I could use your help. I am a stranger here, on assignment. I am Sergeant Lorenzo Toscanini with the Polizia...from Rome, Italy." Patty took a step backward.

"Pal," she said, looking at him very carefully, "if you're from the police in Rome, I'm from the moon. Let me show you something." She withdrew the cop's hat from the Nacosto's take-out bag. "Now, tell me why you're here."

"Like I said," replied Lorenzo, unfazed, "to investigate why Mrs. Saluzzo and that priest, who I'm sure you must have seen, may have staged a robbery in Rome the other day. I suspect criminal activity."

"Really?" asked Patty.

"Oh, yes; perhaps even more so, now. You saw what went on; it looked like someone had broken into the apartment where Mrs. Saluzzo and the priest were dropped off by the taxicab. I arrived just after they did."

Good, thought Patty, *he didn't see Jimmy and his crew.*

"But I did see what looked like a big Lincoln drive off," added Lorenzo.

"So," asked Patty gamely, "what could have gone on here tonight, do you figure?"

She was testing, getting ready to call his bluff a second time; it just might work.

"Gangland stuff, perhaps," said Lorenzo contemplatively.

"You know, don't you," asked Patty, trying her best to stare Lorenzo down, "I need to cover something with you. Impersonating a police officer is a serious offense."

"Of course it is," countered Lorenzo, looking her up and down. "So, you...please tell me...why you are wearing sneakers. You have no radio, no gun. I don't believe you are police...and I do not believe you are telling the truth."

"I'm not a cop, but I am telling the truth," answered Patty. "And I know you have no jurisdiction here...if you are who you say you are. You want answers; so do I. That's why I'm here tonight. You see this hat, this badge?" She still held the hat she'd pulled from the take-out bag. "My father manufactures these––or has them made. My father manufactures a lot of things...covered up a lot of things...maybe even a couple of graves in his time. I'm trying to get to the bottom of a family problem, a death that took place a long time ago. It looks like you're trying to figure out something; let me tell you—what you saw, it was an attempted execution taking place tonight. And my father was behind it."

"Your father? What is he?" queried Lorenzo.

"Everything I'm not."

Lorenzo looked at her carefully. She was obviously a young, spirited person. An American. Lorenzo was not quite yet used to Americans...or their crime problems. He was used to solving his own problems that were mostly caused by Rome's petty criminals, and those that were endured by his long-suffering captain. He drew a deep breath. "Perhaps we can cooperate," he suggested. "It would help me in my mission—and you, with yours."

"That would be good," said Patty. "Let's walk. My name's Patty Callahan, by the way." They walked along once more, sauntering along the sidewalk; the sounds of sirens closing in behind them near Nacosto's eventually fell silent. They found themselves on a street corner in the North End where they paused briefly underneath a gargantuan neon sign hanging from a building. The sign proudly displayed the business name in a vertically arranged column of letters gently pulsating with bright red light. Underneath the name, horizontally arranged, was the word *PIZZA*, and below that, almost as an afterthought, the words *BEER* and *WINE*. The sign cast a warm glow onto the brick buildings across the street.

Patty and Lorenzo exchanged glances. "I'm only looking for answers," stated Lorenzo casually.

"Sure you are," countered Patty, "but I'm one up on you. I'm looking for answers about who killed my aunt, years ago...and to what my father is doing right now, and why he's doing it...trying to get to the Saluzzos."

"Okay," answered Lorenzo. "So...can we work on this together? So many of these things, you know...they involve criminals...they stay in the business for years, many years. They are hard to follow. But I think...from what my boss has told me...there's another player in the game—perhaps this game, the one your father and the Saluzzos, too, have been playing...he has been at it for a long time."

Somewhere far above the pair, perhaps four or five stories up, an apartment window was wrenched open, releasing into the night air the sounds of an old Steely Dan song. The music and the lyrics gently drifted down to the corner. The occupant of the apartment stuck his head out and then dumped an ashtray out the window, presumably before he went to bed. Bright red sparks cascaded down the side of the building, glancing off the bricks and tumbled to the sidewalk, where they briefly bounced around Patty and Lorenzo's feet. "He'll do it again," said Patty, looking at Lorenzo sternly. "Whoever killed my aunt will do it again. And then my father will do whatever he thinks is right...things he's done to harm people before...if he thinks it will set things straight...and then...he'll do it again."

"I think we need to talk more about this," said Lorenzo.

"It's too late," said Patty, looking down at her watch. "I have to go. Can I drop you off some place...and maybe we can we talk tomorrow?"

"Yes," he answered. "I have to find a place to stay."

"There's a hotel not too far away," she said. "Off I-93 on Boston Street, over in Dorchester. I can take you there––it's on my way home. And no funny stuff on the way."

"Okay; please do take me there; thank you," Lorenzo replied. "It's been one long, very long, day." He rubbed his forehead in apparent discomfort.

"I think we need to talk with my father," said Patty. "Let's put it on the docket for tomorrow. Give me your cell phone number. I'll call you." They headed toward Patty's Honda as Lorenzo assiduously scribbled down the number; the car was parked not that far away from the spot where Marvin had just silently and surreptitiously retrieved the no parking, funeral cones.

"You don't trust your father, then, do you?" asked Lorenzo, watching closely for her reaction, but there was none.

"I don't," she said, without apparent emotion.

"Well...can I trust you?" Lorenzo stopped to turn completely around and looked her in the eye.

"Yes," she replied, also stopping. "And right now I'll trust you...but I remember something Ronald Reagan said, back in the '80s when I was a kid: 'Trust, but verify.'"

"I've heard that, too," mused Lorenzo, stifling a yawn. "He said it a lot, back when he was dealing with Gorbachev. It was actually a Russian proverb."

Chapter 24

The Sisters Play
Their Hand

Herman Schmidt—or more exactly, his doppelganger, John Fischer—walked down the sidewalk toward St. George's Cathedral, carrying something that was precious to him. He held it close to his torso within the confines of his jacket, cradling and protecting it. As he did so, approaching and passing through successive arcs of light cast from overhead streetlamps, his shadow at first loomed large and long on the sidewalk, like a stick figure drawn by a primitive cave dweller, then small, as short as a dwarf, eventually disappearing as he stepped underneath each lamppost. The shadows cast by the overhanging tree branches clustered overhead seemed to reach out toward him to rake across his moving figure like long, black, evil fingers as he stepped along toward his destination. It was late—yes...very, very late. So late that he had had to congratulate himself for having finally finished his work and gotten out to find a liquor store still open at this witching hour, in order to properly reward himself. Ahead of him, just beyond an intersection where traffic lights no longer held back traffic but instead blinked red and yellow at lanes devoid of cars, loomed the dark, gargoyle-infested spires and craggy Gothic outlines of the cathedral. Like a glimmer of hope for anyone looking for a sign of life to be found in Cambridge at this late hour, a light glimmered in a basement window of the hulking, dark building.

John crossed the street and headed directly toward the light, much as a ship's captain navigates toward a beacon seen on a moonless night. As he neared the window that was propped partway open, he heard a lively conversation coming from within. He paused momentarily; the conversation stopped, then resumed when he took several more steps farther down the sidewalk. He decided to circle back, walking softly on the lawn so that he could hear the conversation, but not be heard. He'd assumed, wrongly, that he had been alone in the cathedral.

"What's the point of hashing all this out now, anyway, Sister Anna?" asked one of the nuns, Sister Mary. They were seated at a table in the somewhat stuffy basement meeting room of the massive, imposing cathedral, and had its window propped open to gain some fresh evening air. From far down the hallway came the rumbling sounds of a boiler heating hot water. Sister Mary lit a cigarette, took a long, luxurious drag, savoring it, and then slowly exhaled; the plume of smoke drifted lazily toward the open window of the little room. She looked down at her cards, then up over them and across the table at Sister Anna.

"The whole point is," answered Anna condescendingly, glowering at Sister Mary with impatience, "is that we're here to play cards. So, play."

"Right, we are," retorted Mary, momentarily taking her eyes off the deck of cards on the table and stubbing the ash off her Marlboro in the ashtray. "But, the whole deal is, we have to plan this and make it work—or none of us will be coming out of this clean when we come back from Atlantic City on that bus next week."

Footsteps sounded from outside the window, paused momentarily, then resumed their pace. Sister Josephine jumped to her feet, spun around, and looked out through the window. "A man just walked by. I don't know who it was," she reported.

"Wasn't him, was it? That fella workin' on the organ?" queried Sister Mary.

"I couldn't tell," answered Josephine, resuming her place at the card table. "It was too dark."

"Oh, Lordy, Lordy!" said Mary. "That little squirt working upstairs. He's a nuisance, to be sure."

Sister Anna invoked the best Massachusetts accent she could muster, looking around the table for effect, and then stated emphatically: "He's a faht in a mitten!" There were giggles all around the table. "He's only a problem for you because of your vows of poverty...that have you making the rounds upstairs, checking under the cushions in the pews when you hope he's not watching, finding change so you can play poker!"

"I wonder...is he here to spy on us, do you suppose?" asked Sister Josephine. "He looks kind of book-wormy. Someone from the diocese?"

"C'mon, Josephine," retorted Mary. "Why would the bishop send someone here to spy on us? If he's a spy, why then, he's probably spying on somebody else."

"Oh..." offered Anna, "you mean maybe Father O'Donnell?"

The nuns looked at each other in surprise. Then Carmella winked at Josephine and said, "Well...you never can tell! Who knows what he may have been up to!"

"What he needs, that kid," said Sister Mary, "is a good whack with a belt to set him straight. Playing that blasphemous music...sittin' up there solo at the keyboard half the night, sounding those pipes like he's Captain Nemo and he owns the place. Why, if he'd been caught even listening to that trash in our school as a child, he'd have been hung out the second-story window by his heels for a while, to let those demented notions drop out of his head!"

John, now free of his role as Herman, chuckled to himself and decided to ignore further goings-on within the room below. He blithely continued on his way after concluding his eavesdropping, tiptoeing up a walkway and entering the cathedral through a side door. He sauntered down the long, dark aisle, climbed a short stretch of stairs, and sat down heavily on the organist's bench, where he had left a single light on to illuminate the multiple ranks of keys. He raised his eyes, sighed, and reflected briefly on the majestic appearance of the hundreds of the organ's gilded pipes, many of which stretched upward 40 feet or more, almost reaching the vaulted peak of ceiling. He then withdrew the bottle from the paper bag, opened it, and began his ritual––the old ritual of his form of communion––one long forsaken but recently revived, one that would have nothing to do with Sunday services. But one that would, once again, bring him to the point where he could play music from whatever inspired him, whatever came into his head...and awaken the next morning to battle the dragon of sorts, the hangover that would inevitably appear and confront him.

"If it were me," interjected Sister Anna crossly, "he'd have been hung out there to dry for a while, for sure...but from his toenails 'til he repented!"

"I'll bet..." began Sister Josephine.

"Good! It's about time," interrupted Sister Anna impatiently, drumming her fingers on the tabletop.

"No. I'll bet," the other sister continued, this time in a louder voice, "that he drinks up there. D'you know what? I'll bet he was a bed-wetter as a child. Those kids at the orphanage who were bed-wetters...I heard they all became drinkers when they grew up."

"Where are we, girls, on our little secret plan?" asked Josephine seriously, looking around the table at the other three nuns.

"Not so bad," answered Mary. "Old Poppa D'Angelo's car is appraised at 26 grand...our charity raffle is huge this year because of that...the ticket sales for the Caddy just went over $59,000 today. They're all dying to get that car, those folks are. And they all just love our old coach who's donating it. You know the deal: I say we borrow not five, but ten percent off the top, take it to Atlantic City next week on the tour, and shoot to triple our money at the tables, the wheels, blackjack, and the slots. Right? Four of us, four different ways. For two days. That spreads our odds...and gives enough action for everybody." She scanned the other players for a reaction.

"Sounds good," commented Carmella, nodding approvingly, "but, what could go wrong?"

"Nothing's gonna go wrong," said Mary. "This is gonna be an all-expenses-paid, round-trip junket to Atlantic City...with many happy returns. Now, here we go." There was a muffled sound of the deck of cards being shuffled, then crisply cut; it came startlingly close to the sound a kid's bike makes when its owner has cards stuck in the wheel spokes to make noise and attract attention, but not that of his father when he finds his deck of playing cards is missing on Friday night. Each of the nuns pushed a quarter forward into the middle of the table. Mary dealt with the alacrity of a sightseeing tourist feeding pellets to trout at a fish farm, each card making a soft *plop* on the table when it landed.

The sisters picked up five cards apiece and studied them; Carmella tossed in a quarter. Josephine tossed in another. "I'll raise you," said Anna, tossing in two quarters.

"Okay," grumbled Mary, tossing in two herself.

"You know...or maybe you don't," interjected Sister Josephine, smugly maintaining the pious facial expression of a saint's statue carved from pure white marble, "that there is *another* game, don't you? High stakes, big money. Really close...it's down on the south shore."

"C'mon, Sissy Jo," said Mary sternly, "there's no casinos down there. There haven't been since Prohibition."

"Oh, yes," answered Josephine, "there is one. It's what they call a sleazy casino...it's a floater...and they have what they call a 'black ops blackjack club.' It's by invitation only." Mary's eyebrows shot up clear to her wimple in astonishment, then back down."It does exist. It's come back to some of those big old places. I got a guest player's password from one of our parishioners...he's guaranteed to be okay; his brother's a cop. One is scheduled for tomorrow night, down at the Knothole Lounge annex. We could all go as his guests. What do you think?"

"What...are you crazy?" asked Mary. "We could get set up. We could get 'made' in a place like that."

"Fold," sighed Sister Carmella, tossing her cards in the center of the table.

"Call," chimed in Josephine, tossing more coins in, "and you ought to think about it. Less than an hour away. Ocean air. No bus time. And if you want really high stakes for a payoff, there's baccarat."

"Whoa! Hold it right there, girl," admonished Mary. "What kind of people are we talking about gambling with here...James Bond? Bezos? Trump?"

"No," retorted Josephine, "but if you want ROI, not pie in the sky, you might want to look a little closer to home and this gig, rather than the Jersey Shore and gambling with penny-ante bus tour mommas and grandpas on Social Security."

"You're telling me the big money's close to Boston and not in Atlantic City?" queried Anna.

"You bet your rosary beads it is," shot back Josephine. "You know what Willie Sutton said, don't you?" The other nuns looked at her with blank faces. "C'mon! He was a famous bank robber, years ago. A reporter once asked him why he robbed banks exclusively. And he said, 'Because that's where the money is.'"

"We're not bank robbers, Sister Josephine," exclaimed Carmella primly, folding her hands together on the table as if relaxing her knuckles.

"No, of course not," replied Josephine, staring at her and putting on her best look of an angelic expression. "We're...pot hunters." The ensuing guffaws of all four poker players resounded within the little basement room; the noise escaped through the open window but went scarcely farther.

"What do you say, Sisters?" asked Mary, looking around the table. Are we in on this? To give this floating blackjack game a shot before we go to Jersey?"

"I'm in," said Carmella."

"Me too," added Anna."

"Why not, Mary?" asked Josephine.

"Okay," said Mary, lighting another cigarette. "But this has got to fly way, way low under the radar. Get us in."

"All right, then," said Josephine, tossing more quarters into the pot. Mary pulled forth another cigarette from her pocket and prepared to light it.

"Again, Sister Mary?" asked Anna, frowning in obvious disapproval of the vice of smoking.

"Just one more," answered Mary, opening the matchbook and pulling out a match. She looked at it pensively, then looked up at the sisters sheepishly, smiled and said, "It's my only sin."

Upstairs in the cathedral at that very moment, John pondered why, after all this time, he had not heard from his handlers. He took another pull from the fifth of whiskey and mentally relegated Jimmy Callahan and Jerry's defection from the job to the past. After all, the job was done...or at least, Jimmy thought it was. He flipped on the blower switch for the organ and prepared to play from memory a few bars from Beethoven's Fifth. *Captain Nemo, indeed,* he thought to himself, suppressing the urge to laugh as melody rumbled forth from the massive organ. The sound shook the rafters, and the whiskey shook off the ill effects of the last few, rough days. *Captain Nemo would have been proud of me.*

Several miles away from Cambridge, the three Saluzzo brothers were engrossed in earnest conversation as the car they were in—Franky's black Sedan DeVille—sped along Commonwealth Avenue to the midnight meeting that had been arranged. "The old Bay Colony Hotel, right?" Franky asked Bobby, who was sprawled comfortably in the back seat.

"Right," he answered, peering out a side window into the darkness. "Somebody's revived the joint. Reopened about a year ago."

"Who is this guy, anyway?" questioned Charlie, seated beside Franky, who was driving. "I mean...he calls us up out of the blue, says he's got something on the guy who pulled that job on the old man, wants to meet almost at closing time in the lounge...this is some kind of setup." Franky briefly turned to glance at him, turned back, and quickly swerved to avoid an elderly woman and her dog who'd been ambling across a crosswalk, now frozen in fear. Franky cursed and blew the horn at them.

"It was a setup that landed old Dad where he is, stupid," grumbled Bobby from behind him. "Set up for a rap for grand larceny, DUI, destruction of public property. So now we wait for the bail hearing to find out how much it'll cost to get him out of the jam. The lawyer will try to work his magic tomorrow morning and spring him, or he damned well better. Who knows what that will cost? Now...if this guy wants money tonight, I'll make sure we're not throwing it away."

"So c'mon, who is he?" queried Charlie a second time, turning around to look at Bobby.

"Some small-time operator; he did time in Walpole for grand theft auto," answered Bobby. "The ear-hustle on him from the joint is he's got a nice, full-time job now with some very discreet supplemental income."

"Yeah," chimed in Franky, gunning the car to beat a traffic light that was about to change, "that's what I'd like, too...some supplemental income. What's this guy's name?"

"Big Billy Jones. Known on the street as 'The Buddha' but when he was in the bucket doing time in his orange peel suit, the cons called him 'The Great Pumpkin' if I remember right," Bobby replied, matter-of-factly.

"You're kidding me," said Franky, swerving around a slow-moving truck. He peeked in the rearview mirror to make sure he'd cleared the truck, then at Bobby. "Why?"

"When you see him," answered Bobby, "you'll know."

"This is stupid," groused Charlie. "I ain't wasting time tonight talking with some monkey-mouth grad from con college. This is bullcrap."

"Now, you listen to me," snapped Bobby, punching the back of Charlie's headrest.

"No, you listen to me!" Charlie whined in protest.

"You listen to *me*, you two geniuses," Franky hollered, slamming on the brakes. The Cadillac screeched to a halt in the middle of an intersection. He turned in his seat to glare at his two brothers. Late-evening traffic flowed turgidly around the stopped car, drivers gawking at its three occupants. "You want to screw this up? Okay Charlie, you get out right now. Get out, crybaby, and go home to momma. Better get your ass on the subway fast, 'cause it shuts down in half an hour. And while you're at it, go piss on the third rail, just for luck, so you can get a buzz on before you go home." Charlie pouted, stuffed his hands into his pockets, and fell silent.

"Don't want to go?" asked Franky, leering at Charlie. "Didn't think so." He turned back, took his foot off the brake, and the Cadillac moved forward once more.

"C'mon, let's have some peace," snapped Bobby from the back seat.

"Yeah, yeah," agreed Franky, nodding in agreement and contorting his face, rolling his eyes upward and looking at Bobby in the rearview mirror. "Peace, brothers. Amen." He waved his right hand in the air for emphasis like a revivalist preacher. "And let's not forget, while we're at it: Love thy neighbor." There was a long pause, then Franky giggled and added wryly, "Just don't get caught runnin' out the back door!" The three brothers roared with laughter as Franky pulled the car over to the curb near the entrance to the grand old hotel.

The three men stepped from the car and toward the hotel stairway, where a doorman, seeing them approach, jumped into action and opened the thick, plate-glass door. Bobby was already on the phone, ignoring the doorman's welcome. "I'm textin' our man," he mumbled to the brothers, "so we can find him. Okay...okay...here we go." The light from the phone flickered across his face as he read the message. "He's in the tavern, in a booth just outside the restroom doorway." He tucked the phone into the pocket of his jacket. "Let's go," he urged, "we ain't got all night." The brothers walked briskly past the main registration desk and a battery of elevators, down a long, carpeted hallway, turning right at the entrance to tavern, then shouldered their way past the smiling, white-jacketed maître d'.

"We're looking for a friend," Franky said to the surprised man, leaving him standing at his desk, still holding three menus and wondering whether the men were undercover police officers or hit men on a mission.

The three strode past the bar, from which the hum of close conversation could be heard and where late-night patrons were toying with their swizzle sticks, idly stirring ice cubes in their glasses as they sipped and savored the last round of the evening before closing time. The idle bartender, transfixed by a ball game he was watching on TV, could have passed for a department store mannequin. "There he is," grunted Bobby, pointing a finger at an enormous man seated at a booth—so large, in fact, that he occupied most of one double seat—gorging himself on a heaping order of fish and chips. The fat man looked up from his king-size platter, spotted the brothers, and waved them over, still busily stuffing french fries into his mouth with his other free hand. He smiled, displaying several gaps in what had once been a full set of very irregular-looking teeth. The brothers squeezed themselves into the seat opposite the man, Billy the Buddha. "I see what you mean," whispered Franky to Bobby, who quickly dug an elbow into Franky's rib cage.

"So Billy," began Bobby, "What have you got, now that we've dragged ourselves down here at this ungodly hour?" The large man smacked his lips and then wiped them with a greasy, ketchup-stained cloth napkin that would probably never come clean again.

"Hold on, m'man," he said, dropping the napkin on his lap and turning to rummage about in a paper shopping bag perched on the seat next to him. He produced an 8-by-10 photograph and handed it across the table. "I think that's a car—and a man—you are no doubt keenly interested in," he said.

"Callahan," muttered Bobby, "and that Lincoln Mom said she saw. Okay, so you've got a picture—so what?"

"Correction," said Billy, spearing an entire fish fillet with his fork and plunging it into a paper tub of tartar sauce with little regard for the splattering of its contents, "I have *many* pictures of the car and the man. And they're security-camera pictures with times and dates."

"To what do we owe this act of generosity?" huffed Franky sarcastically, staring impassively at the fat man.

"Oh, ho ho!" chortled Billy, shaking the booth as he laughed. "It's not generosity; it's a matter of humanitarianism." The brothers stared at him. "After all, as you can see," continued Billy, taking a bite of fish, "I like to eat. And as they say...if you wanna play, you gotta pay. Maybe you can make a deposit as a show of faith?" Bobby wrinkled his nose, reached into a pocket, pulled out a $100 bill, and tossed it across the table. "More," said Billy the Buddha, munching on the fillet as tartar sauce dribbled from razor stubble on his chin and dripped like melting icicles onto his lap.

"Give *us* more," countered Bobby.

"Try this one on for size," said the Buddha as he gnawed on his fish, handing over yet another photograph, this one showing Jimmy Callahan walking along the sidewalk outside Nacosto's Italian Ristorante. The Lincoln was plainly shown, sitting across the street in a parking lot, with a man sitting behind the wheel. "Nice, right?"

Bobby tossed another bill across the table. "Let's have it all," he said.

"This is an act of faith, you know," sniffed Billy the Buddha, pausing to gulp down the last dregs of beer in his mug. "My faith is in this: that the enemy of my enemy, whose actions have brought some trouble down on me, will be my friend. I can befriend you, but with only one thing at a time." Bobby tossed a 50 across the table. Billy withdrew the last of several photos and handed them over to Bobby.

"And that, my friends...is my act of kindness for the night," Billy said, adding, "You have no idea how much this has hurt me. Emotional distress. Upset stomach. And troubles with my employer, who is totally pissed off at me right now."

"I feel for you," said Bobby, "but let's cut the crap. Don't talk about it to your boss, or bitch about your little problems or whatever or go see a freakin' lawyer about your meeting with us. Your family shouldn't have the shock of seeing your name above the fold in the newspapers some morning. Goodnight." The Saluzzo brothers arose as one and stalked out of the restaurant past the watchful eyes of waitstaff and a security camera whose lens had been aimed at the Buddha's booth the entire time.

In the room beneath the main floor of the Knothole Lounge at Driftwood by the Sea, an alarm disturbed the repose of a young man sitting at a console; he had been monitoring the goings-on on several video screens. The new, automated facial-recognition alarm had jolted him into action; he keyed the pre-assigned call number. "Boss, the new system's got one," he said when the other party answered. "You'll never guess who...actually, it's three." Far down the hall, where the gambling tables had been cleared for the evening and the house's takes tallied, Mikhail Zuckoff answered, animated and shouting into his phone: "What? Who?" Katrina Valenchnikoff came closer in order to listen. "Them? Oh, this is good. The plan is working."

"Saluzzo's boys?" asked Katrina.

"Yes...the three not-so-wise men," answered Mikhail, smiling and wrenching a cigarette from the pack in his pocket.

"This new recognition software works wonders. From our friends in China...very clever folks, those Chinese, don't you think?" he asked, turning to look at her. "Most resourceful," he added, with a wink. Katrina stared at him, not sure what to think...did he know about Zhang? Was he looking for a reaction rather than a response? She denied him one.

"Absolutely," she replied, nodding in agreement, her face completely guileless. Katrina was not one to blink when under fire. And now, perhaps, neither would the Saluzzo brothers be, focused on their enemy and preparing to exact revenge for their father's humiliating disgrace.

Chapter 25

Digging up Bones

All over Dorchester—in apartments, duplexes, and houses, big ones and little ones, tall ones and short ones, in low-down diners and upscale restaurants and in high-rise hotel kitchens—eggs, like daylight, were cracking. In thousands of households and other venues, the new day—and the performance of the daily rituals of dressing, breakfast, dishes, and departures—was beginning. There was the *thud* of newspapers tossed from delivery trucks as they hit front doorsteps and porches. The *pop* of toast springing up in toasters, awaiting butter and jam. The sizzle of eggs and bacon cooking in pans, and the rattle of dishes being brought down from cupboards. The drone of news and weather reports emanating from speakers on televisions and radios, and the grumbles of men, women, and children as they prepared for another day while they listened, complained about the news (or the weather report) and begrudgingly hauled their shoes and socks on. Jets with thundering exhausts, backlit against the pink, brightening dawn sky and heading for far-off destinations soared overhead. Below them, other early morning traffic, daisy-chains of cars with their headlights still on and glistening like diamonds, surged across the bridges spanning the dark waters of Fort

Point Channel. Their sounds drowned out that of the small, silver-gray Honda that pulled up at the litter-strewn curb outside Jimmy C's. Everybody except the two people in the car, it seemed, was headed off to someplace other than Dorchester.

Lorenzo looked out the car window, scanning the hours sign on the front door of the store, to be sure that he and Patty had arrived at the correct opening time. He then glanced down at his pedometer. Had he started off the day right, he wondered, walking around his hotel in order to add some steps? As if on cue, a rotund, elderly man dressed in jeans and a shaggy-looking, fleece-lined jacket soon appeared, opening the store's door from the inside, and proceeded to twist a bundle of keys as he unlocked the steel gate separating the door from the sidewalk and pushed it back. The gate folded upon itself like a collapsing accordion that made little noise except for a mouse-like squeak of rusty protest. He paid no attention to the small car parked along the sidewalk and its two occupants. He disappeared into the depths of the store, and soon its lights blinked on. "That's Marv," said Patty from the driver's seat. "He's Dad's right-hand man. Let's go in."

Patty and Lorenzo stepped out of the car and headed toward the store's entrance, Patty wearing scruffy jeans and a Boston Celtics sweatshirt, and holding a full-to-bursting paper bag containing several items. Lorenzo wore a long, black overcoat, taking care to keep his hands inside his pockets. They entered the store side by side. Marv, just doing cash-in at the register, was caught by surprise at the pair's arrival as he dropped nickels and dimes, counting them as they went, into the open drawer. "Hey, g'morning, help you guys with something?" he asked, looking up from the register drawer, a surprised look suddenly overtaking his face as he saw who he was looking at.

"No," answered Patty, as coldly as a bank robber briskly going about her business. "I'm here to see my dad." There was a clash of coins as Marv clumsily dropped a newly opened roll of dimes into the drawer in astonishment.

"Patty...is that *you*, child?" he asked, quickly looking down at the cash and then staring anew at her.

"Yep, that's me," she said, "plain old Patty. I have business." She and Lorenzo headed toward the stairway to the basement office.

"Hey—wait a minute," Marv implored, slamming the cash register drawer shut. "It's still early...and, hey...you know how Jimmy hates to be interrupted."

"Maybe I don't," replied Patty, turning over her shoulder to glance at Marv. "I haven't spoken to him in seven years...so, how would I know? But I really think I need to interrupt him...right now." Patty and Lorenzo headed down the narrow set of stairs.

Jimmy was seated at his desk with his back turned toward the stairway, his eyes studying the far wall. He'd had to turn his attention away from the newspapers he'd been studying. The big fire downtown was the news of the day. Vince Saluzzo's arrest on charges of DUI and grand theft auto had apparently gone unnoticed by the press, but not by one of Jimmy's old pals, who had casually heard of it on his police scanner when acting as a lookout while his associates were pulling a job. Giggling as he did so, he had gleefully informed Jimmy in an early morning phone call about Vince's bizarre attempt to seemingly put himself to sleep with the fishes. Jimmy, now stuffed full of adrenalin, had skipped breakfast after hearing this. The thought of hopping a plane to a faraway destination in case his scheme was discovered kept interfering with his instincts, which told him carry on and figure out how everything had gone so wrong...why not only Jerry but also Herman had apparently crossed him and deceived him...and what to do about it. Upon hearing footsteps of people descending the stairs unannounced, he spun around. For a brief second—perhaps for the first time in his stint in many years in business—as his two visitors appeared, Jimmy found himself at a loss for words until he recovered and asked, "What in the hell are you doing here, girl?"

"I'm here to see you, Dad," Patty answered, her blue eyes blazing like early evening stars in the twilight of the murky office. "Kinda here to ask your forgiveness...after all, I broke in after hours and stole something from you." Jimmy stared at her, caught off guard. His arms dropped to his sides. She opened the paper bag she had brought with her, and pulled out the cop's hat, badge, and uniform she'd taken the night she had sneaked in.

"What do you mean?" asked Jimmy, dumbfounded. "I haven't seen you in here. Not in years."

"You wouldn't have, Dad. I have the key, the spare gateway key," she replied. "Oh, by the way, don't worry...and don't ask me for it unless you're ready to make a deal. It's in a safe place." Remember," she began, "when I was little, and Aunt Rose gave you that picture of me? When I said that when I grew up, I wanted to be like her? And then I said the same thing about you, to *you*?" Jimmy nodded, feeling somewhat numb. "But...didn't you tell me I should always tell the truth?" she asked, a smirk on her face. Jimmy recognized it; it was his own triumphant smirk, passed down to his offspring.

"Yeah...guess I did...long ago," Jimmy said dejectedly, rubbing his forehead.

"So," asked Patty, crossing her arms defiantly and staring at her father, "what are you going to do? Off me and stuff me in the trunk of your car? Dump my body in a quarry and go on to your next deal? What? Or listen to me?" He resisted the sudden urge to pour himself a drink from the bottle stashed in his desk, in an effort to clear the storm clouds forming in his mind and the headache that was beginning to thump in concert with his quickening pulse.

"So, what the hell is this all about...and who is this guy?" he asked, struggling to retain his usual stoic appearance, pointing a finger at Lorenzo. This was trouble, trouble plain and simple. No, it was going to be double trouble; he could feel it coming on strong.

"Well," volunteered Patty, "first of all...let's start with me. I wasn't seen here the other night, thanks to that uniform I put on, after I got in." She put the hat and uniform back in the bag. "I blended in with all the dressed-up dummies upstairs, so I could get close enough to you to hear what you were saying...every word of it...and I got some notions about what you were going to do to Vince...and decided to look closer. You know, to dig around a little bit."

"Oh, crap," said Jimmy, "what are you talking about? Now that you've come here, today of all days, after I haven't seen you for years. This is not a good time. What is it *you* want? Money? Florida getaway? A condo? Wash your car? Wax it? What?"

"Dad, get real. First, you plan to take somebody out—I hear you planning a murder—and then you line up Mom, who knows nothing about what you're up to, to help you out a little bit along the way. How very convenient and thoughtful of you! You dragged her down enough years ago...and then you left her. But I know you can't leave that thing with Rose alone—and now, neither can I. You had so many secrets—all those things you kept from me and Mom about your business, always the business. And now you've got Mom mixed up in it. She doesn't want to know; she's had enough. But did you ever think I deserved some answers? Did you ever think about what you do could make me lose my job, because of who you are and what you do with your business? That's what *I* want: answers. I have a business too; it's called my life."

"*I* deserve answers, Patty, first of all," replied Jimmy. "Like who the guy sitting next to you is. Let me guess: he's a cop." He glared at Lorenzo.

"I am not with the Boston Police Department, if that's what you think," Lorenzo calmly asserted. "I am visiting from Rome, Italy."

A sardonic smile spread across Jimmy's face. "Oh, now," he said, "this is *really* getting interesting. And you are here...with my U.S.A.–born daughter...why? This is my store...not the Italian-American Club."

"It's difficult to explain," Lorenzo began, "but bear with me, please. Mrs. Saluzzo, who I surmise you surely must know...she was traveling in Italy...in Rome, with a priest. They were robbed in the city...a very strange occurrence, and under circumstances that made me question the truth of the pair's statements to us."

"So?" countered Jimmy, leaning forward and focusing sharply on Lorenzo as if to challenge the policeman to reveal his identity. "And who is 'us'? What are you? Interpol? Secret agent man? Are you charging me? Gonna extradite me to sunny Italy? Good. I could use a vacation. Bring it on." He leaned back and reached for his pack of cigarettes, then tossed it onto his desk. "C'mon, what's your point? Why are you two here like a pair of Mormons out on the last day of a door-to-door recruiting drive?"

"Because," answered Lorenzo, "I have received information leading me and my superiors to believe the Saluzzos are being set up to take a fall. By foreign agents—you could be, too."

"Oh...oh, I see now," said Jimmy, chuckling, and slapping his right hand down on his desk. "My wayward daughter shows up with an attitude after seven years of no communicado, comes into my office with a total stranger, and tells me she wants to come clean because she's done me dirty, breaking into my joint, spying on me all of a sudden with no good reason; then, she has pangs of conscience. She gets into high gear and spins me a hard luck story about the wife of someone who's done me wrong for years. And I'm supposed to love this, right? And do what—help the cause and make everything right for somebody? Her? Seems to me I'm being set up, all right—by you. Get this: I'm not playing your game, Patty. Not for you and your anonymous pal. Whatever your hook is, I'm not biting today. Go find yourself another fish. There's plenty in the sea...just a few miles down the road. Look out, Patty's pal; you could find yourself in there...soon."

"Dad, Dad...can you just listen for a minute?" Patty implored.

"Think about it...why else would I have been told by my boss to follow Mrs. Saluzzo and the good father and watch their movements?" asked Lorenzo. "I need to find out where all this leads. And my department will need to work with your FBI to learn more, and share its information."

Jimmy scratched his forehead, then reached for the pack of cigarettes, paused, and looked at Patty's friend. *Oh, God, the FBI. It was time to think*, thought Jimmy. *Yes, stop and think. Who is this guy's boss?* "Are you two crazy?" he asked Patty, staring at her. He then shifted his glance back and forth between Lorenzo and Patty. "Yeah, that's what I'm asking. You know what I think? You, Patty, and Ellen—who no doubt set this gig up—are as certifiably crazy as two gals in a T-bird going over a cliff together in a movie. And maybe your friend, who's come here today, is too. So...let's have the story." There was dead silence. "Smoke?" Jimmy asked Lorenzo, thinking that his offer might provoke some answers to his question.

"Yes, I do now and then, but don't trouble yourself—not unless you're having one, too," Lorenzo answered.

"Yeah," said Jimmy, "I sure will," withdrawing one and then tossing the pack across the desk to his visitor. "Tell me now...who's your boss?" asked Jimmy. "Let's hear it." He flicked his old Zippo lighter and lit his own cigarette, snapped the lighter shut, and then slid it across to Lorenzo.

"I used to smoke a pack a day," said Lorenzo. "Now it's only a smoke or two each day." He lit up and then passed the lighter back across the desktop.

"Isn't that..." asked Patty, looking at her dad's lighter and then at him, "isn't that Rose's?" Jimmy stared at her through the wisps of smoke that enveloped his head.

"Yeah, it is," he answered. "I still have some of her stuff." Suddenly, the drift of the conversation changed, relieving some of the tension. Jimmy stared at his daughter and replied, "It was Pop's, before that." And then, "It was my granddad's, too." Lorenzo fidgeted in his chair.

Jimmy relaxed somewhat, assuming the air of a storyteller. Telling a story would lighten the mood and allow him some time to think about his next move. Yes, Jimmy was always thinking about his next move. "Let me show you something," he said. He pointed to an old framed photograph hanging on the wall, partially obscured by a jumble of things piled atop a filing cabinet. He stood and pawed them away to better reveal the image. It was a black-and-white photo, decades old, of a classic wooden-hulled powerboat. The ravages of time and handling had chewed away at its edges long before it had been framed. In the photo, smiling men wearing hats and rugged-looking clothing stood on the boat's long, stylish deck, brandishing liquor bottles and guns, tokens of their trade in illegal booze and contraband in the Depression years. Men who had used lethal firepower and a fast boat to serve their cause.

They had, Jimmy knew—all of them, just like him—been immersed too far and too long in an illicit trade to ever revert to being the innocent boys they might have been before they appeared, rampant and in their glory days, before that camera's lens. No wonder that their images had been captured by a man whose finger might have hesitated or trembled a bit just before he pressed his camera's shutter button all of 80-odd years ago, freezing their images until a time when they now appeared, cold, distant, their life forces long departed. But they were once real...deadly earnest in their trade, keenly clear of mind and of any conscience in the day-to-day, sometimes cruel execution of their way of earning a living.

"That was in Prohibition, Patty," her father said, taking his seat again and dragging on his cigarette. A smile wrinkled the corners of his face. He leaned back in his chair and reflected upon the storied past, one that he knew well. "That boat was Granddad's. *Bad Penny*...the fastest rumrunner on the coast in the early '30s. That boat was legend; nobody ever caught old Granddad Mick making a run with that hotshot craft of his. It always came back after a run; that's where the name came from. He made a fortune. Tony Nacosto wanted to get in on the action in the worst way. Tony tried to take him out many times, but in the end Mick put him out of business. Ol' Mick timed it just right; he sold out to the O'Malley family just before Prohibition ended. Nobody ever found out what became of Mick's money after he cashed in and went legit. It sure didn't trickle down to me!"

"Who was Tony Nacosto?" asked Patty, eyes wide now, falling into the narrative like an understudy in a play rehearsal. Lorenzo smoked in silence and listened. He pulled a small notepad out of a pocket and took copious notes.

"Tony was a two-bit wharf rat," said Jimmy, with an air of disdain. "He stole liquor—bottle by bottle—just in off the docks after it landed, from the big dogs in the game, and peddled it to the speakeasies and gin joints. He was a low-down thief...but he got away with it. Then he finally got himself a fast boat and started hijacking loads coming into town, out beyond the coast on the open water. Ol' Mick tuned up Tony's boat one night, for sure. It settled the whole matter."

"Huh?" said Patty. "What do you mean?"

"Blew it up," answered her father. "Tony lost one of his sons who was on his boat that night and the old man learned his lesson. He came back later on with a new attitude, spent some dollar bills, and got into another line of work. Restaurant business. There was peace. And now, the Nacostos are into other businesses...and so are the Callahans." There was quiet in the basement room. "So, give," said Jimmy. "The key, and your silence."

"No Dad," said Patty. "We haven't even started yet. Rose. Tell me about her. You know you owe me."

Jimmy stared at her. She was obstinate...an upstart. She was, indeed, his daughter. "Okay," said Jimmy, turning to a filing cabinet and opening it. "I guess you're old enough to know." Patty and Lorenzo exchanged glances.

"I'm ready," said Patty, "and I'm sure as hell old enough to know whatever you've been holding onto all this time." Her father pulled a bulky manila folder from the cavernous depths of the file cabinet and plunked it down on his desk. Wisps of dust blew around it. Jimmy pulled a faded, withered front page of an old newspaper from the folder and held it up so that Patty and Lorenzo could see it. Up above the tattered fold was the bold headline: "Showgirl Snuffed." And underneath it, the blurb: "Shooter leaves two dead in late-night rampage."

Jimmy sat there, staring at the newspaper. He cleared his throat, not without some difficulty, and began. "It was in the bad old days. Rose had a show...and a good manager...at the club, the Mayflower...back when there *were* clubs in the Combat Zone."

"Excuse me?" asked Lorenzo, perplexed. "A war zone?"

"No," answered Jimmy. "But it did all start during 'Nam. They called it that because of all the guys coming back from tours, whatever, overseas. It was where they went for entertainment and to blow off some steam. Shows, strip clubs, dirty movies––you name it––when they 'got back to the world'.

There were soldiers, sailors, Marines, all in uniform and on leave or rotation, whatever. And there were fights, street action, almost every night. So that's why they called it the Combat Zone. Washington Street. It's all new buildings now, all Chinese restaurants and whatnot."

"So...why? What happened?" asked Patty.

"Dunno," answered her father. He ran his fingers through his hair, put his hands down on the desk, then looked at her with the dazed expression of a man who might have been lifted off the streets, taken back to the past by a time machine and swiftly returned, disoriented and bewildered. "The best I could figure out, someone was shaking down the manager. He was probably being squeezed; the place was starting to lose money. Word on the street was some new high-pressure outfit moved into the neighborhood and picked up the rackets. I tried my best, believe you me, to find out more; nobody would talk. So, my guess is whoever pulled this job knocked off anyone who got in his way––or wouldn't pay. Silence speaks volumes."

"But," said Patty, "she didn't die there."

Jimmy rubbed his forehead, tried to massage away the troubles of times past. He looked up and answered, "Right. That story was a cover. The cops and the feds kept that close. Nobody knew...not you, not anybody else even in the family except me and your mother...Rose knew who did it, and why, and that information died with her. Died right in town. Where the feds put her up."

Their conversation was interrupted by the sound of shouting upstairs. Heavy footsteps sounded on the stairway as Jerry Garrantino rapidly descended it, and then burst through the doorway into the room; he stood before Jimmy and his guests, his face contorted with rage and his fists clenched. One of them held a short length of steel pipe. Marv appeared right behind him. "I couldn't stop him, Jimmy," he yelled. He reached for Jerry and the giant shoved him against the wall, and held him there by his neck.

"You skunked me, Callahan," Jerry growled at Jimmy, as Marv gasped for breath. "You paid me half and left me with the whole job to finish; the last I saw of you was your taillights."

"I paid you half," retorted Jimmy, "and you shoved off. I never saw your ass again, much less Saluzzo's. Half-done. So...*you've* got the beef? Let him go, Jerry. Your beef's not with him." Jerry released his grip on Marv's neck. Slowly. "Marv, we're okay; just go back upstairs and take care of business," Jimmy said. Marv took a deep breath and staggered back up the stairs.

Patty and Lorenzo eyed the large man warily. "Thanks to you and that kid, my dynamic duo," snapped Jimmy, looking at Jerry, "I've never had anything go so bad. The only saving grace in this mess is that everyone except my two guests here believes Saluzzo got drunk and stole the car. His wife isn't talking to anyone—yet."

"So?" asked Jerry. "What does that mean to me?" He patted the palm of his free hand menacingly with the end of the pipe.

"That means," replied Jimmy, "you'd damn well better play along with me—and my little audience here—right now. Because I'm covering for you; I'm paying the price for your screw-up and the kid's. Nothing comes cheap. In a way, I'm kind of glad you showed up here. These people have been looking for you. Identity theft and parole violations are a big deal. Turning you in could get me off the hook."

"What kind of bull are you talking?" grumbled Jerry.

"C'mon, stupid," Jerry admonished. He pointed at Lorenzo and Patty. "Who the hell do you think these people are, and why they're shaking me down?"

Patty, sensing an opportunity to play her cards, pulled the cop's hat out of the paper bag. "Guess who?" she asked, looking at Jerry and smiling. "Your turn," she announced, looking over at Lorenzo. Lorenzo, playing along as well, pulled his badge and holder out from beneath his coat, and smiled. Jerry stared at the hat and the badge in astonishment.

Jimmy looked at Jerry and shook his head. "Good going, Dick Tracy," he sneered at the big man. "All of a sudden now, you just figured out who's who, didn't you? Tell you what," Jimmy continued, "you come back here tomorrow, just about closing time, and I'll settle with you, just to keep your mouth shut. It won't be as much, since my new friends here are deep into my wallet now. But know this: they have others who'll be watching to make sure you don't go wandering off somewhere."

"We have two cars outside, right now," added Patty, who had looked at Jimmy's video monitor for his alarm system and spotted two police cars parked outside. The cops were, in fact, about to have a broken-down car towed away. "Look at the monitor."

"Listen," Jerry said, coming closer now to Jimmy, looming over him. "There are some very real possibilities in this game, if you're playing me. Your luck could run out, in a very bad place. Maybe not the first time, maybe not the second time, but maybe the third time is when someone finally gets your number. Just like that little rat I saw who got clipped at Sergeant Sully's back in '78. Like me, the guy who had it in for him was hot and bothered; he was righteously pissed at his partner. He missed a couple of times, but he finally nailed him. Don't believe me? Those two slugs from his piece are still there, in the wall of that phone booth where that little stoolie sat, beggin' the FBI to take him in. He got his brain drilled when he knew he got made, after he ran out the back door. Baled out and ran...like what you did to me. No loyalty."

"Don't you tell me about loyalty," Jimmy spat back at Jerry. "You can go now, and you can leave the pipe––unless you want to try convincing the cops outside you're a plumber. But just remember...if you don't show tomorrow—if you try to dodge us and start talking all over town to sell your story—you will be found. By me. And then the next time I see your face, I'll be patting it goodbye with a shovel." Jerry took his cue, dropped the pipe on the floor, turned, and trudged up the stairs. There was silence.

Patty was the first to speak. "Dad, do you see what you're up against now? You've got a war started. I can feel it. And I don't want to be around when the shooting starts. Where did you find that clue as to who killed Rose?"

"On the Internet," said Jimmy. "It wasn't a clue. It was a posting on the Classic Crimebusters site. Don't believe me? Here, I'll show you."

He reached for his computer keyboard and mouse and searched for the site, staring into the monitor. "Okay, there's the site," he announced. Patty leaned around her father's desk to see. "Okay, now I'll show you the message board," he said, jigging the mouse around. But it was all in vain; a look of consternation crossed his face. "I don't see it now, damn," he muttered.

"What was the person's name?" asked Patty.

"It wasn't a guy's name, it was a street name. "Something...the bear. Oh yeah, Ivan the Bear." He typed the name into the site's search bar. Suddenly the monitor's screen turned red. A row of skulls and crossbones appeared on it. Jimmy uttered a stream of profanities as he tried unsuccessfully to leave the site—or even shut the computer off.

"Dad, you've just been hacked," said Patty. "You've been had. For all you know, you've started a war based on fake news." Jimmy stared at the computer monitor for a few seconds as though he'd been stunned. Then he recovered his composure.

"If it's a war, it's my war, my rules," replied Jimmy tartly, seemingly unfazed by Jerry's appearance, his daughter's admonitions, and now his computer problems. He turned his gaze toward Lorenzo. "My advice to you, pal," he said smoothly, "is to leave the FBI alone. This conversation here, and what you saw today, never happened. You know what happens to people who call in the feds when they can't settle their own business matters, or when they try to settle someone else's in my business?" There was silence. "Okay, then I'll tell you," Jimmy continued. "They've got a lot of problems...first off, like trying to get someone to start their cars for them in the morning. Know what I mean?"

"I think we're done here," said Lorenzo, standing up. He looked at Patty. She stood and looked at her father.

"I'll call you, probably tomorrow, and set a time and place to get the key to you. I won't come here again," she said. Tell me one thing...who else would know about Rose and what happened back then?"

Jimmy leaned back in his chair and then tilted it back a bit. He stared up at the ceiling briefly and a thoughtful expression appeared on his face. "Jake. Police Detective Jacob Thayer. He was on the force in those days in the Combat Zone. Long retired now—and a big-time crime writer. He lives in Woburn somewhere. Probably the only one of those guys in the P.D. left who'd know about the case.

"*Jacob* Thayer?" asked Lorenzo incredulously. "The crime writer? I've read his books! He's amazing."

"Really?" asked Jimmy. "I think it's amazing nobody's gotten to him yet. He made some enemies back in his day...none of them were my people, though. Maybe you can find out where he is through his publisher. But watch your step. Don't underestimate that guy...or anyone else for that matter. I never did; that's why I'm still here today."

Chapter 26

Two Cops and a Case

The small Honda that had been humming along at 70 since it left downtown crossed the Bunker Hill Memorial Bridge, the strands of its supporting cables strung from its towers appearing like the rigging of a huge clipper ship sailing blithely across the dark waters of the Charles. Patty's car radio was on, playing oldies. The DJ finished a rant about the Saturday morning traffic and then rolled out a 1980s song by Simple Minds. It was hard to forget the smooth, haunting melody and vocalist Jim Kerr's singing, entreating someone not to forget about him, that now flowed from the car's speakers.

"Your aunt, Rose, you just told me about her...she was the dancer, right?" asked Lorenzo. There was no reply from Patty. Lorenzo turned on his phone and fiddled with it. "You like to drive fast, don't you?" asked Lorenzo, looking at her and smiling, hoping to change the subject and whatever it was that was obviously dragging Patty's mood down. Her face looked drawn and haggard. He tried again. Badly. "Speedy—like a silver bullet, no?" Patty shut off the radio and steered straight ahead. She couldn't—wouldn't—forget.

The Honda was amongst the packs of cars in the traffic streaming northward on the Northeast Expressway, threading its way past Sullivan Square and then alongside the Mystic River. Most cars were almost bumper-to-bumper and side-by-side, sometimes veering suddenly to jockey for the lead like pugilistic drivers in a Roman chariot race. Patty turned off the highway at exit 36, and upon reaching the foot of the ramp turned onto Montvale Avenue, then headed west into Woburn. Lorenzo, glancing at his phone occasionally to be sure Patty's car was headed in the correct direction, watched for street signs at each crossroad. "I've got another text from the captain," he announced.

"What is it?" asked Patty.

"He's still asking where I am...but I can't reply just yet without compromising anything. He's confirming there are foreign agents behind the Rome robbery."

"Agents! You mean like, *secret* agents?"

"Yes. But they are criminals, too. One of them is Russian...and the captain says he may be here in Boston now." Lorenzo put the phone away and stared out the window. As if intrigued by what he had learned, and in a hurry to note some details, he reached in his jacket, pulled out an iPad, and started writing on it.

"What are you writing?" Patty finally asked him, turning and taking her eyes off the traffic momentarily and breaking the silence. Jolted by the question, one he had never heard before while writing, Lorenzo looked up at her.

"My novel," he answered. "Inspired mostly by Jacob Thayer's work and his new book, *Found Dead at Dawn*. I've called it *Game On; Bodies Down*, but it's just a working title. Just one of them. I try to write at least 2,000 words a day." The Honda passed through a succession of four-way intersections; each, it seemed, had either a busy filling station or else a fast-food restaurant located near it, with a conga line of cars queued up at its drive-through window. Once beyond them, the car rolled along more slowly, now going through quiet neighborhoods where kids were riding bikes and playing basketball. Parents were outside, too, mowing lawns and setting up backyard pools for the summer season.

"Just *one* of the titles?" queried Patty, looking at him in astonishment at this revelation.

"Yes, I am working on several. Turn left at the next intersection," instructed Lorenzo. Patty slowed to turn onto Green Street and after several blocks turned onto Garner Avenue, with its rows of modest one- and two-story homes.

"I don't see it," she said, looking from left to right to spot the house number Lorenzo had given her.

"There it is," said Lorenzo, pointing to a small house that stood at the end of a short, paved driveway, surrounded by trees. "No wonder we couldn't see it until now. This is fantastic. I had no idea I would ever get to meet Jacob Thayer." He turned to look at her, caught her glance as she looked toward him. It was obvious from the look on her face that his enthusiastic expectations of meeting Jacob Thayer and bonding with him were not going to be under consideration during this unannounced visit.

Patty turned into the driveway and pulled up before the small white cape and a single-car garage. A chain-link fence ran around the boundaries of the lot with the exception of the side facing the street. The curtains were drawn in all the windows of the house, yet the door of the garage yawned wide open; inside it reposed an old, square-looking Ford, a Crown Victoria sedan. Cardboard boxes overflowing with old newspapers were lying on its hood, a lawnmower sat partway under the front bumper, and a lawn rake had been left leaning on one of the car's dusty fenders. Patty turned off the ignition and put down both front windows of her car; no sounds came from the house, but a dog could be heard barking furiously somewhere out behind the garage. It didn't take much imagination, based solely on the volume, for either Patty or Lorenzo to conjure up an image of a large and possibly vicious animal, one that was hopefully restrained by a chain or else held at bay behind the chain-link fence.

"I hope, really hope, that we find something out today," Patty declared, as she withdrew her car keys and stuffed them into her jacket pocket. "I have to work tomorrow—I can't get out of it. I have a flight to Denver. I've begged enough favors from Theresa to cover for my days off, and she's got the same flight assignment tomorrow as it is. Are we good?" she asked.

"As good as can be," he replied, making sure that his badge was displayed properly in its holder, hanging pendant-style from a cord strung around his neck. "I am very much looking forward to meeting this great writer! Let's go." The pair hopped out of the car and warily approached the side door facing the garage. Lorenzo took pains to avoid stepping on any joints in the concrete walkway and glanced at the pedometer he wore on his belt. There was no doorbell button; he stepped up to the door and rapped on its window. The barking suddenly stopped, and the absence of any sounds of life whatsoever coming from either the house, the garage, or the backyard seemed ominous. Patty stepped up to the door and listened as Lorenzo knocked again.

"Looking for someone?" came a soft voice behind them. The pair spun around to find an elderly man standing there; in his left hand he tightly held the leash of a Doberman Pinscher that now bared its teeth and growled at the two visitors. The man's right hand was stuffed in the pocket of his jacket; judging from the sizeable bulge in that pocket, he had more than just his hand in it.

"Yes," asserted Lorenzo, "we're looking for Jacob Thayer, the writer."

"Who wants to know?" queried the old man, peering at them through large, thick-rimmed glasses, tufts of his snow-white hair getting ruffled momentarily by a gentle breeze. The Doberman suddenly lunged at Lorenzo and Patty, almost pulling its master off his feet; he took a quick step forward and jerked on the leash, pulling the dog backward and regaining his composure. "You'll have to forgive him," said the man, now raising his right arm ever so slightly, still leaving his hand in the pocket. "Dillinger gets a little ugly when people show up uninvited and he thinks there's going to be trouble...and I do have trouble controlling him when these things happen; his patience goes right to hell. You know...you could, too, if it's trouble you're after. And Dillinger," he added, staring at Patty for full effect, "is a leg man."

"Look, Mister Thayer," said Patty, "if that's you...we're trying to find out something about my Aunt Rose's murder. I'm Patty Callahan, Jimmy Callahan's daughter." The old man blinked. "My great-grandfather was Mickey Callahan," she added.

"Who sent you?" inquired the man suspiciously as he held back the dog. The animal poised beside the man's baggy trousers and scuffed brown loafers seemed ready to spring forward. "How do I know you're just not some badge bunny digging for dirt in my backyard?"

"Nobody sent us," Patty replied. "I'm trying to settle something...something about my family."

"Oh...your family," replied the man. "Ever-suave Jimmy C. Your dad then. Good businessman, always kept his nose clean...after he got cured of cracking safes by moonlight. No relation, of course, to the famous '30s jail break artist, Tommy Callahan. So, Jimmy C., eh? Grandson of the big-time Prohibition rumrunner Mickey. And I'm talking to his great-granddaughter. Okay, girl...so, since you're so smart, and if you are who you say you are, tell me about a bad penny."

"The *Bad Penny*," answered Patty, eyeing the Doberman warily, "was Granddad Mickey's boat. He named it that because it always came back to his dock unharmed; it always returned. It was his cruiser, a big, fast motor boat he sold after he made his last run."

"Okay," said the man gruffly, hauling back on the dog's collar as it barked and then lunged forward once more. "And whose boat did Mickey take care of on that last run?"

"It was Tony Nacosto's," answered Patty. "He blew it all to hell."

"Well, I'll be," said the man. "And," now looking at Lorenzo, "you, mister brass buttons undercover, who are you and why are you here with her?"

"Sir, I am Sergente Lorenzo Toscanini, of the Rome, Italy Polizia." The old man stared at him as though Lorenzo had three heads.

"Lemme see that badge," he said, stepping closer to peer at it. The Doberman sniffed Lorenzo's shoes, then looked up at him and wagged its tail. "Wow," exclaimed the elderly gentleman as he stared at the badge, paying no attention to the dog. "No wonder I didn't think you were from downtown; you are definitely from *out of* town." He took a step backward and regarded Lorenzo carefully. "Wait a minute now, are you here to talk *Callahan* family business...or 'family' business? Or both?"

"Callahan's," said Patty, glancing nervously down at the Doberman.

"Then that's fine," said the man, withdrawing his now-empty right hand from his pocket, extending it to Lorenzo. "Yes, I'm Jake Thayer. Boston Police Department, retired. And I do know a few things about Patty's aunt. That famous cold case from back in the '70s. Still open." The dog let out a thunderous bark, looked up at Patty, and wagged its tail again. "Never mind him," said Jake, shaking his head. "He's worthless...all show and no go...he's a big pussy. Let's go inside and sit in the kitchen." Jake suddenly broke eye contact with his visitors as he turned and looked about, scanning the neighborhood for any signs of suspicious activity, or for a car, either approaching or sitting parked along Garner Avenue. There were none to be seen.

Jake Thayer opened the door and gestured for his two uninvited guests to enter, then followed them, switching on an overhead light and slamming shut the door. While Patty and Lorenzo stood waiting, he unhooked Dillinger's leash from the dog's collar. He hung up the leash on a peg on the wall, then pulled off his jacket and hooked it over it; a heavy object in one of its pockets clunked against the wall. "Are you armed?" asked Lorenzo.

"Yes, of course...I'm the carrier of my own insurance policy," replied Jake, feigning an innocent look and asking Lorenzo in turn "are you?"

"No," Lorenzo replied, looking around the kitchen. He turned back and smiled at Jake.

"May I say, sir, I follow all of your excellent writing—I have every single one of your books!"

The spacious kitchen was clean; no dirty dishes stacked in the sink or garbage waiting to be taken out. No dust bunnies on the floor. But it was unusual in terms of what it contained besides a table and chairs, cooking utensils, and a refrigerator...and it was less than tidy. A small desk with a computer, keyboard, and notepads stood in one corner by a large window overlooking the backyard, and on its left side stood a stack of blue cardboard document file boxes; a Winchester pump-action shotgun was leaned up against the wall on its other side. Almost every countertop was cluttered with stacks of *The Boston Globe* and back issues of the *Baystate Police and Detective Gazette*. On one side of the kitchen table an enormous Maine coon cat laid, curled up and sound asleep in a low-cut cardboard soda carton. "I know what you're probably thinking," said Jake to his guests, who were staring at the cat. "That's not her litter box; Kittery was a stray when I got her, and I think she must have lived in a warehouse for a long time. She likes to sleep either in a box or on one, like those document boxes. Now and then in the dog's bed, too. C'mon, let's sit down."

That said, Jake roused Kittery, stroked her back, then picked her up and gently deposited her on the floor. The cat twitched its tail, regarding Jake crossly, then stalked over to a large, stuffed dog bed near the desk, entered it, and sat. Dillinger, alert to this invasion of his territory, barked...then padded over and stuck his nose over the edge of the bed, whining. The cat promptly swatted Dillinger's nose; the dog let out a yelp in sudden discomfort, jumped back, and then skulked off down a hallway, presumably in search of a safer place to lie down. "See? I told you," Jake said, shaking his head in mock disgust. "He's totally useless...just a big pansy." Jake sat down heavily at the table. "Pull up chairs, you two," he said, "and tell me more about why you're here."

Patty and Lorenzo exchanged glances. "Who wants to go first?" Patty asked.

"I'll go," said Lorenzo. "First of all, I am here on police business, to investigate why two tourists from Boston were robbed of certain items in Rome a few days ago...and why they lied about what was taken. Also, why someone in Boston ordered a hit on a member of their family who was in Boston while the two were away. It was not successful...but it cannot be a coincidence."

"So," asked Jake, staring at the Italian cop, "who's the mark, the lucky guy?" Patty and Lorenzo looked at each other again.

Lorenzo turned back to Jake before answering. "Vincent Saluzzo," he said softly.

Jake put his elbows on the table, folded his hands together, and then rested his chin on them, posing thoughtfully before he made an observation. "I hope this is not the beginning of another war," he said pensively. "Saluzzo's cleaned up his act a lot and although he's still what we call a person of questionable character, nobody would go after him that way unless it's someone with some real horsepower who wants to take over his rackets and his business, which are worth a considerable chunk of change...or unless his sons have burned somebody badly...which they're dumb enough to do. And they're too dumb to take over from their daddy. They're young enough to have been cooling their heels in their high school principal's office the day I retired, but I've read about 'em." He paused, then asked Lorenzo: "Any more questions?"

"Just one...no, maybe two," answered Lorenzo. He drew a long breath and then let it out. "I'm curious—as an aspiring writer—how many words do you write each day, and what time do you get up in the morning?" Patty frowned in disapproval at this departure from what should have been business.

"What time do I get up?" countered Jake, a puzzled expression overcoming his face. "What does *that* have to do with this?"

"Oh nothing, really," said Lorenzo sheepishly. "I've always read that the most successful writers write at least 10,000 words a day, and they get up early...at 4:00 a.m. That's when they get their best ideas."

Jake coughed, a dry, hacking cough that turned into laughter. It took a minute for it to subside; he produced a faded, dirty blue bandana from his pants pocket and wiped away a tear from one eye...then honked his nose on it and returned it to his pocket. Patty, watching the performance, wrinkled her nose in disapproval. "Son," he said, reaching over to pat him on the shoulder, "that's total bullshit. Writing isn't a Japanese tea ceremony. I never know when I'm going to get up...or if I'm even *going* to get up in the morning. No rhyme or reason to it from day-to-day. The best ideas usually come when I'm polishing off a good bottle of chardonnay, which usually means I'll be sleeping way, way past 4:00 a.m. the next morning. You've got to stop falling for that crap. Okay, Miss," said Jake, turning to Patty, "now it's your turn."

"I'm here," she affirmed, "because I don't want to see a war started either. My dad's ready to start one...one with Saluzzo. He's got the idea Saluzzo is the one who had my aunt killed."

"I see," said Jake. "And how did he come up with this amazing information on a cold case now, after 40 years have gone by?"

"From some posting on the Internet...where he spends a lot of his time, trolling for information," answered Patty. "Something on a message board on the Classic Crimebusters site. A con's deathbed confession."

Jake coughed into his hands. The coughs subsided and then turned into a chuckle. "C'mon, Patty," said the retired detective, looking at her coyly as if scolding her. "In this down and dirty, rough and tumble world of the criminal element, no con ever 'fesses up on his deathbed and rats on another guy. Nobody ever even dry snitches on another guy...even if that guy is the one who's shot him, put him on his deathbed, and the life is running out of his veins. Unless, perhaps, just perhaps, that other guy is dead already and all his crew are dead too. Yeah, we live in an age of information...some of it is good, some is bad...and a lot of it is outright fiction."

"Fact," said Jake, putting both hands, palms down, on the kitchen table. "Rose Callahan was shot at the old Mayflower Club theater on Washington Street; so was her boss, Bernie Finnegan. That was in the fall of '78. I wasn't called right in on that case, but I have notes on it in my files. We who worked downtown knew the manager was into gambling, always paid his debts—smart man—but then agreed to do some money laundering when the theater's business started to slide downhill. We never got the goods on him. It was supposed the two killers were street soldiers, enforcers...but they weren't in with any of the gangs we knew, like the Monument Hill boys. So they were more than likely what you call associates, in the parlance of the underworld types. From the descriptions Rose was able to give, neither man was known to us...and of course, nobody in the neighborhood knew anything about them. Not until one of the two turned up dead, shot through the head; his body was found in an alleyway near some dive bar in the Back Bay area about a month later. And of course, nobody knew anything about that either...although his pockets had been picked clean."

"A cover...a faked robbery, probably," opined Lorenzo as he scratched his chin, engrossed in deep thought.

"Most likely," said Jake, "and a good cover-up for the real motive, too. We never found the bullet; it had passed through the man's head. We of course strongly suspected the body had been moved but could never prove it. The next morning, the FBI called us with information that the man, calling himself Johnny Jackson, had called them earlier on the night we found his body, near midnight. He was offering to turn himself in and turn evidence on his partner, who'd done the shooting at the Mayflower, if he could get a deal. He'd sounded nervous, scared. The call apparently got disconnected before much of anything was said and before a tracer could be put on the line. The FBI fiddled around for several hours, waiting for him to call back and also considering it out of their jurisdiction, but finally got a hold of our office. Too little, too late."

"So, did you ever ID the deceased?" asked Lorenzo.

"Yeah, finally...through dental records and fingerprints. The guy was a longshoreman who must have been recruited to do someone a little favor...I forget his name...he was a small-time fence, a guy who came from Russia originally, got in over his head gambling and was fencing stuff he stole off the docks," proffered Jake.

"Jake," asked Patty, "if you could find out where he was shot and recover some other evidence—like bullets from the same gun—could you find out if that gunman was who killed Rose?"

"Through forensics today, yes," Jake answered. "But, proving it, we don't know where that man was killed."

"I think I might know," said Patty. Jake's eyes grew wide in astonishment.

"How on earth would you know?" he shot back.

"Because Jerry Garrantino told us; he told me he saw a shooting like that. It was at a place called Sergeant Sully's, a bar—it's a restaurant with a sushi bar now, and it's near Kenmore Square."

Jake stared at her, dumbfounded. "Jerry? That big oaf? When did you see him?"

"Yesterday," Patty answered. "He's out...and now, I think he saw that happen."

"Where did he go? Where is he staying?" queried Jake, clearly intrigued.

"I don't know, but I'm betting he'll come back to see my dad again. He told me that he saw someone get shot in the head after the man tried to make a phone call to the FBI from a phone booth. Two slugs missed him before he hung up the phone and ran...and they're still in that phone booth, in its wall."

Jake reached for the telephone near his chair and punched in a series of numbers, first the phone number, then that of an extension. "Murray...that you? How are you? It's Jake Thayer," said the old man. "Listen...no, no, no. I'm not working on a book, not looking for some info; I'm gonna *give* you some info on an unsolved. An old one. One you'll never guess I've got a fresh lead on. We'll have to call in the FBI, too. As they say, it may be nothing, but...you're gonna have to move fast. What do you say...want to crack open a cold one with me?"

Chapter 27

A Clue from the Crypt

"Not that way, you guys...this way," said burly-looking Murray Maloney. He was looking over his shoulder and beckoning Jake and Lorenzo, who had paused to look down a passageway, to follow him. Murray, senior-ranking Boston Police Department detective and cold case team member, a man mentored by Jake while a rookie cop long ago, was the one who had taken Jake's phone call and arranged for this visit to the department's sprawling records storage facility. "Just follow me," he instructed, leading them down an aisle that ran between racks of wooden boxes and then turned into a dark, narrow corridor, one that led farther into the depths of the gloomy, high-ceilinged building. Motion-activated lights in the rafters flickered on one by one and caught the three men in pools of light as they found themselves walking along a pathway that became progressively more difficult to navigate. It was flanked by shelves of storage boxes, some jutting out into the pathway, each one sagging with age and the weight of its contents. All were labeled with the names of specific departments of the Boston police force and the month and the year those records had been placed there. The hands of those who had placed many of them on those dusty shelves—in the days of The Great War, the long, dry years of Prohibition, the jubilant months following V-J Day, or Eisenhower's inauguration—were now folded on their owners' chests, long buried in their graves.

Other boxes of records were stacked on pallets, some piled high, some low. The building had the musty smell of some remote chamber of a long-shuttered library—dank, stuffy, and airless from holding its trove of information safe for generation upon generation. The effect of perusing its aisles was a growing feeling of apprehension similar to that sensed while walking through a strange cemetery, wandering among tombstones and crypts. This one contained not bones but in effect their essence—preserved in dry ink, fading sepia-tone photographs, and crumbling parchment. They were records of the lives of people who had lived and died, many of them departing this earth under horrific, violent circumstances, and whose killers might, in some more recent cases still be at large, roaming free and hungering for yet just one more unsuspecting victim. "There is a backlog," Murray said, stopping suddenly and grunting as he shoved a box back into a spot on a shelf so that the three men could proceed, "in case you're wondering, of about 1,000 unsolved murders just since 1970. That's just Dorchester, Mattapan, and Roxbury."

"Hey, I feel for you, Murray," said Jake with evident sympathy. "Cataloging all this, sifting the info, following up when you get a lead and keeping after cases, no matter how old. Murder Incorporated is one thing; killers anonymous is another. And the newspapers are always on your back, busting your chops all the while when you can't make an arrest right away."

"Hey, Jake," commented Murray, turning around to face his old mentor, "retirement's coming...soon...and I've heard it sucks. Some of the guys who've taken it early come back and volunteer gigs here, helping with records requests, just to keep their hands in it. Otherwise, you know..."

"Yeah," said Jake, "they'd be going 'round the bend."

"I would," answered Murray, turning to look at Jake briefly, then returning his attention to the boxes, thousands of them, stacked from the floor almost to the full height of the ceiling on metal shelving units that sagged slightly under the burden of their combined weight. "You want 1978 and 1979...late '78 assaults and homicide with a deadly weapon, same for '79, right?" he asked.

"Right," affirmed Jake.

"This is all paper?" questioned Lorenzo, obviously astounded.

"Indeed it is, son," said Jake as he shuffled along. "How the hell we did it, got our jobs done—no fax machines, no Internet, cell phones...whatever...I don't know. We just did what we had to. Police work. Nobody does this stuff now. It's all digital. Push a button, and out comes the answer."

"Hey, '78," said Murray, a recollection of days gone by suddenly upon him. "Now, you're calling up some memories there." A thin smile creased his face. Wrinkles caused by his reflection on the past worked upward from the smile, played about his face, and briefly rimmed his eyes, drawing at their corners like a new pair of glasses with too-powerful lenses and providing Murray a sharply-focused, poignant, but vaguely disturbing look into the past. "That was the year of the big blizzard...February. Man, what a storm that was! My job—first one—was at Berkeley Street station that month...we got snowed in...ate, worked...slept at our desks for two days; we were buried. Nobody could get anywhere until the National Guard came in and dug us out. Mayor White was out taking pictures with his Nikon...a film camera...they showed up on the news—remember that?"

"Indeed I do," answered Jake, digging his hands into his pockets to ward off the chill within the vast dark building. Complying with visitors' regulations, he had left his gun at home and come unarmed, but he felt another reassuringly smooth, hard, cold piece of stainless steel in his pocket—his flask, a companion he traveled with when he was not keeping close company with its larger brethren at home.

"A man had to trust his instincts back then," asserted Murray, halting and hitching up his belt that sagged and drooped around his hips under the weight of the gun and perhaps also the cumulative effects of too many power lunches during the years. He pulled a small flashlight from his gun belt, scanning the shelves for the file boxes the three men were looking for. "And use his brains. Cooperate. Today, there's electronics, like the automobile ignition disruptor that'll stop a fleeing car dead. There's inPursuit, that new Intergraph software we got going; the computer brings all this shit together...in a cruiser, on a desktop—makes a matchup easy. It overhauled everything we used the past 40 years or so...since the years you're looking back into, guys. And then, maybe even then...not all of it. It's not science. Hell, I'm a cop, not a scientist." He turned around and faced Jake and Lorenzo, as if looking for their approval. They nodded gravely.

"When I came in, in '58," commented Jake, glancing about as the men walked slowly along, "there was no 9-1-1, no radios, except in cars...we had call boxes, telephones."

"No 9-1-1?" asked Lorenzo, looking at him quizzically. "How did someone call the police?"

"Oh, we had a phone number," answered Jake, with a chuckle. "You dialed DE8-1212. The 1212 was easy to remember—not so the DE8. So when Leo Sullivan was commissioner, we started putting up billboards all over with those numbers on them, so the public would get the message. That was about 1960."

In silence, the trio walked forward again, then halted when Murray, beaming his small flashlight back and forth in a searching pattern held up his right hand. He extended all five fingers as the commander of a company of soldiers does when exploring hostile territory, suddenly spots trouble, and orders his men to stop. "Here we are," he said. "This is the '60s through '70s section." He paused, turned slowly to look at the boxes on the right, then on the opposite side of the aisle. "Jake...my God...will you look at that now!" he exclaimed, pointing at one of them. "That box there...the name on *that* one brings back some memories."

"Yeah," said Jake, staring at the cardboard box that was sagging with age, bulging with documents, and upon which someone had scrawled in black magic marker and capital letters the name Barboza. Several question marks appeared beside it.

"Who?" asked Lorenzo, quite innocent of the named criminal's extensive history, "is that?"

"He *was* Joseph 'the Animal' Barboza," said Jake, turning to Lorenzo. "Never heard of him? Hit man...wild man...killed more than 20 people...at least, that's how many he claimed to have killed, back in the old days. No doubt that's why this guy has a whole box of documents here, just for him. He was mixed up in the McLean-McLaughlin wars, back well before your day. He was legend...and he sure as hell kept the department busy."

"Yeah...you could say that," opined Murray. "He was a crazy man, even back in the '50s; as a young guy he beat up people in the streets for no reason, down in old Scollay Square...you wouldn't want to cross him...and that gold Oldsmobile of his, with the 400 engine—our guys called it the James Bond car. Full of tricks, weapons hidden inside secret compartments in the doors, and that thing could lay down a smoke screen and go like hell if you were after it and were trying to catch him. My dad was a beat cop when he was in his prime, back in '65, and told me all the stories. Barboza was a street soldier for the big guys...but he didn't play by the big guys' rules."

Jake looked at Lorenzo in order to gauge his reaction. "What did he do...and what happened to this man?" Lorenzo inquired, an astonished look on his face.

"Barboza testified in the murder of Eddie Deegan, the master break-in artist," Jake answered as he withdrew the bedraggled blue bandana from his pocket, gave his nose a honk as if to punctuate the story while thoughtfully looking about the storage building, and returned the soiled bandana to his pants pocket. He obviously relished telling the story. "Deegan was a burglar extraordinaire, a lot like Patty's father was in his early days. Eddie...they called him Teddy...was found shot dead in Chelsea, interrupted while he was pulling a nighttime B&E...died in a backdoor alleyway with a screwdriver—tool of the trade—in his hand. Anyway, a screwdriver's no defense against three guns, is it?"

"This was before my time, but I've read about Teddy," said Murray. "Go on...tell our guest from across the pond the details."

"Right. Barboza turned on the mob...who he worked for...and framed four of its guys he hated. Sang a story to the feds—he threw those four under the bus—and he got shot dead after he got relocated to the left coast. It's said the FBI knew all along his testimony was false, but he gave them traction in their moves against the mob and was actually the first guy to enter the Federal Witness Protection Program, back in '69," added Jake. "Sometimes it's what happens to informants. They talk too fast before they think. Then, they wind up dead." He paused and reflected upon the years gone by since the days of the turbulence and mayhem his recollections brought to mind. "We're in the right section, as far as the years go, I guess." He looked around, then, for effect, stepped toward Lorenzo. "Do you know if that's the deal with your friend's aunt?" he asked.

"That she talked too much before she thought about what she was going to say?"

"Sir," answered Lorenzo, "I honestly do not know. I'm in a bit over my head here."

"Well, here we are," announced Murray, pointing at one box in particular. "Go knock yourselves out." He stood back and watched as Jake took a box marked 1978 homicide off the shelf and faltered under the weight of it; Lorenzo grabbed it, saving it (and Jake) from tipping over. The two men lowered it to the floor. "Crap," said Murray, "nothin's easy, is it? I'll help you guys. C'mon, let's take this fancy-ass dish of tidbits from the past over to the table." Helping to pick up and support the sagging underneath of the file box, he steered it together with Jake and Lorenzo over to a nearby bench. They dropped the box onto it and lifted the lid.

Jake ran his fingers over the tabs of the file folders. "Okay, let's start with January, just in case anything's misfiled," he said, looking at his watch; it was 9:15 a.m.

Some two hours later, the bench had become littered with stacks of folders. The three men pored over them and their contents. Looking for some comic relief, Lorenzo joked, "Whatever became of the saying that X marks the spot?" as he sifted through a pile of yellowed papers and looked up at Jake and Murray.

"Well, kid," grumbled Jake, sometimes it does, but in a treasure hunt like this, you've gotta start at the beginning with the letter A, then B, then C...sometimes, you've gotta go damn near through the whole alphabet in this game, before that X is revealed to you. And then, even then...you go dig some more." Jake delved into the box and pulled out more folders.

"Wait...wait, wait, wait!" exclaimed Lorenzo excitedly as he picked up a small, pocket-size card that had dropped out of a folder onto the bench along with several documents. He held it up where Jake and Murray could see it; it was a longshoreman's ID card. "Look at this, please. Issued by Captain of Port, Boston. It's for Johnny Jackson."

"That's one of our guys," exclaimed Jake. "Now, we're getting somewhere!" Jake pulled the silver flask from his jacket pocket and slammed it down on the table. "Want a snort?" he asked Lorenzo. Lorenzo looked at him and countered, "Why, yes, as long as you do."

"Hell, yeah!" said Jake, spinning off the top, taking a swig, and sliding the flask across the bench toward Lorenzo, who paused—and looked at his American counterparts.

"This would be strictly forbidden in my department," Lorenzo said, "but...since I am in yours, why not?" He took a drink and immediately coughed, thumped his hands on the bench, and took a deep breath. "That's strong!" he said emphatically.

"Hell, son," replied Jake, laughing at his discomfort. "That's whiskey straight, with no artificial additives or preservatives. Whaddya think it was...Chianti? And this ain't my department anymore, it's Murray's. I'm retired; I've got no jurisdiction here!"

Murray roared with laughter. "I'm gonna leave you two now," Murray announced. "Almost lunchtime, and I have to check email. I'll come back in an hour to make sure you two haven't passed out." He pushed back the chair he'd been sitting in and rose to his feet.

Lorenzo rummaged farther down in the pile of papers. Another longshoreman's card from the same time period as Johnny Jackson's, issued to one David Mikhailov appeared...as did the homicide report on Jackson. "Wait a minute," he implored. "There must be some reason these two cards are here close together. Would you run them through inPursuit...FBI... most wanted...Interpol, please?"

"Sure," said Murray. "I'll be back at ya in an hour or so. D'ya want pizza, some KFC or something?" he asked the two men.

"No, we're good," replied Jake. Murray hiked off toward the distant doorway.

"Keep digging, kid," advised Jake, turning his attention to the folders. "It's a good start. We're past A, B, and C now." Jake pulled the flask across the table and took a swig. "Want some liquid lunch, kid?" he asked his Italian partner in the investigation, who nodded his assent. He passed the flask back toward him. "D...that's the next letter...is for drink," Jake said, looking at Lorenzo and smiling. "What do you say...let's have one."

It was just a few minutes later when Jake found the homicide report on Johnny Jackson. "Look at this, son," mumbled Jake. Lorenzo leaned over to read the document Jake was straining to look at through his bifocals. He read from the tersely-worded report written in cop jargon: "Officer was dispatched by emergency call, report of body found—single gunshot wound to head, rear alleyway Brookline and Burlington Avenues, officer arrival time 2:37 a.m. 12 October 1978. No ID on body, white male, approx. 5' 10". Entrance wound back of head, exit front, shot close range. Reporting officer interviewed Donald Smith, DOB 1-16-24, Roxbury resident, night watchman Burlington Boston Apartments—last made rounds approx. 12:00 p.m. 11 Oct. and states body not present at that time. Subject heard no sound of firearm discharge. Consider deceased was possible robbery/execution victim, pockets had no contents. Lack of pooled blood at scene indicates deceased shot elsewhere. OCME coroner arrived 3:46 a.m. 12 Oct. & signed release for transpo to Southern Morgue, Albany Street, autopsy. Full report to be made to BCI and Homicide Squad when fingerprints rec'd, OCME."

Both men sat in silence for a moment. "Let's see what else is in that folder," Jake said, pulling it across the bench. He withdrew a flimsy document with badly-faded, typewritten purple letters on it.

"What is that?" asked Lorenzo curiously, peering at it.

Jake laughed, coughed for a moment, and then answered, "That's a teletype. Back before there were fax machines, you could sit and type a message on the teletype machine, and it would go over the wire, a dedicated line, to another department or whatnot and their machine would print it out. Let's see what it says."

The message read:

AU
  -807
  9087 FILE 181 PD BOSTON MASS 10-15-78
  TO APB
  DAVID MIKHAILOV, MISSING FROM HIS APARTMENT SINCE 8-00 AM
  AS OF 10-14-78 DESC AS W-M-18-5-10-150-BLONDE HAIR – BLUE EYES-
  FAIR COMP - WEARING JEANS – BLACK JACKET – BLACK BOOTS – FLUENT IN RUSSIAN – DRINKER – CARD PLAYER/GAMBLER – CIGARETTE SMOKER –MAY BE OPER 1967 MUSTANG BLACK – MASS AL3145 - BODY DAMAGE RIGHT FRONT FENDER – OWNER JOHN JACKSON – TAFT ST/DORCHESTER
  AUTH LT JACKSON BARRY DIST C-1 9-10 AM
  RPB MHG AM LINE C

"So…Johnny boy goes missing, then David a couple of days later…and David's got John's car. Okay, so now we've got some breadcrumbs to make a trail," said Jake. He rifled through the folder. "Wow," he said, pulling out a black-and-white, 8-by-10 photo.

There was the black, '67 Mustang, sitting in a parking lot at the MBTA's Riverside station. The driver's side door was wide open and its window smashed; someone had drawn a circle on the part of the photograph showing the driver's seat, where a sizeable dark stain could be seen...presumably from blood. A crumpled black jacket was on the passenger seat. "Jackson car/ Mikhailov MP 181 / 10-1-78" had been typed on a piece of paper and pasted to the back of the photograph.

"Looks like someone must have had it out for David," opined Lorenzo.

"Not so fast," cautioned Jake. "There's more." He reached into the folder again, saying, "Well, well. Lookee here." Jake produced a fingerprint ID sheet. "The post-mortem fingerprints of one John Jackson, shot and killed October 12, 1978. Fingerprinted by the Office of Chief Medical Examiner October 13. It says here he was identified by dental records; he'd had a filling done a month earlier, and ID'd by his parents, naturalized citizens from Russia. He changed his name from Savansky after he left high school, joined the Army—from what I see here—got a dishonorable discharge, and then went to work on the docks. And, here's one more thing."

Jake produced a police department memo typed on cardstock; he read from it: "Tips line call received 10-17-78, 10:15 p.m., memo dictated by officer Lou Berenza 10-18-78, viz: Caller: 'You are looking for David Mikhailov, right?' Officer Berenza: 'Yes, please go ahead.' Caller: 'Do you know where Morse's Pond is? Out on Route 9?' Officer: 'Yes, I do, go ahead.' 'Well, look on the bottom...that's where you'll find David.' Call ended 10:16 p.m." Jake turned the card over and read the document stapled to it. "There was an extensive search," he said to Lorenzo, looking up at him. "They dragged the whole pond. No body was ever found. Hmmm...interesting." From far off within the building came the sound of a door being opened and slammed shut, then the sound of footsteps approaching. Murray appeared, carrying a red, white, and blue cardboard pizza box; he set it down on the bench amidst the mass of papers.

"I know you guys didn't want anything, but I took pity on you two slaving away down here and bought you a tomato pie," he said, hitching up his gun belt and smiling. "Dig in—this one's on me."

"Pizza?" asked Lorenzo. "Fantastic. *Grazie mille*! Thank you so very much! Is it Sicilian style or Neopolitan?" The expression on Murray's face momentarily resembled that of a schoolboy who'd just been asked to recite the Gettysburg Address from memory.

"Kid," answered Murray, suddenly laughing so hard he had to hold onto his belly momentarily, "I'm Irish...what the hell do I know? It's a pizza and it's red stuff and cheese—that's all I know!" Jake pawed open the box and grabbed a slice; Lorenzo did the same. "I got news for you guys," said Murray. I ran the photos from those two longshoremen's cards. We got a hit on one of them. The face is the same...but the name's different. Mikhail Zuckoff, new to this country some years ago...caught up in a gaming raid...paid his $500 fine and went his way."

"Holy crap," muttered Jake, pulling out his blue bandana, wiping away tomato sauce that had dribbled onto his chin, and reaching for the photo ID and report Murray held. He looked up at Lorenzo. "I think we've got letters D, E, and F now, kid," he said. "Let's keep going."

Over on Maple Street in Chelsea, FBI Special Agent in Charge Bob Tranten had succeeded, finally, in clearing his desk of a massive accumulation of 502 forms and other paperwork. What had to be dealt with had been dealt with, and what had to be delegated had been delegated. Bob took pride in his work...after all, he was known as a clean desk man, the master magician of the disappearing paperwork act and the empty in tray. It was time for lunch, albeit a late one. Bob rolled down his shirtsleeves, buttoned the cuffs, and was about to rise from his desk and head for the cafeteria when his desk phone beeped; he was being paged for an incoming call. "Yes?" Bob responded on speakerphone, turning to reach for his jacket. It was Myrna, staff office manager, on intercom.

"Bob, I have someone from the Italian Carabinieri who wants to talk with you. It seems they are looking for an Italian policeman from Rome who's gone missing in your district...and they say you might already know something about it. Bob? Bob?"

Chapter 28

The Bad Penny

The seat, and its cushion Patty was sitting on seemed to be
rising and falling...rising and falling. Patty opened her eyes
and found that indeed it was; she found herself seated in the
open stern of a long, old-fashioned wooden powerboat. It was
the dead of night and the big, mahogany-hulled craft bobbed
up and down, tugging gently at its dockside lines in a city harbor. Through the darkness she could just discern the shadowy
forms of men moving stealthily about, far forward on the
boat's open deck. One of them struck a match and two others
huddled with him briefly as they all lit their cigarettes over it;
the men's gaunt faces momentarily glowed with a fiery orange
hue like those of demons joining forces in hell as the match
flared...and then was snuffed out. The three carried on a conversation in low tones as they smoked, while another stood
atop the helmsman's small forward cabin, looking toward the
docks and a long row of warehouses that stood beyond them.

A small, yellow light glowed from within the boat's binnacle
in the cabin, but no other forms of illumination showed on the
sleek craft, other than the orange pinpoints of light from the
men's cigarettes. The boat's two powerful straight-eight engines rumbled below the deck and shook the boat slightly as

they idled away, their exhaust bubbling out from twin ports just below the waterline, making a muted grumbling sound as if the boat was in protest of being tied up at the dock, waiting impatiently to get underway and go to sea.

At the far end of the docks, twin beams of light from the two round, yellow headlights of an old car poked around the corner of the warehouse block and headed for the boat, becoming larger as the sedan grew closer. It had apparently been raining earlier and the auto, a big, shiny-black car of ancient origin, all of 80 years old, perhaps, splashed through puddles of standing water as it came. It slowed briefly...briefly enough for a shadowy figure to emerge from his dockside place of concealment behind a pile of crates and to jump onto the car's passenger-side running board. The sedan skittered to a stop on the dock opposite the boat and the man, who had a rifle slung across one shoulder, dropped off and quickly opened the back door of the sedan. He brought out a Gladstone bag and, after closing the car door, carried the bag over toward the boat; the driver, draped in a trench coat and topped with a gray fedora that was cocked at a jaunty angle, emerged from the car and slammed his door shut. "Mickey!" called one of the men on the boat to the driver, "We've been waitin' for ya, lad!"

"Toss 'em the swag-bag, Grady," said Mickey Callahan to the man carrying the Gladstone. The man pitched it to the uplifted hands that were waiting below, and the fellow who caught it swiftly stowed it in the boat's cabin. In one spry movement, Mickey stepped off the dock and onto the boat's deck. "Are you ready, boys?" he asked the men who gathered around him.

"We are," answered the man who'd stashed away the Gladstone. "*Bad Penny*'s all tuned up and gassed. We're set to make the run, and the Canuck hasn't called the date. We're as good as can be."

"Good work, Tommy," said Mickey. "Those guys seem to be good fellows and treat me square."

"Of course those boys do," chuckled Tommy. "Our dollars are worth more up there than theirs are!" The men guffawed as Mickey lit a cigarette and then tossed the spent match overboard. "Word out tonight is Nacosto's got his boat on the water," warned Tommy solemnly.

"That rat-ass bastard," commented Mickey, frowning and pausing to spit over the side of his boat in disgust. "That hijacking son-of-a-bitch. Let's only hope the Coast Guard has their Cutter out tonight and takes him on. The bastard might be laying for us out there right now, for all we know." The men all nodded gravely. Tommy hitched up his gun belt and his trousers, and looked about nervously.

"Well, boys, this is our last run," said Mickey. "So, be on your guard tonight; be sharp. You know O'Malley's buying me out tomorrow and he's a good man. Any of you who want to work with him can go work with him and he'll be square with you...or you can stay with me, and there'll be plenty to do. It'll be the same pay. And no hard feelings or stepped-on toes; I mind my business and he minds his. You all know that. Any questions?" There was silence. "Okay then, let's go," Mickey commanded, stepping toward the helm, taking the wheel, and placing his right hand on the twin throttles. "Cast off, Grady!" The man on the dock handily spun the lines off the dockside cleats, tossed the lines on board, and gave *Bad Penny*'s bow a hard shove with one foot to swing it away from him. Just as the boat's twin engines growled a stronger, deeper tone and as the boat moved forward, Grady dropped onto the aft deck with catlike agility.

Bad Penny cruised slowly through a harbor where other boats her size were docked, and then threaded her way through an assortment of tramp steamers anchored for the night, awaiting the attention of stevedores come morning. As the boat reached the harbor's open channel, Mickey pushed forward a bit more on the throttles and all 16 cylinders of brute power below the engine house hatch responded heartily to his command with a throaty roar. Patty tried to move but couldn't budge. It was as if she was moored, as the boat had been to the dock, to the cushion she was sitting on. She wanted to call out to her great-grandfather, now intent on urging *Bad Penny* forward to its mysterious rendezvous. Wanted to talk with him...but found she couldn't speak. A cold, salty breeze now buffeted her face, tugged at her hair and pulled it backward, making it flutter like a flag. The boat passed a distant lighthouse from which a white beacon swept around in circles; Mickey swung the boat in a wide arc. The faraway city and its docks soon hove into view, seen as if by a jewel thief in the dead of night—strings of tiny glittering pearls and diamonds, lines of shimmering rubies and emeralds lying on a jet-black dresser top. It was the top of the deep, black ocean *Bad Penny* was racing across toward her destiny.

The boat turned again and then resumed a straight course. In the distance glowed the running lights of a tramp steamer; a red light on its port side and two white lights on its topmasts. "There he is!" exclaimed Tommy.

"Okay, give him the light!" hollered Mickey. Tommy stood on the foredeck and flashed a prearranged spotlight signal to the distant ship; a few seconds later, his signal was answered with a blinking white light. Mickey pulled the throttles back and the boat slowed in its approach of the vessel. He motored closer, steered to starboard, and let his boat drift; the foreboding mass of the big ship now towered over *Bad Penny*. A mesh of rope had been hung down over the steamer's steel-plated side, and Mickey skillfully brought his boat within a few feet of it; Grady snared the mesh with a gaff hook and pulled the boat toward it until he could make *Bad Penny* fast to it with a line. Unseen hands aboard the ship lowered a line with a hook secured to its end, and Grady then made it fast to the Gladstone bag and gave it two tugs; the bag was swiftly hauled upward and taken aboard the steamer.

"Here we go, boys!" yelled Grady, looking upward. "Now, look alive! Here it comes!" Patty watched, fascinated—still unable to move, other than to twist her head to change her view—as a winch aboard the steamer whirred and a boom swiveled out over *Bad Penny*. A rope sling containing perhaps three-dozen wooden crates was lowered from it onto *Bad Penny*'s polished deck. Under his watchful gaze, Mickey's crew hurriedly pulled the crates—crates of name-brand Scotch whiskey—from the sling and distributed them evenly around the deck. Grady gave a tug on the line as soon as the sling was emptied, and the winch whirred again, pulling the sling upward.

"Look out below, Yanks," called out a voice from the steamer's deck as the now-empty Gladstone bag was tossed over its railing, landing with a *plop* in Grady's outstretched arms. Mickey pushed on the throttles and *Bad Penny* turned its rudders to the steamer and sped away into the night. The whole exchange had taken no more than five minutes.

"Off without a hitch," remarked Grady to Mickey.

"So far," said Mickey laconically, looking over his shoulder as the lights of the steamer faded into the distance and soon went over the horizon. "Keep a close lookout, you fellows!" he added sharply, with just a hint of Irish brogue in his voice.

"Mick!" yelled Tommy, standing, legs far apart to steady himself high atop the cabin, peering into the darkness behind the boat with a huge pair of binoculars pressed to his eyes. "We've got company! There's a boat coming up on us—fast!" Mickey reacted by turning to port; all hands aboard got a view of a dark mass speeding along perhaps 1,000 feet behind *Bad Penny*, white water churning at its bow like a bone in the teeth of a mad dog.

"Who is it, Tommy? Coast Guard?" yelled Mickey.

"It's Nacosto!" came the sharp reply. Mickey turned hard to starboard and shoved the throttles forward; the two big engines bellowed and their propellers churned the water into foam, leaving a long, narrow wake behind. *Bad Penny* dug in; her bow pointed down and she plowed through the tops of the waves now, her hull slamming up and down on the water. And then shots rang out from the pursuing craft; bullets whistled overhead, one of them clipping the staff on the stern and sending splinters flying.

"Make smoke, boys," ordered Mickey, "and make it fast!" Grady grabbed and unplugged a rubber vacuum line leading into the engine compartment and Tommy, who now had a small can of kerosene in hand, plunged the line into it. Thick smoke immediately billowed out behind the boat. Mickey glanced back over his shoulders, straight astern at the pursuing craft...and Patty stared back at him. *He's looking through me*, thought Patty. *Looking right through me...why can't he see me?*

"We're gonna come about, boys," he called out. "You know what to do." Grady fetched his rifle and the other men each grabbed a Thompson submachine gun from underneath the boat's seats, eased off its safety, and pulled back its bolt. They gathered around Patty. Mickey pulled the throttles back and as *Bad Penny* lost way, he quickly cut the wheel hard to port and then gained headway, doubling back through the smoke screen...and stopped. Nacosto's boat suddenly appeared and quickly slid past before her crew could get off more than three or four shots, all of which missed. Her skipper realized his mistake too late as he finally slowed and swung his boat ponderously around after speeding by his mark. His craft, a black cabin cruiser, momentarily hove to before coming about and wallowed heavily in the chop behind *Bad Penny*, its entire length exposed to the guns assembled at her stern. Mickey beamed his boat's spotlight at the cruiser.

"They asked for it—let 'em have it!" roared Mickey. Five tommy guns and Grady's Browning automatic rifle chattered in anger, and a barrage of bullets raked the cabin cruiser that had been following *Bad Penny*, tearing it apart from stem to stern. One of the bullets found a frightful home, as it bored into and raised a spark in either the boat's fuel tank or a can of gasoline carelessly stored on board the deck...and the dark boat exploded—violently. A massive fireball sent a shock wave and a blast of heat toward *Bad Penny*.

"Go!" bellowed Grady to Mickey. "Go, go, go!" *Bad Penny* dug her heels in and surged ahead as shards of broken glass, pieces of splintered burning wood, and metal fittings rained down on the water and on the deck near Patty as the ammunition on board went off like lethal strings of firecrackers.

The men, their guns, the cabin of *Bad Penny*—all were lit with a fiery red light from the burning hulk of the hijacker's vessel. Once more, *Bad Penny* sped along as if the devil himself was after her, hammering up and down across the waves...and then, one gigantic wave broke over the bow, engulfing the boat. Patty felt herself falling. She heard the boat's bell ringing. She reached for the boat throw cushion...hers, but it eluded her grasp. Everything, Patty, the boat, the boat cushion...were all dropping like a stone, going down into the depths of the deep, black ocean. "We're going down," she moaned, "we're going down..."

"Patty...Patty! Wake up!" hissed the disembodied voice, one she seemed to recognize. The boat was falling into a vortex...but Patty somehow rose to the surface, as if pulled upward. A woman's voice called again. Patty blinked and awoke. Theresa, her friend and fellow flight attendant on the flight to Denver, was shaking her shoulder. "For God's sake, I'm glad I woke you up before you said *that* any louder!" The 727 they were flying in was being jostled, bumping up and down over rough air; the red fasten seatbelts signs were on. Patty peeked around the corner from her jump seat. Ronald, who had the tail end was walking the aisles, checking seatbelts, and picking up empty cups, dropping them into a trash bag. As usual, prissy, ever-fastidious Ronald stuck his nose up and extended his pinkie on the hand he used when picking up litter. Two girls sitting together close to the aisle were giggling at him. "Don't worry; I already got the front," whispered Theresa.

"Ladies and gentlemen," announced the captain over the intercom, in clipped, fighter-pilot-banter with just a hint of Texas drawl thrown in, "we're encountering some turbulence and I'm asking you to please fasten your seat belts and remain seated until we gain some altitude and get above this rough air." The jet's engines rumbled and the great plane ascended to a safer level...and Patty was safely lifted out of her dream, her Great Granddad Mickey's boat...and the year 1932.

Chapter 29

The Sit-down at
Double Deckers

The three Saluzzo brothers, Franky, Bobby, and Charlie, sat quietly. They were playing cards, smoking, and drinking—the three things they seemed to do best when unsupervised or not bothered by their family obligations, in a booth toward the rear of Double Deckers. Double Deckers was a dark, low-ceilinged lounge in Charlestown that had red-and-white-checkered vinyl tablecloths and matching curtains that blocked out most of what little sunshine filtered through the grimy windows. The walls were dark pine paneling, decorated with photographs of famous entertainers—Dean Martin, Frank Sinatra, Tony Bennett, and others—displayed in the kind of cheap plastic frames one would buy at a discount drugstore. The menus at Double Deckers were short in length, but the bar tabs totaled up at day's end were invariably long. It was mid-afternoon, just after three, the time when kids were getting out of school, pouring out of schoolhouse doors like small fry entering the rushing stream of life. It was also when thirsty adults who swam with their own school of fish—the big ones, those who prefer to explore the earliest of happy hours when the alcohol first begins to flow and who act like children—began to rise to the surface and gravitated toward small neighborhood dive bars like Double Deckers.

Double Deckers was named for its burly-looking proprietor, Doug "Deadeye" Decker. Doug, a former liquor control officer who lost his job in a scandal and later became an insurance salesman of sorts, had lost an eye in a fight over a 'policy' with an upset 'customer' back in '94. Doug settled the matter and then realized considerable wealth gained from severance pay he received from the 'insurance firm', which was glad to have had his services; after all, when all was said and done, the client had disappeared without a trace. He then decided to try his hand in retail business...and called in some favors. "I have to do something," he said when he signed the lease of the property and launched Double Deckers. "I might as well do something I know and love." Doug wore an eye patch, and as he advanced in years and became more and more far-sighted, he still refused to wear either reading glasses or, in the extreme, as he stated, "...a damned monocle. I'm an American." As a result, the measures of alcohol "Deadeye" poured were quite liberal, as he could not always focus on what he was pouring. If you were drinking at Double Deckers, they said, and saw two of Doug, it was more than likely that it was your lucky day and he'd been pouring you doubles. You'd better not complain.

"What time is this guy comin' anyway?" asked Franky, looking across the table at Bobby, with a look of impatience on his face. Bobby set down his cards—carefully, face down and close to him—pulled his right shirtsleeve cuff up, and consulted his Rolex.

"At 3:30," he said. "It's only 2:50 right now. Hey, Charlie," he said, elbowing his brother as he turned toward him, "why don't you go downstairs and make sure we've got everything set for our guest?"

"Yeah, okay," grunted Charlie. "Don't you mess with my cards, you stiffs." He got up, stretched, and sauntered off toward the back of the bar, cracking his knuckles as he went.

"Don't you just love him, Franky?" asked Bobby. "Yeah," said Franky, "to pieces. Just the way you'll wind up some day. Just make sure when that day comes...whoever does the honors keeps your carcass parts off my doorstep."

"Crap," answered Bobby, "that's special...that's why I love you like a brother."

Charlie descended the stairs leading to the dank basement of Double Deckers. The musty smell of damp concrete permeated the still, lifeless air. He turned to the right and entered a small room he had asked to be set aside for his purposes; Doug had cheerfully obliged to this request. There, under a bare light bulb dangling from the ceiling stood a chair filched from one of the tables upstairs. It sat upon a bright-blue, plastic tarpaulin. Charlie nodded; it was ready. He heard footsteps; someone was descending the stairs. It was Doug's dishwasher and garbage boy. The pimply-faced teenager looked into the room, gawked at the chair, stared up at the ceiling, expecting to see a leaking pipe, then at Charlie, and asked, "Whoa...what's up with this? Have I got some kinda problem here?"

"Not at all, kid," stated Charlie, looking back at him calmly, hands stuffed casually into his pockets, with a warm smile on his face but cold daggers in his eyes. He withdrew his hands and cracked his knuckles again. "As long as you ain't sittin' in that chair, you won't have a problem. Now, get your ass upstairs and forget about what you saw."

Upstairs at the bar, happy customers sat and ordered drinks; "Deadeye" Doug was busy, pouring them fast and loose. Pickled eggs and Polish sausages were being served up as appetizers, filched out of brine in big glass jars with tongs and dropped onto paper plates. Hot dogs and Doug's signature Double-Decker Burgers were brought over from the grill in grease-spotted paper baskets and handed over to customers, who thoughtlessly reached across each other's plates to get them, in the course of which they frequently bumped elbows and shoulders as if they were rival taxicabs brushing each other's fenders in heavy traffic. Doug's establishment was not known for fine food, or for fine manners. Downstairs, Charlie pondered his next move, one drop...onto that tarp...at a time. He and his brothers had acquired the rights—all of them—of the recently departed loan shark known as Freddy "The Fish" Funarlo, including Freddy's receivables. Among them was a sizable loan whose final payment was due. As owners of Freddy's estate, the Saluzzo brothers were calling this in. And Charlie, thinking ahead about being persuasive enough to affect payment in full, had prepared a seat downstairs for the borrower. A good one.

Bobby's phone rang. It was Maria. "What's up, Ma?" asked Bobby. "I'm kinda busy."

"Don't you 'Ma' me," snapped his mother. "I'm in a very bad mood. Where are you? Why aren't you here at the office?"

"Where, Mom?" asked Bobby, pretending he was having trouble hearing.

"At the office, where you should be. Where are you—at some dive bar? You're not, are you?"

"No, Mom; I'm having lunch...late. With the guys."

"Well, you need to get down here," Maria said. "We have some problems. And I am not taking over total responsibility for your father's business...you need to step in."

"What...what...what..." began Bobby, pulling a pen out of his pocket and reaching for a cocktail napkin in order to write notes down.

"Your father can't make bail," said Maria, "we can't even make payroll. Somebody's had his hands in our pockets...our accounts have been hacked and money drained off, eighty grand, almost overnight, from just one account."

"Jesus," exclaimed Bobby, genuinely astonished.

"Stop, stop, stop with that language," implored his mother. "Don't use the Lord's name in vain. We need to raise $30,000 bail, and the bondsmen won't touch us. You and your brothers have to pony up and get him out. Or else...well...you know how he gets when things like this happen. I don't have to tell you." There came a loud *click* as Maria hung up on Bobby.

"What?" Franky asked Bobby.

"Trouble. Big time," Bobby answered. "Ma couldn't make Dad's bail...must be the lawyer can't do anything. We need to get our hands on cash—fast. More than what we can collect today."

"What do you want me to do about it?" asked Franky, eyes wide.

"Think, genius," barked Bobby. "Think."

Franky's phone rang; he jolted and quickly answered it. "Mister Saluzzo?" queried the caller.

"Yeah?" replied Franky.

"This is Principal Jay Forward calling from John Paul Jones Memorial High. No need for alarm, but there's been an incident involving your son Dominic."

"Is he okay?" Franky asked innocently, his suspicions of foul play instantly aroused. Usually, his son was the cause of it, and considerable collateral damage.

"Oh, yes," said Jay, "*he's* fine...the other boy in the scuffle...not so fine."

"Yeah, so?" asked Franky.

"You need to come to my office, please," said the principal, "right away. There have been some problems with Dominic's behavior, which I have already brought to your attention...but your son is now in danger of being expelled. And by the way, he's in detention today because of this incident...we really need to talk, you and I, before this boy goes home. He's not going anywhere until you get here."

"Okay...I got it," replied Franky. "I'll be there in a few minutes." He put the phone away in a pocket of his coat.

"Hey, Franky boy...where do you think you're going now?" queried Bobby. "The party just started."

"School. I gotta get Dom out of a jam," Franky replied in a huff, standing up and buttoning his coat.

"You'd sure as hell better be back here within half an hour—before our guest gets here—or you'll be taking his place downstairs," chimed in Charlie. Franky, feeling as though his day had suddenly gone to hell, hustled through the doorway of Double Deckers and sprinted down the sidewalk a short distance to his parked car. Things were getting worse; he saw there was a parking ticket plastered on its windshield.

***

"Principal Forward will see you now," said the gray-haired woman at the school's visitors reception desk as she looked up at Franky, studying him through her horn-rimmed glasses quite carefully as she did so. There was something she distinctly disliked about him, but she couldn't quite put her finger on what it was...despite his overly-polite manners and the expensive (and rather expansive) suit he wore—still perhaps a size too tight for his ample girth. He exuded the air of a slick used car salesman or a wily carnival pitchman.

She put down her telephone, got up from her chair, and walked over to the frosted-glass door on the opposite side of her desk. She opened it, glanced inside, and then motioned Franky to step into the room. "Our principal, Mr. Jay Forward," she announced, smiling at Franky and holding that smile just long enough for him to enter and close the door behind him.

Jay, dressed in slacks and a white dress shirt, sleeves rolled up, and loosened necktie dangling from his open collar, was the very picture of a harried, hardworking man with a tiresome desk job. He arose and shook Franky's hand. "Mister Saluzzo, good of you to come so promptly," he said, a thin smile flashing briefly across his wrinkled face as if suddenly forced upon it. "Have a seat." Franky sat down heavily, wedging himself into a green, leather-covered armchair that seemed a tad too small and also seemed to be pitched forward at a precipitous angle. There was something uncomfortably familiar about being in the hot seat in front of a high school principal's desk. The tilting chair, and his nerves, were keeping him on his toes.

"You're welcome. This gonna take long?" he inquired. One of Jay's bloodshot eyes twitched in reaction.

"Well," replied Jay, picking up a pencil and tapping it thoughtfully against his cheek, "I'm sure you're a busy man. I'll be as brief as I can. Your son's in serious trouble." He set the pencil down and picked up a manila folder, opened it, and leafed through the pages of reports it held. "We're almost done with this semester and already Dominic has been in three fights. Today's was a clash over a card game in a locker room. The other boy suffered bruises and a broken lip. The players were your son and three other kids...all of whom sneaked out of their study halls or cut classes. I'm worried not only that your son likes to start fights...but he may also have a gambling addiction."

"Gambling?" blurted Franky, genuinely astonished. He tried to squirm in his too-tight chair and struggled not to steal a glance at his watch.

"Yes," replied Jay, "he's been caught playing online poker using school computers, and on his phone during classes. Don't get me wrong, Dominic excels in algebra. But overall, he's a smart kid who won't apply himself to studies. He's on the verge of failing history and his English teacher has disciplinary problems with him. He smokes in the boys' room whenever he thinks he can get away with it. The track coach is begging his teachers not to fail him—they need him on the team. All around, he's a good kid with some bad habits; the kids who know him say he's a wicked sharp card player...and has a nasty right hook when he starts swinging."

Franky let his head droop to affect a look of shame, one he had perfected in dealings with Maria. He shook his head for added effect. He then rolled his eyes upward and looked at Jay. "You're sure this is not a mistake?"

"No," replied Jay, "and I'm worried—deeply worried—whether he stays in school or not, that he's going to fall in with the wrong element."

"What element?" queried Franky.

"The criminal element," answered the principal. "He could very easily wind up becoming a member of some gang—drugs, weapons, extortion...violence. Is that what you want?"

"No sir," said Franky, as meekly as he could. He then straightened up in the chair, as if suddenly inspired by something...a resolution, perhaps. "Sir," began Franky, "let me just say that I will not be the one, to...I will not break my promise to you today—I promise to take responsibility for straightening my boy out. Time is short, and I have to go to an important appointment now, but I swear to you you'll see a change in him. Where is my kid?"

"He's outside in my secretary's office, waiting for you," answered Jay. Franky arose, leaned forward, and shook Jay's hand again.

"In light of all the bad things I hear my boy has done, his bad behavior and his shameful habit you've brought to my attention," Franky said, shaking his head in disbelief and then looking straight at Jay with eyes wide open, "I am ashamed, I am surprised, and I humbly apologize to you for all that he has done and what he did today...I honestly don't know where he gets it from."

***

"Get in the car!" Franky ordered his son. The two of them stood beside Franky's car in the parking lot. The proverbial clock was ticking. Ticking like a time bomb.

"Will if I want," said Dom, shoulders hunched in disregard of his father's order, hands jammed down into his pockets.

"You'd better want," barked Franky.

"Great, Dad," retorted Dom. "So I gotta get in this P.O.S., right out in front of everyone, huh? I wouldn't want to be seen in this car dead."

"That could be arranged—easier than you think," muttered Franky, fumbling with his remote and unlocking his Sedan DeVille. "Get in." His son got in and slammed the door hard enough to make a sound like a rifle shot. This mini-drama did not go unnoticed by the small group of kids loitering nearby. Franky got in on his side and slid behind the wheel.

"Why don't you make my day complete and make me ride in the backseat so I look like a total nerd?" nagged the boy, turning right to bare his teeth and grin at the group like a comedian does when he's blown a punch line performing before a live audience.

"Shut up," said Franky, starting the car and peeling out of the school's parking lot. "I don't give a shit what those lot lizards over there think about you."

The car headed south as if headed toward Boston. "Hey...where are you going?" asked Dom. "This isn't the way home."

"I ain't takin' you home," replied his father. "We're goin' someplace else."

"Dad, don't be a dink. Don't mess with my head, okay?" asked Dom, turning toward Franky, at first leering at him and then putting on his most-pissed-off-of-all faces.

"You messed with me and you made my day," Franky said. "Maybe I should return the favor. We're not going home."

"Oh...oh...oh!" chortled Dom. "I think I get it. So this must be 'take your son to work day,' right, fatty-daddy?"

"You gotta lotta balls to say that to me, boy," groused Franky, as he put his foot down and the car hurtled along a busy avenue, with Franky trying desperately to beat the traffic light ahead that was fast changing to red. "Trust me, I'm gonna bust 'em for you before this day's over. After that, believe you me; I'll hand them to you on a platter."

"Oh, yeah, big guy; justice is served hot, not cold, huh?" asked the boy.

"Yeah," retorted Franky, swerving around a parked garbage truck. "Justice like, you being grounded."

"Maybe so," giggled Dom, "but you won't stop the game. I'm going."

"What game are you talking about? Don't you bullshit me," said his father, steering around an elderly man using a walker who was trying to cross the street and proffered an uplifted middle-finger salute to him as he sped by.

"The poker game. The floater tonight...the big one down on the south shore," said Dom, looking dreamily out the car's windows at the brick buildings flitting by. "It's big money." He turned and looked at his father—gave him a hard look, one that Franky thought only a person well beyond his son's years could muster. "You don't know what I do—do you?"

"Sure, I know. You screw up in school, piss off your teachers, then the principal, and then I have to come and bail you out," said Franky, not taking his eyes off the street.

"Bullcrap. I'm in the game. I'm a winner," retorted the kid, crossing his arms defiantly and staring out through the windshield.

"What crap are you talking, son?" asked Franky.

"Dad, let's get serious here; how about the Mitsubishi twin-turbo I bought last summer, huh? How do you think I paid for it? You sure as hell didn't think about it, did you?" Franky was silent. "Wanna know?" asked Dom, turning toward Franky. "I bought it with money I won in poker games." He uncrossed his arms and leaned back in the seat in smug satisfaction. "Wanna know what the best part is?" he asked, looking at his father. "I did it without you."

"How?" asked his father, his radar up, genuinely interested now.

"Good memory. And, an algorithm," Dom explained.

"Huh?" muttered Franky, clearly puzzled. "Algorithm?" He pondered the word briefly, searching in vain for its meaning. The closest thing that came to mind was the rhythm method, and his regret now he hadn't practiced it about 16-odd years ago with Dom's mother.

"Oh c'mon; don't you know what that is?" Dom sputtered, incredulous. He started laughing at his father. "It's math. It's a way to develop sets of rules to work out problems. For example, you use it to figure out how the house wins, like it does in baccarat, and then apply it to your game. Whatever your game is."

"Oh...yeah, yeah...now I get it," replied Franky. Wheels were turning in his head now, possibly as fast as the wheels turning on his Cadillac, speeding toward the lounge. "I get it now. Duh. It's the math. Like they said when Clinton ran in '92: 'It's the economy, stupid.'"

Dom turned and looked at him. "Yeah, stupid," he mumbled. And, after a small pause, "Who's Clinton?" he asked, a blank look on his face.

Franky didn't answer; he was thinking—hard. "Where is this game?" he inquired.

"Some resort. I'm going with Billy McCart. He goes to school over at St. George's. He lifted some kind of club member's pass and some cash from his dad's wallet. Each player's allowed one guest, so, he can get me in. We can pass for 18, no sweat."

"Where do you get your cash?" asked Franky, glancing at him. He noticed his son was grinning at him like the Cheshire Cat.

"Just use your imagination, Dad," his son said. Franky could feel the blush creeping up his cheeks as he drove. The answer was obvious. What a fool he'd been. It hadn't been his wife snitching bills on him, after all. Dom had obviously betted he never would have suspected his own son. So, there it was; it was Dominic all along.

"So," asked Franky, turning onto a side street, "if I were to stake you some real money—big bills—let's say I gave you five grand, for example. What kinda return are you gonna give me on my money?"

"Return? What crap are you talkin', Dad?" chuckled Dom "Me, playing high stakes poker for you? What's in it for me?"

"Two percent—and you get your car back. Now."

"No deal. That's not an offer; that's an insult. And I'm already being insulted by having you drive me around in this pimpmobile."Dom had his arms crossed and his chin stuck out.

Okay," said Franky. He bit his lip. "Tell you what—three percent, and the car...if you more than double the money, you get four percent."

"Look...I may be a dumb-ass kid, Dad, but I'm not gonna make a dumb-ass deal. Ten percent or nothing—and the car," countered Dom. He lolled backward in his seat and made pretense of studying the car's headliner.

"Look, this is my best offer. Five percent—and the car—and six if you get more than double the money." There was a long pause.

"Okay," said Dominic, nodding. "That's more like it. Deal."

Franky pulled up near Double Deckers and worked the Caddy into a tight, handicap-only parking space. "Gimme the tag that's in the glove compartment," said Franky to his son. Dom produced a parking permit that had been filched from another person's car; Franky hung it from the rearview mirror. "C'mon, let's go! Hustle!" he urged.

"Where to?" asked Dom, looking up and down the street, expecting to see a name-brand fast-food restaurant, a diner or else a hotel's lounge entrance.

"In there," answered Franky, pointing at the Double Decker's grubby-appearing front door and cloudy-looking front window. "We've got no time to lose. And I'm gonna tell your two uncles all about our deal; you should be proud."

The pair entered, walked to the booth where Bobby and Charlie were waiting, and joined them. "Hey, hey, hey...what's up with this?" Bobby groused. "What's young Dom doin' here?"

"I'll tell you later," huffed Franky. "He's in with us on bringing in some cash."

"Look," whispered Charlie, tapping Bobby on his shoulder. "Here comes our guy." A spectacled, middle-aged man wearing jeans and a bowling jacket had just entered Double Deckers. He was carrying a small black briefcase and glanced nervously over his shoulder as he made his way toward the Saluzzos' booth.

"Bobby!" he said, upon spotting him and flashing a huge smile that was worthy of a toothpaste commercial. "Good to see you! Hey, now...who are all these other guys? I thought this was our deal."

"My brothers," said Bobby. "And one young son here...we all deal together...you got everything you promised me?"

The man suddenly looked crestfallen. His shoulders slumped. "Almost...almost," he said. "I came so close...I just need a couple more weeks. Look, I gave Freddy all the juice on time. Every time. Twelve percent is a ball-buster. I'm an honest man. I need to catch up. I brought what I could. Maybe...you guys could give me a break?"

"Oh," said Bobby, a faint, sardonic smile appearing on his face, "I'll bet we can...tell you what, let's go somewhere where we can have a little privacy. This young guy here don't want to hear your business; he can hold down our table while we talk and give you a receipt. Something you can go home with." Franky, Bobby, and Charlie arose and headed toward the stairs to the basement; Bobby in front, the man with the briefcase behind him, and the two other Saluzzo brothers following.

"Cool," muttered Dom under his breath.

A waitress came over to the booth where Dom sat, carrying the brothers' fresh drinks—three of them—on a small tray. Her cheap perfume had the pungent, overpowering aroma of an air freshener in a motel bathroom. "Where did they all go?" she asked, looking around, perplexed, then down at him.

"Downstairs with some guy; they'll be back up in a while. I'm just holding down their booth," he said, looking up at her and giving her the most gracious smile in his extensive repertoire of innocent expressions as she set down the drinks. She picked up the empty glasses one by one and placed them on her tray.

"Well, I haven't seen you in here before. Get you something?" she asked.

"Yeah, a Coke," Dominic said softly. No sooner had she turned her back on him and sauntered off than the boy sampled the liquor in each of the three glasses in succession, taking his time and obviously savoring the contents. Two old cronies sitting side-by-side at the bar happened to notice Dom sampling the booze.

"Oy," said one to the other, "that kid's got some chutzpah."

"So what do you know?" asked the other scornfully. He stabbed at the squiggly dill pickle on his plate with a toothpick, like a fisherman trying to spear a small, slippery fish that was being elusive.

"He's a mooch, just like those other three chumps sitting with him," said the first man.

"You know them?" quizzed the other.

"Oh yeah, I know those guys," came the reply. "The boy's dad, real well. You know, there's an old saying."

"How old?" came the response. "Older than even you, maybe?"

"Uh huh," said the first man, pausing to tip his head back as he raised his glass to let the last drops of his Manhattan trickle down to his open lips. He wiggled the glass and at last, the cherry broke free. It rolled down into his mouth and disappeared like an eight ball rolling into a corner pocket of a pool table at the end of a game. He chewed on it briefly, and then spat out the stem into his glass. He wiped his lips with the back of his free hand, looked at his companion, and said, sagely: "Like father...like scum."

Chapter 30

The Pickups

"He's over there," Father Clancy O'Donnell said to Dave Dobson, pointing to a far, dark corner of the cavernous St. George Cathedral. "Sleepin' it off, most likely." He said this softly, as he knew that the sound of one's voice often carried quite well within these historic quarters due to the somewhat mysteriously-generous acoustical properties of the grand old building. It was also because he was not on the pulpit this morning, preaching to his flock in a loud enough voice, as he usually did, to keep them from nodding off or letting their thoughts turn toward any form of temptation. "That boy seems to keep to himself...except for havin' an affair," he added gruffly. The elderly priest then absent-mindedly scratched his bristly shock of white hair, unleashing a blizzard of dandruff that glimmered in the early morning sunlight streaming through the window, and quickly settled in stark contrast on his black jacket.

"An affair?" asked the FBI agent, squinting at the priest, wondering what else the old man knew about John Fischer and his alias, Herman Schmidt...and if the priest was in on Fischer's assignment. Dave had elicited many confessions during his career with the FBI, but never one from a priest.

"An affair," said Clancy smugly, his square jaw now jutting out like a craggy rock formation, "with the bottle. I've kept the sacramental wine under lock and key since that lad's been working here...and now that the job's done, I'd been hoping he was going to leave. So, now...*is* he leavin'?"

"Oh, yes," replied Dave, the agent. "He'll be leaving here to-day—with me."

"Very well then, sir," said Clancy. "I'll be in the rectory next door if you need me for anything." He reached out, grasped the agent's hand, and shook it with surprising strength—almost with the strength a bulldog grips an adversary it has in the clasps of its teeth. "It's been an honor to meet you. It's not every day the FBI comes callin' at St. George's!" The priest beamed at him, most likely, thought Dave, in gratitude for Dave relieving him of the imposter hit man. Most men who deal with the criminal element and survive their encounters learn not to express fear, if they are to survive...since it's said criminals can smell it. Father O'Donnell probably smelled not just alcohol but danger on his guest and was glad to be rid of him.

"Thank you, Father O'Donnell, for your cooperation," said Dave, turning and stepping purposefully toward the corner the priest had pointed to. Within a minute, he reached the pew where John Fischer, the man posing as the contract killer Herman Schmidt reposed, sprawled like a dead man on the cushions. He was snoring almost loudly enough to shake the rafters and the departed in the heavens above. He was barefoot; his shoes, socks, and jacket lay on the floor beneath the pew in a jumbled heap. Dave grasped the sleeping man's shoulders and shook him—hard.

There was no response, other than a brief snort, a cough, and then the resumption of the snoring. Dave slapped him on one side of the face...then the other. John Fischer's eyes opened, then blinked—bright red—like brake lights. "FBI," Dave announced, taking a business card from his pocket and tossing it on John's chest. "Time to wake up." John's eyes opened—and stayed open this time. He fumbled at the card with his right hand, finally picked it up, and peered at it, bleary-eyed.

"So," he said groggily, "you've come for me. And this is an...FBI card...thank God." His head dropped back onto the cushions and he let the card drop to the floor.

"What did you think it was?" asked Dave sarcastically.

"I thought for a minute," John mumbled, looking up at him with what appeared to be a dazed and rather genuine expression of gratitude, "it might be the ace of spades."

"C'mon," ordered Dave, grabbing John by the collar and pulling him upward, "we've got to get going. Where's your gear, your weapon, and all that? And don't lie to me...I know you've got some iron on you." John struggled to his feet and searched for his socks and shoes, almost pitching forward onto the floor in the process.

"Weapon?" he asked, with uplifted eyes. Just the effort to move his eyes caused John almost unbearable pain. No matter where he looked, a huge black spot blotted out the center of his field of vision.

"Yes. Whatever it was they outfitted you with. And the ammo. Go get it—now." Sounds of happy kids playing baseball over on Corcoran's Playground drifted through an open window in the cathedral and lifted the mood somewhat, but not for John.

"Oh, wait...I've gotta put my shoes on," John said. He fumbled briefly then succeeded after a while, in putting each shoe on the correct foot. "Gun's down here." He reached farther back under the pew and grasped a long, black metal tube, an old organ pipe that had been made into a carrying case with a handle that was stoppered at each end. He brought it forward so Dave could see it. "Barrel's in this one," he said, handing it to Dave, "along with all my pipe-cleaning rods. Bullets and stock...they're in the other one. You know, the bullets...my signatures." He reached under the pew once more, almost falling over as he retrieved it, this one much larger and without a handle, and rolled it out toward Dave. "That's my claim to fame," he stated. He then promptly passed out and collapsed backward on the pew, spread out like a rag doll.

"I guess this," observed Dave, as he stooped down and reached out to grasp the tube before it rolled down the aisle of the cathedral like a pipe bomb gone astray, "is not going to be my day." He looked at John, sprawled out on the church pew, the man who was now his charge, and muttered, "Okay, gung-ho guy; it ain't gonna be your day, either."

* * *

By mid-morning, enough information had been elicited from John Fischer, as he slowly became lucid and could relate details about Jimmy Callahan and his plot to take down Vince Saluzzo, to garner the attention of the Boston Police Department, once the FBI quickly shared this information. The police department, as it turned out, had some information to share with the FBI concerning the long-unsolved Callahan murder case and a certain person of Russian descent—suspected of being implicitly involved in that case—who was operating a business in the South Shore area. And the FBI, reaching further into that certain person's background, found some very interesting material.

The search warrant for evidence in the cold case of Rose Callahan's murder was the very first thing served at the sushi bar near Kenmore Square, right at opening time. Upon entering, Murray and Jake were accompanied by two other police detectives and a forensics expert. They soon made their way to the telephone booth located in the back of the barroom. It was eerily silent inside the old building that had seen so many tenants during the decades. The pool table lay empty of billiard balls; the paddle fans overhead sat idle. "What is it you guys are looking for, anyway?" asked the bartender, tagging along with Murray like a puppy as he strode toward the telephone booth.

"Stuff," answered Murray. The bartender was getting on his nerves.

"What kinda stuff?" inquired the bartender, twirling the first, spotless-white and otherwise unsullied dishtowel of the day in his right hand. He seemed anxious.

"Bullets," grumped Murray, as he stopped by the pay phone booth and looked around him. There were several easy chairs, a pool table and an old Wurlitzer jukebox with an "out of order" sign on it in the room. The bartender glanced nervously at the staircase next to it from time to time. The carpet on its steps was heavily-worn.

"Bullets!" exclaimed the young man. "Nobody's ever been shot here...at least, not since I've been here. Oh my...just think, gunplay!" he gushed, sounding excited, wringing the dry dishtowel as if for dramatic effect.

Murray stared about him...and sniffed. Something was wrong; he could simply smell it. "What kind of place is this?" he asked, looking farther about. There was scant evidence of the kind of food-service equipment that could really support a small neighborhood bar, the kind he was familiar with.

"Oh," replied the bartender, looking vaguely amused, "it's a sushi bar."

"What's upstairs?" asked Murray, looking toward the stairway.

"Oh," said the bartender, almost giggling as he replied, "we have rooms." Murray sniffed again. No odor of fish. Yet something was definitely fishy about this place and the giggly bartender standing before him who was obviously nervous about something.

"Dig into that pay phone, Joe," Murray said to the forensics man, just as a young man dressed only in black undershorts sneaked down the stairway in bare feet, peeked around the corner at the policemen and the bartender, and quickly darted back upstairs, but not before Murray caught a glimpse of him. Murray turned to the barkeeper and asked, "What was this place...before you guys...I mean you...started this business here?"

"Pizza parlor," answered the man, "for a while, and before that—long time ago, I mean like really, really long ago—some old Army dude had a joint here, crazy man. Sergeant Sully's, I hear they called it. He died in the VA, Agent Orange or some crap like that—he had it bad. And the place went up for auction."

"We're on 'em, Murray," announced Joe. "You were right; here they are. Two slugs in the wall." He took several close-up photos of the bullet holes. Then, with a pair of forceps, he reached into one of the small round holes in the wall of the telephone booth, pulled out a dried-up wad of chewing gum and a wrapper, then grappled with something the way a dentist struggles to pull a bad tooth that won't let go. He made a face, grunted, and finally pulled out a mangled bullet, depositing it into an evidence bag. "One down, one to go," he announced calmly. He then pulled out the other bullet after a brief tussle, placing it into a second bag. "Okay, sport," he said, turning to Murray. "Let's take these to the lab and see what these slugs will tell us. The brass...the lead...it all talks to me."

"C'mon, man," said Murray, stone-faced. "Cut the crap, bullet whisperer. And don't listen too hard to those slugs if they talk to you when you're driving and get distracted, Joe. You could wind up being buried just like them...in a guardrail. And we won't volunteer to pull your sorry ass out of it. Too much trouble...and you'll be in way too deep, and in too many pieces to put back together."

***

It was just after 9:30 a.m. when Murray got the message that the FBI wanted to liaise—and quickly—with the police department on the Callahan case, and to keep it quiet. The bullets taken from the phone booth matched the ones from the Rose Callahan murder case. And the suspect matched the identity of a figure in international underworld crime circles who moved a lot of weapons. A joint raid was being planned for that evening to take the suspect into custody. Murray acted quickly upon the message he received, which requested a preliminary meeting at the junction of North Beacon and Cambridge streets. He immediately sanctioned it. "Let's roll when you're ready, Chuck," Murray said to his understudy, a corporal who'd played college hockey and had seemed headed for a career with the Boston Bruins before deciding he'd like a little more danger and excitement in his life—for more than just one season a year. He was about to get some. "Get us a car," said Murray, "plain wrapper."

Over at the FBI office in Chelsea, Dave brought Bob Tranten up to speed on the recent developments, as John Fischer slowly came to in the interrogation room and gave forth relevant information on how he'd been primed to play the part of Herman Schmidt, and play along with Jimmy Callahan. Dave had chosen the location for the meeting wisely, or so he thought, as it was at a crossroads within easy traveling distance for all concerned, and in a setting not frequently trolled by the media. "Let's go for it, Dave" said Bob. "Can we use your car? I'd like to be as discreet as possible."

"Sure," replied Dave. The two men walked downstairs into bright sunlight and the melodious sounds of early May birdsong as they left the overhang of the building and entered the parking lot. "It's over there," said Dave, pointing toward an old, black, rather nondescript Mercury Marauder four-door. "It's my son's car. He has reserves this week, and my car's in for warranty repair—airbag replacement. So, I'm using his."

"He must be a good kid," commented Bob. "Army reserves, huh? Good to have boys like your kid Scott who do the job. Doing a service to our country."

"Yeah...it is, Bob, even if he does still live at home at 21...but that kid's a real party animal. He was out last night until 2:00 a.m. He just shipped out this morning...I put him on a bus. I wouldn't let him drive." He pulled the keys from his pocket and, after fumbling with them briefly, unlocked the door. He opened it, and in his haste to jump in, dropped the keys onto the floor.

"Hey—let me in, okay?" asked Bob impatiently. Dave fished for the keys on the floor and found them...together with an empty beer can. He grasped the keys and shoved the beer can underneath the driver's seat where it would not be seen. He sat down, keyed the ignition, and the Mercury grumbled into life. Dave unlocked the passenger-side door and after Bob got in, Dave steered the car through the security detail, waved to them, and then turned out onto Maple Street, heading toward Center Street, Route 1, and the rendezvous.

"There's nothing wrong with a kid having his own car, right?" asked Bob.

"Right," answered Dave, as they drove along. "It all goes toward responsibility. It's what makes a kid into a man." As the car headed down Maple Street and made a turn, heading toward Route 1, the empty beer can rolled toward the front of Dave's seat and clanked against the seat anchors, which thankfully prevented it from rolling out between Dave's feet and making a startling appearance.

"What was that?" asked Bob, listening intently.

"Probably the exhaust system," said Dave dismissively. "Loose pipe or something. Scott did some work on the car last weekend."

There was silence for several minutes and then Bob cleared his throat and spoke. "Kids can worry you sometimes...like, with parties, cars, and stuff," he mused philosophically. "Take my daughter, Linda, for instance...she's just turned 17."

"Hey," commented Dave, "Your gal Linda's an honor student...straight As, right?"

"Right. But she's got a new boyfriend; I've met him three, four times maybe. Nice kid. But..."

"But what?" queried Dave, shooting a glance at him. He slowed the car to a stop at a red light.

"He took her out shopping the other day...bought her a fancy black dress. They're going out on the town tonight."

"Yeah, go on." Dave set the car into motion again, slowly enough to prevent the concealed beer can from giving itself away.

"It's a strapless evening dress. I just can't get my mind off it; I mean, she's only 17...wearing that kind of thing. It's...weird. My wife's having a conniption fit over it. Says it's risqué. And I hate fancy French words, Dave." Bob frowned and stared ahead at the traffic. "I hate 'em."

The black Mercury sped along onto the Route 1 on-ramp and merged with traffic, accelerating as it did so; the beer can rolled around again and clanked against the back of a seatbelt anchor bolt this time. "There it is...I heard it again," said Bob, his interest piqued. "Maybe you'd better have security check this rig out."

"It's okay, I'm sure of it," answered Dave. Small beads of perspiration were appearing on his forehead. He switched on the radio and tuned into an easy listening station, hoping the sound would cover any further clinking and clanking noises.

"What? Elevator music? I thought you were a classical music geek."

"Hey," replied Dave, taking a stab at levity to lift the mood, "it's like the guys driving along in that TV series, *Supernatural.* You know the rules, right? The driver picks the music; the shotgun shuts his cakehole."

"Okay, good one. I guess I had that one coming. So, anyway—what's your take on that strapless go-go girl dress of Linda's, Dave?" Bob peered at Dave apprehensively, awaiting an opinion.

Dave thought a minute and then chuckled before turning to him to answer. "Boss, with all due respect...I'd say...if she can hold it up, she's old enough to wear it!" There was an awkward moment of dead silence. Then Bob guffawed and slugged Dave in the right shoulder——hard enough to make the car swerve a little before he could recover.

"Dave, I gotta hand it to you, that's pretty damn good. That got me down off the fence...that's good enough to tell the wife when I get home!"

***

The Mercury arrived at the junction of North Beacon and Cambridge streets a few minutes later. Dave was chagrined to see that there were no street-side parking spaces. He steered the car into a small parking lot between two buildings behind the apex of the intersection, where he spotted Murray. Beside him stood his corporal, Chuck, plus Lieutenant Evans Lancaster, evening shift commander of the state police, and Evans' sergeant, Emily Watkins. All except Murray were in uniform, standing beside their cars. Murray was the first of the assembled group to speak as Dave lowered the car's window. He was beet-faced, primed for action and furious.

"What the hell were you thinking, Tranten?" he asked Bob. "Are you trying to make us look bad?"

"What do you mean?" Bob asked innocently, looking around. "Am I wearing the wrong color necktie? Wrong time of day? What? This seems like a good spot."

"Sure as hell it does," countered the detective. "Look where you guys set us up for this," he said, waving his right hand. Dave and his boss looked to the left: there was the world-famous Twin Donuts shop. To the right, just across the parking lot was a Dunkin Donuts franchise. "Great PR," spat Murray. "Set us up for a meet in between two donut shops. We're getting our chops busted already...look; here we go again."

An Allston Police Department car approaching on North Beacon Street slowed down, ostensibly so the two cops inside it could get a better look at what was going on. Upon spotting Murray, the driver honked the horn and the cop riding shotgun gave the detective a big smile and a thumbs-up; the prisoner in the back gave Murray the finger. Then, a school bus stopped at the intersection for a red light. A kid in the back slid down his window and yelled out: "Mmmmm! Donuts!" The whole busload of kids could be heard laughing.

"I'm going in to get a coffee," said the lieutenant to Emily. "Want anything?"

"Yeah, sure," said the sergeant. "Plain donut and a large coffee, black. Thanks! I'll stay here to make sure these people don't kill each other."

Murray came closer to the car's open window, then leaned inside...so far that Dave could smell coffee on his breath. "Nice going, guys," he groused. "You've made my day. And I see you guys are driving a beater that's older than my grandmother. I guess times are tough at the FBI, huh? We got rid of the '04 cruisers years ago. It must be humbling to be seen driving around in an old heap like this."

"Well, Murray," said Bob, a wicked smile slowly spreading across his face, "not really. It's already humbling to be seen here in public—with you. Lucky for you I had to get out of the office today and come here."

"Oh, so...they can't stand you either?" Murray remarked sarcastically. There was a brief pause, and the other cops looked on expectantly to see what would happen next that might demand their immediate intervention. "You're a pain in my ass, Bob," added Murray, smiling now, "but it's kinda nice to be working with you again. Who's this stiff behind the wheel?"

"Just some alky I picked up off the streets because I couldn't find another driver. Probably got an empty beer can or two under his seat for all I know. Say hello to agent Dave Dobson; he's my right-hand man." Murray and Dave shook hands. Dave felt as though he was shaking slightly inside his skin...a feeling that took a few moments to subside. In the meantime, he left a succession of sweaty palm prints on the car's steering wheel.

An elderly woman dressed in filthy sweatpants, decrepit sneakers, and a grubby parka patched with duct tape waddled by. She was pushing a shopping cart loaded with laundry and empty soda cans along the sidewalk, and paused briefly to look at the gathering of law-enforcement personnel. She blinked, then stared at Murray with the glazed-over eyes of someone who is addicted to reality-show television and rarely leaves the house during daylight hours. "I bust my ass taking in laundry to make a living," she hollered at him, "and you guys ain't out fighting crime; you're loafing around eating donuts and drinking coffee. I think we need Batman or something. Screw you all." She waggled her head in disgust, spat on the sidewalk for good measure, and shuffled off.

"Nice going, Bob," muttered Murray. "Now, I'm a comic book villain. And Batman's the hero. You...you're a zero."

The lieutenant emerged from one of the two donut shops carrying a tray with two large coffees and two donuts. "Their donuts are killers, Emily," he exclaimed. Just a split second later, a large man in dark clothing, carrying a bag burst forth from the doors of the other store and pelted down the sidewalk, heading west along Cambridge Street.

"Stop him!" someone outside the store yelled. "Shoplifter!"

"Chuck!" commanded Murray. "Go take that man down!" As a pro football fan, Chuck knew the rules of play—but hell; there weren't many when the other guy didn't observe them. And although he'd never played professional football, Chuck was an avid runner and could make a flying tackle almost as well as anyone else on his high school football team could. The fleeing man tossed something onto the front lawn of a gray, three-story apartment building as he ran; it was a handgun. Two seconds later, Chuck tackled the fleeing man, toppling him quicker than a logger fells a mighty pine tree in a forest just at quitting time. This event did not go unnoticed; there were plenty of people around to hear Jerry Garrantino go facedown with a muffled *thump*.

"Good time for that guy to take a little dirt nap," commented Emily, giving Chuck a thumbs-up. "Now for the habeas grabbus."

Chuck wrestled briefly with the big man, finally cuffing him. "What's in the bag, dummy?" asked Chuck, securing the giant's hands.

"Donuts, soul food for you morons," Jerry said.

"What did you pitch back there? A piece?"

"Nothin'," answered Jerry.

"Let's go," said Chuck, "and see the complainant." Not without some difficulty, he hauled the big man to his feet, and finally got a good look at the man's ruddy face. "Well, I'll be...you're Jerry Garrantino...we've been looking for you. Violation of conditions of release, among other things. Boy, do I ever love this job!"

"Really," snarled Jerry. "So, is that a Glock in your sock...or are you glad to see me?"

"Oh, yeah," said the cop. "I am glad to see you. You sure as hell are a charmer."

"Why don't you kiss my ass," grumbled Jerry, "and we'll call it a romance."

Murray, huffing and puffing from the effort, caught up with Chuck and his prisoner after sprinting along the sidewalk as quickly as he could. "Grab that bag, Murray," said Chuck. Murray stooped and retrieved the bag full of donuts.

"Take this," Murray said, handing the bag to Jerry. "You might need it. It's a long way off until lunchtime at the jail." He walked Jerry back to the parking lot. The store manager quickly made out a complaint of retail theft; Emily, meanwhile, had retrieved the discarded handgun, a Beretta, from the lawn of the apartment building.

"So Jerry, why rip off five bucks' worth of donuts and take a chance on being caught?" asked Murray. "You do know cops hang around donut shops, right?"

"I just couldn't help myself," replied Jerry, "and, like you cops, I never pay retail."

Bob's phone rang and he answered it. He listened carefully for quite some time before shutting it off and pocketing it, without saying a word. He motioned Murray over to his side of the car, lowered the window, and imparted to him the information he'd just learned. "We went to tap Callahan's phone—Saluzzo's, too—and found out both of them, all their lines, have already been tapped and compromised...by that Russian guy. David Mikhailov...Mr. Z...Mikhail Zuckoff...whatever, now we know it's all the same guy. We'll monitor these from now on, but the Russian's, also. He's even managed to get a bug inside Saluzzo's office. Looks like he's behind all of this stuff," Bob continued. "Let's regroup downtown."

Jerry had meanwhile been read his rights and placed in the backseat of Murray's police car. Although his hands were cuffed––now, in front of him––the big man was finishing off a powdered sugar jelly donut. Red jelly dribbled down his chin and there was white sugar spread around his face. He leaned back in his seat, looking for all the world like a man who'd been shot and left to die in an abandoned car. "Lieutenant!" called out Emily. "He's eaten half the evidence! Murray's taking him in! What should I do?"

"Oh, hell, Emily!' said the lieutenant in mock disgust, taking a swig of his coffee. He looked at Jerry, sprawled back on the seat of the black Dodge Charger police car like a corpse. "It's no big deal." He paused, then grinned and added, "Leave the donuts, take the Beretta."

Chapter 31

Hook 'em and Book 'em.

Dom Saluzzo deftly flicked his car's shifter with his right hand while grasping the steering wheel with the other as he double-clutched and then tromped on the gas. The Mitsubishi's engine screamed at high revs as he shifted out of overdrive down into fourth gear—then again as he went for third. He jerked the steering wheel to the right, pulled onto a highway exit ramp, and then shot straight down to the foot of it where—oblivious to traffic—he yanked the wheel hard to the left. He gunned the engine; the low-slung car skidded neatly across the intersection sideways before he quickly corrected course, scattering oncoming cars to either side of the road. He then sped toward Driftwood by the Sea, now and then cautiously eyeing the rearview mirror for any police. Billy McCart, strapped into the passenger seat like a hapless crash-test dummy, was jostled around like a rag doll in a rocking chair caught in a tornado. "You shit!" he hollered to Dom. "I'm sick! You're gonna make me hurl! Why the hell did I ever say I'd help you?"

"You're right—you are sick; you're one sick bastard, Billy!" said Dom, taking his eyes off the road briefly enough to glance at his accomplice, leering at him gleefully in the gathering darkness. The glow of the green dashboard lights made his pale face appear like the visage of a sneering goblin. "But you're the master card player, Obi Wan. You have taught me well. You gotta stay with me. Through thick or thin. Now, tonight, we're gonna play some awesome hot cards."

"Yeah, we are, man," answered Billy. "Just...slow down, Dom. Cripes, my lunch is comin' up for air." The sun had set about an hour or so ago, and the fast, early '90s sports car swung around a sharp corner like a dark black bat going after a bug at twilight. It soon swooped into the entrance of the resort, where Dom swiftly steered it toward a roosting spot in the parking lot.

"This car's too small for me, Dom," said Billy as he unfolded his six-foot-tall frame from the Mitsubishi, after untangling himself from the intertwined seatbelts.

"Tell you what," replied Dom sarcastically. "When we leave here, since you're built like a giraffe and like to keep your yap open...I'll put the top down so you can stretch out, stick your head up, eat bugs, and bark at the moon." Billy stepped out of the car and stretched to his full height, his brawny limbs appearing like girders forming a substantial building, one that seemed almost the size of the Prudential Tower.

"Where do we go from here?" he asked Dom.

"Dunno," commented his poker-playing partner as he stepped out of the car and straightened his necktie, carefully checking out his reflection in the window of the car parked next to his. "Let's just go where the lights are and check it out."

The lights, as well as the sounds of music and laughter emanated from The Knothole Lounge; in fact, lights poured out of every window like illumination from a carnival's tents and amusement rides. Dom and Billy padded along the stone pathway and stepped up to the twin doors leading into the lounge.

Billy grasped one of the two big brass door handles, shaped like leaping dolphins, and pulled mightily. The door heaved open without a sound; the two boys stepped inside and the rather sullen-looking maître d' standing stiffly at his desk, like a watchful border crossing guard at a small European country, greeted them. His chin ratcheted up and his white collar seemed to clinch his neck like a tourniquet. Small wonder that his face looked pink. "Reservations?" he queried imperiously.

"We're not here for dinner," said Billy. He presented the club card he'd filched from his father's wallet.

"Mister...McCart?" asked the maître d', studying him carefully, then taking the card and inspecting it thoroughly to make sure it had a chip embedded within it.

"Yeah," answered Billy, straightening up the collar of his coat and fingering the necktie he had liberated from his father's bedroom closet.

"Okay," said the maître d'. "And...this fellow with you is?"

"Dominic Saluzzo," answered Billy. "Here as my guest."

"Very well," said the maître d'. "But first, gentlemen, please sign the club register. And also print your names beneath the signatures." Both of the boys complied, scribbling their names and signatures onto an iPad that was handed to them. They started to leave the foyer and to head for the main hall. He then led them down a short hall toward an archway in the wall, where he swiped Billy's purloined card in a small, cleverly-concealed reader imbedded in a door that was lettered "Broom Closet." It quickly opened, and he handed Billy's card back to him. "Quickly, please," he urged, pointing the way inside as he looked back over his shoulder.

"We're in!" exclaimed Dom as he and Billy clattered down a short stairway and then strode across the floor of yet another foyer and into the basement game room of the building, an annex of The Knothole Lounge. In fact, if the truth be known, it was the *old* Knothole, the one of the Prohibition days that had remained hidden away for so many years, far beyond (or more exactly, beneath) the revenuers' prying eyes.

"Thanks to me, you hump," said Billy, looking around nervously and slowing his pace.

"Hey," said Dom, grabbing Billy by his jacket lapels...the ones that belonged to Billy McCart's father. Dom could sense Billy's hesitation. The pair halted. "Don't you go weird on me. I got big bucks riding on this. You can go play your penny-ante game; I can go to mine," stated Dom, staring at Billy fiercely.

"Looks like we're gonna have to," whispered Billy as he turned away to direct Dom's attention somewhere rather than by pointing. "Look over there." He shifted his gaze more closely into the room; Dom's followed.

Roughly 50 feet away from them sat none other than Jay Forward, principal of John Paul Jones Memorial High. Jay had a lit Chesterfield dangling from his lower lip and was apparently trying to engage a much-younger woman—perhaps even a teenager—in conversation...most likely to convince her to gamble with him. Jay had, by the looks of things, been trying do this for some time and been buying drinks in the process; there was a considerable pile of small change and an ashtray with several butts on the table before him. The woman was a stunning young redhead, dressed in high heels and an evening gown, who was having none of it. The conversation, going on over dice lying idle and being impatiently eyed by a crowd gathering by the roulette wheel, quickly died on the gambling table—like a patient being taken off life support. "All bets are off," said the girl loudly, and she stalked off in a huff. A dejected expression now hung on Jay's heavily wrinkled face, making it sag so badly he resembled nothing so much as a sorrowful basset hound that had been denied a tasty doggie treat.

"Hell," whispered Dom, "that ain't my gig tonight. I'm not playing that table." He fidgeted, now more than a little bit nervous upon spotting Jay.

"Maybe you can play one *I* don't want to even go near to," said Billy. "Look yonder at that table and those penguins from St. George's holding it down. Go for it, Mister Big Cojones; show your stuff and play poker with them." He pointed far down the hall where two nuns sat at a table, drumming their fingers on it and glaring at each other. Another stood at a poker machine, plying it with tokens; a fourth stood by the baccarat table nearby. "I'm not goin' down there." The two boys looked at each other for a moment.

"Hey——every man for himself," said Dom. He sauntered down the aisle toward the cashier's booth, chin up, chest out to get his chips, hoping there would be some mercy for Billy at Jay's table. Dom didn't know that he could expect none from the sisters...or who might join them.

"Five thousand in," said Dom softly to the blonde woman behind the screen in the cashier's cage, putting on his most affable smile and maintaining his laid-back posture, which he had practiced after watching a clip from the James Bond movie *Casino Royale.*

Avoiding eye contact with her now, he gazed nonchalantly to his left and then to his right, as if seeking an audience of admirers. In fact, he was looking to see if there was anyone else in the room he recognized, other than Jay. He then reached inside the breast pocket of his brand-new jacket, one he'd bought off the rack at a Marshall's discount store few hours ago, for the wad of bills his father had given him. It wouldn't budge. The woman stared at him warily, almost as if she suspected he might draw a weapon from his pocket.

Dominic forced a laugh. "I know I've got it," he said, scrounging deeper to extract the money. "It just doesn't want to leave!" He tugged the bundle of hundred-dollar bills free at last and placed them on the counter, then he flashed another smile at her, just for luck.

"Well," she said coyly, a cunning smile appearing on her face, "tell me what you want. I'm sure it's not just one brown chip, is it?" She picked up a glass of liquor, looking at him meanwhile and waiting for his answer. "You know we are not playing checkers here," she chuckled, now turning her head slightly and giving him a sly look. "You are too old for that, no?"

"Yeah, we're sure not playing checkers," answered Dominic, playing along and taking a stab at injecting some humor into the exchange. "But nonetheless...gimme all black, hundreds. You know, I'm a cautious guy."

"Oh, but of course," she answered. As she reached out and grasped the pile of bills with sudden alacrity, Dom noticed one of her wrists was adorned with a bracelet that bore Chinese characters. She counted the bills carefully but as quickly as a banker would on a Friday afternoon just before closing time.

Seizing this opportunity, Dominic let his gaze pass quickly over her fair face, blonde hair, and cleavage amply displayed by her low-cut black dress, the complete picture of her figure below that point unfortunately obscured by the countertop. "Which table are you playing?" she asked, matter-of-factly.

"That one over there, I guess," replied Dom as he stroked his chin thoughtfully, striving to look naive and gesturing toward the nuns' table. "They look kinda honest to me." Then, he collected his chips. "It's been nice talkin' to ya," he said to the woman and shuffled off toward the game table. Katrina, the cashier, hailed her boss on the intercom.

"Z, that kid you warned me to look out for––he's headed to table 15," she said.

"Yes," said Mikhail. "I got an alert as soon as he signed in and his name came across the screen; he's one of the Saluzzos. But now that I see 15's overhead camera has stopped working, I'll have to put Dimitri, not Sergey in at that table." He cursed softly at this discovery as he briskly rolled his chair back from his desk within the basement office. He motioned the elderly, bespectacled man standing nearby who'd been watching Dom on another game room monitor to step closer. "Dimitri," he said to the man, "you heard it; the camera's out, so I'm sending you in. He's our mark, that kid. Bring him on...bring him in...then make him lose...lose big. Now, gear up, and get out there on the floor."

"Okay, what cards—you tell me?" asked Dimitri, a quizzical expression on his narrow face, despite the fact he knew full well what was expected of him. Mikhail rolled his chair back to his desk and pushed an intercom button. "Katrina, what cards are they playing, table 15?"

"Bay State, red back, number 23, specials. Well worn." Dimitri walked over to a cupboard and grasped a deck of red-backed playing cards that had a rubber band around it. He pulled off the rubber band and methodically sorted the cards into four distinct piles—diamonds, hearts, clubs, and spades—on a nearby desk. And then stuffed each suit into a different, commodious pocket of his rumpled tweed jacket, highest card on the top of each suit. Dimitri exuded the bemused appearance of an absent-minded college professor who had slept in and just tumbled out of bed, gotten dressed in a hurry, and rushed to the university only to find he'd missed his own class. This had actually happened several times to Dimitri, one good reason why he was no longer a professor of mathematics in his native Russia.

"Done?" asked Mikhail, impatiently. He looked down at his wristwatch and frowned.

"Done," mumbled Dimitri, plucking the cuffs of his tattered Oxford dress shirt out from the sleeves of his baggy jacket as he headed for the door. "Aces high," he said, sighing wearily as he left for the gaming tables.

"Mind if I join you two ladies?" Dom asked the two scowling nuns he had spotted a moment ago, as he approached their table.

"Well," began Sister Carmella, but Sister Mary kicked one of her shoes under the table, cutting off her attempt to possibly tell the young man not to bother.

"Not at all, young man" replied Sister Mary, forcing a look of benevolence to wash across her face. "We're glad to have some company." *He looks young and pretty innocent,* she thought. *Brand-new suit; he's got money. Deep in the chips, too; pockets are sagging.. It could be our lucky night tonight.*

"Welcome," said her partner at the table. "I am Sister Carmella and my companion here is Sister Mary. We are of the Sisters of St. George."

"I'm Dominic Saluzzo," said the young man, beaming at the sisters. "I'm glad to know you." He took a seat. No sooner had he sat down than he felt someone tap him on the right shoulder.

"Room for one more?" inquired the owner of the bony finger, an old man dressed in baggy trousers and a rumpled tweed jacket who had shambled over while Dom was talking. Dom spun around to look at the man's face. It was thin, and as creased, gray, and worn-out as a dirty old dish rag lying in a laundry basket. The man smiled broadly, exposing overly-large false teeth. He looked like an ancient, swaybacked horse that was ready for the glue factory.

"Sure," said Dom, managing a small, polite-looking smile. He looked over the man's jacket as the gentleman took his seat. *Older dude, retired. Maybe even a teacher,* thought Dom. *Poor guy, probably going to be pissing away his Social Security check tonight. Some people just can't help themselves.* So, Dominic decided that he'd be kind to him. Maybe let him take a little bit of cash home; after all, the guy probably needed bus fare and would need to buy himself a bottle on the way home. Dom could be kind, if the situation warranted it. Dom studied the man more closely now, looking at his pockets; they bulged with unknown contents. *Could it be chips galore, or money in those moth-eaten pockets?*

The man, Dimitri, put a few yellow-and-green chips on the table. "Deal?" he asked Sister Mary sweetly. Mary frowned at him, looked at her watch, shuffled the cards, and deftly cut the deck. At this the old man's sleepy eyelids shot up like two window shades being suddenly yanked on a sunny morning. *The old man has money, that's it,* thought Dom. *He's a sly old dog. Almost fooled me with his act.* So, Dom would be kind. He would bring the old guy on, let him win a few hands, and then go after that loot that was dragging down the old man's pockets. And the old man would lose—big time.

***

"This is what I do the most of on these gigs—waiting. I wait." said Murray morosely. It was dark outside Driftwood by the Sea now, and darker still inside the idling, unmarked police cruiser. Only the soft lights of the police radio glowed within the car. Murray sat, sprawled behind the wheel, a fast-cooling paper cup full of coffee in one hand. Jake sat beside him riding shotgun, fondling the .38-caliber revolver he had in his pocket. Behind them were Patty and Lorenzo. "How's everything back there in steerage, guys?" asked Murray. The large man twisted ponderously in his seat like a bull walrus on a beach, turning around to check on his pups, in order to look at Patty, and then, Lorenzo.

"A little tired," volunteered Lorenzo, "but I'm okay if you guys are." He stretched his legs, then fidgeted in his seat.

"I'm okay," said Patty, stifling a yawn.

"It's probably gonna be a while before our guys go in," stated Murray, putting his coffee down into a cup holder and then hauling up his left shirtsleeve to get a look at his watch. "FBI came in at the last minute and wanted oversight; they're going in with the staties. We've only got the back door to watch here."

"I don't know how many times I've been on stakeouts and all-night parties like these," said Jake, reminiscing about his long career with the police department. "Can't say as I miss those days." Despite his reticence, he almost sounded wistful.

"Well," observed Murray, "you also wrote enough about 'em, didn't you? You wrote 'em into that first book of yours, *Catching the Indecent Dozen*."

"Yeah, guess I did," confessed Jake, nodding. He felt the .38 to make sure the safety was on.

"You know," said Murray, looking over at him, "that's just about my favorite book. I keep it in a special place. Did I ever tell you that?"

"Well," countered Jake, "No. But don't tell me you keep it close to your heart. The back pockets of your pants aren't that big."

Murray snickered. "Nah. I keep it in the magazine rack in the bathroom...right next to the can."

"Good for you. And if it's still got all the pages, I consider that an honor."

The bright, clear landing lights of a jet airplane appeared in the sky, making Patty suddenly think about her job, her family, and to question what she was doing here in a police car on a stakeout, with two cops and a crime writer, taking valuable time off when she could be working...working toward her early retirement. The value was in what the outcome would be...the value would be in the truth she had been looking for, for years.

And Lorenzo, what was he in it for? Patty glanced at him; he was pondering something too. Resolving something he'd been sent to investigate. Jake? Old school. Digging up old bones...wait a minute...*she, Patty* was the one digging up old bones. Murray? Murray being Murray. Doing his job. A job? What was a job? And who above who, was honest? She remembered something she'd read about someone who was a Channel 7 news beat reporter back in the '70s, Jack Kelly, who reportedly said, "If you want a story on a gangster, go to a cop. If you want a story on a cop, go to a gangster." Patty had gone to both the cops...and to her father, for answers to her questions. She wasn't quite done yet.

The radio suddenly buzzed with information. Tersely-worded chatter between armed state police units entering the resort ensued. "They're going in now with the search warrant," Jerry announced. "We're probably not gonna see anything here, way out back tonight, but if we do, remember...I'm betting my badge on you guys being discreet. You're not here...know what I mean? I'm backup for a take-down that's out of my hands. After they make the pinch, we'll roll out front, and we can walk around and see what's what, and who's gonna get a catered breakfast in a holding cell downtown tomorrow."

***

Inside the fortress-like basement of the Knothole Lounge, pandemonium ensued among the guests as the secret entrance was noisily breached and members of a state police SWAT team, weapons drawn, swarmed into the game room; they were accompanied by FBI agents Dave Dobson and Bob Tranten. Each agent wore a blue uniform and a bulletproof vest. Their intrusion did not go unnoticed by the men in the gambling parlor's control room. An armored steel door quickly dropped down with a thud and shuttered the cashier's cage, preventing any entrance. The top of the bar quickly overturned, dumping the liquor—bottles, glasses, and all—into a pit, and returned, blank and empty; the roulette wheel and its table neatly folded up and disappeared automatically...or so it seemed...like a Murphy bed folding up into a wall. "Our money!" screeched Sister Mary in horror as she saw what was happening. "They're taking our money!"

Dom jumped to his feet, bumping the table and scattering cards and poker chips onto the floor. He turned and ran—then stopped momentarily to look behind him. The old man in the tweed jacket was sitting calmly at the table as though nothing had happened. Then the poker machines disappeared, dropping down into recesses in the floor. Sister Anna jolted back from the machine she had just been feeding tokens into as it dropped like an elevator in free-fall and was quickly concealed by a sliding tile panel. Mr. Z, seeing the approach of the officers from the screens in his office control room, had given the doomsday order: "Shut it down! All of it! Now! And bring me the cash from the cage!"

Denied the chance to gain access to the cage, the two FBI agents turned their attention toward questioning people. People who, if nothing else failed, would be charged with being present at an illegal gambling site. "Where is he? Where is Zuckoff?" demanded Bob of a young woman with red hair, who looked as though she'd been poured into a stylish black formal dress. She looked familiar. In fact, even the dress looked familiar to him. She had her back turned toward him as if she were hiding—impossible to do, really, under the circumstances—and was holding her hands over her face as if in shame. "Turn around! FBI!" demanded Bob sharply. "We need to talk to you."

The young woman turned around. "Dad," she said, looking into Bob's eyes, tears rolling down her cheeks "I am so, so sorry."

"Linda!" bellowed Bob, staring at his daughter in wide-eyed astonishment. "My God! What are you doing here?"

"Dad," she said, wiping tears from her eyes, looking at him for some sign of pity, "I can explain."

***

"Nothing doing—yet," observed Murray, listening to all the goings-on via radio.

"Murray," said Jake, turning toward his protégé, "you'd best keep an eye on that building. Every rat's got to have a back door...a second rat-hole. An escape hatch. He's a clever bastard. My guess is, if Z thinks he's got a clean break tonight...he'll go for it. He's new school—so he'll probably leave his pals behind to save his own skin. And, he won't come back for them." Murray put the cruiser into drive and slowly maneuvered it to get a better look at the resort's warehouse. Almost as soon as he did, a garage door in the building opened, and a car shot out of it. Before Murray could react, the vehicle, a black Mercedes, had rocketed out of sight around the corner of the resort's complex.

"C'mon Murray!" Jake urged. "Get after him! It's gotta be him!" Murray grabbed the radio's mic and keyed it, advising all units he was giving chase.

"Just sit back, guys," he advised as he turned on the vehicle's concealed blue lights, buckled his seatbelt, and put the car into gear, "and watch the show." The cruiser surged forward. "This bastard's gonna lead me on a merry chase, of that, I'm sure...even if it isn't our suspect. Buckle yourselves in," he advised. He steered off in the direction the Mercedes had headed.

"I thought everything was sealed off?" asked Lorenzo.

"It should be," answered Murray, "but I can't take chances. Besides, there are civilians outdoors at the resort who could get hurt, the way he's driving...unless he gets stopped."

"Looks like I'm already takin' a chance," groused Jake, looking at Murray, "riding this slow boat with you!"

Murray hauled the cruiser around the corner of another warehouse and put his foot down; the car sped down a road that was bordered on one side by a tall, chain-link fence; an open field was on the other. Far ahead of them in the gloom, the bright red brake lights of a car briefly flashed. "That's him," said Murray. "He's driving with his headlights off. Probably looking for an open gate." He got on the radio once more and

320 PHILIP R. JORDAN

advised he was in pursuit of a black Mercedes with its head-lights off, and to use caution.

"Suspect not sighted," advised a state trooper shortly, after the call went out to other cars on the scene of the raid. "Do not pursue. Contain if possible and advise."

"Bullcrap," muttered Murray. The Mercedes had disappeared. "He's given me the shake but I'll find him." He slowed the cruiser as it neared the end of the road, and then turned back the way he'd come. As the cruiser neared a padlocked gate in the fence, the Mercedes shot out of the field and across the road, bursting through the gate. It tore it off its hinges and plunged into the darkness beyond. Dragging along behind it, raising sparks, was a long, mangled strand of chain-link fence wire and a pipe—then, it was gone.

"Damn!" cursed Murray, who'd braked sharply and almost stood the cruiser on its nose to avoid a collision.

"Punch it!" hollered Jake. "Go get that bastard!" Murray launched the big Ford cruiser through the opening and keyed the radio's mic. "Four-five, seven-seven," he called. "Seven-seven pursuing black Mercedes. Eastbound on Atlantic Avenue, request 10-78." In the backseat, Patty and Lorenzo both braced themselves as the cruiser jostled when its tires pounded over the broken gate and steel posts that lay on the pavement.

Lorenzo tapped Jake in the shoulder. "This is interesting," he observed. "In Rome, our procedure calls for..."

"Kid," groused Jake, turning around momentarily to give him a look that would have paralyzed an attacking mountain lion, "when in Rome, you Romans can do what you Romans do. Here, we do it this way." Jake settled back in his seat, pulled the Smith & Wesson from his pocket and slowly, idly turned the cylinder round and round as he peered through the windshield, looking for any sign of the fleeing Mercedes. It had been a long time since he had fired that gun. Jake found that the palms of his hands were itching.

The cruiser sped along, its flashing blue lights casting tall, flickering shadows on the houses along the avenue. There was no sign of the Mercedes. "I think I've lost him," grumbled Murray, as he took his foot off the gas. The cruiser slowed to a stop at an intersection.

"Look," exclaimed Lorenzo, "over there...along the curb." There, on the corner of the avenue and a side street lay a long strand of wire and a bent piece of silver pipe. "He's gone down that street." Murray punched the gas and drove the car down the street. It was lined with parked cars; none of them were the Mercedes.

The cruiser reached the end of the street and Murray made a right. "I'm going to double back," he announced. He circled the block and turned back onto Atlantic, shutting off the emergency lights. "Looks like we're out of the game," he said glumly.

They drove along in silence for a minute, heading back to Driftwood by the Sea before Patty spoke up. "There's something wrong about this," she announced.

"Why?" asked Murray.

"Just a hunch," she replied. "I think he hasn't gone that far—yet."

"Why not?" asked Jake. "He's probably headed for Route 3 right now. He might even ditch that car and steal one...or maybe he's got a safe house somewhere, or another car stashed away. I wouldn't doubt it."

"I've lost him," Murray announced on the radio to the other units.

What Patty heard next came across as clearly as if it had been heard on the radio—but it hadn't. It was as if someone sitting beside her—not Lorenzo, not Murray, not Jake—but Mickey Callahan, sprung from her dream, who spoke those words straight into her ear: "Keep a close lookout, you fellows!" Tugging at her seat belt to gain some slack, she reacted by turning around to look behind the cruiser. There, not more than two car lengths away was the dark mass of a vehicle following them.

"He's behind us!" she yelled to Murray. "Look out!" A small flash of orange flame appeared from the pursuing car and a bullet splintered the back window of Murray's cruiser.

"Go, Murray, go!" yelled Jake, frantically unbuckling and discarding his seatbelt.

"Get down, everyone!" Murray bellowed. He swerved and the cruiser's tires howled in protest as he turned off Atlantic Avenue and accelerated, trying to escape his pursuer. Another bullet hit the trunk of the cruiser with a resounding *thunk*. Jake, meanwhile, had lowered his window and was twisting around, now backward in his seat, his revolver in his left hand. "No Jake, no!" commanded Murray at seeing what his old mentor was up to. Murray twisted the steering wheel to dodge another shot fired from the Mercedes behind the cruiser.

"Dammit, Murray...grow a pair, will ya?" Jake spat back at the big man. Jake pulled back the hammer on the gun, leaned far out the window, and took a shot—then another.

The cruiser and the Mercedes were fast approaching a junction with a four-lane highway, brilliantly lit with several streetlights; the traffic lights suddenly glared red. "Now that I can see you," growled Jake, "I've got you." He fired again; the Mercedes spun out of control, performing a 360-degree spin before jumping the curb and hitting a fire hydrant and an electric transformer outside an office building. The first object ripped apart the car's suspension and punctured the gas tank in the Mercedes. As it reposed on a neatly-manicured lawn, with Murray and Jake approaching, weapons drawn, the second object's shattered circuits and bare wires caused the gasoline trickling from the tank to explode.

Lorenzo and Patty jumped from the cruiser, but there was little they could do to help. The heat from the burning gasoline was intense enough to force them to stay back.

"Get out! Get out of the car—now!" bellowed Murray at the burning hulk of the Mercedes. There was a thumping sound heard over the sound of approaching sirens;

Mikhail Zuckoff was kicking his door open. He at last succeeded and tumbled out of the car onto the ground and rolled away from the Mercedes. Twisting in pain, he slowly, agonizingly rolled over once more; a gun was in his right hand. Murray quickly stepped forward, kicked the weapon away, grabbed the man by his collar, and dragged him farther away from the fire. Katrina Valenchnikoff, meanwhile, bruised and bloodied, had crawled across the driver's seat and emerged partway. She fell, turned, and tried to drag a large bag—no doubt containing cash—from the car's backseat by its strap. The bag wouldn't budge.

"Leave it!" hollered Jake, darting forward and grabbing her, shielding his face from the searing heat with one arm. "If it's money, forget it. Get out—now!" Two state police cruisers sped up to the fiery scene and quickly stopped. The uniformed troopers hopped out and rushed over to where Murray was tending to the two injured people who were now lying on the pavement a safe distance from the burning car.

"There they are...good show," observed one trooper, "but who are those three?" pointing at Lorenzo, Jake, and Patty.

"Civilians who stopped by to assist," replied Murray, lying quickly but magnificently about his passengers. He added a suggestion: "You could help me out here," as he applied cuffs to Mikhail, who glared at him sullenly.

"You know what the difference is between an elephant and a police car?" Mikhail asked. Not taking the bait, Murray fastened the cuffs in silence. "Okay," snickered Mikhail, "in a police car, the asshole's in the front and the trunk's in the rear."

"Shut your smart mouth, or *you'll* be in the trunk," Murray retorted, jerking him to his feet.

"Mirandize him, you guys," said Murray to the troopers. "Her too," he added, pointing to Katrina, who was sulking and picking pieces of broken safety glass from her hair and dress.

"What are you charging us with?" demanded Mikhail coolly.

"Attempting to elude a police officer. That's good for starters," said Murray matter-of-factly. The taller of the two troopers then strong-armed Mikhail over to a cruiser, opened the back door, and pushed him inside, in the process rapidly shoving his head down to clear the roof the way a bartender shoves a cork into a wine bottle at closing time.

"Murray?" asked Jake, "Call someone for me, will you?" His voice was suddenly shaky. Murray quickly turned toward the old man, who now had his right hand on his chest. "Too much excitement...I think you'd better call the wagon for me." He collapsed and fell before Murray could catch him.

Chapter 32

The Wake Up Call

B oston is a colorful city. From the North End to the South End—and from Boston Harbor to Back Bay—colors abound in every imaginable shade, shape, and form. Take, for example, the red colors; the various shades alone are enough to astound one, observed in the many brick facades of places such as the famous Old Union Oyster House, Robinsons Brewery, and Bell in Hand Tavern. Then, there are the wildly variegated hues of browns, blues, and mauves in the lumpy-bumpy cobblestones on Acorn Street in Beacon Hill. And the shades of green verdigris on the copper sheathing of the ornate, rounded bay windows on buildings in North Square and the lush greenery of the Public Garden come May, when the first of many springtime fun-seekers hop on board the swan boats to go paddling lazily about the garden's pond.

But today, it was raining, and it seemed as though the rain had washed away the colors, causing them all to go trickling down the storm drains along the streets and to disappear as quickly as watercolors being rinsed off a paintbrush. Boston—including its Dorchester neighborhood—seemed monochromatic in the gloomy overcast. The streets were gray, the skies slate-colored, and the many three-story apartment buildings abounding in Dorchester seemed to have been dulled to shades of ash; as gray as the pigeons that scuttled about like bobble-head toys along the curbs. Long, dark, Navy-gray battleships of clouds floated slowly overhead and periodically fired off salvoes of thunder, lightning, and heavy rain. Occasionally, the sun would try to burn through those massive clouds, briefly appearing to rain-drenched citizens below like the dull glow of a distant lantern spotted by hopeful, desperate men trapped deep within a coal mine—then it would disappear, as if exhausted by the futile effort.

Jimmy stood at the front counter of his store and looked out at the street; rivulets of rainwater coursed down the front windows. "Hell of a day, ain't it, Jim?" commented Marv, who was standing behind him, fiddling with the detail tape on the cash register.

"Sure is," Jimmy replied. He was preoccupied with more things than Marv's concerns about the foul weather.

"Word on the street is," continued Marv, "the cops and a couple of feds picked up your ex-pal Jerry Garrantino." Jimmy, taken by surprise, spun around and looked at Marv. "But I doubt he'd sing, as stupid as that guy is."

"Marv," said Jimmy, "I'm not so sure what to bet on any more." Jimmy looked out the window. A white van lettered for A to Z Plumbing was parked in front of the three-story apartment building across the street and just two doors south of Jimmy's store; the van had been there since Jimmy had turned the key in the lock of his store this morning. This was not a good sign.

Suspicion that surveillance might be going on in his neighborhood always put him in a state of high alert. The presence of the A to Z van was especially suspicious because the man who owned the apartment building was himself a plumber. A plumber Jimmy knew, who in fact owned the E-Z Go Plumbing Company; his tenants would have no good reason to call one of the building owner's competitors. Jimmy went down to his basement office, walked over to a row of filing cabinets, reached down behind them, and found an old, leather Gladstone bag. He opened it and rummaged through the contents, at last finding and pulling out what he'd been looking for: a pair of rather large, military-issue binoculars. He took them upstairs, stepped to the front of the store well back from the window, and raised them to his eyes, studying the apartment building the van was parked in front of. He moved his gaze slowly from window to window, passing from ground floor to the second, then to the top floor. Not a soul was to be seen; most of the curtains or shades were drawn. And then, he saw it—on the third floor—in a room where the curtains were partially parted. A large camera, mounted on a tripod, was pointed directly at him. Dimly seen behind the camera was a man in a white shirt and necktie, drinking coffee from a paper cup. "Feds. I should have known," Jimmy mumbled to himself.

"What?" asked Marv. "I didn't catch that."

"I should have known it would rain all day," said Jimmy, in as louder voice. In short, as he now realized, he should have known the feds would get involved sooner or later. Now, with Jerry Garrantino out of circulation but no doubt sitting under bright lights and perspiring profusely in an interrogation room, all bets were off as to when the heat would come down. There were other things concerning Jimmy also.

The computer expert who had visited Jimmy's store this morning had confirmed what Jimmy suspected. "You've got a virus," the computer geek, a young man, announced authoritatively as he pushed his horn-rimmed glasses back up onto their perch on his bony nose. Jimmy frowned. "Oh, yeah; how bad could it be? Well, let's put it this way," the kid had continued condescendingly, "if your computer was a hospital patient and I were the doctor, I'd be shopping for a coffin right now, like, for an 80-year-old patient who's coughing up blood.

Somebody's hacked your email, gotten in, and probably stolen your info...maybe even your identity. Probably some troll in Eastern Europe. Nobody makes upgrades for an operating system as old as the one you have. You need a new computer." Jimmy had paid him and sent him on his way. Jimmy was beginning to believe he would need a new identity—not a new computer—and soon.

"Marv," Jimmy announced, "I'm going down to Kay's for lunch in a few minutes. I'll be back in a while." He trudged back downstairs and over to the filing cabinets, and dropped the binoculars into the bulky Gladstone bag. Its leather surface was dusty and fissured with cracks from ages spent in storage. It was a hand-me-down from Jimmy's father and had once belonged to *his* father, Mickey Callahan. The binoculars landed amidst a collection of ancient newspaper clippings, family photographs, a battered old hat, and other items that had been languishing there since Mickey gave up on his rumrunning trade and cashed in his chips, as the saying goes, long years ago. Beside the bag was a small, badly scuffed boat throw cushion, a small lifesaver that had belonged to *Bad Penny*, Mickey Callahan's boat. Jimmy grabbed it and stuffed it into the bag.

There they all are; the family Callahan archives, thought Jimmy, as he bent over and snapped the bag shut. He stood up and stared down at the bag for a few moments. *Maybe it's time to take a cue from old Mick and get out while the getting's good.* Jimmy put on his leather coat and headed back up the stairway. Before leaving the store, he paused long enough to remove the thumbtack that held an old, faded photograph to the wall. He stuffed the photograph into a pocket of his jacket, turned the collar up, put his head down, and headed out the door. Pelted by raindrops and driven by a sense of urgency, he strode briskly along the sidewalk toward Oh, Kay's! Bar and Grill several blocks away. It was time to make a phone call—the call he secretly hoped he'd never have to make. But it had to be done...and if he was being observed, he was definitely not going to risk making the call, or any others today for that matter, from his office phone. He made an effort not to look over his shoulder until he was two blocks away from the plumber's van; to his great relief, no one was following him. Yet.

***

Oh, Kay's! Bar and Grill had been founded in the early 1960s by a woman who had left a career in one type of service industry to enter another: food service. The word *okay* has been used many times in business names to enhance the business's credibility, but this was actually not the case with Oh, Kay's! Those who knew the owner, Kay, from the old days when her original business was run out of her home, maintained the bar's name came from an expression that customers could frequently be heard exclaiming at odd hours of the evening, whenever the upstairs windows in her house had been left open.

Jimmy had been a customer at Oh, Kay's! Bar and Grill since the days when he had been a young man, trying to establish himself as a boxer at a gym and an arena nearby. Getting "K-O'd at Oh, Kay's!" was the term Jimmy's crowd used for the fellows who stayed out late, drank over their limit, and went down under the table. But then again, being "out for the count" meant little to some of these denizens of the bar who simply couldn't—or wouldn't—count their drinks, much less their blessings at being so generously accommodated and sedated.

In his younger days, Jimmy had decided to end his boxing career after leaving Oh, Kay's! late one night. It was the night he lost a prize match to Bernie O'Sullivan, a match there was a lot of money riding on. By the sixth round, Jimmy was hanging on the ropes, bleeding from a cut on his lips and suffering from a badly-bruised, rapidly-swelling right cheek, which Bernie had tenderized like a veal steak with several hammer-like punches. Jimmy, determined to get revenge, gathered up his strength, lunged off the ropes, and into one of Bernie's trademark left hooks; Jimmy went down for the count. He came to several minutes later, finding himself seated in his corner with his manager Harry Hanrahan bandaging him up, and with the seats in the auditorium emptying out. "Patch me up, Harry," Jimmy said wearily, "and get me outta here. Just don't wrap me up so I look like King Tut."

It was roughly half an hour later when Jimmy limped through the door at Oh, Kay's! and gingerly took a seat at the bar. Kay herself came over and served him a shot of whiskey straight away. "You look like crap," she said. "What does the other dog in the fight look like tonight?"

"He's still fat and sassy, Kay," said Jimmy, knocking back his drink. "I let him get away easy this time. He got away—just like Toto in the *Wizard of Oz*."

"You lie like a rug," said Kay, winking and pouring him another shot. "Next thing you'll tell me is he ran away with his tail between his legs, too." Jimmy was discreet enough for once not to make a wisecrack and ask Kay if she'd seen Bernie's tail recently.

The next morning, Jimmy awoke to find himself lying on a sofa, covered with a blanket that smelled faintly of mothballs and cigar smoke. A massive headache throbbed and pounded away behind his eyes with the steady, earth-shaking cadence of a steam-powered pile driver. His knuckles ached, and there was something stuck to his right cheek. He reached up and touched it; it was a gauze bandage. Although the effort caused excruciating pain, he rolled his eyes far enough to look around, and then recognized the room; it was his manager Harry's living room on Mt. Vernon Street. Just then Harry appeared, bending over him. "Ah, the mummy awakes!" he exclaimed.

"What...what the hell happened?" asked Jimmy, bewildered, attempting to sit up.

"Well," said Harry, "you lost the fight, in case you don't remember. Then you went over to Kay's place. You drank three shots, had four beers, and passed out. Kay's cook and I dragged your sorry ass back here and dumped you where you are. Kay says you owe her $14.50 and that a tip would be appreciated."

***

Four blocks away from his store, Jimmy stopped and turned as if to peer into the window of a butcher shop. He cautiously shifted his gaze to the left, far up the street from the direction he had come in; no one was following him, either on foot or in a vehicle. He tromped on, turned the corner, and found himself at Oh, Kay's! Bar and Grill. Bright red, blue, and yellow neon beer signs glimmered from behind the rain-soaked window panes, and Jimmy could hear the sounds of laughter and the rumbling of an old Bobby Darin song playing on the stereo inside. A car sped by, dowsing the sidewalk with rainwater as it splashed through a puddle. Pigeons wobbled along the sidewalk like wind-up toys, oblivious to this watery interruption in their perusal of the neighborhood. Jimmy stood, rooted to the spot momentarily. He saw it now, clearly. How he'd painted himself into a tight spot—just like a wind-up toy that walks into a corner and keeps on walking...like those pigeons, as if in denial of their circumstances. It was time to stop and think. Jimmy entered the bar.

Kay, sprightly as ever, even at the ripe old age of 80 (and that figure was only guesswork on Jimmy's part) spotted him at once from where she sat on a gilded chair, poised like a dowager queen holding court from behind a chrome-plated cash register. "Jimmy!" she hollered. "What brings you out on this crappy day?" Heads turned at the bar as the court's many self-appointed jesters pricked up their ears and began to listen.

"Just walking for my health, Kay," he said, managing a wan smile. "And I decided to come over for lunch. Is it okay if I use the phone?"

"Oh, I don't know," said Kay, shaking her head. "Are you a credit risk? Didn't pay your bill? Got disconnected?" She cackled briefly like a fairy tale witch gleefully stirring a cauldron of vile potions, then sat back on her gilded perch and waited for his response.

"Hey, you know I pay my bills. I started when I paid off that $14.50, plus tip and interest!"

"Go ahead, hon," Kay said, giggling and lighting a cigarette. "You know where the phone is."

Jimmy noticed that Kay was playing solitaire, with the cards laid out on the countertop behind the display rack of after-dinner mints and candy bars next to the cash register. "Are you running an honest game back there, Kay?" he asked. "I hear you're a wicked card cheat!"

"Hon," replied Kay, peering at him over the rim of her reading glasses, "I never was good at fooling myself. The first time I knew enough not to fool myself was back in '63. I knew it was time to fold 'em. Four years on my back was enough time to spend saving up to start a business." Jimmy nodded. "And you," she said, her forehead wrinkling in curiosity, "where have you been all this time? It's been ages since you've been in." She moved her cards a bit, slowly, and looked up at him, staring at him with the aplomb of a fortune teller doing a tarot reading. "You're not in trouble, are you?"

"No, Kay. I've just been busy." Jimmy wished he hadn't provoked the conversation and stoked Kay's curiosity. *Christ,* he thought, *does she have a crystal ball under the counter?*

"You hardly ever come out of that basement office of yours, do you?" she inquired. "That's too much like Punxsutawney Phil...or maybe like old Adolf in the bunker, right at the end—you know, when the Russians were closing in on him."

"Thanks, Kay," said Jimmy, "I'll try to get out more often. "I'll have my usual...which I confess I haven't had in a long, long time." Kay grabbed a waitress's pad and scribbled an order on it.

In order to use the phone at Oh, Kay's! one had to run the gauntlet. In other words, one first had to step behind Kay's chair, wiggle through a narrow doorway, and then pass between the bar and the liquor rack—with all the patrons watching—and then, farther on, between the bar and the grill, to gain access to the backroom where the telephone hung on the wall. "Here," said Kay, turning around to face Jimmy as he stepped behind her ornate chair, "give me a hug." Embarrassed, Jimmy stooped and briefly hugged the elderly lady. Getting an armload of old Kay wasn't exactly what he had in mind in visiting today.

"You haven't changed a bit, Kay," Jimmy lied to her, after letting her go.

"Hey, hon," she giggled, winking at him and reaching for her glass of vodka, "what you see is what you get. No nips or tucks, no artificial ingredients or fillers...still going after all those years, and with the same liver, too!"

Upon reaching the telephone, Jimmy peeked around the corner into Kay's office and the storage room; they were both empty. Jimmy pulled a scrap of paper from his pocket, read the number, picked up the phone, and punched in the number for Nacosto's Italian Ristorante. "Jimmy Callahan here...let me talk to Sammy," said Jimmy. There was a short pause before Sammy Nacosto got on the line. "Sammy," said Jimmy, "there's no bad blood between us. Our families made peace long ago, and so I'm going to lay something out for you; I'm selling out. When we made peace, we always had the deal that if one of us wanted to move on and move out, the other guy could buy in and come out stronger. It's just business. I'm ready, but I want to move on it. Tomorrow. Where? Okay, yeah...that makes sense. When? Alright. I'll bring just one of my people. Just cash...right."

Jimmy hung up the phone. He picked it up again and dialed the number for Patty's cell phone. He had a plan now. He knew he could never make things right with her. But he had to talk with her before anything else went wrong.

He didn't tell her that she was part of the plan.

Chapter 33

Family Matters

L orenzo awoke, rubbed his eyes, and rose from the large, soft bed in his dark hotel room. He tossed the sheets aside and glanced at his wristwatch to check the time, the early hour expressed in three tiny, glowing numbers. His bedside alarm clock had not yet sounded; he'd awakened upon seeing a crack of daylight appearing between the drawn curtains at the window. Apprehensive about not missing his morning flight back to Italy, and curious to see what the weather was doing, he padded barefoot to the window and tugged the curtains apart. The rosy glow of the sunrise greeted him, causing him to blink, and it bathed the room in its low-level light.

Although it was still early morning, with the sun about to make its way over the horizon, hundreds of commuters already scuttled busily along the distant highways. Their vehicles appearing like lines of swarming, tiny black ants diligently heading off en masse to do their daily chores for some unseen master. Farther away to the northeast was the hub of Boston. Its tract of land, like a giant hand upon whose back the downtown buildings sat, seemed to reach toward the sea, the long wharfs along Commercial Street extending into the water like its fingers. The downtown buildings, many still displaying lights on signs and in windows, appeared like a string of glitter-ing charms on a bracelet, strung on the wrist of dark land that separated the waters of Fort Point Channel, calm, murky and oily-looking, from the Charles River far beyond.

Patty had said goodbye to Lorenzo the night before as she dropped him off at the hotel. She seemed preoccupied, her thoughts no doubt filled with concerns about going to the meeting her father had asked her to attend today; Lorenzo had tried to talk her out of it but Patty had resolutely refused. Lorenzo thought she was more than a bit like her father, stub-born to the core and not given to changing her mind once she was bent on a course of action. Willing to take a calculated risk, too, like impersonating a police officer and having no great moral qualms about it. "Stick with Jake Thayer," Lorenzo had advised, smiling, "and I'll bet you can solve any mystery you have a mind to."

She smiled back. "It's just one more," she replied. "Maybe this will be the last one concerning my family." Her handshake was firm and resolve showed in her eyes. *That's her*, Lorenzo thought, *Jimmy's daughter...how did the Americans say? A chip off the old block.*

After they parted company yesterday, Lorenzo had tried to come to grips with how to handle his return to Italy and his desk job—if he still had one. On one hand, he had failed to accomplish what he had set out to do, to find what Mrs. Saluzzo and the priest had been up to. And, he had delayed his response to the captain's orders to return to Italy. On the other hand...he had been complying with the captain's first or-ders: to follow the pair and not report until he had the facts. Furthermore, he had taken a part in solving a crime that was among Boston's oldest cold cases, and also in the arrest of the perpetrator, charged not only with murder, but also with money laundering, illegal gambling, and cybercrimes. Perhaps Lorenzo still had a job, and his rank, after all...but then again, maybe not, he mused. It could be worse, much worse, than he could imagine. *I could do better than this, having this job,* Lorenzo thought.

He gazed out the window and saw movement nearby in the parking lot of a discount lumberyard and home goods store. Men in ragged-looking, castoff clothing were lining up on the sidewalk by the store's parking lot gateway, shuffling about and smoking. He watched as a truck loaded with roofing materials and lumber left the loading dock, drove toward the open gate, and stopped beside it. The driver leaned out the window and beckoned to the first two men in line. After what was apparently a brief conversation involving some hand waving, sign language, and negotiation, the men got into the cab of the truck and it drove off. *Those are men looking for work,* thought Lorenzo, *for hire by the day.* It was still chilly at this hour; the men standing in line in their rough, ill-fitting clothes rubbed their hands and stamped their feet in an effort to feel some sense of warmth. *Well,* thought Lorenzo, thinking now about coffee and the breakfast awaiting him in the hotel's lounge, *I could do a lot worse than being a sergeant, or even a patrolman, too...if I had to be one again.*

***

"If that's what he told you...don't piss him off," Jake Thayer said to Patty. He was sitting up in bed—a good sign, given his previously critical condition—holding a paper cup of ginger ale and sipping it through a straw. He set the cup down on a bedside tray. "You've just got to obey the conditions to gain their acceptance, but remember: there's no trust." It was quiet in the hospital this morning, and sunlight streamed in through the window of Jake's room. The other patient in the room, a part of the cardiac care ward, had gone out for a slow stroll down the corridor with one of the nurses. He was probably counting floor tiles and, in the process, taking in a world-class view of the nurse's legs, Jake thought to himself. Lucky guy.

338 ~ PHILIP R. JORDAN

"How could he do this?" asked Patty. "I mean—I told him I'd bring him the key, but he doesn't want to meet at his place."

"Well, Patty, it sounds to me like it's a setup for something bigger. Maybe your dad wants you for a witness...do you think he wants you as collateral for some kind of exchange?"

"He wouldn't dare," answered Patty, shaking her head—and her hair in the process. She gathered it up, ran her fingers through it thoughtfully, and then stared at him.

"So, he said to go to Moakley Park, at noon, right?" Patty nodded. "And then look for three guys sitting together in lawn chairs, way out in the middle, with an empty chair for you, right?" She nodded again. "And—wait; I'm sure he must have said 'Come alone.'"

"That's right; he did," answered Patty.

"Uh huh," grunted Jake. "This thing is a meet that's been sanctioned. You're not brokering the deal, so either he is...or somebody else is," observed the old man. "And you—you've got something he, your dad, wants."

"Yes," answered Patty. *Of course; there's always something Jimmy wants.*

"And, it must be he's with some guys who want something, too. You'd better take Dillinger; you're taking care of him anyway, which I'm glad of, but take him for your sense of security."

"There are some things I can tell him now," said Patty, wrinkling up her nose. "Now that you've told me Jerry's talked—and what he's said, so that I know. We all know now—that Zuckoff is undeniably the person who shot Rose."

"Right," said Jacob. "Jerry sang like a bird, given the prospect of spending any more quality time in prison than he might have to. All circumstantial evidence...and all the forensics evidence...point to Zuckoff."

"So maybe today, I can still stop my father from this perverted war he's got going on in his head...and whatever else he's trying to cook up today."

"You need to give him that key," said Jake, coughing slightly. He reached for the ginger ale and the straw, and took a drink. "That ends your complicity in anything. And convince him to end it...whatever it is he's up to. Let me know how it turns out."

***

It was 11:50 when Patty pulled into the parking lot just off William J. Day Boulevard. Beyond it were the waters of Old Harbor, and on the shoreline along Carson Beach people were sitting in loungers, lazing in the sunlight. They were watching a father and his young son running to and fro, flying a brightly colored kite that skittered back and forth, tormented by strong winds in the clear blue sky, high above the sand. "C'mon, Dillinger," said Patty to Jake's Doberman, snapping a leash onto his collar. "It's time to meet my dad."

Patty led Dillinger out of the Honda, locked it, and headed across the boulevard and into the park. To her right, Patty could hear the *bonk!* of tennis balls being hit back and forth on courts and to her left, the sounds of a baseball game in progress on one of the park's several diamonds. Far beyond her, in the middle of the green space in the park, Patty spotted three people sitting in lawn chairs. Beside them was a vacant chair. Her chair.

"What the hell?" she said to herself. She quickly reined in Dillinger as he lunged at a scampering squirrel, and started walking toward the three people in the center of the park.

She looked over her left shoulder; there was no one following her. Behind her was only green space, the boulevard, and at the far, south end of the park, a traffic rotary and a state police station. *Well, I guess that makes this somewhat safe,* she thought. As she neared the three people seated in the lawn chairs, she recognized her father; at his feet was an old Gladstone bag, the one she had seen in his office. The other two men sitting with him were strangers. One was her father's age, a tall man with a bony-looking face and aquiline nose. He looked calm and composed; his hands were folded in his lap, and he was chatting amiably with her father. Patty recognized him as the man she had seen on the video monitor the night she had slipped into the manager's office at Nacosto's. The third man was younger—perhaps not quite her age—and was fiddling with an iPad, as if ignoring the conversation.

"Okay, Dad," she said as she neared the group. "I came alone...almost," she added, pointing at Dillinger.

"Good," said her father softly. He held up one forefinger, pressing it to his lips. Apparently, Patty had interrupted a conversation.

"And there we were," said the calm-looking man, looking out toward the beach, ignoring Patty for the moment, "out fishing, up on Squam Lake in New Hampshire...me, the little kid rowing the boat, and Granddad Tony...and the state fish and game commissioner, with whom my granddad was having a fine conversation, while they drank their beers and fished." He turned to face Jimmy, smiling, then adding, "A good time, right?"

"Right," answered Jimmy, nodding his head.

"So the old man, and his pal," said the calm-looking fellow, "weren't catching anything. So old Granddad, ever impatient, reached into his tackle box, see...he pulled out a stick of dynamite...he lit it, and he heaved it into the water. *Ka-boom!* Up came all the fish they could ever want, and he started to net them. And the fish and game commissioner..."

"He's got his panties in a bunch, now, right?" laughed Jimmy.

"Right. He had a fit. 'You can't do that!' he yelled. So Granddad turned around...he waited a minute, like he was going to reach into the cooler, crack open another beer, and give it to the guy to calm him down. But instead, he lit another stick of dynamite. He spun around, stuffed it into the commissioner's pocket, and said to him: 'Hey—are you gonna sit there and bitch all day, or are you gonna fish?'"

Both the calm man with the bony-looking face and Jimmy guffawed; the other, younger man remained absorbed in whatever was on his iPad. Once the laughter ended, Jimmy looked at both of them and said, "Guys, meet my daughter, Patty Callahan. Patty, this is Sammy Nacosto and his son, Eric."

The elder Nacosto, who had been telling the story, rose to his feet, leaned over Jimmy and shook Patty's hand briefly, almost methodically. The overall effect for Patty was that of someone arriving early at a wake and being greeted by the owner of the funeral home, who obviously was bored and had nothing better to do at the moment. "Thank you so much for coming," he said. "It means much to me that each of our families can meet—each of them with the father and his only child—without anyone else, as a show of good faith. It goes toward trust...given our troubles in the past. It is a gesture I appreciate and respect." He looked down at his son. "Eric," he snapped, "please say hello."

"Hello," parroted Eric, looking up at Patty momentarily. "Nice to meet you." Sammy glared at him briefly; his son returned the look. Sammy then turned back toward Patty and smiled as though nothing had passed between him and his son. Dillinger the Doberman whined, walked around in a tight circle, laid down on the grass, rolled his eyes upward at Patty, and sighed, as if resigning himself to attend this meeting.

"Dad," asked Patty, looking at her father quizzically, "what's going on? I thought this meeting was just about me giving you that key, right?"

"Right, just like you promised. Can I have it now, please?" He expectantly held out one of his hands.

"I'm not so sure now," she said. "I told you I wanted answers. And it seems like lately, I've had to find a lot of them on my own. Now, what is this meeting really about?"

"What's it about?" Jimmy asked. "It's about me getting out of business...I'm selling the store and the business to Sammy and his son, Eric. Eric does the financial stuff; he's working on the closeout right now." Eric continued to doodle on the iPad.

"Wow. So, you're getting out. Good for you. Where's *my* easy out?" huffed Patty.

"Hey, this is what you wanted—what Ellen wanted—all along."

"What *I* wanted? What Mom wanted? Please, this is about what *you* want. You want out of a mess you got yourself into."

"What I want? To make things right where there was a wrong...when my sister was killed. And you know by who."

"Oh, yeah," snapped Patty, "you still think it was one of the Saluzzos, right?"

"Ah! That bunch," scoffed Sammy. He raised one hand from the arm of his lawn chair and waved it dismissively, as if he were waving off a troublesome fly. "Vince—that mooch. And his wife Maria, the oh-so pious, generous one, right? I'll bet she makes change from the collection plate in church. And young son Charlie? The kind of son who goes to a family reunion to pick up girls?"

"No," interjected Patty, "it wasn't any of them."

"Yeah? Then who did push the button?" asked Sammy, sitting still and staring at her as solemnly but expectantly as an owl perched on a tree, watching for prey. "I remember reading about that. No one would ever talk about it."

"A Russian mobster, David Mikhailov," asserted Patty. "He's just been busted, running an underground gambling parlor on the south shore—Driftwood by the Sea—under the name Mikhail Zuckoff. The police put everything together."

"What? Holy—" exclaimed Sammy, straightening up in his chair. "The Russians—the damned Russians. I heard that they were coming in here and setting up shop. I should have known something was up with that place. He's taken enough people out of the hospitality business and ruined them. But—you didn't hear that here." He looked about, as if to make sure no one else was within earshot. "He tried to pull his game on me, but it didn't work. He's a sly one...crazy like a fox. But no one takes Nacosto's away from me by pulling the wool over my customers' eyes. Eric took care of all that trash he and his crew tried to spread on the Internet." There was a long pause. He slowly turned in his chair and stared at Jimmy. "He didn't try to pull one over on you, did he?"

"I've had a lot of stuff pulled on me," said Jimmy. "Look what my daughter's pulling on me right now. But no—that guy, I've never heard of him. My business is clean."

"Oh, really?" commented Patty. "I've heard enough."

"Hey, Judge Judy!" blurted Sammy. "Let's button it and wrap this up. I'm not sitting in family court here. I need those keys. Let's get this deal done." Patty, her temper almost coming to a boil, pulled the old, brass MBTA key from her jacket pocket and handed it to Jimmy, who pulled another key from his pocket, then handed both to Sammy Nacosto.

"There you go," Jimmy said. There was a dazed expression on his face. "Do you want to see what's in the bag?" he asked.

"What *is* in the bag?" asked Sammy, tilting his head back as if sniffing for something rotten that would spoil the whole deal.

"All the old stuff from Mick's rum boat, the boat your grandfather bought from O'Malley," answered Jimmy. "Your family got a bum deal; Mick had the goods on the politicians and found out Prohibition would end sooner than anyone ever thought. He screwed O'Malley and then O'Malley woke up and dumped it on your granddad. You're entitled to this stuff."

"Oh, yeah? Pangs of conscience? Where the hell did Jimmy C get pangs of conscience?" Patty wondered aloud.

"Oh, go ahead; express your inner Ellen!" remarked Jimmy. "Rock on, girl; this is just great for business."

"Keep it," said Sammy. "I've got what I want. And I've got no time to watch an early edition of Family Feud. Eric, give

Jimmy the package." Sammy stood and scanned the area; anyone approaching them in the huge green space would immediately be noticed. "Check your drone, too," ordered Sammy. Eric
consulted his phone, and a drone that had been hovering high
overhead buzzed closer, then took off and performed a series
of meandering circles.

"Nothing," said Eric laconically. Satisfied that no one was
watching or listening, Sammy sat back down.

"Okay, Patty," Jimmy said to his daughter, looking at her
earnestly. "You want family history? You want all the stuff
from the past? You got it." He pushed the old Gladstone bag
toward her feet.

"Thanks, Dad," she said bitterly. "I'm second best, huh?
What the hell...I'll take it." She stared at him. "My inheritance,
I presume? It's probably all I'll ever get from you. But I never
had expected much...from a father who has no moral compass.
With you, it's all about business. And, you know what? I'll bet
you wouldn't have a legitimate business for anything, would
you?" Dillinger sniffed the bag carefully and nudged it playfully with his nose. Jimmy stared at Patty, before giving her, for
once, an honest answer.

"Not for all the money in the world. I guess...I just can't help
myself."

"We're almost done here," announced Eric crisply. "Jimmy,
just sign here please." He presented the iPad and a stylus to
Jimmy, who signed his name on the screen and then handed
them back. Eric handed him a padded envelope, from which
Jimmy extracted several large bundles of currency and stuffed
them inside his jacket.

"So," he said, "we're done, right?"Jimmy asked.

"Correct," answered Sammy. "We're done. Once more: Marv
and all your boys are staying on the job, right?"

"Yes, they are. One more thing; that box you told me you'd kick into the deal, for my protection, the electronic disruptor, or whatever it's called."

"Oh yeah, the box," said Sammy. "Eric, put that thing down and give Jimmy the box. What are you watching now, anyway?"

"Baseball," groused Eric. "Terrible game. Bottom of the seventh inning and Cleveland's skunked 'em, 5 to 1. Damned Sox." He pocketed the iPad, reached down under his chair, and grasped a small cardboard box; he pulled out a device that looked somewhat like a radar gun. He handed it to his father, who passed it along to Jimmy.

"What," asked Patty, "is that thing?"

"Cop stuff, high-tech stuff," answered Sammy. "Experimental." A faint smile played on his face. "You aim it at a car, pull the trigger, and it stops the car dead. All electronic. It won't work beyond a range of 50 or 60 feet—but it works. The versions on the street, what few there are, are all mounted in police cars, but this one's hand-held."

Jimmy's brow wrinkled. "Is it hot?" he asked.

"Not really," chuckled Sammy. "The cops don't even know it's missing yet."

"So we're done here, right?" Jimmy asked. Sammy nodded.

"I'm not done," chimed in Patty. She grasped the open Gladstone bag and peered inside. There was the framed photograph of *Bad Penny* that she had seen at her aunt's beach shack...the boat throw cushion she'd sat on as a child...an old fedora hat...a bundle of old newspaper clippings, yellowed with age...and a pair of large, military-style binoculars. She snapped the bag shut, grasped the handle, and stood.

"The Callahan family archives," she said, staring at her father. "How thoughtful of you. Now, I am done." She picked up Dillinger's leash and gave it a gentle tug; the Doberman stood, stretched, and wagged his tail. Jimmy stared back at her. Patty turned her back on him and began to walk back to her car.

"That's it, huh?" asked Jimmy. "Walking away?"

"Why not?" countered Patty, not turning around. "You did...years ago. And now, I'll bet you're going away."

"I sure as hell am," replied Jimmy, following her. "Right now..." he paused to look at his watch, "there's a fire breaking out at my house. Awful thing. A bad one. I don't know if anyone will even be able to find my body after it's put out."

"I won't look," snapped Patty. "I won't waste my time any more than I will right now, talking any more with you."

"Mexico's good this time of year," said Jimmy. He stuffed the disruptor under his jacket, like someone concealing a handgun. "What do you want to stay in town for? Want to keep that flying job for? Your health? Meet a guy? Get married again? What?"

Patty stopped and spun around. "Don't you patronize me," she snapped. "Don't even think about inviting me on your escape from reality."

"Escape? Me?" He paused, spreading his arms wide, gesturing like a waiter summoning diners to a table. "Hell...I was going to offer you 20 percent."

"Twenty percent? Twenty percent of what? And why?"

"Twenty percent of the sale. Cash. It's real. For assisting with the sale. And being discreet."

"Oh, oh oh oh," replied Patty. "You're trying to buy my silence, huh? Oh, God, I really like that. Thanks, but no thanks. I won't work in your world. You don't get it, do you? I don't work on a percentage or a pay-per-story basis. You don't need a daughter—never did. You need a spin doctor with a criminal mind. To make everything pay—for you. Your way."

At that, Jimmy waved his hands in the air, scattering pigeons as he did so. "You want to see crime? You want to see crime pay?" he blustered. "Go to law school; go get yourself a law degree!" Dillinger cringed and whined; the dog—and Patty—kept on walking.

"I just saw crime pay," said Patty, intent on reaching her car quickly, "while you sat there and got what you think you're due, while Nacosto sat there like he was General Grant at Appomattox." Jimmy's face flushed crimson.

Patty and Dillinger reached the curb by the boulevard and stopped. Dillinger looked up at Patty and wagged his short tail. "You don't care, then, do you?" Jimmy asked his daughter. "About money? Let me tell you...if you were born broke like me and Sammy, money would be very important to you."

Patty turned around and looked at her father. "*You* don't even know, don't even care, do you?" she asked.

"What?" responded Jimmy.

"Why your sister Rose got killed, do you?" Jimmy just stood there, staring at her while she spoke. "Because she knew too much about someone who was a criminal...and she was going to come forward to help convict him. You know what? Right here, right now, I'm going to quit while I'm ahead. I don't know you, can't say as I ever did. All I know is, Jimmy is for Jimmy." She turned her back on her father and headed for her car.

Jimmy stood for a while and then sat down on the curb. Watched Patty go to her car, unlock the doors, toss in the Gladstone bag, and get Dillinger safely inside. Watched as the car started, turned out onto the boulevard, and then saw a Cadillac Sedan DeVille with three men in it abruptly pull out of a parking spot and follow Patty's Honda, which soon went whizzing by. Jimmy pulled the disruptor from his pocket, fumbled with it, and released the safety. And as the Cadillac neared, he made out the figures of the three Saluzzo brothers inside it...then held up the disruptor and pulled the trigger.

There was no noise...until the Cadillac's engine abruptly stopped running, and the man behind the wheel, Franky, panicked and hit the brakes. The car skidded in a small arc and caromed off the side of a street-sweeping truck before smashing into a row of parked blue-and-black cruisers at the state police barracks. The response from the police was almost immediate; officers poured out of the barracks and swarmed over the Cadillac and its occupants, dazed and briefly pinned in place by airbags, like angry bees protecting their nest. "Good going, guys," muttered Jimmy. "You chumps took the bait. I guess sometimes if you want to fish, you've got to use dynamite." He stood up, stuck his thumb out, and almost immediately hitched a ride with an old man driving a newspaper truck.

"Where ya goin'?" asked the elderly gent, chewing on a toothpick as he eyed the road ahead, and, in the rearview mirror, the Cadillac's encounter with law enforcement.

"Somewhere else. Anyplace else," said Jimmy, looking tired. He felt the bundles of bills stashed within his jacket, checking to make sure they were still there, and then smiled. To him, it seemed as if the sun was somehow shining just a bit brighter than a minute ago. He looked through the truck's windshield at the open road ahead, settled back in his seat with a sense of resignation, sighed, and said, "It's the only place left to go to."

***

It was early afternoon when Patty's Honda pulled into the driveway of Jake Thayer's Woburn home and came to a stop. Dillinger, his head stuck out the open backseat window, yelped excitedly. "Oh, you big baby," said Patty, looking at the Doberman in the rearview mirror. "Yes, you're home, but not for long. Let's go inside and feed Kittery...then, you're off to the vet's to be boarded." Patty stepped out and opened the back door of the car, reaching inside for Dillinger's leash. She was momentarily in shock. "Oh, no! Dillinger...you bad dog! What have you done?" she exclaimed. The Gladstone bag she had tossed into the car had apparently sprung open and its contents were strewn on the seat of the car. The old fedora had been crushed; Dillinger was sitting on it. A brittle old newspaper, now almost shredded to ribbons, sat beside the dog. And Dillinger, now looking sorrowful indeed, had been busy on the ride home from Boston, chewing on the old boat cushion as if it were a doggy toy. One side of it was ripped open and wet with saliva.

"Come on! Out of the car, now," ordered Patty, tugging gently on the Doberman's leash.

Dillinger nimbly hopped out and then sat, looking up at her and wagging his tail. "What a mess," commented Patty, reaching into the car and grabbing the boat cushion. As she did so, two small oilcloth bundles, each roughly the size of a man's hand and sealed with what looked like brown wax, tumbled out and fell to the ground. Puzzled, Patty held up the cushion, looked inside, and shook it slightly; like a robin's nest being pulled apart and emerging piecemeal from a birdhouse, a mesh of old, rotted cloth, pieces of yellowed paper, and what may at one time have been several handfuls of horsehair emerged and fell to earth. And yet more of the strange, small bundles came out, plopping onto the pavement. There were eight of them in all. Dillinger pounced on them.

"No!" Patty yelled. Dillinger cringed, laid down, and emitted a long sigh. He whined and rolled his eyes at her. Patty dropped the empty boat cushion and picked up one of the bundles, turning it over and over in her hands. "What *is* this?" she pondered before finally succumbing to an overwhelming sense of curiosity. She bent it in her hands and it yielded to the pressure, at first cracking, then crumbling into several pieces, some of which fell to the pavement.

She stared in astonishment at what was revealed to her, now that the remnants of the bundle's covering were mostly gone: a stack of musty-smelling, odd-looking $100 bills.

It took several seconds for Patty to come to her senses, lift her head up, and look about to see if someone was watching her, but the street nearby was empty of cars and people. She knelt, gathered up the remaining bundles, and stuffed them into the boat cushion, together with the money. She stood, pulled the spare key to the house from her pocket, grasped the boat cushion and Dillinger's leash, and headed to the back door, which she quickly opened. Kittery greeted Patty with a loud meow and then greeted Dillinger by taking a swipe at his nose that thankfully missed the mark. Patty unhooked his leash and the Doberman made a beeline for his dog bed; the cat jumped up on the kitchen table.

"Yes, yes, Kittery, I know; you're hungry and your food's in the fridge," said Patty, pausing to stroke Kittery's head; the cat soon emitted a purr of contentment. Patty laid the old boat cushion from *Bad Penny* on the table and slowly opened the bundles, one by one; they all contained $100 bills that were redolent of must from the decades they spent in storage. "Well, Dad," said Patty to herself softly, clutching a stack of bills that were made when her great-grandfather was a young man and FDR was in the White House, "I guess I've got one up on you. You never could figure out what old Mick did with his fortune. Mystery solved; it just trickled down to me...I guess *I* just can't help myself. You made your fortune today...I guess I've made mine, too."

Kittery yowled insistently now, hungry as ever, and brushed against Patty's hand. "Oh, all right, kitty," she said. She grabbed a spoon from the dish rack, brought out the reserve can of cat food from the fridge, spooned the contents into a clean dish, and set it beside Kittery's water bowl. Kittery launched herself from the table and pounced on the dish like a lion about to savage a wounded gazelle. *Just exactly like a lion*, thought Patty. *And now...I'm being just exactly like Dad.* She looked up and caught sight of her reflection in a mirror hanging a darkened room down the hall. There, where the shades were pulled and the curtains tightly drawn, her image seemed to float above the floor like some glowing, ghostly apparition sent to haunt her. She noticed there was a smirk on her face. She looked away from it, turning her thoughts inward. *This isn't my fortune*, she thought as she stared at herself anew in the mirror and saw that the triumphant, almost evil expression that had been on her face a moment before had vanished. *It's Ellen's fortune...Chloe's, too. No, Jimmy, I don't want to be just like you.*

Chapter 34

The Last Word

Hal Hemmerman, editor of the *Baystate Police and Detective Gazette*, stopped writing and reached for the steaming hot mug of coffee beside his desk. Without taking his eyes off the computer monitor for even a second he reached out, grasped the mug, and took a swig. The mug left a dark brown circle on the advance copy of a book it had been resting on. The book was, like many Hal received in the mail virtually without fail every week, yet another crime novel sent to him by some PR maven in a big city publishing house. Although Hal was not disposed to write and publish book reviews in the paper on a regular basis until and unless the mood struck him, the publishers nonetheless fairly showered him with galley proofs and advance copies. If nothing else, the novels provided Hal with what he once referred to as his "bathroom reading material," but excerpts sometimes handily provided inspiration on days when Hal was struggling to hammer out a dramatic, attention-riveting headline or a snarky-sounding blurb for an important story when press day was just around the corner. A story like this one, the one he was working on feverishly. And now, he'd hit a dry spell—nothing was coming to him.

He set the mug down on the novel, leaned back in his chair...and then it came to him.

Something from one of old Jacob Thayer's novels. He sat bolt upright, leaned over the keyboard, and stared at the text on the screen before him, scanning what he'd just written about the raid at Driftwood by the Sea. He clicked on the image of the four Sisters of St. George being escorted from the gambling parlor by a cop, and then he clicked back on the story, entering the bold headline: "Nuns the Wiser." Below it, he entered the blurb: "Sisters Shown Mercy After Raid, Face New Questions in Auto Raffle Scam." Hal leaned back, stretched, and reached for his coffee once more. Beside the mug rested a well-smudged glass, still harboring the faint aroma of scotch; a puddle of water from melted ice cubes lurked in its bottom like the remnants of a glacier that had come to ruin. The glass had seen active duty well into the final hours of the previous evening as Hal worked late on his editor's note, and also on the contents of the now-empty liquor bottle in his office wastebasket. Hal's phone beeped; someone in the office was paging him. He picked up.

"Amber alert!" came the warning from the caller. The caller was Chuck, the newspaper's ace photographer and Hal's confidant. Chuck was warning his boss about the approach of Amber Grossenbaur, the elderly and rather truculent production manager.

"Thanks Chuck!" chuckled Hal. "I thought I heard the distant clatter of tank treads, and maybe even a sabre. What was she doing just before she left? Sharpening a knife?"

"She had a jar of something open on her desk...and she was rubbing something from it on her face," answered Chuck.

"Well, what was it?"

"Some kind of lotion. What did you think it would be? An aphrodisiac, you lucky dog?"

"Crap," said Hal in mock disgust. "I was hoping it was vanishing cream." He quickly hung up the phone and turned his attention toward the monitor once more.

Sure enough, footsteps soon sounded in the hallway outside Hal's office, and then Amber appeared in the doorway, pouting at him, her form looming large and blocking the sunlight that had been streaming through the hallway window. "That article...you said you'd have it in half an hour," she groused. "That was 45 minutes ago." She peeked at him peevishly over the rims of her reading glasses.

"Sorry. Just finished it," said Hal. "I'll send it to you right now." He looked down at his keyboard, clicked a few keys, then looked back up at her and flashed a toothy smile. "There—sent." The computer emitted a whooshing sound that momentarily made Hal wish he were onboard a jet plane leaving Boston, the office, and the impending deadline behind.

"Okay, what about the piece on the Callahan murder and the Russian guy...and the car chase?" she asked. "Are you finally signing off on the layout now?"

"I really think we need to go with two pages now, not one," Hal answered. Amber glowered at him and placed her hands on her hips. Her lower lip was now jutting out, a sure sign of impending conflict.

"If you knew all this and had Chuck's pictures, and all the police reports, why didn't you tell me what you wanted before I laid it all out?"

"Sorry," replied Hal, looking sheepishly down at his keyboard, then at the wastebasket, where the open neck of the scotch bottle peeked out like a glazed-over eyeball, lurking beneath a crumpled copy of yesterday's *Globe*. Hal judiciously rolled his chair back slightly to block it from Amber's view. "I just want to make sure that when this runs, everything looks good," asserted Hal.

"It will," retorted Amber. "This newspaper isn't my first picnic. Don't worry; *I'm* what makes *you* look good."

"Well...it was a long night last night," added Hal.

"Well," commented Amber sarcastically, "it's going to be a *long day* today. You can count on that." She stuck her nose up, turned on her heel, and left in a huff.

The phone beeped again. Once again, it was Chuck on the intercom. "Yes?" Hal asked.

"You won't believe this!" sputtered Chuck excitedly. "It just came over the scanner. The state police station at Moakley Park has been attacked."

"What?" exclaimed Hal, instinctively reaching for a pen and a pad of paper. "How?"

"Three men in a car...they drove through a barricade into the compound's parking lot and wiped out five cruisers. Nobody's been hurt, but there are charges pending. The cops are viewing it as an act of domestic terrorism."

"My God!" exclaimed Hal. "What do we know about the perps?"

"Plenty, Hal There are three guys...and, get this: they're the Saluzzo brothers!"

"Chuck!" Hal roared. "What are you doing, sitting there? Get your ass down to Moakley Park and get some pictures! Take whoever's on call with you to get the story!"

Hal stood up and looked into the small mirror that hung above his desk. He had placed it there long ago to avoid being startled when people walked quietly into his office unannounced and interrupted his train of thought. Today, that train of thought was a juggernaut rolling along down the tracks of crime-publishing history toward fame and fortune, gaining speed with every moment. Hal looked at his reflection and suddenly realized he had two days' worth of beard on his face. His eyes looked like stoplights and his rumpled white dress shirt, untucked as it was from his trousers, resembled the expanse

of a distended accordion. But that didn't matter. The next issue—his issue—was going to knock the proverbial ball out of
the park. He smiled and mouthed the words he'd been longing to utter as long as he'd been in publishing...the words that
otherwise perhaps only an overly-stressed laundry worker on
overtime might appreciate: "Stop the presses!"

* * *

The plane leaving Logan Airport gained speed; cone-shape,
bright yellow and orange marker lights flicked by the cabin
windows in quickening succession, turning into a blur, like
lines of guardrail posts seen from a speeding car. Patty's plane
lifted, and the sound of its tires rumbling across the concrete
runway ceased; the aircraft rocketed upward at a sharp angle—sharper than usual—pressing the passengers into their
seatbacks. Soon—with a muffled *thunk* and a *bump*—its landing gear retracted. A strange rattling noise like the sound of
loose marbles scattering down a sidewalk seemed to come
from under the seats in the front of the first-class section,
then abruptly stopped as the plane accelerated and veered to
the right, soaring aloft into the pre-morning sky above Boston.
It executed another turn, and was off on its way to its western
destination. Yet another sound emanated from first
class––the sound of a little girl crying.

Patty's plane, still gaining altitude, was now approaching
central Massachusetts and homing in on radio beacons on the
dark mountaintops that lay ahead in the Berkshires. No lights
appeared below; cloud cover masked the glow otherwise emanating from the towns thousands of feet beneath the plane
where neon lights of diners and coffee shops buzzed into life,
waitresses scuttled about filling coffee cups, the earliest of
early risers were waking, and morning editions of newspapers
were being delivered. A woman sitting in row five waved Patty
over to her. "My daughter," she said smiling, nodding toward

the diminutive girl seated next to her holding a coloring book, a little girl whose distressed face looked much like a pot of pea soup about to come to a boil, "wants to talk to you."

"Something the matter, hon?" asked Patty, looking down at the little girl, all of five years old. The girl's face was turning crimson and puffy; the misty warnings of teardrops soon to come were in her eyes.

"I lost my crayons," she blurted, "when the plane went up. They're all gone...all of them. I want to draw and I can't now. I can't." A storm of tears of tropical proportions now formed and trickled down the girl's cheeks.

"Maybe you can help?" asked the girl's mother.

"I'll see what I can do," answered Patty. She went back to her jump seat, stood in the center of the aisle and addressed the passengers: "Folks, can I have your attention, please? I need your help here. One of our small passengers has lost some crayons. Would you please check under your seats and give me any crayons you happen to find?" There were giggles, some laughter, and a puzzled look from Theresa, Patty's co-worker.

Some 50 people suddenly heeded the request, many banging their heads against the seat rests in front of them as they explored the floor with their fingertips. "I've got a blue one and a green one," reported a soldier in row seven, holding them aloft triumphantly.

"I've got one that's purple," exclaimed a lady in the seat behind him.

"Hey, I've got three of them," said a kid farther back, holding them aloft.

"Avocado!" yelled a girl behind the kid, waving a light green crayon. "Crazy '70s color! Dig it!"

"Got one, too," said a man in a turban behind her. "Red, ruby red." Patty walked down the aisle, collecting the crayons and thanking people who had turned them in. She brought them back to the little girl in row five and put them in her tiny hand.

"Oh, thank you!" said the little girl, smiling up at her. She took them and immediately began doodling with them in her big coloring book.

"How old is your daughter?" Patty asked the girl's parents.

"She just turned five years old yesterday," said the father, putting down his magazine. "The coloring book and those crayons? They're her favorite present. From her grandfather. Would you believe that? I gave her a game toy...but she likes to draw. And she's starting to write...her spelling's very good, in fact." The little girl stopped doodling in her coloring book.

"There, I'm done," she announced, looking at her mother, then at Patty. "You know...when I grow up," the little girl said in adoration, eyes wide, big and blue, looking straight up at Patty, "I want to be just like you! Look, I wrote it here, right under your picture." Her parents smiled and nodded in approval. The girl held up the coloring book and turned it around so that Patty could see the illustration the girl had been working on. It was a stick-like caricature of a woman in a red uniform, with blonde hair, blue eyes, and a funny-looking nose. To Patty, it was as startling as the image of herself she had seen in the mirror in Jake Thayer's house.

The deck of the airplane suddenly seemed to fall out from underneath Patty, and she rocked backward on her heels momentarily. Reactively, she looked out the closest window. Far below her was the distant countryside, warming to the first rays of sunrise. It was a patchwork of different fabrics: the brown corduroy of furrowed fields, the stippled, dark green cotton of pine forests, the smooth felt of lush meadows and pastures, and the tan, course canvas of rock. And weaving through it threaded the silver needles of the rivers that sewed those patches together and made them the whole quiltwork of land that the plane and its passengers rose above. Here, there were no gangsters, crooks, or con men, no ghosts or evil secrets. There was only the land and the sky as the day dawned

and the world turned on its heel anew, presenting an innocent, peaceful new face to whoever would embrace it, while
the other half was obscured by the black of night. But that was
the way the world was—and the figures of the Callahan family's past that haunted Patty's memories, too—living half in
the light, the other half cloaked in darkness.

"What was that?" asked the little girl's mother, surprised by
the airplane's jostling.

"Just some turbulence," answered Patty, smiling at her reassuringly. "We'll get over it. What's your daughter's name?"

"Carol," answered the girl's mother with a sweet smile, regaining her composure.

"Well, Carol," said Patty, kneeling down and looking straight
at the little girl, who was still smiling at her, "you've got to
think about something. If you're going to be just like me when
you grow up, now honey, who's going to be just like you?"

* * *

Half a world away from Boston, Lorenzo Toscanini shuffled
along in a long, single-file line of passengers disembarking
from an airplane. The flight from Boston, with one stopover
along the way, had been long and tedious. Absent any form
of entertainment other than his recollections of the past few
days spent in America, Lorenzo had fiddled with his novel, now
surpassing 100,000 words. It was stored on his tablet, stowed
away in the pocket of his coat. Upon clearing customs—after answering the inevitable questions, enduring the delays,
the yakking, fidgeting, and grumbling of fellow passengers as
they fumbled for and then produced their passports—Lorenzo
stepped from a gateway into the main concourse and almost
immediately spotted his boss, Alberto Pellegrini, standing in
a throng of people. He was in full dress uniform, and—to
Lorenzo's great relief—it was still a captain's uniform.

"Good to see you, Lorenzo!" the captain exclaimed, slapping Lorenzo on the back and seizing his luggage. "Let me have that...you look exhausted."

"Oh, not so bad," replied Lorenzo. "I could have taken that." The captain made a dismissive clucking sound.

"I know how it is with those long flights," he said. "They take more out of you than you realize. Tell me, how was it in America, working with their police?"

"Interesting, to be sure," replied Lorenzo. The two men walked toward the end of the concourse, then outside into a compound reserved for police and emergency vehicles.

"This way," said Alberto, leading the way toward a small, ungainly-looking blue police vehicle. Awkwardly diminutive, it looked for all the world like a wind-up toy that should have a giant key sticking out of its rooftop.

"What—a Panda?" exclaimed Lorenzo in surprise.

"Yes, Sergeant, a Panda 4x4. There have been some changes since you've been away. Hop in," said Alberto gravely. "You're lucky you still have your sergeant's stripes...and I, my captain's bars."

He opened the vehicle's driver-side door and squeezed himself into the seat behind the wheel, closed the door, and twisted his key in the ignition. Lorenzo sidled into the passenger seat and slammed his door shut; it made a sound like an empty tin can being rapped with a fingernail. Alberto drove the quirky-looking Panda past the security post where two guards were standing; one of them nudged the other with his elbow and they both snickered as they waved the Panda through. Lorenzo pulled the tablet from his pocket and fiddled with it. "What are you doing—writing again?" asked Alberto, glancing at the sergeant.

"Yes," he answered. "I just had to add a few things I just thought of."

"What about?" queried the captain, now eyeing the roadside a hundred feet or so beyond, where a large woman with long blonde hair was apparently struggling to change a flat tire on a white Alfa Romeo convertible. There was something that seemed oddly familiar to him about the vehicle and its driver, something that matched a description he knew that he had read or heard of, but that he couldn't quite remember. The captain slowed the Panda and turned on its emergency lights as he prepared to pull over and assist the unfortunate motorist.

"Those Americans," said Lorenzo, not looking up, engrossed in his writing. "Some of them...are as crooked as they come."

Acknowledgements

Writing can indeed be a cathartic process. I'll vouch for that. But it is often said that for a writer's friends, co-workers or neighbors who are asked to read first-draft copies of a writer's work——and agree to do so——it can sometimes be another kind of process, much too unrewarding for them to bear. I have heard humorously-exaggerated tales of such long-suffering people, who supposedly put down those draft copies in disgust or dismay, emptied out their homes and quietly moved to other states in the middle of the night, wearing huge smiles of relief on their faces and leaving no forwarding addresses behind. That said, I am indebted to several people I will now mention, who read drafts for *As Crooked as They Come* and offered their valuable crits and corrections. To their credit, they still live near me, too, and in fact still speak to me on a fairly regular basis.

I am indebted to my wife, Edie, for the many valuable suggestions she offered as I wrote and edited this book, and also to two former co-workers from my time in the 2010s as editor and publisher of *Vermont Magazine*, Marisa Crumb and Michelle Boisse. My thanks as well to former co-worker Darci Webster for her input, to Billy Thieleman for his helpful information on all things nautical, to Abilash Rasheed for his help with the cover images, and to my *consigliere* Romey Romagnoli for advice on all things Italian. Finally, I am grateful to Captain John Zink of the Bennington County Sheriff's Department (retired) and to Will Davis, a retired New York State corrections officer; both of these men told me some very valuable things about criminals. Those remarks and observations sparked something important: the ignition that ultimately started up and drove my creation of the characters in this book.

Philip R. Jordan is a native Vermonter and hobbyist photographer. As a young man, he worked at various times as a freelance photographer, decorative painter, antique picker, store manager and tractor mechanic following college. He then entered into a three-decade career as a salesman traveling throughout New England, and afterward spent more than another decade with *Vermont Magazine*, retiring as its editor-in-chief and publisher in 2019. He has written books on transportation subjects, such as *Rutland in Color* (Morning Sun Press, 2003), has been a columnist for *This Old Truck* magazine, and been a contributor to *Old Cars Weekly*. He lives in a quirky old one-room schoolhouse in Sunderland, Vermont together with his wife, Edie, and just can't seem to stop writing and taking pictures. He is a member of the League of Vermont Writers.